The House on Schellberg Street

The House on Schellberg Street

by Gill James

Chapeltown Books

British Library Cataloguing in Publication Data

A Record of this Publication is available from the British Library

ISBN 978-1-910542-23-1

This edition published 2018 by Chapeltown Books
Manchester, England

All Chapeltown books are published on paper derived
from sustainable resources.

Contents

Renate, 22 December 1938 6:30 a.m.

Renate reread the letter while she waited for the paint to dry.

22 December 1938

Dear All,

This is such an exciting idea! I'm really glad you asked me to be the first. I had thought of waiting a week or two, until I'd got something to report about the Christmas holiday and the new school. But in the end I couldn't wait. The sooner I send it on to Anika, the sooner it will go round to the rest of you. And the sooner I'll get it back to read all of your news.

I hope you all like the book I chose.

It's going to be a glorious Christmas this year, anyway. Two weeks of snow, in Stuttgart, they say. We are off to stay at Oma's house on Schellberg Street for Christmas as usual. I'm looking forward to those walks through the hills again – it'll be such fun in the snow. And I'll be seeing my cousins and my friend, Hani.

We lit the Adventskranz at coffee time yesterday afternoon. Wilma had made a lovely one with fir branches and fat white candles. Mother had baked one of her famous Apfelkuchen. She makes them so nice with big chunks of apple and lots of cinnamon. My favourite.

I love this time of year. Even father seemed in a brighter mood than usual. Both he and mother have been so serious-looking recently. There's something wrong, I think, and they won't tell me what. Do you remember that fuss mother made about me going to Mostviel last summer? Well, it's gradually got worse. Father looking more and more worried, and mother cancelling dinner-parties and refusing to go to the opera. I hope they're not falling out or anything.

But yesterday they got into a bit of the Christmas mood. I almost choked, though, when the telegraph boy came round.

"Heil Hitler!" he said.

*And my father replied "Heil Edler!" Thank goodness the
boy didn't notice. But I was going redder and redder, trying
not to giggle. After he'd gone I almost spat the whole
mouthful of Apfelkuchen out.*

*That scene repeated itself at dinner. Father knows very
well that I hate spinach, and that I just hide it in my mouth
until I can get rid of it later. He kept trying to make me laugh.
Then it happened: a great explosion of green all over the
white table cloth. Mother made a terrible fuss and muttered
something about young ladies in her day. Wilma was trying
not to laugh, I could tell! Father just roared.*

*It'll be funny in January, all being in different places. I'll
see some of you at the Gymnasium, next autumn. I'm looking
forward to hearing all about what the rest of you do at your
new schools, and about your Christmases.*

So I'll finish now and get this in the post!

Love to you all,
Renate Edler

Yes, it was going to be a lovely Christmas. She smiled when
she thought of Hani. She would have appreciated the Apfelkuchen.
She liked her cake – and it showed. Renate looked down at her own
thin arms and tutted. She looked so bony! If only she could curve
a bit, like Hani. Oh, it was going to be such fun staying with her
for the few days before Christmas.

The picture was dry now. Renate carefully glued it into the
little exercise book. This was exciting. She placed the book into
the brown envelope and neatly wrote Anika's address, before
making her way down to the kitchen.

Wilma was there, preparing the breakfast.

"Are there any stamps?" asked Renate.

"On the shelf in the hall. Why don't you leave that, and Johann
can take it when he calls?"

"Oh no!" replied Renate. "I have to take this myself. It's
special."

"Well, don't be long. Your mother says you have to pack. And wrap up warm – it's bitter out there."

"I've done my packing," replied Renate. She'd decided to wear most of what she was taking; layers that she could peel off. The train was always so cold at first, and then, usually when they were almost there, it would get unbearably hot and stuffy, because by then it would be absolutely packed with people.

She walked quickly to the post-box at the end of the street. It was such a promising day with the sun was getting higher in the sky. Something ran in front of her, into the nearby woods. It was much too quick for her to see what it was.

So some of you aren't hibernating, then, she thought.

She felt like skipping but thought that perhaps she was a bit too old. Nothing could spoil this day, though. Not even the huge swastika on the fence opposite.

The house was oddly quiet when she got back: no wireless; her father was not arguing loudly with the newspaper like he usually did; and Wilma was not singing in the kitchen. She could hear her mother and father talking softly but urgently in the dining room. The usual smell of strong black coffee and warm bread greeted her as she went into the room, but the coffee cups were empty and the rolls were still in the basket. Both of them jumped when they saw her. They stared at her, then looked at each other and then back at her. Her mother gazed straight into her eyes and opened her mouth to say something. Her father turned away. Then she noticed her mother's lip wobbling as tears formed in her already red eyes.

Hani, 22 December 1938 11:30.a.m.

"It looks bigger now that all that junk's gone," said Rikki. "I suppose there will be room for the trundle-bed. You'd better put some of the spare curtains up at the side window. You don't want anybody looking in. And I think I know where there are some extra blankets."

"But nothing at the sky-light," said Hani. "Because we'll be able to look up at the stars then. It's going to be so lovely."

"I hope you two girls won't catch cold sleeping out here," said Rikki, frowning slightly.

"Oh, Rikki, you worry too much." Hani put down her pile and gave her former nanny a hug. "Nobody's going to catch cold. We've got feather beds, haven't we? And that little stove is quite efficient. It's going to be so cosy."

"I don't know," said Rikki. "You do get some funny ideas. Wanting to sleep out here when you've got such a lovely room."

"Yes, but it'll be such an adventure," replied Hani.

"If you say so," replied Rikki, with a sniff. "Now, I'll just go and get young Wilhelm to clear this lot up. Then he can go and get the trundle bed."

"Nice cosy little den you've got here," said Wilhelm a few minutes later, after he'd brought in the bed and she'd helped him to straighten it out. "You two'll be set up just fine." He pushed his wild blond curls from his forehead and wiped the sweat from his face.

"It's great, isn't it?" said Hani. She'd always liked Wilhelm. He always seemed more like an older brother than one her father's workers. But now she just wanted him to go away, so she could get on with the room.

"Anything else I can do?" he asked.

"No, no, not at all, thank you," replied Hani, gently stroking the curtains and blankets Rikki had sent down. Why wouldn't he just go away? She couldn't wait to get started making the garage room the cosiest of places.

Rikki had already swept the floors clean, done away with all the dust and polished the small window and sky-light until they shone. All there was left for Hani to do now was to make the room look pretty.

In no time, the bright yellow curtains framed the little window. On top of the normal bed-rolls she stretched out two red blankets. There were so many cushions she didn't think she would be able to use them all, so she put three on each bed and dropped the rest on the floor.

This is really comfy, she thought. We can use the cushions as seats. It's going to be so good.

There was nothing more she could do now. It really was perfect.

The smell of cooked chicken coming from the kitchen was making her hungry. Fantastic!

Must be about half past twelve, she thought. And she'll be here by two. I wonder whether Rikki has made some strudel. If not we could go to Kellerman's on the way back from the station.

She really wasn't sure whether she could bear to wait the extra hour and a half, but at least lunch might take her mind off it.

"Your mother says you're to eat downstairs in the kitchen with me and Wilhelm," said Rikki as Hani came out of the bathroom from washing her hands.

"Why?" asked Hani.

"She and your father have something to discuss," replied Rikki.

"Do you know what?" asked Hani. Why didn't they involve her in their discussions? She wasn't a child anymore. Besides, she wanted to find out more about what was going on, because she knew it was something not so nice.

"Now take that frown off your face, young missy," said Rikki, frowning herself. "You know your mother and father work really hard, and they don't often have time to sit down and talk, let alone have a meal together."

Hani sighed. "I suppose so," she said. "Anyway, what are we having? It smells delicious."

"Chicken casserole and dumplings," answered Rikki.

"Now that sounds good," said Wilhelm as he came through the back door.

13

"Yes, but not until you've washed that muck off your hands, it won't be," said Rikki.

"Look, I'm sorry if I was a bit impatient earlier," said Hani. "Only, you know, I wanted to… well."

"No problem," replied Wilhelm. "I had work to do in the garden, anyway. Look." He held up two muddy hands.

"Bathroom. Now!" hissed Rikki.

"Heil Rikki!" cried Wilhelm, raising his right arm stiffly out in front.

Hani shuddered. Rikki looked as if she was about to faint. Her face had gone quite white.

"Don't you joke about that, young man," she said quietly.

"No, sorry," replied Wilhelm, darting out of the kitchen before Rikki could say anything else.

They ate in silence, all three of them looking down at their food. Hani felt strange. December was such a lovely time. The weather was just as it always was at this time of year – cold, but clean and fresh. Everything seemed so normal. Yet it wasn't. There was something about to happen and Hani couldn't be sure exactly what.

"That was great," said Wilhelm as he wiped his plate clean with a slice of bread.

"Yes, there's seconds," said Rikki. "Though I don't know how much longer we'll be able to say that."

Wilhelm looked at Hani and winked.

"She's coming round," he whispered. "She likes me really."

Hani watched Rikki ladle more of the sauce on to Wilhelm's plate. She would have loved some more herself but she didn't have Wilhelm's excuse. He'd been working in the garden all day. She'd done very little – unless you counted the prettying up of the garage room, although Wilhelm and Rikki had done all the heavy work. Besides, if she didn't lose a bit of weight soon, she would get another lecture from her mother.

The doorbell rang.

"I'd better go and get that," said Wilhelm. "They won't want disturbing."

Rikki sat very still, just staring into space. Hani didn't know whether she should say anything.

"It was the telegram boy," said Wilhelm ten minutes later. "A telegram for upstairs."

Rikki flinched.

"I don't think it was anything too important," said Wilhelm. "They didn't look very worried when I gave it to them."

"Ah, well, we'll see," said Rikki.

Hani hoped it wasn't to do with Renate. Perhaps she was sick? That would be awful.

Oh, stop worrying, she told herself. It's probably only something to do with one of their meetings. But the uncomfortable feeling would not go away. It was no good pretending things were all right. Things were just not all right at the moment.

She saw Rikki and Wilhelm exchange a look.

"What's the matter?" she said. "Do you think there's something wrong?"

They didn't have time to answer before they heard footsteps coming down the stairs. Hani's mother came in, holding the telegram in her hands.

"I'm sorry, darling," she said. "Renate won't be coming." There were tears in Frau Gödde's eyes.

Hani's heart sank. "What is it?" she cried. "What's the matter with her?"

"It's… it's nothing too serious," her mother stammered. "She's perfectly safe. Just come on upstairs, will you? Vati and I need to talk to you."

If it's not too serious, why is she crying? thought Hani.

It seemed to take forever to walk up the stairs to the main lounge. Her mother didn't look back once, and it reminded Hani a bit of being shown into the dentist by Herr Schröder's assistant. She never looked at you nor did she ever smile. At least mother smiled occasionally, but obviously not today.

"Sit down, Hani," said Herr Gödde. "We need to talk to you about Renate."

"She's not ill, is she?" cried Hani. "What does the telegram say?"

Her mother raised her eyebrows and mouthed something at Hani's father. He nodded. Frau Gödde put her hand to her mouth and handed Hani the telegram.

```
Renate unable to come stop chicken pox
stop
```

Hani felt the relief as a great stone being lifted from her chest as she read the telegram. Renate was ill, but it was nothing much. So she would be coming soon – when the spots had gone. She couldn't very well go on a train all covered in spots.

"Well, she will come when she's better, won't she?"

Her parents didn't answer. They just frowned. Why were they so bothered? It was just chicken pox, wasn't it?

It was only later, when she was back in the garage room turning the telegram over in her hand and looking sadly at her cosy den, that she remembered. They'd both already had chicken pox. Here, when they were seven. You were only supposed to have chicken pox once.

Suddenly the winter had lost all its charm.

Renate, 22 December 2:30 p.m.

"What's going on, Wilma?" said Renate. "Why was Mutti crying this morning?"

"I expect she's just worrying about the packing," said Wilma. "You know what a tizzy she gets into when she has to pack."

"I suppose so," said Renate.

"And I expect she's bothered about leaving your father on his own," said Wilma. "It's not very nice, families being split up at Christmas."

"Vati's not coming to Stuttgart?" said Renate, alarmed. She had been looking forward to spending time in Oma's rambling house on Schellberg Street, and the few days before staying with Hani. Christmas without Vati?

Before Wilma could answer the door opened. It was Mutti.

"Renate, I need to talk to you," she said.

There was something about the tone of Mutti's voice that Renate didn't like.

"You may have wondered, perhaps…" her mother began. "You may have noticed…" She folded her hands and closed her eyes and then started again. "Have you ever wondered if we might have Jewish connections?"

Renate couldn't believe what she was hearing. What did Mutti mean? They couldn't possibly have anything to do with Jews could they? That would mean… that would mean they would have to give up all sorts of things.

"Yes, my dear, I'm afraid it's true," her mother continued. "I am Jewish, and so is Oma – but not your father. You and I and your Oma will have to leave Germany after Christmas and go and live in England. A lot of very kind people have done all sorts of things to make it possible for us to go there. You will have to go first."

"What? On my own?" cried Renate.

"Yes, I'm afraid so. But I shall be following very soon. Your uncles are waiting for you in England and will take care of you. But Vati won't be able to come too – he won't be allowed to leave

17

Germany." Her mother's voice broke and she added almost in a whisper. "Go and think it over in your room. I… I want to be alone for a bit."

Renate couldn't move. She stared at her mother. They were Jewish? She and Mutti were Jewish? She knew that it was very difficult for Jewish people living in Germany and was getting worse all the time. Everything had been just the same as normal, except perhaps for Mutti's strange moods. But they didn't look at all like the Jews they'd seen down in town. Those men with the big hats and the long sideburns and the women always dressed in black. Mutti just looked like any other German woman.

"Renate, I told you to go," said Mutti. "I need to be on my own."

Somehow, she managed to will her feet to move. She left the lounge and set off for her room. As she crossed the hallway, she caught her reflection in the long mirror but she could see nothing different. She was not a racial disgrace or a contamination. That's what they said the Jews were, didn't they? She pushed her shoulders back and held her head up. "I'm just the same as ever. I am not a disgrace. I am going to England and I shall like it," she whispered.

Her father came out of his study and stood beside her. He put his arm around her shoulders. "It's for the best," he said.

"But I can't speak any English," said Renate.

Renate, 28 January 1939 9:00 a.m.

Hans Edler suddenly roared with laughter. "Well, well. That spotty little Hitler-fan might have actually saved your life by being so pedantic. Or maybe even our dear Father Brandt, the old soak."

"Hans!" Mutti said sharply.

"Well, getting a new passport now, you know—"

"Shh!" her mother said.

He just shrugged his shoulders, then looked a bit more serious and said "You take care now."

Renate had had her passport for two years now, since she went on a school trip to Italy. She remembered going with her father to get it.

"But the birth certificate is wrong," he'd argued with the official. "The fool of a priest who christened her was drunk at the time. She is supposed to be Renata Clara – Renata ending in 'a', not 'e' and Clara with a 'C' after both of her grandmothers. Not Klara with a 'K'. Renate with an 'e'."

"Well, you should have found a priest who wasn't drunk," said the young official.

Renate remembered his eyes: blue and lifeless. He'd looked beyond them, not at them.

"She was born in a thunderstorm, six weeks early. We didn't think she would live," her father replied in a raised voice.

The younger man hesitated for a moment. Then he slapped the application form down on the table. "Oh, go round the corner and get her an adult passport. She's old enough anyway."

"One of Hitler's trumped-up youths," her father had mumbled as they joined another queue in the passport office.

When they were eventually shown into the office, Vati recognized the official. He was Herr Müller, one of his old school friends.

"But Hans," said Herr Müller slowly, "even if the birth certificate is wrong, we must put on her passport exactly what it says there. Of course, in the privacy of your own home and amongst your own family and friends, you can call her what you like."

"Yes, you're right of course." Vati sighed. "But I just can't stand the attitude of Hitler's young bully boys."

"Yes, I know, I know," said Herr Müller. "But we still have to obey the rules." He turned to Renate and winked. "Now, the passport will be ready very soon."

Three weeks later he personally handed the passport to Renate. "There," he said. "Your very own grown-up passport. That should last you quite a long time. You'll be a pretty young woman by the time you need a new one, I've no doubt."

Then Herr Müller had looked at her father and said quite seriously. "You know, I think it was a good thing to get her an adult passport. You never know how useful that might be one day."

Renate hadn't understood what he'd meant then, and still didn't now, though she supposed it was useful for this trip.

"That's the biggest we've got that you'll be able to carry," said Mutti. They were putting the last of her things into the suitcase. Renate was wearing her best dress under two extra jumpers.

"Surely it won't be that cold there?" Renate said as she pulled on even more layers.

"It is a damp place, surrounded by water," explained Mutti. "Not that all these clothes will keep out the coldness."

"I'm not really Jewish, am I?" asked Renate.

"Wear your blue sweater on the boat," Mutti said. "Even with your thick coat on you'll be cold."

Renate, 28 January 1:00 p.m.

She was still standing on the station platform, waiting for the train that was supposed to have left just after eleven. It seemed as if the weather knew what was happening and sympathized. The bright sunshine had gone. She shivered as she looked up at the black clouds that blotted out the sun and threatened rain, not snow. It was bitter. At least it meant she was glad of all the extra layers of clothes under her thick winter coat. She still thought that at any moment she would wake up and find this was just a horrible nightmare.

At last, a train pulled into the station and stopped next to the platform where they stood.

"You all have your identity cards or passports, don't you?" asked Fräulein Gottlieb. "Remember, if any officials get on to the train don't say anything unless they speak to you. If they ask any questions, answer as simply as you can, and of course, politely."

Oh yes, thought Renate. I wouldn't be without it.

She'd had to say goodbye to Mutti and Vati in the waiting room as they weren't allowed on the platform. The SS guards had told them that there was to be no hugging or kissing and no crying. Oddly, she hadn't felt like crying. She'd done plenty of that over the last few weeks. Now it didn't feel real. She wondered whether Mutti and Vati were still watching. She couldn't see as there were too many other children on the platform.

Fräulein Gottlieb and the other escorts started shuffling the children on to the train. Renate found herself in a compartment with an older boy, a pair of twins – one boy and one girl about her age – and a couple of little girls.

"Jakob, you're in charge," said Fräulein Gottlieb. "And you two older girls please help Christa and Irmgard if they need anything. Please all make sure your tags are visible at all times. And if anybody asks you about the violins, Adelinde and Erich, remember to tell them that you have passed grade eight." She scuttled off to the next compartment.

The twins had very small suitcases with them. That must have been to make up for the violins. She wondered whether she would go to a family that had a piano. She didn't play all that well, certainly not grade eight, but she would like to keep on trying.

Jakob stood up and opened the window. "Everyone's on now," he said. "I expect we'll be going in a minute."

Suddenly a young woman rushed up to him. "Please take her," she said, handing a bundle to Jakob. "My sister will pick her up when you're in Holland."

"But—" Jakob went to protest.

It was too late, though. The train was pulling out of the station.

"What is it?" asked Adelinde.

"It's a baby," said Jakob.

Renate's stomach did a somersault. Somebody had given them a baby to look after: a baby who was not supposed to be on this train. "We'll have to hide it," she said.

"Under a coat," said Erich.

"But make sure she can breathe," said Adelinde.

The baby was good and slept peacefully. Jakob kept her on his lap but carefully covered by his coat.

"Would you like me to hold her for a while?" asked Renate.

Jakob shook his head. "The mother told me to take care of her."

The train was beginning to pick up speed. It didn't seem that anyone wanted to talk. She was glad: she needed to think about all of this. It was too ridiculous. She couldn't be Jewish. Neither could her mother or her grandmother. Besides, being Jewish shouldn't mean that she and her mother had to move to a country where they didn't even speak the language. Then she'd remembered what had happened back in November to the synagogue and all those shops and other businesses owned by Jews.

No, she didn't want to think about that. She closed her eyes. The motion of the train soon made her fall asleep.

It was dark when she woke up. The train had stopped and Jakob was staring ahead looking rather worried. The baby was still asleep but making little whimpering sounds as if she would wake any moment now.

"We're almost at the Dutch border," said Erich. "I expect they're making sure we're not taking anything valuable out of the country."

"If the baby starts crying, will one of you two start making a noise?" said Adelinde to the two little girls. Christa nodded then whispered something to Irmgard.

The compartment door suddenly opened.

"You will all show your papers at once," said the official. "And open all cases and bags."

Renate a shuddered as she saw the sinister black uniform. She avoided looking directly in his eyes.

They took their suitcases from the luggage rack. Erich handed Jakob his.

"Can't you get your own case?" the official asked Jakob.

"I've hurt my wrist," said Jakob.

The official raised his eyebrows and shook his head. "What is in those cases?" he asked, pointing up at the luggage rack.

"Those are our violins," said Erich.

"Show me," said the official.

Erich took the two cases down and he and Adelinde opened them.

"They must be worth a mark or two," he said. "Do you play them?"

"Of course," said Adelinde. "We have both passed our grade eight exams. We hope to join an orchestra in England."

"Show me," said the official.

Adelinde and Erich exchanged a glance.

They took the violins out of the cases and carefully tuned them.

"Bach's double concerto?" suggested Adelinde.

Erich nodded. "One, two three."

They started playing. Soon the notes were dancing around each other. They were brilliant.

How did they get those notes out their violins? Renate had tried it once. It had sounded terrible. If she should be lucky enough to have a place with a family that had a piano she would practice for at least an hour every day.

Even the SS officer watched the twins open-mouthed.

Unfortunately, though, the baby also heard the music and wasn't so impressed. She began to whimper more restlessly. Renate nudged Christa.

The little girl began to howl. "I want my Mummy, I want my Mummy."

It worked. The music and Christa's whining was louder than the sounds the baby made.

"All right, all right," said the official. "That's enough noise. You may keep your violins." He scowled at them and moved on to the next compartment.

It was easy enough to stop the music, but the baby was another matter; Christa wouldn't be able to keep up the noise for much longer.

"Try putting your finger in her mouth," Renate said. She'd often seen mothers do that to crying babies and it seemed to sooth them.

Jakob pulled a face but did as she suggested. It calmed the baby a little but she still grizzled quietly.

Some children were made to get off the train and carry their suitcases into one of the waiting rooms.

Renate hoped the officers weren't going to make them stay here. She wanted the train to start moving again now. She wanted to get out of Germany.

At last, though, the children came back.

"They're all there," said Adelinde. "I counted – twenty went out of this carriage and twenty came back."

"I wonder if they've been allowed to keep all their stuff, though," said Erich.

"Get in quickly, scum!" shouted one of the SS officers.

Renate held her breath as she saw one of the girls drop her suitcase. It came open and her clothes fell all over the platform. She stopped to pick them up. The SS officer kicked her.

She yelped.

"Get on with it, you piece of filth," said the officer. "Or you'll have to stay here." He pushed the girl on to the train.

The suitcase and most of its contents remained on the platform. The officer picked up the case plus a handful of the contents and threw them into the carriage. The doors were shut and the train started to pull out of the station. A broken doll was left behind.

"At least they should be friendlier at the next stop," said Jacob. "We'll be in Holland in a few moments."

The door of the compartment opened again. It was Fräulein Gottlieb. "Well, done," she said. "You all handled that very well. How is the baby?"

"You knew all along?" said Jakob.

"Of course," said Fräulein Gottlieb. "I told the mother to give her to you, but I forgot to give you her milk and spare nappies. I've been so busy with some of the smaller children who have been very upset. Some of them don't travel so well either. But here they are now. Can you try and get her cleaned up and fed before we hand her over to her aunt?"

The incident with the violins and the crying baby had really broken the ice. It turned out that Adelinde and Erich had left a baby brother behind and knew all about nappies and feeding babies.

"At least she's a girl so she won't pee in your eye while you're changing her," said Erich.

"True," said Adelinde. "But this nappy is not too nice."

"Give it to me," said Jakob. He opened the window and threw it outside. "I hope it lands on some Nazi scum."

They all giggled.

In no time, they were chatting away with the baby gurgling contentedly. It turned out that Adelinde and Erich were also very good at singing and soon had them all joining in. Renate didn't know the words to some of the Yiddish songs but she soon picked up the tune.

"So you're not really Jewish?" said Jakob.

Renate shook her head. "I'd always thought I was German and Catholic."

"But the Nazis didn't," said Jakob. "Because you have Jewish blood." He shrugged. "It doesn't bother me that you're not kosher."

"No, we're all in the same boat," said Erich.

"We soon will be, quite literally," said Adelinde.

Half an hour later, the train stopped again.

"I expect it will be the Dutch officials now," said Jakob.

Renate's stomach did another flip.

"I expect they'll be kinder than the Germans were." Jakob pointed out of the window. "Look, we're actually at a station. I'm going to get out and find this little one's mother."

Then he and the baby were gone.

Renate heard the doors of the compartments opening one by one. She could hear women talking softly rather than the harsh voices of border officials.

Theirs opened. A lady appeared with cups of hot chocolate and another held a tray of little cakes. A third carried fluffy blankets and a fourth had some cute teddy bears. The four ladies made a fuss of them, handing them the drinks, cakes and blankets and a couple of the teddy bears to Christa and Irmgard. They seemed so kind and friendly, although Renate couldn't understand a word they were saying.

The chocolate was delicious. The cake was like nothing she had tasted before – so sweet and spicy – making her realise how hungry she was. She was glad of the blanket, too. It wasn't that she was cold with all the layers, it was rather that the softness of it was so soothing. However, she couldn't stop the tears pricking at her eyes.

It had all been such a shock. Finding out she was Jewish and that she had to go away. Then realising that she wasn't all that Jewish. Yet there were people being kind to her: the Dutch women and Adelinde, Erich and Jakob who had had to leave parents and brothers and sisters behind. At least her uncles would meet her in England and her mother would come over later. But what about Christa and Irmgard? Would they be allowed to stay together? They were so young to be away from their parents.

The Dutch women collected up the mugs and waved cheerily to them. No Dutch officials at all got on. The train began to pull out of the station even though Jakob had not got back.

The tears began to flow freely. Renate could not stop them. Adelinde put her arm round her, Christa held her hand and Irmgard patted her arm.

The compartment door opened and Jakob was there.

"Hey, Renatechen," he said. "You didn't think I'd deserted you did you?" He held up a bag bursting with fruit and sandwiches. "She wouldn't let me go and she's given us enough food for an army."

"It's all right, Renate," said Fräulein Gottlieb, now standing behind him. "It's good to cry. You'll probably feel better."

She really began to sob now.

"On the other hand, I could tell you one of my jokes," said Erich, "and that might make you laugh." He frowned. "Or perhaps not."

Now she was alternatively laughing and crying. Fräulein Gottlieb was right. It did make her feel better. In no time she was only laughing and the rest were joining in.

YOU THINK A BABY AND A COUPLE OF VIOLINS WILL SAVE YOU? DO YOU THINK WE'RE IMPRESSED? TCH! FILTH. YOU'RE ALL FILTH. GO ON. GET AWAY WITH YOU. ALL OF YOU. GO. AWAY FROM THE FATHERLAND. GOOD RIDDANCE.

Renate, 29 January 1939

They made their way into one of the already crowded lounges. People sat on top of suitcases, on the floor, or squashed three to a seat on the uncomfortable wooden benches.

"You could go and have a look around the boat if you want," said Fräulein Gottlieb. "Put your things in your cabin first. But I want you in bed within an hour."

Renate was sharing a cabin with Adelinde, Christa and Irmgard. Jakob and Erich were sharing with two other boys.

"I'm tired," wailed Christa.

"Me too," said Adelinde. "Shall we go straight to bed, girls?"

Christa nodded. Irmgard didn't say anything. She placed her hand into Adelinde's and stuck her thumb in her mouth.

Renate felt wide-awake, though. "I'd like to have a look around. I'll see you soon."

"Give me your things, then," said Adelinde. "I'll put them in the cabin."

Renate waved to the three other girls and set off across the crowded inner deck. She didn't think she had ever seen so many people crammed into one space. Warm body odour and sea air made for a strange mixture of smells. She had never been on a boat as big as this – should she call it a ship? This ferry that was going to take her to England. People were still getting on. Would this – ferry – be able to hold them all?

It was hard to breathe in here. A slight breeze drifted from above her head. She noticed a staircase – which was more of a ladder made of steep steps with only air between them – which led to an opening in the roof above her. She made her way up the rungs.

Outside it was cold. The shore looked close. She shivered. It wasn't just the cold, though; she would not see her own country for a long time and now she was going somewhere she didn't understand. She still didn't really understand either why she was going there, or what being Jewish meant.

The boat started to judder. There was a loud creaking and

groaning, the sound of chains clanking and shouts from the men working at the side of the harbour. The town began to move backwards away from them. The breeze now became proper wind. Renate could hardly keep her balance. The boat rolled from side to side and then as it turned out of the harbour, it started to go up and down like a seesaw. One moment the line where the sea and the sky met seemed to be up above her head, the next minute she was looking down at it. She couldn't work out where she was and began to feel dizzy. Perhaps it would be better if she sat down.

She made her way carefully down the steep steps which kept falling away from her then rushing up to meet her feet. Once she slipped and banged her hip into the rail at the side.

The warmth flooded over her as she arrived on the lower deck. For just a few seconds it felt good. Then the smell of the closely packed passengers made her feel slightly sick. Yes, she should go to the cabin. Perhaps if she lay down she would feel better.

She tried to push her way through the crowds. It was even more difficult now, as the boat was moving up and down and from side to side at the same time. She struggled to keep her balance.

"Watch what you're doing," shouted one man angrily as she accidentally trod on his foot.

"I'm sorry," she managed to mutter as she then almost fell on a woman who was trying to feed a baby.

The boat lurched to one side and then rose up in the air, crashing down suddenly, then juddering for a few seconds before once more springing up. She saw a small door in front of her and hoped that that was what it looked like. And even if it wasn't, at least she might be on her own in there so no one could see what she was about to do. The ferry veered to the other side. She pushed the door open and just made it in time into one of the toilet cubicles, where she vomited straight into the pan. Perhaps that would make it better now.

It didn't. Time and time again, the acid yellow fluid came out of her mouth. Still the boat moved around in every direction. Then it got worse. And finally there was no more yellow fluid to come out of her stomach into her mouth but still her whole body went into spasm and she retched with every movement of the boat. This journey was going to take forever. Twelve hours, Fräulein Gottlieb had said. Twelve hours of this. The boat rocked. Her stomach retched. She wasn't alone, she could hear. Then she could smell other people's vomit. That made her feel even worse. Finally not able to hold herself up straight, she sank to the floor. With her chin propped over the side of the toilet basin, and even as the retching continued, she felt her eyelids close.

She must have fallen asleep for now there was a different sort of rocking. Somebody was shaking her.

"Renate! Renate!" she heard a voice cry. "Oh, you poor child. Why didn't you come and find me?"

Renate looked up to see Fräulein Gottlieb's bright eyes looking into hers.

"Too sick," murmured Renate. "Had to stay by the toilet."

"My dear, I'm so sorry," said Fräulein Gottlieb, helping Renate to her feet. "My poor, poor girl. Just look at you. Let me help you get cleaned up." She tried to tug the creases out of Renate's crumpled dress and coat. "When Adelinde wished me goodnight from the cabin, I assumed you were all there. Then I was busy with one or two others who were also feeling sick. On my break, I only meant to close my eyes for a moment... then the rocking motion of the boat, you know... it always sends me to sleep. Adelinde came to find me because you hadn't got back to the cabin. She was worried."

Renate noticed the boat was not moving so violently now – just rocking gently, like a cradle; soothing. And she felt so tired... oh so tired. She would love to curl up now and be in a soft, cosy bed but Fräulein Gottlieb was working at a vomit stain on the skirt of her dress, and the smell of other people's vomit would have put her off sleeping.

"You should have come to get me," said Fräulein Gottlieb, "if you felt so poorly. I'm supposed to be looking after you."

"Come on, let's go and get some fresh air," said Fräulein Gottlieb. "We ought to be able to see some land now."

Renate had stopped feeling sick at least. But she was so weak, and her legs were wobbly. The ferry was going really slowly now, and the rocking from side to side had almost gone completely. They were just going up and down gently. Even so, she had to lean on Fräulein Gottlieb as they made their way across the deck. Other white faces looked at her and she was at least glad that she wasn't the only one who had felt so bad. No one smiled and many people frowned. Were they all dreading arriving in England as much as she was?

"You go up first," said Fräulein Gottlieb, when they arrived at the staircase. "Then I can catch you if you fall."

It took Renate all her strength to haul herself up to the last step of the steep stairway. The cool wind took her breath away at first, but then she realized that it also made her feel better. The sun was shining now and there were no clouds in the sky. Perhaps this would be all right, after all. It was hard to believe it had been so grey and cold when they'd set out.

They really were not far from land. The first bit of the harbour wall was just in front of them. Renate could see some big cargo ships moored there. Cranes were loading huge crates on to their big decks. Beyond that, black shiny roofs and white buildings were gleaming in the sun. She had to shade her eyes to stop the glare.

"Well," said Fräulein Gottlieb. "Here we are. Your new home. England."

"Home?" said Renate. That sounded final.

"Your uncles will be there to meet you," whispered Fräulein Gottlieb, "once we're in London. They'll know how to keep you safe."

Renate looked again at the town. It seemed to offer her no welcome.

THEY'RE WELCOME TO YOU. YOU'RE ALL FILTH. HAVEN'T EVEN GOT SEA-LEGS. A PROPER GERMAN WOULD KNOW HOW TO SAIL. A PROPER ENGLISHMAN WOULD KNOW HOW TO SAIL. NOT YOU. A MISCHLING. YOU'RE NOT EVEN A PROPER JEW. SO YOU'RE MORE THAN FILTH.

The Smith Family, 29 January 1939

"Well, at least it meant that they didn't hold you up for too long at customs," said Uncle Ernst, looking with slight disgust at the stained coat. "I don't know what that woman was thinking of, letting you go off on your own."

"She was really kind, actually, said Renate.

Uncle Ernst sighed. "Yes, indeed. And the poor young lady has had to go back to that awful regime. You're right. We should be grateful. We'll get you to the Smith family as quickly as we can. They'll soon get you sorted out and cleaned up."

"What are they like, the Smiths?" asked Renate.

"Very kind," replied Uncle Ernst. "They have a son John, who is in the sixth form at grammar school and an older daughter who is a nurse and works away from home."

"So… you think it will be all right?" asked Renate.

"Of course it will," replied Uncle Ernst. "Now, let's go and find a taxi." He marched her towards the taxi rank.

Uncle Ernst did not offer to carry anything so she had to struggle with her case all by herself.

There was something about the way that Uncle Ernst stood that made the other people waiting for taxis get out of his way, and they were able to pile into the first one that arrived.

Renate thought she heard him say something like Eely. A place named after a sea creature, then. She wondered how far that was going to be.

Renate noticed the big red buses and square black taxis that she'd always been told were everywhere in London. They were just as she had imagined. They didn't see Big Ben though, nor Nelson's Column, and before long all she could see was row upon row of houses. They weren't like the ones at home. They all looked the same – built of red or black bricks, with their chimneypots lined up like soldiers on parade. Most of them didn't have gardens, or only very tiny ones.

"I'll see you settled in with the Smiths," said Uncle Ernst. "I won't stay long though. I want to get back to my hotel as your uncle Rudi and I have a meeting there early this evening."

Why were her uncles living in a hotel? Were they going to go back to Germany and leave her here?

"Aren't you going to live in England too?" she asked. Was she really going to be all alone in this strange country?

Uncle Ernst turned and smiled at her. "I shall stay in London until your mother is safely here and settled in," he said. "Then I shall be going to some of the other Steiner school sites. Your uncle Rudi is going to Canada soon. So, for the moment at least, we are living in a hotel." He turned once more to the driver and said something else she didn't understand. "Not long now," he said turning back to her.

The taxi eventually stopped. The driver mumbled something to Uncle Ernst who took out his wallet and handed some of the strange notes and coins to him. The driver unloaded Renate's case without smiling.

"Come on," said Uncle Ernst as the taxi moved away. He put his arm around her shoulders and propelled her towards the house, which looked just like the ones she had seen on the journey. When they moved towards the front door, Renate realized that the house was bigger than it had first looked. It did have a front garden, even though it was quite small and consisted mainly of a tiled path. A light suddenly went on in the porch.

"We've been spotted," said Uncle Ernst. "The Smiths live in the first floor flat. And a nice Polish family live on the ground floor."

The front door opened and the path flooded with light. Renate could see a small woman with slightly greying hair. She looked a little older than her mother. A faded flowered pinafore covered her skirt. She spoke in an animated whisper to Uncle Ernst.

Renate could not understand a word. Uncle Ernst answered the woman firmly and before Renate had a chance to try and work out what they were saying, she was shuffled inside and up the stairs. A man and a boy a few years older than her were sitting in the lounge.

Renate noticed that they were both very smartly dressed in ties and jackets. They stood up as soon as she and her uncle came into the room and shook hands enthusiastically with Uncle Ernst. Her uncle said something to them and Renate heard her own name.

"Renate," he said, turning now to her, "this is Mrs Smith and Mr Smith and their son, John. They will make you very welcome in their home. I'm sure you're going to be very good for them."

Renate held her hand out to shake theirs then pulled it back again quickly and looked down at the floor. She couldn't expect them to touch her in that state. Then Mrs Smith seemed to explode and made noises that sounded like a hen clucking. She was bundled out of the room and down a corridor then into another room, which she guessed was going to be her bedroom. Mrs Smith, who Renate now noticed had very kind eyes, indicated that she should get undressed. She then started rummaging in her suitcase and took out some clean clothes. She opened a cupboard and took out a thick blanket, which she wrapped around Renate and marched her out of that room into the bathroom. She started running a bath. She left the room and came back a few minutes later with a smelly paraffin heater.

After Renate had finished her bath, Mrs Smith helped her to dry her hair. Soon she was dressed in clean clothes. Mrs Smith bundled the dirty ones up and made some gestures with her arms, which Renate guessed meant she would wash the clothes.

"Well, you look a bit more respectable," said Uncle Ernst as she came back into the lounge. "I guess I should make my way back now and see whether that younger brother of mine has not got up to any mischief."

"Uncle, don't go," said Renate, suddenly panicking. "I can't speak English."

"You'll soon learn," he said. "And anyway, John speaks a little German. But you're to use it for emergencies only. It's really important that you learn to speak English as quickly as possible."

John said something to his mother. Renate guessed he was translating into English. Mrs Smith laughed and smiled at Renate. Perhaps Uncle Ernst had been right. The Smiths seemed kind.

Even so, Renate felt really odd as her uncle left the flat. John grinned at her whilst Mrs Smith went downstairs and showed him out. Mr Smith sat there, quietly puffing on his pipe. She heard the front door click shut. Mrs Smith was already talking as she came into the room but Renate couldn't understand a word. Yet she did understand that it must be something about her, because Mrs Smith smiled at her again. Then she pretended to be eating and drinking. Renate guessed she was offering her food. She shook her head. She really wasn't hungry yet. Her stomach was still a bit sore, and everything was so strange here.

A little later, she did manage to eat and drink something but it tasted odd. Not long after it got dark, she managed to indicate to Mrs Smith that she wanted to go to bed. Mrs Smith led her along to the big bedroom she'd shown her earlier.

Renate shivered as she got into her pyjamas, but once she was in bed it was quite cosy and warm, though the bed was funny: it didn't have a normal featherbed roll. It had sheets and blankets and a puffed up thing which was a bit like a roll but which went over the blankets, and then there was another cover over that that had tufty ridges on it that made a pattern. And the pillows were oblong instead of the normal square… but never mind. It was comfortable in there.

Mrs Smith bustled out of the room again, leaving the light on. Renate knew she ought to get up and switch it off but felt too sleepy. She was just beginning to have funny, dream-like thoughts, when the door opened. Mrs Smith came in carrying a tray and Renate could smell hot chocolate. She sat up in bed. Mrs Smith handed her the mug and a plate on which were two very thin, very brown biscuits.

Mrs Smith sat on the bed while Renate drank the chocolate and ate the biscuits. The chocolate was a little bitterer than she was used to, but it was still very nice and comforting. She had never tasted anything like the biscuits. They were not all that sweet and tasted very much of wheat. They had a nice texture and melted in her mouth. This was just right, after that long journey.

When she finished, Mrs Smith took the plate and cup off her

and tucked her into bed. Thank goodness she didn't make her get up again and go and clean her teeth. Mrs Smith rubbed her cheek gently. She went over to the door, waved once more and switched off the light. She left the door open a little.

Renate snuggled down into the welcoming bed. Nothing mattered any more. She was safe here. Sleep was going to drift over her any minute now and then the whole world would go away. The Smith family would guard her from any harm while she slept. Maybe it would be all right… for the moment, at least.

NICE ENGLISH FAMILY HERE, RENATE. WHAT DO YOU SAY? THEY'RE GOOD PEOPLE AREN'T THEY? THEY'RE GIVING YOU A HOME. ARE YOU GRATEFUL? DO YOU DESERVE THEM? EH? A NOBODY LIKE YOU? WHAT HAVE YOU DONE TO DESERVE SUCH KINDNESS?

Renate, 1 February 1939

"Nice, isn't it?" said Uncle Rudi.

He was right. This looked as if it should be a stately home. The bright sun made the white walls gleam. Yet that was definitely the sound of children's voices from some sort of play area behind the building. She couldn't make out what they were saying, of course. They were shouting in English. So odd, as well, that it was just off a busy London street.

The Headteacher's office looked as if it should belong to the Lord of the Manor. Mr Brown sat behind a huge carved desk and an equally elaborate carved cupboard filled half of the wall behind him. He wore a very smart suit, a white shirt and a neatly knotted tie.

Renate could not understand what Uncle Rudi and Mr Brown talked about.

"It's all right," said Uncle Rudi. "They are sure you'll be very comfortable."

"But what about my English?" asked Renate. "I won't understand anything. And what will they think of me being German?"

Uncle Rudi said something to Mr Brown, who flinched a little, smiled broadly, and then said something to her uncle.

"They won't mind at all," explained Uncle Rudi. "All Steiner school pupils are open-minded and accepting of others. And being amongst people of your own age you will soon learn the language."

I don't think it'll be that easy, thought Renate.

"Then I'll be off," said Uncle Rudi. "I have to get to my meeting." He smiled briefly at Renate. "Be good."

Mr Brown opened the door for Uncle Rudi and smiled at Renate. He mumbled something to her and gestured that she should follow him.

As she walked behind him along the corridors everyone was looking at her, she was sure. She felt sick. Perhaps it was the dirndl-type pinafore she was wearing – really no different from the gymslips some of the younger girls had on, but the girls her age wore ordinary skirts and some of them were even in overalls. Whilst several of the younger girls wore plaits, hers were tighter, somehow, and some of the girls her own age were wearing their hair in a modern loose hairstyle. She kept her eyes on the ground, but even so, she knew they were talking about her. The conversations would stop, and then start again only quieter. If anyone should speak to her, she would give the game right away.

They arrived at a doorway. Mr Brown smiled. "Your classroom," he said.

Renate was amazed that she had understood. She couldn't think what to say. She just about managed to nod and smile. At least the classroom was familiar. It contained rows of desks just like the one at the Wilhelm Löhe School. The blackboard, though, was astonishing, displaying an elaborate chalk drawing of a tiger. She had never seen such a colourful picture anywhere, let alone on a blackboard.

A teacher arrived. Mr Brown beamed at her. Renate managed to make out that she was called Miss Thompson. She was quite young and very pretty. Renate thought. She wore what looked more like a Sunday dress than something practical for school, but there wasn't a mark on it. The classroom was neat and tidy too. She grinned at Renate.

"Hello," she said, followed by something Renate couldn't understand. She recognised the word "school" though and thought the teacher might be asking her where her old school was.

"Nuremberg, in Germany," said Renate, trying very hard not to sound German.

The light went out of her teacher's eyes. Just for a split second. Then she smiled again, but not as warmly as she had at first. She turned away from Renate and talked to Mr Brown. Renate was sure they were talking about her.

The other members of her class arrived. They were surely younger than she was?

Miss Thompson started talking to the students. Renate knew they were talking about her again. She heard her name followed by one or two gasps and out of the corner of her eye, she could see some of the pupils nudging each other. The whispering began again.

Miss Thompson said something to a tall girl, without looking at Renate. Renate worked out that the girl was called Christine.

"Yes, ma'am," said Christine. She turned to look at Renate but very quickly looked away again.

The lesson began. Renate was relieved that the attention was no longer on her. A few moments later, a couple of the boys started tittering behind her back. Miss Thompson frowned at them but she didn't say anything.

Christine was very polite and for the rest of the day made sure that Renate knew where everything was and what she had to do next. It was hard work though. They had to use a lot of gestures and sometimes it was really difficult to understand. As soon as she had sorted Renate out, she left her to go and spend time with her real friends.

The time went slowly at first. She wanted the day to end, because this was so uncomfortable though no one was unkind to her. Even so, she wasn't sure whether she was looking forward to being back home with the Smiths. They were lovely, but it wasn't really home. Then she found that she was concentrating so hard on understanding everything that the time went quickly.

Next she was looking at the instructions that Uncle Rudi had written on the scrap of paper about where to catch the train, how to get a ticket and where to get off. She made her way down the drive whilst the sun was beginning to set. Most of the other students were going home in small groups full of laughter and excitement, and some were sliding on the icy patches. She walked on her own.

Why did she have to be Jewish? Or German?

Seconds later, she saw the London Transport sign. She waited a few minutes for her train and was soon sitting in the carriage staring at the blank faces of the people who had left work early.

SO WHAT ARE YOU, REALLY, RENATE? WE THINK YOU'RE JEWISH. THEY THINK YOU'RE GERMAN. HOW FUNNY! THEY THINK THE GERMANS ARE THEIR ENEMY. WE KNOW YOU'RE EVERYBODY'S ENEMY.

Anika, 5 February 1939

Dear All,

Aren't Renate's pages pretty? I think she's really set the tone for us. Now we'll all have to write neatly and put in lovely illustrations. Straight away, though, look, I'm going to spoil it with my untidy sprawl. I can't help it. I do try to write neatly, but it just won't come out right. You know, I've never been any good at writing. I am really going to make an effort with this, though. It is such a lovely idea. It'll be such a record. And easier than each one of us keeping a diary.

How was everyone's Christmas? The snow has been fantastic. Fritz and I went out skating on the river lots of times. When we weren't out, we played cards. I'm getting really good at whist and Fritz is now teaching me to play bridge. He says I'm a natural. I do keep beating him. He gets quite stroppy about that sometimes.

Homework seems a thing of the past, though I expect they'll soon be piling it on once this term gets going properly again.

Well, I'll finish now and get this into the post. Looking forward to hearing from you all, dears.

Best wishes,
Your Anika

Hani, 10 February 1939

Hani pulled off her old shirt and skirt and slipped on the Bund Deutscher Mädel uniform. She looked in the mirror. Actually, it wasn't bad. The navy-blue skirt was long enough to make her look a bit slimmer. And it did fit. The waistband didn't cut into her. The shirt was beautifully white. Would it stay like that? Surely Rikki would help to keep it white? The short sleeves would be a bit of a problem in this cold weather, but she could wear the little flying-jacket even when indoors, and the great coat would probably do the trick for outdoors. Pity they weren't blue like the skirt. They were that same ugly brown the boys had to wear.

And this black neckerchief? What was she supposed to do with this? She held it up under her chin. Ugh! Funeral colour and how on earth was she supposed to tie the wretched thing?

There was a tap at the door.

"Come in," called Hani.

She was surprised to see her mother standing there. She'd expected Rikki to be back to check up on her and to see that she hadn't put any creases into the carefully ironed shirt and skirt.

"My, oh, my," said Frau Gödde. "Don't you look the smart one?" Her eyes were wide open and a little smile played on her lips.

I can look smart sometimes, you know, mother, thought Hani. "What do I do with this thing, Mutti?" she said, waving the neckerchief at her mother.

"Here, let me do it," said Frau Gödde. She took the piece of black cloth and folded it neatly, then slipped it under Hani's shirt collar. "You'll need this as well," she said, taking the small gold-coloured ring off the bed. She pushed the two ends of the neckerchief through the ring and pulled it up to just under Hani's shirt collar. "There!" she said. "Even better. Look."

Hani did not recognise the grown-up young woman in the mirror. Was that really her? Did she really look that good?

"A proper Deutsches Mädel," said Frau Gödde. She took

Hani's two hands into hers. "Now what I'm telling you is very important. You must do everything they ask you to do, even if you don't like it. Except, if they ask you to do something you know is wrong, then you don't do it. Talk to me and Vati about it. And whatever, we will always love you and we will always be on your side."

"Of course," mumbled Rikki. What was wrong with her mother? You had to be a member of the BDM. Everybody knew that. What on earth could they ask her to do that could be wrong? It was all about hiking, camping, singing songs and learning how to cook, wasn't it? How could there be anything wrong with that? She pulled away from her mother.

"Good. That's all settled then," said Frau Gödde. "And you'd better get going. You don't want to be late for your inauguration ceremony."

It was stuffy in the town hall. Hani wondered why she had been so bothered about the short sleeves on her shirt. She was plenty warm enough now. So warm she felt dizzy and hoped she wasn't going to faint. She knew that even if she couldn't help it, Gisela Schmidt, their group leader, would somehow make her feel as if she had done it deliberately. The fanfares and the drum rolls had been quite fun at first but now the speaker was droning on and on. Hani wondered whether if she moved her neckerchief ring down a bit she would feel a bit better. She slid it down a few centimetres.

A finger prodded her back. "Sit still and stop fiddling," whispered Gisela. "Do your tie back up. You're a disgrace to the Führer."

She would have to try something else to take her mind off how uncomfortable she felt. Then she remembered her mother's trick. "If there's someone who makes you feel a bit nervous, just imagine them sitting on the lavatory." The image of the tall blond Hitlerjugend leader, sitting with his pants around his ankles was almost too much. She wanted to giggle. She must concentrate or she would be in trouble. She tried to listen to his words, but she really could not make out what he was talking about.

He pranced up and down the stage, in front of the portrait of Hitler. Now, then, what about him on the pan with his pants down? That was just too much. She coughed to disguise the giggle rising in her throat, but then she got a real tickle. She started to cough more violently. The leader stopped talking and glared at her.

Gisela thumped her on her back. "Will you stop showing us up?" she hissed.

Hani felt her cheeks burning. She was sure everyone was looking at her. She looked down at the floor.

The leader resumed his march across the stage.

Hani took a deep breath and closed her eyes. His voice now almost made her want to go to sleep. At last he finished, and then they were all on their feet singing the song that they'd been practising for weeks. They remained standing while one of the boys being initiated into the Hitlerjugend read the pledge.

"We affirm:

The German people have been created by the will of God.

All those who fight for the life of our people, and those who died,

Carried out the will of God.

Their deeds are to us holy obligation."

They all answered: "This we believe."

How does that work? Hani wondered. Is he saying that we are God's chosen people? She wasn't at all sure whether she believed in God or not, but if she did, wasn't she supposed to believe that he loved everyone?

"We will never forget that we are German," the boy carried on.

Hani answered with the others: "That is what we want."

Except it wasn't. She hated all of this. Then that was more or less it. The SS man who had opened the ceremony spoke for just about one minute.

More rubbish, thought Hani.

They sang two more songs they'd been practising and those carrying the drums and flags filed out, singing the last verse. Hani and all the other new initiates followed them. She was so glad to get into the fresh air even though it was quite cold. She would have to go back in to get her great coat but for the moment, she was going to enjoy the coolness.

All the other girls were chatting excitedly. Hani couldn't think what there was to be excited about. Now she was going to have to start attending even more of the silly meetings. She was getting hungry. She'd said she'd meet her mother here – but should she get her coat first? They hadn't discussed that. There would be a really long queue at the cloakroom by now. What should she do? All she wanted was to get home and have some supper.

"Hey, Johanna," called one of the other girls. "Hello, anyone at home?" The girl had now started wobbling her arm.

"What?" said Hani. Nobody ever called her Johanna these days. She turned to look at the speaker. It was Trudi Müller, a girl from her class at school. She was a funny little thing with pale grey eyes and white wispy hair that even today had not behaved well: several strands had come loose from her thin plaits. She was always very serious.

"There's going to be an At Home next Thursday. In the common room at the Hitlerjugend hall," said Trudi.

"What?" said Hani. What on earth was an At Home?

"It's compulsory," said Trudi. "It starts at 6.30. Be there or you're in trouble."

At that moment, Frau Gödde arrived. Hani felt relieved to see her mother. Perhaps now they could get her coat and go home.

"Mutti," she said. "Do we really think God likes only the Germans?"

"Pardon?" said Frau Gödde. "Leave this until we get home," she whispered.

Trudi was staring at them, frowning slightly. "Frau Gödde," she said, "I was just telling Johanna about the At Home. She has to come to it!"

"Oh, so what's that all about?" Mutti asked.

"Oh, we talk about German heroes, we practise our songs – and learn some new ones – and we plan what we're doing about next year's camps."

"That sounds very jolly, doesn't it, Hani?" said Frau Gödde, slipping her arm into Hani's. "I'm sure she'll enjoy it."

I won't.

"You will make sure she's there, won't you Frau Gödde?" said Gisela Schmidt who had now wandered over to them. Gisela, Hani noted, did not have a hair out of place and there was not a single crease in her uniform.

"Of course," said Frau Gödde. "Now come on. Let's go and get that lovely warm coat of yours before you catch pneumonia."

Hani didn't get this at all. Her mother seemed to approve of the Bund Deutscher Mädel now, yet at home she said she should think for herself. Didn't that mean you shouldn't believe everything you were told at these meetings?

"Take care. You must take care," her mother whispered as they made their way towards the cloakroom.

Helga, 18 February 1939

Dear All,

I agree. Renate's pictures are lovely. I wish I could paint and draw like that. I can bake. Does that count? It's a bit difficult to put cake into a letter in an exercise book, though.

Yes, Christmas was good, despite everything. I managed to get flour and dried fruit to make a Stollen and I made Christmas cookies. The trouble is, they all say that my cakes and cookies are so good that I shall have the job of baking for the family forever more, I think.

Oma spent Christmas with us and naturally therefore all the family came. All my aunts and uncles and my cousins. It was great having the little ones around. I just love playing with them. I think later I would like to work with children.

Even Fasching has come and gone and we are well into Lent. Did you see the posters for the ball in Munich? It did look rather grand. Oh, that will be the day, when we can all dress up as elegant young women and go to the Faschingsball on the arm of a nice-looking young man. Nobody celebrated much round here. Mutti says it's because no one has any money.

Have you all given something up for Lent? I think it's difficult to give up something when you've pretty well had to give up everything anyway. No more baking, Mutti says. And I've stopped making 'flower' arrangements from what I can find in the garden. It gives me plenty of time for getting on with homework. They seem to give us even more here than they did at WL. Ah well... only another half year of school for me.

Looking forward to getting all your news. I wonder how long it will take before the letter gets back to me?

Take care, all,
Your Helga

Hani, 28 February 1939

Hani sighed and started pushing the bike. The tyre was completely flat. She'd pumped it up but seconds later it was down again. It must have a puncture but she couldn't see what had caused it. Oh no. That meant she would be late getting home and would be late for her BDM meeting and then she'd have to listen to Gisela Schmidt's sharp tongue….and Trudi Müller's gloating.

The first bit of her journey was uphill and soon she was sweating despite the cold February air. She wished she knew someone nearby who might help her fix the puncture. Vati had showed her dozens of times how to do it but she was still pretty useless at it.

If only she was still at the Waldorf School! It was nearer to home. Even if she'd had no bike at all she would have been home from there by now. She realised that she wasn't actually that far from her old school. If she turned down the next street she would be able to walk right past it. Not that she really wanted to do that. She had a couple of times before and it had been quite depressing to see it all shut up.

But another thought was that she was not that far away from Haus Lehrs in Schellberg Street. Surely it would be all right to go there and ask for help? Mutti had said she shouldn't go and disturb Frau Lehrs as she was very busy. Hani wondered just how busy an old lady like Renate's grandmother could be. But then, knowing Frau Lehrs, anything was possible. She was always helping the old folk – how funny when she must be at least 70 herself – or visiting the sick or trying to cheer up people who were sad. Hani was sure she would have some news about Renate, but Mutti had definitely said she was not to bother her.

She was really getting worried about Renate now. She'd written a couple of times and had no reply. It must be something worse than chicken pox. She knew she'd already had that. So, if she went to House Lehrs, she could ask about Renate as well as getting some help with her bike.

A few moments later she turned into Schellberg Street. Hopefully one of Renate's uncles would be there. Or probably that boy who worked for them – what was his name? Christoph? Surely somebody would be able to help her?

And then there she was, standing in front of number 20, her mouth dry and her heart thumping. She wasn't really quite sure why she felt so nervous. Probably because she was doing something her mother had told her not to.

The outer door was already open. Hani propped her bike against the wall and stepped into the porch. She thought she could hear people talking inside. They sounded like young people. What was going on? She stepped forward and rang the doorbell. The voices stopped. She waited and waited. Nothing seemed to be happening, although she knew there was somebody in there. The door was definitely open and she hadn't imagined those voices had she? Why didn't somebody come? She went to ring the bell again and then heard footsteps coming up the stairs from the cellar. Someone opened the door a crack, A face appeared in the small gap. Christoph!

"Oh it's you, Fräulein Gödde." He unhooked the chain. "I'm afraid Frau Lehrs is very busy. Perhaps you could call back later?"

"It's my bike," said Hani. "I've got a puncture and I can't fix it. Can somebody help me? I'm going to be late for my BDM meeting and I'll be in trouble."

"All right, then," said Christoph. "Come round the back. Quick as you can, I'll meet you in the garden." He slammed the door shut.

Hani wheeled the bike round. Her heart was thumping. There was obviously something wrong. She hoped it was nothing to do with Renate. And what were those voices she had heard?

Christoph was already by the back door when she got there.

"Let's take it into the shed and I'll look at it there."

It was quite warm inside the shed, which smelt of wood and creosote. Hani watched as Christoph took the tyre off the bike and looked at the inner tube. She felt useless.

She ought to be able to do that.

"Oh dear," he said. "This is bad. This is really bad. It can't be repaired. You'll need a new tube for this. Can you leave the bike here? I'll get you one later and fix it. Then perhaps you could pick your bike up after school tomorrow?"

Oh no! She was never going to get home now!

"Hey, cheer up," said Christoph. "I'll go and ask Frau Lehrs if I can take the car. I'm sure she'll say yes. Then I can drive you home. Go home in style or what? Your neighbours will have their eyes on stalks."

Hani nodded.

"Just wait here then," said Christoph. "I'll not be long."

But he was a long time. Ten minutes at least went by. She was going to be late now, whatever happened. Perhaps he was getting into trouble for even asking. Perhaps she'd go and find him and say that it was all right after all. It didn't really matter about the stupid BDM meeting. She could walk home. She'd just have to be late. She didn't want to put them to any trouble.

Besides, it was getting cooler now in the shed. It had seemed so warm at first. But now she needed to move around a bit.

The kitchen door was shut but not locked. Hani turned the handle and walked in. It was tidy, as usual, but somebody had obviously been busy. Twelve cups and plates were drying on the rack over the draining board. Who had Frau Lehrs been entertaining, and where was Christoph?

"Christoph," she called. "It's all right. I can walk home."

There was no reply.

She thought she could hear people talking again. Yes, definitely. They were down in the cellar room. She thought she recognised one of the voices.

She pushed open the door to the cellar. The voices became louder. She made her way down the steps.

"It all right Liesel," she heard a man's voice saying. "We're here."

Hani opened the door into the cellar room. The chattering stopped. Christoph was sitting on the floor, holding Liesel Schuhmacher. There were all the other children from the Special Class and Doctor Schubert.

"Ah, Hani Gödde," he said.

"Sorry I left you so long," said Christoph. "Liesel had another seizure and they needed my help."

"How very nice to see you, my dear," said Frau Lehrs. "And yes, of course, Christoph will take you home in the car."

"It's all right. I'll walk," said Hani. She blushed at the thought of her own stupidity. She'd never once thought about what had happened to the Special Class. It was obvious they weren't at the Gymnasium with her. She hadn't given them a single thought.

"No. No question of it. And I'm sorry I've not been in touch," said Frau Lehrs. "But you can probably see why. We've been busy."

"How's Renate?" said Hani. "Is she better from the chicken pox?"

"Ah," said Frau Lehrs. She looked away.

"It's only me," called another voice that Hani recognised. "Shall I come down?"

Clara Lehrs grinned at Hani. "Don't worry. It will be all right," she whispered.

"Only I've managed to get a good supply of pencils and paper from that new printer in town. They'll deliver it tomorrow," called Frau Gödde as she came down the stairs. She opened the door. The colour drained from her face and she gasped as she saw Hani.

"Don't worry, Frau Gödde," said Clara Lehrs very quickly. "She only came because she had a puncture. Christoph is going to mend it for her."

"So why exactly does Frau Lehrs have the Special Class in her house?" asked Hani as she sipped her peppermint tea. She was back now from her BDM meeting. She'd got there just in time. It hadn't been so bad, in the end. In fact it had even given her one or two ideas. Then Mutti had said she wanted to talk to her – preferably after Rikki had gone to bed. So here she was, sitting in the kitchen in her nightie and dressing-gown. For once, she didn't mind the peppermint tea. There was something odd going on and she wanted to find out more. Her mother had opened the conversation by reminding her of what had happened that afternoon.

"Because the Waldorf School closed and there was nowhere for them to go," said Frau Gödde.

Hani couldn't believe she hadn't thought of that. She'd been so preoccupied with getting used to the new school and all these activities with the BDM that were so much more demanding than the Jungmädel had been, that she hadn't given a thought to what might happen to the children in the Special Class.

"Isn't there a special school for them?" said Hani.

"Unfortunately no," replied Mutti. "I don't think the authorities quite know what to do with them. They really wish they weren't there at all."

"So what would happen to them if they didn't go to Haus Lehrs?" said Hani.

"They would just have to be educated by their parents," said Frau Gödde.

That would be hard. They'd all been used to the children from the Special Class at the Waldorf School and the Special Class children had been used to them. But Hani could see that they would be hard work. Doctor Schubert was really the only teacher who could do a lot with them. It would be strange to think of them in a big school with lots of other children like them. But not going to school at all – that was even worse.

Hani remembered some of the things they'd discussed at their BDM meeting. They had been talking, hadn't they, about doing charitable works, about helping others? Couldn't she help Frau Lehrs? Would than count?

"Mutti, couldn't I help Frau Lehrs and Doctor Schubert?" said Hani. "We're supposed to think of a charity to support for next week."

Frau Gödde shook her head. "You'll be at school when they're at school," she said. "And besides, it's a little bit dangerous."

Dangerous? How could helping less fortunate people be dangerous? "What do you mean?"

"Well, strictly speaking, the school is breaking the law," said Frau Gödde. "You mustn't tell anybody about it. The only people who know are those at Haus Lehrs, Vati and I and now you."

So, she was being let in on a secret.

"I'd still like to help," said Hani quietly. Liesel had been one of her best friends until she'd started having the seizures and acting so strangely. "And anyway, the Special Class lessons go on for longer because they don't have homework. Perhaps I can go there after school? And I can always do some things for them in my spare time – whatever Frau Lehrs or Doctor Schubert needs."

Frau Gödde stroked Hani's hair. "You're a good girl, Hani," she said. "All right. You can help a little. But your school work and your BDM work come first. And you must be careful to tell absolutely no one about all of this. No one at all. Promise?"

"I promise," said Hani. She took a last sip of her peppermint tea. It was completely cold now. She shivered.

Sabine, 28 February 1939

Dear All,

I think this is such a good idea, and it is so good to share everyone's news. Yes, I've been enjoying the winter, too. I've been ice-skating every evening with my brother and his friend Thomas. Thomas is such a good skater. He's also showing me how to do some ice-dancing moves. That's something I would really like to take up seriously, I can't afford to go to the big rink in town and take lessons, so I'm hoping the cold will hold out.

Still, if the snow does melt, I can start training again for the area athletics championships. Herr Schmidt is going to train me again this year, even though his activities with the Hitlerjugend are keeping him very busy. He actually doesn't think he will be called up for the army because of the injury to his leg, though he does think he might be called upon to train some of the soldiers. He thinks he'll be able to do that near here, so he'll still be able to go on with my training. Just why are so many people joining the army now? It seems that they can't get enough through military service.

Well, Georg will be doing his military service soon. Mutti seems to be really worried about it, and yet when Günter did his five years ago, she didn't fuss.

Father says I must work hard at my sport, but that also I should remember the duties of a young woman. He tells me how proud he is of my mother – always working hard for the family, making lots of lovely homemade food and doing her duty by going to church. I think I'd find that all a bit dull, really, and I'm glad it will be a while before I have to be a good German house wife.

Well, I'll finish now. I look forward to hearing from you all.

Sabine

Renate, March 25 1939

"Still no news from Doctor Edler?" Mrs Smith asked Mutti that morning.

She had moved into the little attic room above the Smiths' flat a few weeks before. Uncle Ernst and Uncle Rudi had left so they really were alone in England now.

"Oh, I don't need him," Mutti replied. "I am a woman of independent means. I look after myself. After all, he shouldn't mix with the Jews."

But Renate missed her father and she knew Mutti did too. She'd heard her crying sometimes at night. She felt like crying herself sometimes. School was all right, though, except that still no one spoke to her. Not even the teachers. She really would have so liked some proper English friends. Nobody was unkind, but nobody seemed to want to include her in things.

Even school life couldn't be peaceful forever. Miss Thompson did at least know all about Renate, even if she didn't quite know how to be with her. When she arrived at school that day, there was no Miss Thompson, but Mrs Barlow who taught English to the pupils in the Upper School. Miss Thompson had flu apparently.

"Oh!" she said when she saw Renate. "I didn't think... well... I thought maybe you wouldn't be taking part in this lesson."

On the blackboard was a detailed picture of an angel speaking to a young woman.

Some of the others had come in by now and had started to stare at Renate.

"I mean, doesn't your mother mind you learning these things?" asked Mrs Barlow.

What did she think? Her mother had been a scientist, for goodness sake. She didn't believe in all those things. Neither did her father for that matter, and she wasn't so sure herself, either, though it was quite nice sometimes to believe that there was a god who looked after you and cared for you. Angels were a nice idea as well.

But if they were going to bring up now that she was Jewish...
It was bad enough that they all knew she was German. She didn't
want to be different. She wanted to be the same.

"We don't believe in all of that, really," she said, very aware
that her German accent had returned and was stronger than ever.

One or two of the others were crowding round now, staring.
What did they think? She was just ordinary, wasn't she? Just like
them really, or at least, just like her friends back in Germany.

"You can sit out if you want to," said Mrs Barlow.

Renate looked at the board. That angel really was beautiful and
the girl he was talking to looked not much older than herself. She
didn't know what to say.

"Why shouldn't she do this lesson?" she heard one of
Christine's friends whisper.

"I think perhaps she's Jewish," she heard David reply.

Renate turned to face them. David looked away and Christine
blushed. How did they know? How did they know and what did it
matter? She wasn't really Jewish. She was German, and she was
trying to learn to be English.

"Yes, fine, then," said Mrs Barlow. "Right then, sit down if
you're staying."

Renate sat down, and listened again to the story of the angel
Gabriel speaking to Mary. It was a story, that was all. A story. One
she rather liked, actually.

The lesson came to an end. They had sport afterwards and she
threw herself into a game of netball. Fortunately, the PE mistress
herself picked the teams. If it had been left to one of the girls,
Renate was sure no one would have picked her. She hadn't played
netball before, but she did rather like it, and soon managed to score
three goals. Maybe that would take their minds off whether she
was Jewish or German or just a freak. Still no one spoke to her.
Christine just nodded.

"Mutti," she said when her mother came in that evening. "Why
does being Jewish make us different from other people, when
we're really the same?"

"We are the same," replied Frau Edler. "It's just that Herr

Hitler and his cronies think otherwise." She shrugged.

Renate could tell it was not a subject to be discussed.

YOU DON'T GET IT DO YOU? THAT JUST SHOWS HOW STUPID YOU ARE. TUT. TUT. WHEN IT'S SO OBVIOUS. THE BLUTSCHUTZGESETZ SAYS SO. YOU'RE A JEW BECAUSE YOUR GRANDMOTHER AND YOUR MOTHER ARE JEWS. A FILTHY JEW. IT'S ALL IN THE BLOOD.

Charlotte, 5 April 1939

Dear All,

Isn't time a funny old thing? It seems to go too quickly yet it also seems to go too slowly. I mean, it doesn't seem five minutes since that last afternoon in Miss Braun's class, when we had to be sent home because the heating broke down. Yet so much has happened since. Do you know what one of the other girls said to me the other day? That she remembered my name first because of my hair. I always knew it was a mistake having red wiry hair. Everybody notices it. Liesel – who has now become a very good friend, but not yet as good as some of you – said it's not just the colour, but also how bushy it is, even when it's in plaits.

The new school is so much bigger than the Wilhelm-Löhe school. There's always something new going on. But you can also feel lost in a crowd.

Ursula gave birth to twins just three weeks ago, so now I am an aunty. She's named them Hanna and Lotti. They are quite sweet and have wonderful blue eyes like their father. Their hair looks blonde at the moment. It's so strange, being an aunt. It makes me feel quite grown-up.

We now have my grandmother living with us. She has become completely blind and cannot manage any more on her own. She is good company. She has such good stories and always a wise word or two to say. She doesn't like Herr Hitler one little bit.

Well, I think I'd better finish now and get this posted on. I look forward to the rest of your letters.

Until the next time,
Yours,
Charlotte

Hani, 12 April 1939

Hani and two of the other girls were unloading the tents and the other camping equipment into the Hitlerjugend store. It was all so neat and tidy. She couldn't believe the boys had managed that. I suppose it's what they teach them to do, she thought. She was hot and thirsty and her lovely white shirt was getting dirty. Goodness knows what Rikki would say. Why on earth they'd had to change back into their formal uniform she had no idea.

"We have to keep up appearances," Gisela Schmidt had said. "The Führer expects us to look smart at all times." Well, blow the blooming Führer. He was a nutter. Hani blushed at the thought and hoped that none of the other girls were mind-readers. She hated the way some of them seemed to be in love with Adolf Hitler. One of the girls had even said, "I would love to go to bed with him and make babies." Gross! He was old enough to be her father, wasn't he? Older, even. And he didn't even have the blond hair and blue eyes that everybody seemed to think were so important. What colour were his eyes? She wasn't sure.

"Come on ladies, get to it," barked Gisela. "What is it, Fräulein Gödde? Day dreaming again? Move it."

At least she was fitter now. She could move more easily. All the marching and sporting activities with the BDM were helping, plus cycling round to Haus Lehrs. With the general lack of food she was much slimmer now.

Ten minutes later, they were done.

"You can't go home yet," said Gisela. "We're going to have a short meeting first. So, inside, ladies please, and set out the chairs in a circle."

"Darn!" whispered Hani. She had promised she would go round to Haus Lehrs as soon as she got back and help get the craft trays ready for the next day. Reluctantly she made her way into the hall.

"Why are you looking so sulky, Johanna Gödde?" said Trudi Müller. She squinted up at Hani. As usual, much of her fine white baby hair had escaped from her plaits. She looked so funny Hani found it hard not to laugh. "You're not going to be a good Reich's citizen if you're not willing to put in the effort. And I bet you can't get yourself a good Reich's man. Not with your dark mouse hair. At least I'm nice and blond."

Trudi's hair was more like old-lady white, and actually a bit like baby hair as well. How would that be attractive to a man? Hani tried to ignore her.

"Come on you two," shouted Gisela. "Hurry up and sit down."

Hani took her chair and put it into the circle as far away from Trudi as she could. She went to sit down.

"Just a minute," said Gisela. "Come and stand in the middle and let's have a look at you."

Hani felt her cheeks go bright red again.

Gisela came and stood next to her. "This, ladies, is an example of what we don't want to do. Just look at the state of this uniform. Shirt untucked and covered in dirty marks." She wrinkled up her nose as she looked at Hani.

Well, what did she expect if she insisted on them unloading dusty camp equipment in their full uniforms?

"And this skirt is an absolute disgrace," said Gisela, pulling at Hani's waistband. "If it's become too big for you, take it in. All young German women must be handy with a needle and thread."

Hani looked down at the floor. She couldn't bear to see the others looking at her. This was the sort of thing that Rikki would normally do for her. But recently Rikki had also been up to something secret – something Mutti seemed to approve of – and some of the household tasks had been neglected. She guessed she'd better learn to sew.

"Go and sit down," hissed Gisela. "But don't ever turn up to a meeting looking like that again."

Hani returned to her seat. She tried not to look at the other girls but suddenly there was a giggle from the other side of the circle. Hani looked up to see Trudi smirking at her.

"Right," said Gisela. "I'm not going to keep you long. I promise. You've all worked very hard. Well, most of you have."

She glared at Hani. "That, of course, is very good. That will help the Fatherland no end. But it is time to think about how we can strengthen the German people even more. I want you to go home and talk to your parents about the Reichsbürger and the Blutschutzgestz." She paused to look round at all the girls. "I'm pretty certain everybody here is all right and has nothing to worry about. But we all have to be aware of who the state enemy is and how to avoid them."

A few of the girls gasped and exchanged worried looks with each other. There was a general mumbling. At last one of the girls put her hand up. "What do you mean?" she said.

"Well, you remember what happened last November?" Gisela said.

Hani closed her eyes. She remembered walking with Vati through the middle of town that cold November morning. There were lots of people hanging about in groups. There was glass all over the pavements. Café Kellermann, her favourite café, had all its windows smashed and the remains of the prettily crafted cakes had been trodden into the ground. The word 'Jude' had been painted on the door. She was shocked. She hadn't realised the Kellermans were Jewish.

A man came running along the street. "The synagogue's on fire!" he shouted.

Hani and Vati turned the corner and there it was. Bright orange flames were lashing into the sky. Firemen were spraying the buildings next door.

"They're trying to stop the other buildings catching fire," Vati explained.

But why weren't they trying to put the fire at the synagogue out?

"Why has all of this happened?" Hani asked.

"Some people don't like Jews," said Vati.

"Why not?" asked Hani.

"Shh!" said Herr Gödde. "We'll talk about it when we get home."

A policeman who was standing nearby came over to them.

"Heil Hitler!" he said, raising up his right arm smartly.

Herr Gödde frowned, waving his arm limply. "Heil Hitler!" he mumbled.

"Best if you take the young lady home, sir," the policeman said. "She doesn't need to see what's happened to the scum."

So they'd gone home. Vati had gone straight to his study when they got in. He'd never explained to Hani why some people didn't like the Jews. She hadn't dared to ask him again. He'd been so pale and looked so worried. Was Gisela now going to give her some sort of explanation?

The girls were listening in silence now; all eyes fixed on their leader.

"Well," Gisela continued. "That was only right and proper. This was the people's way of dealing with state enemy."

One of the girls put up her hand. Gisela nodded that she could speak.

"Why are Jews the state enemy?" said the girl.

"They steal our jobs, they take our money, and they live in the houses which should be ours," replied Gisela. "Remember: they killed Jesus Christ and still deny that he was the Messiah. And above all, they are vermin. Filth."

But Jesus was a Jew anyway, wasn't he? thought Hani. And how could Gisela say that the nice people who used to run that café were filth? They were lovely. Always so kind and friendly. The café was always spotlessly clean. And the two little girls had the prettiest blond hair. What Gisela was saying didn't make any sense.

"Anyway, what is most important is that none of you have anything to do with anyone who is not of pure Aryan blood. Anyone befriending Jews – or even Mischlinge – people who have two grandparents who are Jewish or in any other way non-Aryan – will also be seen as enemies of the state. You must let the authorities know of anyone who is doing this. You can let me know if you prefer and I can pass on the information."

Gisela looked at all the girls one by one. One or two shuffled uncomfortably.

"Good," said Gisela. "That will do for today. We can take this up again next time. Can we tidy the chairs away please?"

One or two girls began to make comments as they dragged the chairs across the floor. Hani couldn't hear what they were saying because of all the clattering. She was aware, though, that Trudi Miller was staring at her. "I know somebody who talks to Jews!" Trudi pointed at Hani. "I've seen her going into Haus Lehrs on Schellberg Street."

"Are the people who live there Jews?" asked Gisela.

"Mutti says she's known the family for years. Herr Lehrs was a soldier in the war with my Opa. She says Frau Lehrs' name used to be Loewenthal. They're Jews all right." Trudi smirked at Hani.

"Is this true, Hani?" said Gisela. "Have you been to Haus Lehrs?"

This didn't make any sense. How could Frau Lehrs be Jewish? She was a Christian, wasn't she? Hani's mouth was so dry she couldn't speak.

"Well," said Gisela. "Did you go to Haus Lehrs?"

"I went there one day because I had a puncture," said Hani. "I thought they might help. Frau Lehrs' granddaughter is one of my friends." She shouldn't have said that. "I haven't seen her for a long time, though," she added quickly. "She lives in Nuremberg and she's had chicken pox, badly."

"Hopefully very badly," said Trudi. "Or maybe she doesn't live in Nuremberg anymore. Perhaps they've sent her somewhere more sensible for Jews. Your friend's partly Jewish, a horrible Mischling. And you're an enemy of the state because you mix with Jews."

What were they saying? There was nothing bad about Renate, nothing at all.

Hani had to get out. She had black clouds in front of her eyes. Something nasty was going to happen.

"Excuse me," she mumbled and pushed past the other girls. Everything was a bit of a blur but Trudi Müller's leering grin was all too clear.

She just made it outside before she vomited on the grass. Some of it landed on her skirt.

Her friend Renate was a Mischling and might not be living in Nuremberg any more. She had never really believed it about the chicken pox. One thing was certain, though. Mutti, Vati and Frau Lehrs must finally tell her the truth.

Gerda, 12 April 1939

Dear All,

It's really good to get all your news. I've really enjoyed reading all your letters. It's odd, though, thinking that Renate's letter was written before Christmas and now Easter has come and gone as well.

Easter was quite a celebration for us, actually. Vati killed a chicken so we had a nice roast dinner. Hans was back from his military service. That means he will be able to help on the farm. Mutti and Vati have been letting me help quite a lot. I wish I could do that full time. Still only three more months of school. Vati wants me to go to the agricultural college next year. School again, I suppose. Still, it's bound to be interesting. Thomas wants to go as well. He'll have to wait ages before he gets to work on the farm. Properly, I mean. He does a few little jobs, like cleaning out the chickens and sweeping the yard. Vati keeps saying he won't be able to start for years. I don't really get why. He's only a year younger than me. Of course, I guess he'll have to do his military service, too. I suppose we're lucky, really, having so much fresh food to hand. The potatoes will be early this year, father says. Potatoes in spring!

I've been knitting again. No new wool though. I've had to unravel some old jumpers. I made scarves for Hans, Thomas and Vati. Mother has even got me knitting socks for the menfolk! That's complicated. But it's really not too hard once you get the hang of it.

Well, I'll finish now. Do all hurry and send me more news. I'm so looking forward to the next round of letters.

Gerda

Renate, 15 April 1939

It was raining heavily. They'd all been allowed into the building early. Renate made her way into the welcome warmth of the classroom. The others drifted in gradually. Today there was no Miss Thompson. Instead, sitting at her desk, looking through some of the student's work was an older lady with dark hair greying at the edges. She looked up and smiled at Renate.

"Good morning," she said, seeming to speak particularly to Renate though she was looking at everyone. "I'm afraid Miss Thompson has been called away. Her father has been taken ill. My name is Elsie Cohen. I'll probably be teaching you for the rest of this term. I retired from this school at the end of last year." She smiled and shook her head. "Alas, all those hours of freedom – they were not to be, and here I am again. And now the first thing I want to do today, before we even start Main Lesson, is to get to know you all a little."

One by one, she asked all the students to talk about themselves and then she asked them a few questions. Renate found it interesting. She found out all sorts of things she hadn't known about the others. Judging by the look of surprise on some of their faces, it was a similar experience for many of them. At last it was her turn.

"So, Renate," she said. "You are here from Germany. Perhaps you could tell us a little about your life there." Elsie Cohen smiled encouragement at her.

Renate told them all about the school there, which was so different from this one, and about the exercise book with the letters, and even about the way her father used to say 'Heil Edler' instead of 'Heil Hitler'.

"Why does everyone say 'Heil Hitler'? asked David.

"Do you know?" Mrs Cohen turned to Renate.

She didn't know really, though she, like her father, had always found it rather ridiculous. She shrugged and shook her head.

"I think people have to, or they would be in trouble," said Mrs Cohen. "And tell us, Renate, what do you miss from home?"

"Apfelstrudel, my friends and my father," said Renate in a tiny voice. Tears were stinging at her eyes. Christine put an arm round her. Then the sobs came. Christine squeezed her harder. She felt so silly, but she was glad of the younger girl's attention.

"There now, there now," said Mrs Cohen. "Oh you have been so brave. But it's all right not to be brave all the time." She stroked Renate's hair. She turned to the rest of the class. "Does anyone have any idea why Renate has come here?" she asked.

No one answered.

"Do you know yourself?" asked Mrs Cohen gently.

"It's to do with me being Jewish," stammered Renate.

"And so what's that, being Jewish?" asked Mrs Cohen.

"I don't really understand," said Renate.

"Neither do I," said Mrs Cohen quietly. "Neither do I. And look at me. Could you get a more Jewish name? And I couldn't feel more English if I tried. Roast beef, Yorkshire pudding and good old London town."

One or two of the students tittered a little.

"But you know," continued Mrs Cohen, to all the class and not just Renate. "If your mother is Jewish, you are Jewish, whether you like it or not. And unfortunately, a lot of people don't like Jews and the reasons they don't aren't always logical."

"Is it because the Jews didn't accept Christ?" asked David.

"Perhaps, in some cases," replied Mrs Cohen. "But a lot of people who don't like Jews are not particularly Christians anyway. And isn't it particularly unchristian to reject anyone?" She turned to Renate again. "Is your mother a practicing Jewess?"

Renate shook her head.

"So, you're really German not Jewish, but it seems that the Germans won't let you be German." She turned to the rest of the class. "You see, Renate is labelled Jewish because her mother is Jewish, and she in turn is Jewish because her mother is Jewish. Neither of them can help that. Renate was born in Germany. Her father is German, so she is also German. She cannot help that either." Mrs Cohen paused. She looked at the rest of the class. "Just imagine if someone tried to stop you being English."

There was complete silence.

"Mmm, about time we got on with Main Lesson, I think," said Mrs Cohen.

The class worked quietly. The lesson seemed to go very quickly, though Renate wasn't really concentrating all that hard. She was trying to sort out what Mrs Cohen had been saying.

"What a hard-working class!" said Mrs Cohen when they heard the bell ringing in the yard. "What well-mannered children. Now you shall all go out and enjoy the sunshine. I see the earlier gloom has gone."

The others started putting their things away. Renate carefully blotted her work and then closed her exercise book neatly.

"But I'd like to talk to you for a few minutes first, Renate, before you go to break," said Mrs Cohen.

They waited for the others to finish leaving the room.

"Do come and see me if any of this gets you down or puzzles you," said the teacher. "I've been mainly lucky, but there have been moments, even so. And goodness knows what is going on over there. I think it is going to be very bad." She paused. "The other students, you know, they are quite kind and open-minded. I think it's just that they don't know what to say or how to be with you. Please forgive them."

There was a huge lump in Renate's throat. She couldn't speak. Mrs Cohen gently touched her arm. "Go and join them now," she said. "I think they may want to see you."

David was standing by the door when she got outside.

"Hello," he said, blushing right up to where his hair parted. He didn't seem to know what else to say. Then his face lit up as if he'd had a sudden bright idea. "I don't suppose you'd like to play cricket, would you? We always play cricket at break-time. Except in the winter when we play football." He pushed his hair away from his forehead and blushed even deeper. He shuffled from foot to foot. "No, silly idea, I guess. Girls don't play cricket, do they? Oh! You don't play cricket in Germany anyway, do you?"

Renate couldn't think what to say. It was really the first time anyone at the school had invited her to join in anything.

"Do you like sport?" asked David. "Only... I watched you playing netball. You seemed pretty good. Did you play that in Germany as well?"

"I used to play handball," said Renate. "And I've always been good at running."

"Yes. Handball. Of course. Handball. You know, I've always wanted to learn how to play that? Could... could you show me some time?"

"Of course," said Renate. "It's easy. You only need a ball and people. But perhaps you could show me how to play cricket?"

"It's... it's... a bit complicated, I'm afraid," said David. "And the bat is quite big and it might be a bit heavy." He glanced over to where some of his friends were now watching. They were standing with their arms folded and they were grinning. "But if you can run well, you'll be fine," he said as he turned back towards Renate.

"All right, then," said Renate. She didn't tell him that her cousin Gottfried knew how to play cricket and had already shown her. He'd spent many months in England when he was a student and cricket had been one of the things he liked best. She already knew how to hold the bat and hit the ball and she had even had a go at bowling. She hadn't been bad at all.

"Right, chaps, I've found our twelfth man," David shouted to the others.

"She's a girl!" Renate heard one of the boys say in disgust.

"And what's wrong with that?" shouted Christine.

"Why shouldn't girls play cricket?" cried Anne, one of Christine's friends.

"Yes, why shouldn't they?" echoed another.

There was some general cheering from the girls. Some of the boys were shrugging their shoulders and shaking their heads.

"Are you sure you don't mind?" asked David, looking worried.

"No, I think it will be fun," replied Renate.

They put her into bat straight away.

"Bet she won't last long," she heard one of the boys mutter.

Wouldn't she? She'd show them.

She remembered the weight of the bat and how to angle it to get the most power behind the ball. Gottfried had been a good teacher. And of course, she could run. Soon she was lobbing the balls well out of sight, and the boys fielding had to work hard.

"Go, Renate!" she could hear the girls shouting from the side of the pitch. "Show 'em."

She was beginning to feel hot and a little short of breath, but her arms and her legs still felt strong.

"Edler! Edler!" chanted some of the boys, who were waiting for their turn to bat.

They didn't get a turn, though. By the time the bell rang to mark the end of break, her score was thirty, not out.

"You were fantastic," said David patting her back as they returned to the classroom. Several of the other boys also crowded round.

"They ought to have her on the team," mumbled one of the others

She parted company from David as they made their way towards the toilet blocks to wash before going back in. Christine was waiting for her, with two of her friends.

"You were great!" said Christine. She looked up towards her eyebrows. "I wish I could run like that." She hesitated, and then took a big breath. "But anyway, I was wondering… would you like to come to tea on Sunday? Anne and Joyce are coming as well," she added pointing to her two friends. "If you come on the underground or the bus, Dad will take you back in the car afterwards."

"It would be lovely if you could come," said Anne. "We're so lucky to have a friend who plays cricket as well as the boys. It must be really funny for you being here… you must miss your friends."

"We want to get to know you better," said Joyce. "We should have been nicer to you before… We didn't understand… about Hitler and all that stuff…"

There was an awkward silence.

"Will you come? Please?" Christine squeezed Renate's wrist.

Renate grinned. "I'd love to come. Should I bring some

Apfelstrudel? I'm sure I can persuade Mutti to make some."

"What's Apfelstrudel?" said Joyce.

"Apple strudel," said Renate. "A bit like your apple pie but the pastry is much thinner. You have to roll it out so that you can see a newspaper through it. And there's much more apple!"

"Oh yes, please bring some," said Christine.

SO, YOU THINK YOU'VE FOUND SOME FRIENDS. OH YES, THEY'RE NICE ENOUGH. BUT ARE YOU? YOU'RE NOT LIKE THEM ARE YOU? NOT REALLY. SO YOU THINK A BIT OF APFELSTRUDEL WILL BUY THEIR FRIENDSHIP? ARE YOU SURE IT WON'T JUST MAKE THEM THINK THAT YOU'RE GERMAN? WILL YOU EVER FIT IN ANYWHERE AGAIN? REALLY?

Erika, 22 April 1939

Dear All,

We are missing you, but we suppose we have each other for company. The new school's a bit boring, I'm afraid. Still, we did our usual trick of fooling the teachers. I went along for Gisela's singing lesson. And she did my detention. I'd got it for shouting out in class. I'm so glad she got to do my lines. Well, we've started dressing differently, so there. Except for school. And for BDM. Oh, obviously we have to dress the same there.

Are all the rest of you going to BDM? What do you think? I'm enjoying some of the activities. Next week we're going to be building some rafts with the boys from the local Hitlerjugend. Then we're going to raft down the river and have a picnic. We're looking forward to that.

I'm not sure about all the words, though. All that stuff they keep on about.

Well, I'll hand over to Ilse now. I look forward to the next letter.

Erika

Ilse, 25 April 1939

Dear all,

    Oh yes, I was so relieved when Erika went to my singing lesson for me. We've thought of her going all the time until Frau Mecker says I'm good enough and tells Vati and Mutti they can stop paying for lessons. Trouble is, dare I open my mouth to sing? Well, Erika says she will help me. She's actually giving me private lessons. Anyway, they'll be glad not to have to pay any more, I guess.

    Anyway, we're going to have to stop all of that soon. Our class teacher now can tell which one of us is which, when we're together at least. And because we've decided to dress differently.... Well, they're going to have it easy.

    Mutti is cross with us about that. "Why did I bother having twins if they want to be different from each other? Girls, you are identical twins. Behave like them!" Huh!

    Yes, we're both looking forward to the rafting with the boys. But Erika is especially keen... you see there is one boy called Kurt. He's very tall, blond hair, blue eyes... and Erika would do anything for him. She really blushed the other day when he came out of the baker's as she was going in. He saluted and she was too befuddled to answer back. It's a good job no one was watching.

    She'll kill me if she knows I've told you this. So, I'm getting this posted off straight away to Renate. By the time the letter comes back again... who knows... maybe she will be over Kurt.

Until the next time,
Take care everyone,
Ilse

Anika, 25 April 1939

The back door suddenly banged. Anika dropped the card she was holding and knocked most of the others on the floor as she bent down to pick it up. Drat it! For the first time ever she had almost completed a game of clock patience.

"Mutti!" she heard Fritz shout. "Mutti. Where are you? I've got something to tell you."

It sounded urgent whatever it was.

Fritz came bursting into the sitting room. "Where's Mutti?" he asked. His eyes were sparkling and his face was bright red.

"What is all this fuss about?" asked Frau Müller as she came into the sitting room, wiping her hands on her apron.

"We found old Jakob Kohn in the woods," shouted Fritz. "Dead. Somebody had shot him."

Anika gasped.

"Oh no! Oh, God in Heaven," said Frau Müller, putting her hand in front of her mouth and sitting down.

"Why?" asked Anika.

Frau Müller just shook her head and rocked backwards and forwards. "Oh, no, no, not here," she whispered.

"But who would want to kill him?" asked Anika. Herr Kohn had become old and weak and a bit strange since he'd closed the shop after his wife died. He didn't deserve to be shot, though. She remembered how kind he'd been when she was a little girl. He used to give her sweets from one of the brightly coloured jars on the counter when Fritz and his friends had been teasing her. He'd always told her such funny stories as well to cheer her up.

"It's probably because he was Jewish," said Frau Müller softly.

"There was blood all over the place," said Fritz, his eyes sparkling even more brightly. "They'd shot him in the head."

Anika felt sick. How could anyone do such a thing? Why should you shoot somebody just because they were old and strange, or Jewish? Perhaps he had a lot of money?

"His head was all gooey and there were maggots crawling all

over him," said Fritz, pulling a face.

"That's enough," said Frau Müller standing up suddenly. "I think you and I had better have a quiet little chat about this." Her face had gone red now and she was pointing towards the door. She marched Fritz out towards the hallway.

"Don't let me ever hear you talking like that again about something so terrible," Anika heard her say.

Then the kitchen door slammed. She heard Frau Müller and Fritz talking quite loudly but she couldn't quite make out what they were saying.

The doorbell rang. Frau Müller opened the front door. She then said something to the visitor, but Anika couldn't make out what. The door to the sitting room opened and Frau Müller showed in a little woman who looked as if she had been crying. Anika recognized her straight away as Wilma the maid who worked for Renate's parents.

"Tell her yourself," said Frau Müller. "You can explain exactly what you know."

"This came in the post, for Renate," said Wilma. The tears were forming in her eyes again. "Only she's not here anymore."

"Well, no she's in Stuttgart, isn't she?" asked Anika, remembering that Renate had actually given them her new address in Stuttgart. Trust Gisela and Erika to send it to her old one. But surely Wilma knew where Renate was staying? Couldn't she have just sent it on?

"No, she's... she's..." The older lady couldn't speak now.

"Come on sit down," said Frau Müller, leading Wilma towards a chair. "Fritz," she called. "Bring Wilma a glass of water." She put her arm around the older woman.

Fritz came in with the water. Wilma got herself back in control.

"She's gone to England," she managed to say at last.

"England?" said Anika.

"Yes, you see, she is Jewish," said Wilma. "She and her mother are Jewish."

"Never!" cried Anika. "I can't believe it."

Wilma nodded.

74

"And her poor father can't go and join them," said Wilma. "He's working for the government. Not allowed to leave the country." She shook her head and sighed. Then she looked sharply at Anika "I hope you didn't mind me looking in your book to find your name. I had to ask one or two people about where you lived."

"I'll make some tea," said Frau Müller.

Anika, 3 May 1939

Dear All,

I have the most amazing news. Renate has gone to England! Apparently, she is Jewish! Who would have thought it? How come we didn't know?

I decided to write to Fräulein Braun and ask her what she knew. She has replied and I've put her letter in here, to all of you. I think it would be a good idea to include her in the circular letter, don't you think? You can all put in your replies and if we all agree, the next time it comes to me, I'll send it on to her instead of Helga.

There has been some excitement here as well. Do any of you remember Jakob Kohn? You know, he used to run the little sweet shop in our village. Fritz and his Hitlerjugend friends found him dead in the forest. They thought he'd been shot – there was so much blood everywhere. But now everybody is saying he was only hit on the head. And it's even possible that he did it himself by walking into a tree. His next-door neighbour said he often went out at night. He was always talking to himself. He became very peculiar after his wife died and he shut up the shop. Poor Herr Kohn. He was always such a nice man. I'm really glad, though, that he wasn't shot because he was a Jew. How could anyone do such a thing?

Well that's all the excitement. And I'm sorry it wasn't nice excitement.

Looking forward to your news.

Your Anika

Hanna Braun 28 April 1939

Dear Anika,

What a delight to receive your letter and then what sadness to read inside it. But do let's keep this all in some sort of perspective. Renate is not really any more Jewish than you or I. I'm sure she certainly doesn't feel at all Jewish. There are strange things going on at the moment, and it's wise to be cautious. But let's just hope it's only the work of madmen and that even they will come to their senses.

As for Jakob Kohn, I am sure you are right and it was just a tragic accident. From what I've heard, he was quite demented. We ought to care for our old folk better. Yes, he had a very Jewish name, but like Renate, we hardly thought of him as Jewish did we?

I am so pleased that you have decided to set up this circular letter. It is an excellent idea. I would love to join in – if you will have me. I do like to keep in touch with my former pupils and this is such a good way of doing that.

Just a little word of caution. Be a little careful of what you put in here. It may seem that none of the officials would be interested in schoolgirls' exercise books, but who knows what they might soon do in the future? Or what might happen if our precious little book should be lost in the post. So, just talk of your everyday lives, and the things you are achieving, and only of personal sadnesses – hopefully there will be none.

Well, I've started my new school. It is a very small private school and also under threat of closure. But for the time being I have my own little class.

Be brave and be good, all of you.
Thinking of each and every one of you,
Your Hanna Braun

Hani, 7 May 1939

Hani was bored. Even though school and the BDM meetings gave her plenty to do, she wasn't really doing anything she enjoyed.

"Why can't I go back to Haus Lehrs?" she said. "I'll be really careful."

"I know you want to help," said Frau Gödde, "but it's just too risky."

"You're always doing things to help people," she replied. "And Vati doesn't like doing the 'Heil Hitler'."

"But he does do it," said Frau Gödde. "And he knows when and how to be discreet. You're not mature enough to do that. Look how you told those despicable girls about Renate."

How could her mother think she was nothing but a silly child? She would show them. She had already become an excellent schoolgirl and a model BDM member. But none of that mattered. What she'd been doing with the Special Class was real work.

This was all just so unfair! "Oh, I'm going out," she cried.

"Where are you going?" Mutti shouted after her.

"I don't know and why should you care?"

She stomped out of the house and slammed the door behind her. She really had no idea where she was going but soon found herself at the local sports ground, watching some people she vaguely knew play tennis.

"I didn't know you were into tennis," said a familiar voice.

Hani turned to face the speaker. "Christoph!" Then she felt her cheeks burn. She'd never noticed before how good-looking he was. But then, she'd never seen him with bare arms or bare legs before. The white shorts and shirt really suited him and showed up his faint tan.

"I'm not," she said.

"So what brings you here?"

"I've just had a row with my mother."

"Oh dear, that's not a good idea," said Christoph.

"I'm so bored with everything," said Hani.

"You should come back to Haus Lehrs," he added. "We need you. When are you coming back?"

"I can't," said Hani. "That was what the row was about. One of the BDM girls saw me going there and she knows that Frau Lehrs is Jewish."

"Oh dear. That's a shame."

Neither of them spoke for a few minutes.

"I know," said Christoph suddenly. "We can disguise you as a boy. Then your little friend won't see you going there again. And the nosy neighbours won't know who you are either."

"What?" said Hani, laughing.

"Yes, you could be my younger brother. Hans Tellermann. The girls wouldn't recognise you. Nor the Hitlerjugend boys."

"You're not serious are you?" asked Hani.

"Naturally I am," said Christoph. "I could meet you here next week with some of my clothes."

"Do you think it would work?"

"Why shouldn't it?"

Could it work? Hani wasn't sure.

"Ah, look. It's my turn to play."

Hani looked to where he was pointing. Three of the four young men who had been playing on the middle court were walking off now. The fourth one stayed on the court and waved to Christoph.

He turned back towards Hani. "I'll bring the clothes, right? Meet you here the same time next week?"

It was worth a try, she supposed. She nodded.

She watched Christoph play a couple of sets and then slowly made her way home. She'd have to apologize to her mother, she knew, but she might be able to get back to working at Haus Lehrs. Fancy that! Now that was something to look forward to.

Hani, 14 May 1939

Hani looked at herself in the mirror. It really worked. The trousers fitted her well. The shirt was a little big on the shoulders but otherwise it looked good. Christoph had found her a whole pile of other clothes so there would be enough for several changes a week.

These are really comfortable, she thought. I could get used to this. There was a problem though: her hair. What could she do with that?

The door to her bedroom suddenly opened.

"Goodness," said Frau Gödde. "If it wasn't for your hair, you would look just like a boy. What on earth are you doing?"

Why didn't her mother knock when she came into her room? She really could be annoying.

"Where did you get all these clothes?" said Frau Gödde.

"Christoph gave them to me," said Hani.

"Christoph?" Frau Gödde suddenly looked very serious. "Why?"

Hani sighed. "I really want to go back to Haus Lehrs and carry on working with the Special Class."

"I don't understand," said Frau Gödde. "What has that got to do with these clothes?"

"Hans thought I wouldn't be recognised by the likes of Trudi and Gisela if I looked like a boy."

Frau Gödde raised her eyebrows. "I don't know," she said. "It's so dangerous."

"You still go," said Hani. "Why shouldn't I? I want to help as well."

"I know. But there are so many risks."

"I know I was a bit careless before," said Hani. "But I didn't realise how bad it really was. I've been very good since, haven't I? A model German girl."

"You have, you have," said Frau Gödde. "Vati and I are really proud of you."

"Well why won't you trust me then?"

Frau Gödde frowned and pursed her lips. "Hang on a minute." She went out of the room.

Hani looked in the mirror. She held her hair up over her head again. Could she make it work? Probably not! Anyway, her parents would most likely not agree to her going back.

A few moments later, Mutti came back into the room. She was holding a man's cap.

"It's one of Wilhelm's," she said. "I don't suppose he'll mind. Try it on."

Hani placed the cap on her head.

"Here, like this," her mother said, scraping Hani's hair up and fixing it with the cap.

"Gosh!" said Hani, as she saw herself in the mirror.

"Yes. More Hans than Hani, I'd say."

Neither of them spoke for several minutes.

"You are being much more sensible now," said Frau Gödde at last. "But we have to be so careful." Then she smiled and hugged Hani. "And I'm really proud of my brave, thoughtful little girl."

"Not so much of the little," said Hani. "And I'm big enough for you to tell me what really happened to Renate."

Frau Gödde sighed. "All right. She's gone to England. There's a special scheme for Jewish children. She's been especially lucky because her mother has been able to go and join her. Not all the children have that chance. But she was on her own for the first couple of months."

"England?" said Hani. "But she doesn't speak English."

"No, but she's at a Waldorf School," said Frau Gödde. "You know they'll treat her kindly."

Renate was at a Waldorf School? Unbelievable. Hani almost felt jealous but then remembered it must have been really funny for her friend, finding out that she was Jewish and then having to go away like that, on her own, to a country where she didn't speak the language.

"Perhaps you can ask Frau Lehrs more about it when you go back," suggested Frau Gödde softly.

Hani, 2 June 1939

It was a glorious day. The sun was streaming down and the sky was a deep blue. Not the slightest hint of a cloud; just enough of a gentle breeze to stop it being too hot. It was such a pity that they couldn't take the children outside to play. They just daren't though.

Hani could feel her cap falling off her head. It was really making her feel hot. She wanted to pull it off completely. Not yet, though – not until she was inside.

She wheeled the bike up the path and put it into the shed and then made her way as quickly as possible to the back door. She wasn't so sure how convincing her disguise was close to, and they didn't know whether they could trust the neighbours. In the kitchen, she resisted the urge to look at what was baking in the oven and making the place seem so warm and welcoming. She caught a glimpse of herself in the mirror. Now that she was a little taller and a little slimmer – despite Frau Lehrs' excellent baking – Christoph's clothes fitted her well. She would have to do something about her boobs soon if they carried on growing at this rate, but at a distance at least, she no longer looked like Hani Gödde. Here she was Hans Tellermann; Christoph's younger brother, if anyone asked.

Once indoors she got rid of the cap. She took it off and slipped it into her pocket so that it would be handy if she needed it in a hurry.

She could hear Doctor Schubert's voice coming from the cellar. The class seemed to be going well and it was clear the children were listening attentively. There was a note on the hall table addressed to her in Frau Lehrs' handwriting.

Dear Hans,
Can you please wash out the paint tubs and see if the pictures are dry? It will be nice if they can take them home today. I'm sorry I can't greet you personally. I'm having a

meeting with Dr Kühn this afternoon. I hope we'll be finished before the children go home.

Clara Lehrs

Hani smiled to herself. She loved the way Frau Lehrs took her disguise so seriously.

The paint pots were, as she expected, already in the utility room. Hani smiled at the sight of the children's paintings all pegged on to the line as if they were washing. They were so colourful. That was something you could always say about children from the Waldorf School: they certainly knew how to draw and paint.

Soon all the pots were drying on the draining board. She carefully checked each of the paintings. They were all dry. Frau Lehrs would be pleased. The children would be able to take them home today. She stacked them up neatly. Then, she would just have time to put the pots away and take the pictures downstairs. She wondered whether the meeting with Dr Kühn had finished. What could that be about? All she knew was that Dr Kühn had come to her school now and then, and he was something important to do with the Waldorf schools.

She stacked the paint pots into the cupboard and picked up the pile of paintings. The door to Frau Lehrs' study was just opening as she came out into the hall.

"I'm glad we've been able to settle this so quickly," said Dr Kühn. "We can get the money into your bank account in about three weeks and then the house will be mine. No need for you to worry any more. I'm just sorry that I can offer you so little."

"Oh, Doctor Kühn," said Frau Lehrs. "Not a problem. You are just doing what has to be done. And better that you have Haus Lehrs than it goes to a complete stranger."

Hani gasped and dropped the pile of paintings on the floor. Frau Lehrs was selling the house? What was going to happen to the Special Class? Where was she going to live?

Dr Kühn turned towards the door. "Ah, my dear Fräulein

Gödde," he said. "Let me help you." He came out into the hallway and started to help her pick up the paintings. "Frau Lehrs has told me all about the good works you have been doing here. Splendid. Splendid. But maybe I shouldn't call you Fräulein Gödde. Hans, isn't it? Well done, that man. Good. Good. Do give my regards to your parents."

He handed Hani the paintings and reached for his hat and coat from the stand. "And now ladies, I wish you good day."

"Thank you so much. For everything, Doctor Kühn," said Frau Lehrs, as she let him out of the front door.

"Leave the paintings on the hall table, my dear," said Frau Lehrs. "You've had a shock. Go and sit in the lounge and I'll bring you a glass of lemonade. That cheesecake should be ready by now as well. I'll get Christoph to deal with the pictures."

Hani went into the lounge and sat down on one of the overstuffed sofas. She'd only been in here a couple of times before. Frau Lehrs was very house-proud and she and Renate had always been worried they'd make something dirty or untidy. Since she'd been working at the house, there'd been no time to sit down at all.

This room was so lovely though, with the light streaming in through the windows. Hani looked at the photos on the piano. There were ones of Frau Lehrs and her husband, when they were younger; there was one of Renate's parents on their wedding day; there were even a couple of her and Renate playing in the garden at the back of the house. And then there were the lovely paintings on the wall. What was going to happen to all of this after the house was sold? Where was she going to live? It would have to be another big house, and wouldn't that cost as much as this one? It didn't make any sense. Frau Lehrs loved this house. Hani knew that for sure.

"Here we are," said Frau Lehrs, as she came in carrying a tray holding two glasses of lemonade and two slices of cheesecake. She placed the tray on the small table in front of the sofa. "Do tuck in. This cheesecake is rather splendid, even though I say so myself and I shouldn't."

Hani took a sip of her drink. She could hardly swallow it. She didn't think she would manage to eat any of the cake, even though she knew it would be good.

"I really didn't want you to hear that," said Frau Lehrs. "We had meant to keep it a secret from everyone." She took a bite of her cake and then frowned. "Though I suppose eventually everyone will find out. Your parents know, of course. Perhaps I should tell Christoph after all. Hmm."

"But what's going to happen to the Special Class?" asked Hani.

Frau Lehrs laughed. "Of course. You think I'm moving. No, no. Not at all. Everything will carry on as normal. I'm renting a room from Doctor Kühn but I shall live here as I've always done and the class will carry on as normal. You won't know the difference. I promise."

Hani found she could swallow again and she thought she might be able to eat a little of the cake after all.

"In fact," Frau Lehrs continued, "with the money I get for the house I'll be able to spend a little more on the class. Yes, it's all to the good."

So that was it. Frau Lehrs was running short of money. Unbelievable. Mind you, she was always so generous to others. Perhaps she'd been a bit too generous?

"Anyway, that will get them off my back for a while now. They have what they want. Haus Lehrs will belong to a proper Aryan German. And I'm sure things are going to get easier now. The worst is over."

So it wasn't just that Frau Lehrs needed the money. What had Gisela said? That they, the Jews, were taking our houses? Was that it? But she still couldn't think of Frau Lehrs as a Jew. It was stupid. She was the most Christian and the most German person Hani knew. She let her fork drop on to her plate.

"Oh, but you're not eating your cake," said Frau Lehrs. She sighed. "I know what will cheer you up. I'll just pop and get something from my study."

Hani wanted to go home. Perhaps Vati would be able to tell her why Frau Lehrs had to sell her house. Or perhaps he wouldn't.

He'd refused to talk to her about the day they'd seen the synagogue burning. Maybe Mutti would be a better bet?

She guessed it would be very rude to leave without pretending to be cheered up by whatever it was that Frau Lehrs thought would do the trick.

A few seconds later, Frau Lehrs came back into the room, holding a letter. Hani recognised the handwriting. Her heart missed a beat.

"This is Renate's latest letter," said Frau Lehrs. "I've not got round to burning it yet. And I promise from now on I'll let you read every single one until I turn it into boiler fodder. You know, she would love it if you would write to her but I think it's best not to, though. I promise that I'll give her some news about you every time I write."

She placed the letter on the table.

"There," said Frau Lehrs. "I'll leave you to read in peace. The parents will be coming for the children any minute now and I want to make sure they all take their paintings home. And do eat up your cake. Don't take this trying to look like a boy too seriously. You're getting terribly thin, my dear."

Hani's hands were trembling as she opened the letter. She'd so wanted to hear from Renate, but now that she had some news she was a little afraid to look. There were such strange things going on. Perhaps the news would not be all good. Or perhaps Renate would be very homesick. Oh, she hoped Frau Lehrs was right and that the worst was over. But you couldn't be sure, could you? Renate was certainly better off in England.

She took a deep breath and started to read.

Sunday, 14 May 1939

Dear Oma,

You'll probably be pleased to hear that my English is getting better and better. I can now follow all the lessons really well. I don't mind any more that I'm working in a class for children a year younger than me. Because the work is easy it helped me to understand the actual language. I can understand what the teacher is saying now and I can answer questions. I can even write quite well, though it's still a bit difficult to follow what the other children are saying when we're out in the yard. They speak so fast!

I've met a super new teacher called Mrs Cohen. She came to teach us when our regular teacher, Miss Thompson, was called away because her father was ill. She managed to explain to the rest of the class that I'm German and Jewish at the same time. She also helped me to understand that I'm not peculiar because I feel so mixed up about who I am. It's the same for her because she's more English than Jewish. She's really nice.

You'll never believe it. I'm actually going to play in the cricket team! My class mates can't believe how well I understand that very English game. Thank goodness for cousin Gottfried. I'm so glad he spent all those weeks last summer teaching me what he'd learnt in England. And of course, I can run.

The girls in my class are getting very friendly now, and I'm regularly invited to tea by one or other of them. The other day Mutti made a wonderful Apfelstrudel. My friend and her family really enjoyed it.

Mutti is quite happy now because we have found a little delicatessen not far from the flat. It was the Polish people who live in the ground floor flat who told us about it. Of course, it is Polish, not German, but all the same, we can get some things we miss: salami, black bread (yes, we actually miss that. Who'd have thought it?) and cheesecake. Of course, Mutti makes an excellent cheesecake, almost as good as yours, but you can't buy quark in England. And the people at the Polish delicatessen do get quark, but they use it all up in the cheesecake. The nearest you can get to it is a sort of cream cheese, but it's just not the same. So we just have to buy the cheesecake.

Mutti is well and sends her love. I expect she will write to you again soon. Have you seen anything of Hani? Does

*she know what has happened to me? I'd love to write to her
but Mutti says it's best not to.*

> *I'll write again soon,*
> *Your loving granddaughter,*
> *Renate Edler*

Hani refolded the letter. She could feel a heavy weight lifting
from her chest. Her friend was doing all right. In fact, she almost
envied her. She seemed happy at the Waldorf School. It sounded
as if things were better in England than they were here in Germany.
No BDM for Renate. All she had to do in her spare time was play
cricket, go to friends' houses for tea and eat cheesecake.

Cheesecake! That piece of Frau Lehrs' cheesecake was sitting
staring at her. How could she resist? She couldn't, now that she
knew that Renate was all right. She picked up the plate and fork
and started to eat the cake.

It was melt-in-your-mouth good. Smooth, creamy and lemony.
Oh, she hoped that the one Renate and her mother were getting
from the Polish delicatessen was just as good. Yes, Frau Lehrs was
definitely an excellent baker. The cake was gone in no time. Hani
was just swilling it down with the last of the lemonade when the
door opened and in came Frau Lehrs.

"Good," she said. "You've finished. I hope you liked the letter.
And I see you liked the cheesecake in the end. Could you put those
things in the kitchen now? And then come and help get the children
ready to go home? Oh, and you'd better put the letter in the furnace
when you come down."

A few moments later Hani was in the basement about to put the
letter into the fire that heated the boiler. She hesitated. She wanted to
keep it. Should she? It did seem a shame to throw Renate's letter away.

She heard the voices coming from the classroom.

"Hans will give you your pictures," she heard Frau Lehrs say.
"Just be patient."

Hani opened the furnace door and dropped the letter inside. She
picked up the pictures and hurried to the classroom.

Renate, 18th June 1939

"Mutti!" Renate called. "I'm back. I've got something to tell you."
She was holding the note that Mrs Jenkins had given her for her
mother explaining all about it. She had been invited by Christine's
family to go on a camping holiday in Kent. Mutti was invited too.

Silence. Then she heard the voices from the side garden. Her
mother was talking to the people from the flat below. The
Hanusiaks had taken to inviting them on fine afternoons to join
them in the little garden that went with their flat. Sometimes
Renate would amuse Marek and Tatiana, the twins, by playing hide
and seek or a ball game. Even though they were only six, she really
enjoyed being with them. She loved her new English friends but it
was so good to spend some time with other people who had had to
leave their homeland far behind. The Hanusiaks had also lived in
Germany and Renate often forgot that they were Polish and not
German at all.

She quickly went into the bedroom to change out of her school
clothes into something more comfortable. She could play with the
twins for a while and then the Hanusiaks might invite them to listen
to the wireless tonight.

"It was such a shock," she heard her mother say, as she went to
go through the gate into the small garden at the side of the house.
"I was waiting to see Klaus – that's a cousin of Hans, my husband.
He was going to get me some papers – just in case I ever needed to
get away in a hurry. In fact, it was Klaus who warned us that it
might be an idea to leave while we still could. Well, anyway, they
were all perfectly polite. It was still fine to be Jewish in those days,
if you weren't actually a practising Jew. They showed me into this
small room – a sort of waiting room, I suppose. Klaus's office led
directly off it. There was another door on the other side. It suddenly
opened. And there he was."

"Really?" said Frau Hanusiak "And does he look like his
picture?"

"Well, his face is the same," said Mutti. "With that silly little moustache. But he's actually not as tall or as dignified as I thought he would be. In fact, I'm not sure who was more scared – me or him."

"So what did you do?" asked Frau Hanusiak.

"Well, nothing really," said Mutti. "He was only there a few seconds. They'd obviously shown him into the wrong room. Someone came in just after him. They went ever so red and they bundled him out again. And I didn't manage to salute him. He didn't salute properly either. He tried, failed, then nodded his head and clicked his heels together. Not as if he meant much by it though."

"Good heavens!" said Frau Hanusiak.

"It's just as well he was so flustered," Mutti continued. "Otherwise he might have noticed I'd done my husband's trick of saying 'Heil Edler!' Then there would have been trouble."

"Sensible man, your husband," said Herr Hanusiak.

"But it's what I had in my bag that was interesting," Mutti whispered. She nodded her head and raised her eyebrows.

Renate ducked behind the gate and stood absolutely still. If they saw her, they would stop talking about this at once and she would never get to hear this story.

"I had a small revolver in my bag," Mutti continued. "I'd taken to carrying one all the time. Things were getting difficult, you know. It seemed a sensible idea. Don't know whether I'd have ever dared use it, though."

"You could have killed him there and then," said Frau Hanusiak.

"Pity you didn't. Pity you didn't," said Herr Hanusiak, shaking his head. "It would have done the whole world a favour."

"Oh, there are plenty of Germans who wouldn't agree with you," said Mutti. "Besides, it never occurred to me. Not until after. A long time after, in fact. Funny though, how the great man actually looked more like a scared rabbit than a powerful leader."

The grown-ups laughed. Renate's heart was beginning to thump. Had she really understood that right? Her mother had been in the same room as Herr Hitler? And she'd had a gun in her bag and she could have killed him?

"Trouble is," said Frau Hanusiak suddenly more serious again, "even if he does behave like a timid animal, he's actually a nasty little man with a lot of power."

So, Herr Hitler was alive and well, despite her father's silence about him. And people still didn't like him. Some people at least. What was more, her mother might have been tempted to have a go at killing him. Then what would have happened?

Renate slipped away quietly.

SHOOT THE FÜHRER? SHE WOULDN'T HAVE IT IN HER. AFTER ALL, SHE IS A JEWESS. AND EVEN IF SHE HAD DONE YOU CERTAINLY WOULDN'T BE HERE NOW, RENATE. A JEWESS CAPABLE OF USING A GUN? OH, PLEASE!

Hani, 10 July 1939

"Do you think there will be a war?" Christoph was pinning up some of the children's work on to the walls. They had invited the parents to come in for the last half hour of the day so that they could celebrate the children's progress that year. It was the nearest they could do to having an end of year party.

Hani remembered how they used to mark the end of the year at the Waldorf School: concerts, the summer fete, the sports day and the parent/teacher meetings. All they had at her new school was a parent / teacher meeting. It was all a bit miserable, really.

At least they were trying to do something here.

"Well, do you?" asked Christoph. "Do you think I'll have to go and be a soldier?"

"Oh, I hope not," said Hani. Christoph couldn't be a soldier. He was too young, surely, and needed here. There was so much to do and neither she, nor Frau Lehrs, nor Dr Shubert could lift some of the heavier children who couldn't walk up the stairs. It would be awful. They would be at war with England and that meant she would be at war with Renate.

"But I think it will happen, don't you?" said Christoph. "They'll never let old fury-chops get away with stealing his Lebensraum from other people."

"What did you call him?" asked Hani, trying not to giggle.

"Fury-chops," said Christoph. "Suits him, don't you think?"

"Yes, but don't let anybody else hear you saying that." She tittered. "Good name, though."

But old fury-chops had already been stealing Lebensraum from people. He'd made Frau Lehrs sell her house to Dr Kühn for a silly amount of money. That was the worst sort of stealing because he'd actually made it look as if he was doing a good thing.

The doorbell rang.

Hani exchanged a glance with Frau Lehrs.

"Children, quiet now," whispered Frau Lehrs.

The children sat as still as statues. It had been drilled into them that if ever someone rang the doorbell they were to keep absolutely still and absolutely quiet. At least they seemed to have understood that well. When their parents came to fetch them, they tapped the front door lightly three times.

Doctor Schubert nodded to Christoph who had gone white and seemed glued to the ground.

"Go on," mouthed Dr Shubert. "Go and see what they want. Now!"

Christoph's face now went bright red. Then he sprinted up the stairs.

They heard him open the front door.

"Good afternoon," they heard a voice say. "SS Obersturmführer Poll. I understand that this is the residence of Dr Emil Kühn. Is Doctor Kühn at home today?"

"I'm afraid he's at the office today," said Christoph.

"Well, may I come in and wait for him?" said the officer. He didn't seem to give Christoph any choice. He barged right into the house.

"If you'd like to wait here, sir," said Christoph. "I'll let you know as soon as Doctor Kühn arrives."

Christoph then came back down the stairs.

"I've shown him into the lounge. I didn't know what else to do."

"Leave this to me," said Frau Lehrs.

"Clara, you shouldn't," whispered Dr Shubert.

"It'll be fine. Trust me," said Frau Lehrs. "Hans, you go out the front and warn off any of the parents until I've got rid of him. Wait until I'm in the lounge, though."

Hani watched Frau Lehrs go up the stairs.

"Ah, Obersturmführer Poll," said Frau Lehrs. "Isabella Kühn. I'm afraid my son is away at his office at the moment. He will be here soon. May I offer some refreshment whilst you wait?"

The lounge door clicked to. Hani made her way up the stairs as quietly as she could. Before she got to the front door, there were three taps. Her heart was thumping and her hand was trembling as she went to open the door. It was Frau Schumacher, Liesel's mother.

"Oh I'm so looking forward to this," Frau Schuhmacher started to say.

Hani shook her head vigorously, put her fingers to her lips and pointed to the lounge.

"Oh," gasped Frau Schuhmacher. She seemed to freeze on the spot.

Suddenly there were more footsteps running upstairs.

"Mutti," shouted Liesel.

This was a disaster.

Frau Lehrs opened the lounge door.

"Ah, Hilde," she said. "She has been such a good girl. I'm sorry I can't ask you to stay for some tea but I have company at the moment. Do give my regards to your mother."

Obersturmführer Poll poked his head out of the door. Hani showed Liesel and her mother out. She tried to keep her face turned away from the SS officer.

"Isn't that one of the children from the old Special Class at the Waldorf School?" asked Obersturmführer Poll.

"It is indeed," said Frau Lehrs. "It is so difficult for the parents now that they have no school to go to. Liesel's grandmother is a very dear friend of mine. I was helping her daughter out for a few hours."

"Will your son be very long?" The SS officer sounded impatient.

Frau Lehrs turned to Hani. "Hans, dear, will you ask your brother to cycle round to Dr Kühn's office. I'm afraid the telephone isn't working. And then carry on with what you were doing before."

Hani nodded, still keeping her back to the two of them.

"That boy is so sullen," said Frau Lehrs as she closed the lounge door. "I don't know why my son keeps him on. But I suppose until he is settled in…"

Once the door clicked to again, Hani dashed down stairs.

"You're to go and get Dr Kühn," she said to Christoph.

"But I don't where he is," Christoph protested.

"He'll be at his old office at the Waldorf School," whispered Doctor Schubert.

Hani and Christoph rushed as quietly as they could upstairs and out the back door. Christoph got his bike out of the shed and Hani made her way to the front of the house just in time to see one more of the mothers making her way up the street.

Hani walked as quickly as she dared towards her.

"It's all right," said Frau Schröder. "The others have heard. Frau Schuhmacher told us. If you let me know once all is well, I can soon tell everyone."

Hani nodded. Frau Schröder turned and walked away slowly. Hani walked briskly back to the house. She let herself in through the back door and crept as quietly as she could down to the basement. Several of the children had fallen asleep. The ones who were still awake sat absolutely still, just staring.

They're being really good.

"The problem will be if one of them wakes up suddenly and doesn't know where they are," said Doctor Schubert. "Let's hope Doctor Kühn gets here soon."

What seemed like hours later, but Hani realised was only ten minutes, the back door opened again and she heard two sets of footsteps.

The lounge door opened. "Ah there you are, Emil," said Frau Lehrs. "Obersturmführer Poll is here to see you."

The lounge door closed again.

"Now what?" whispered Hani.

Doctor Schubert shrugged. "He may want to inspect the house. Make sure everything is in order. You do know that today Doctor Kühn takes over ownership."

Hani tried to swallow but couldn't. She knew Frau Lehrs had said she wouldn't notice anything different but it still didn't seem right.

The lounge door, clicked again. Perhaps he was going.

"And the Jewess is still living here?" said Obersturmführer. He started shuffling some papers. "Klara – with a 'K' – Sarah Lehrs?"

"Klara with a 'K', Sarah Lehrs?" whispered Frau Lehrs.

"Yes, we insist on German spelling," said the officer, "and all

Jews who have no Jewish name are assigned the name Sarah or Israel. For convenience."

"I see," said Frau Lehrs. "Very sensible."

"Clara with a 'C' Lehrs is renting a room from me for the time being," said Dr Kühn. "She is out shopping at the moment. You know that it can be very difficult. She will probably be some time."

"That is satisfactory," said the officer. "Now, can we proceed with the tour?"

Another ten minutes passed by very slowly. One of the sleeping children murmured. Then there was a little tap at the door.

"It's only me," said Christoph. "I'm locking you in. Don't worry. I'll let you out afterwards."

Oh great. So now they were locked in as well.

A few moments later, there were three sets of footsteps on the stairs.

"And all of the furnishings are your own?" asked Obersturmführer Poll.

"Oh, no, no, no," replied Doctor Kühn. "I arranged to keep them with Frau Lehrs."

"The woman obviously has excellent taste," said Frau Lehrs.

"Especially for a Jew," said Obersturmführer Poll. "I hope you got it all for a fair price."

"Extremely fair, I would say," said Frau Lehrs.

"Anyway, as you can see, all there is down here is a boiler room," said Doctor Kühn.

"What about this door?" asked the officer, rattling the handle.

Hani bit her lip. Peter, one of the boys still awake, looked at her with big brown frightened eyes. Hani put her hand on his shoulder and her fingers on her lips. He relaxed a little.

"Oh, Frau Lehrs couldn't find the key," said Doctor Kühn. "She's not used this room for years. She thinks it's full of old junk. We're going to get a locksmith to come and open it. You do appreciate; we couldn't really start doing anything until today."

"Very well," said Obersturmführer Poll. "All seems to be in order. This can of course only be a temporary arrangement for the Jewess. I'll leave you in peace. Thank you for your time. I can see myself out." He clicked his heels. "Heil Hitler!"

"Heil Hitler," mumbled Doctor Kühn.

The front door slammed. Christoph ran down the steps and unlocked the door.

"You can breathe easy, now, children," said Frau Lehrs.

Maybe, thought Hani. But what was all this about it only being a temporary arrangement for Frau Lehrs? "Oh bugger old fury-chops," she said. "I'll give him 'Heil'!"

All eyes were looking at her. Christoph's mouth was open.

Frau Lehrs gave a little titter. "Old fury-chops?" she said. She giggled again. One or two of the children began to snigger.

Within seconds, everybody was laughing loudly. Tears were streaming down Hani's face when she remembered about Frau Schröder.

"I suppose I'd better go and telephone her," said Frau Lehrs after Hani had managed to stop laughing long enough to tell her.

Hani wondered how she was going to manage that. Frau Lehrs was still giggling as she made her way up to the hall.

Renate, 18 August 1939

Renate lay back and closed her eyes. She could hear younger children splashing at the water's edge below her on the beach. She could feel the sea breeze on her face and taste the salt on her lips. This was heavenly. Christine and her family had been so right about this being a good place to camp. Even Mutti seemed to have relaxed and she was certainly smiling a lot – and getting quite sun burnt. Oh, it was such bliss just lying here. She was quite tired after her swim that morning and a wild ball game on the beach with Christine and the others. But it was a nice kind of tiredness. A seaside kind of tiredness. Such a pity that they had to go back to London tomorrow.

She sat up and looked at the scene below. She normally enjoyed countryside holidays more, but perhaps that was it. She lived so far away from the coast in Germany, and then it was always the cold, windy North Sea coast. Here it was milder. The breeze kept you cool, rather than cold, and those flat brown sands were lovely.

It was the best possible spot here, overlooking the beach, but with trees behind them for shade. It really was relaxing, living out of doors all the time. Different again from the Landschulheim where she'd been on many trips with the school, and different from staying at her grandmother's or Hani's place, which was much too civilized. This was fun.

She looked over at Christine who was still dozing and looking so peaceful. Well, that wouldn't do. She took a long stalk of grass and started to tickle Christine's face with it. Christine wrinkled her nose and then started pawing at the air. It took a while before she opened her eyes, by which time Renate could not stop herself from laughing.

"What are you doing?" screamed Christine. She was startled at first, but it didn't last long. Soon she was giggling just as much as Renate.

"I'm hungry," said Renate, "and it's our turn to do the lunch."

"Oh no," groaned Christine. "Why can't we go on a hotel holiday, and be waited on all the time?"

"Because you'd soon get bored, and you'd have to keep clean," replied Renate. "It wouldn't be half so much fun."

"All right, then. Let's get on with it," said Christine.

Seconds later, they were buttering the crusty bread Christine's mother had bought that morning and making cheese and tomato sandwiches.

"There's Victoria sponge for afters," said Christine.

"As long as somebody put the lid on the tin properly last time," said Renate. "Or the squirrels will have got it."

"Oh, and those nice plums," added Christine.

In no time at all, there was an inviting lunch spread out on the grass.

"This looks great," said David. "Not bad for girls."

Renate was so hungry she didn't worry about the others. But as she ate and started to feel less hungry, she began to ask herself where her mother and Mrs Jenkins were.

She was about to take a second slice of the Victoria sponge and then decided that would be greedy and she ought to leave some for the grown-ups, knowing that Mutti particularly liked Mrs Jenkins' cakes. She sighed and stood up.

"I'm going to look for our mothers," she said to Christine, "before I'm tempted to eat all their lunch."

She wandered over to the tent her mother was sharing with Mrs Jenkins.

"Mutti, Mrs Jenkins," she called, "are you coming for lunch? There won't be any left if you don't hurry up."

"We'll be out in a minute," Mrs Jenkins cried.

She could then hear them talking. She listened very hard but couldn't make out what was being said – just the odd word here and there.

"I really don't know... if only he could... by this time next year."

No, she couldn't hear all the words, but she did recognize the strain in her mother's voice. Just like the time she had refused to go to the opera, and when she'd not wanted Renate to go on the school trip. The same tone of voice. The same whispered conversations.

"Come on," she heard Mrs Jenkins say at last. "Chin up, for Renate's sake."

The two women came out of the tent.

"Ah, Renate," said Mrs Jenkins brightly.

A little too brightly, Renate thought.

"Do you know," continued Mrs Jenkins, "your mother and I have been absolute pigs? We ate two ice creams each this morning, the weather was so nice. We need to go for a walk, now, to get rid of the rolls of fat."

"But there's the Victoria sponge cake," said Renate.

"Oh, you young people can have our share," said Mrs Jenkins.

Mutti only looked at the ground.

"Come on then Käthe," said Mrs Jenkins, slipping her arm into the other woman's. "Best foot forward. Let's walk off all those pounds."

They set off. Renate's mother did not even look at her.

Renate's appetite had suddenly gone. "Why does she have to be so moody?" she said to Christine.

"Perhaps she's worried about your father. And your grandmother," Christine suggested.

That was probably it. It wasn't unreasonable.

"Come on, though," said Christine. "We've just got to enjoy this sunshine."

Renate nodded.

"And that's you girls out," shouted Roy as the ball hit Renate's leg.

She was quite relieved actually. She'd been getting tired. Christine's brothers had arranged a game of French cricket for the afternoon and she soon got lost in the game. All her effort was going into hitting the ball hard and running as fast as she could.

She flopped down on the grass.

"Look, our mothers are coming back," said Christine.

"What time is it anyway?" asked Renate.

"Just after four," said Edmund, looking at his watch.

Frau Edler was smiling again. Her hair was windswept and she laughed as she tried to get it under control.

"There you are, see," whispered Christine.

So, now it seemed fine to carry on enjoying the last day of their holiday.

The day continued well. There was another delicious meal plus more swimming, and as the evening fell, Renate and Christine decided to go for a walk in the cooler air. They seemed to get new energy, and before they knew it, they were at the other end of the bay, making their way back across the cliff top.

"Isn't it lovely how the moon makes the tops of the waves silver?" said Christine.

"Oh yes, it is," replied Renate. She was getting quite good at English now and could chat almost fluently to Christine.

"I wish we could stay here forever, don't you?" said Christine. "No more school. Wouldn't that be grand?"

Renate didn't reply. It was lovely here, but she did miss Germany – and her father and her friends, of course.

"Well, what do you think?" her friend asked.

"I don't mind school," Renate answered.

"I suppose it's all right," said Christine with a sigh. "We'll be back there soon enough. I suppose we've just got to make the most of it. Tell you what; I'll race you back to the campsite."

She set off. Soon, though, Renate was catching her up. Seconds later, she was overtaking her. She thudded along the path and then cut off the corner and went through the woods. She was quite out of breath by the time she arrived and actually limped along the last few metres.

Mrs Jenkins and Mutti were sitting on camp chairs under a lamp which gave them enough light for their card game. But they seemed to have abandoned it.

"It's really not looking good," said Mrs Jenkins.

"No," said Mutti. "You can't trust any of them. Those politicians are all the same. German ones. English ones. All the same."

"Renate, you could have waited," shouted Christine as she ran out of the woods. She flopped down on the ground, out of breath.

Renate noticed the grownups exchanging a worried glance.

"Would you two girls like some cocoa before you turn in?" asked Mrs Brown.

"Definitely!" shouted Christina. "I need to get my strength back after that run."

"I'll go straight to bed," said Renate. There was a huge lump in her throat, and she thought she was going to cry. It looked more and more as if war was really going to happen: war between England and Germany – she and her mother on one side, her father on the other. Unbelievable.

She pretended to be asleep when Christine came to bed half an hour later. She kept her eyes shut tight as she heard her undress and then switch off her torch. Soon, Christine was snoring. Renate knew she would not sleep. It had been such a perfect holiday. Now it was ruined.

SO, YOU THOUGHT YOU'D GET AWAY WITH IT BY COMING TO ENGLAND. OH NO. WE'RE STILL GOING TO GET YOU. YOU SHOULD KNOW THAT BY NOW. YOU CAN'T HIDE FROM US.

Renate, 22 August 1939

It seemed like just an ordinary day but it wasn't. They'd all been called into school in the holiday, and now everyone jostled for places on the train. The businessmen read their newspapers. People avoided looking at each other. There was the normal chatter, no more and no less.

"Cool for the time of year," she heard one woman say.

"Typical English summer," replied her companion.

Nothing's unusual, then. But she couldn't help reading the headlines on the newspaper articles. BELGIUM SEEKS TO STAVE OFF WAR WITH THE GERMANS. With the Germans. No! That was her. Yet nobody on the train seemed to realize. She hoped they saw just another schoolgirl on her way to school. Because that was all she was. Except, she shouldn't be going to school on the 22nd of August.

The journey seemed shorter than normal today, and in no time at all she was stepping off the train, then a few moments later standing at the entrance to the school. She took a deep breath as she started to walk up the long avenue. What would the others think? What would they say to her? Everyone had been so friendly recently. They seemed to have forgotten that she was German. But what would they think now?

Tom and Daisy, two of the children from the infants were playing outside.

"Hello, Renate," called Tom. Renate and Christine had sometimes helped in their classroom during wet playtimes.

"Hello Tom, hello Daisy," called Renate, relieved to see them being so normal.

"I'm going to build a tree house with my daddy next week," said Tom, rushing forward to take Renate's hand, "so that we can climb up into it and see the Germans coming."

Well, there's one already here, or hadn't you noticed?

"My Daddy thinks he'll have to join the army," said Daisy. "I hope he doesn't. I don't want him to go away. He said I'd have to be brave and look after Mummy."

So maybe things weren't so normal. At least they didn't seem to think it was anything to do with her. Would the older children think the same?

Well, she was about to find out. Christine and David were standing in the doorway. Christine waved. Renate's heart was thudding as she made her way towards the door. Daisy seemed to have forgotten her worries and was skipping cheerfully along beside her.

"Hello," said Christine. She paused and looked down to the ground. "How's your mother?" she asked in sudden rush.

Renate shrugged. She couldn't think what to say.

"It can't be very nice for you both," said David.

"No," murmured Renate. But then, it wasn't going to be exactly nice for any of them.

The bell rang and Tom and Daisy scooted off towards their teacher. Renate, Christine and David ambled slowly towards their form room.

"I suppose it's all going to get different now," said David.

Christine and Renate exchanged a glance.

Anne and Joyce were waiting for them inside.

"What does your mother think of it all?" Joyce asked Renate.

"She hasn't said a lot," replied Renate. "I think she's worried about my father."

And so am I, she thought. She knew he didn't like Herr Hitler, and she knew that recently he'd been pretending that none of it mattered all that much. But it did now. He might get into trouble.

"At least we can look after you," said Joyce, squeezing Renate's arm.

Mrs Cohen was already at her desk when they arrived in the classroom, and she looked quite serious.

"Sit down, sit down, class," she said. "As quickly as possible. There are no lessons today. There is a lot we have to tell you and there is a lot we have to do. And we'll all be going into the Great Hall with the rest of the school in about half an hour."

There was a general mumble from the class.

Mrs Cohen waited patiently.

"Yes, yes," she said. "These are unusual times. But listen now. It looks as if the war is certain so the school *is* going to be evacuated and we shall be relying on you older students to help with the little ones."

If there had been a little mumbling earlier, there was now a general outcry.

"Where shall we be going?"

"Will we all be going to the same place?"

"Will we still go to school together?"

"Yes, yes, yes, I know," said Mrs Cohen, nodding her head. "Big news. But in some ways you are luckier than the students who go to ordinary schools. We shall be going to Minehead."

There were even more gasps of astonishment. Renate looked at Christine.

"It's in Somerset, by the sea," Christine mouthed and shrugged her shoulders. Her eyes, too, were round with surprise.

"We shall be moving the school into a lovely old house," explained Mrs Cohen. "And you will be billeted with local families. You really are going to have it easier than some of the other London school children."

Renate's heart was beginning to sink. What would happen to Mutti? Would she be able to come too? Or perhaps they would not want to take her to the school in Minehead.

Christine was talking excitedly to Joyce, Anne and David.

"Won't that fresh air be lovely?" said Christine. "We'll be able to go for such long walks. Oh, it'll be so nice to be by the seaside. Away from the dirty London air."

Renate's heart lifted a little. Maybe it would be all right.

Mrs Cohen was smiling. "Now, now," she said after a moment or two. "Settle down. We now need to go into the hall and listen to Miss Faversham."

"Miss Faversham?" asked Christine.

Renate was also surprised to hear the name of the Deputy Headmistress instead of Mr Brown.

"You'll see, you'll see," said Mrs Cohen, waving them along.

"Come on now. To the hall!"

Miss Faversham was waiting for them. About half the school was already there, and they watched impatiently as the rest filed in. Miss Faversham looked even more serious than Mrs Cohen had earlier.

"Where are all the men?" whispered Renate.

Christine looked around, surprised to see no male teachers present. She raised her eyebrows and shrugged.

At last, the whole school was there. The talking subsided and everyone was looking at the Deputy Headmistress.

"Well," began Miss Faversham. "You have all been told about the move to Minehead. We shall be departing, by train, next Friday. You will attend school as if it were a normal school day on Thursday when full instructions will be given about travel and living arrangements."

There were gasps from the younger pupils. School had not been supposed to start until the 4 September. Miss Faversham's lips twitched into a half smile. Then she looked very serious again.

"We shall be tucked away at the seaside, safe from any attack on the capital, should we go to war," she continued. "And I'm afraid the seniors' holiday will be cut short. We shall need you in every day to help with the packing. Please wear your oldest clothes." She paused. "You may notice that my male colleagues are missing. They will help over the next few days, but they have all decided to volunteer their services for the war effort, including Mr Jenkins and Mr Thomas, who will take on home-guard duties and will help to keep the home fires burning in our beloved London. We are sure that all our students will make every effort to make this move go as smoothly as possible. Seniors, you are to remain in the hall. All other pupils are to return to their classrooms with their teachers. Those of you who are certain that a parent is at home will be sent home. Some of the seniors will organize games for the rest of you. I wish you good day."

Miss Faversham nodded and walked smartly off the stage.

Any excitement Renate may have felt earlier at the prospect of going to the seaside was now replaced by dread. Britain might soon be at war with Germany. Her new home might be at war with her old home and anything could happen.

DO YOU REALLY THINK YOU'LL GET AWAY WITH IT THAT EASILY? SEE, YOU DON'T EVEN KNOW US GERMANS ALL THAT WELL.
GO ON, OFF TO THE SEASIDE. YOU WON'T ENJOY IT, THOUGH.
WE'LL STILL GET YOU. THE SEA CAN'T SAVE YOU.

Sabine, 27 August 1939

Dear all,

The summer has been busy. I've been training every day with Herr Schmidt. Two hours every morning. Of course, he's very busy with his Hitlerjugend group. And his work. He thinks the war is certain.

So, everything has stopped now.

Still, if I might boast a little, I did win the silver medal for my 400 metre sprint in the Youth Championships.

Of course, we haven't really been on holiday this year. Everyone is so poor and with this talk of war... but we did manage to go to the Schliersee for a few days, where we swam and enjoyed the sun.

The wild berries have been fantastic this year. We've collected blueberries, wild strawberries and now the blackberries are full and juicy. Back in July we collected elderflowers and made elderflower fritters. Oma showed us how to make cough syrup from the flowers as well.

"There is no need for anyone to starve," she said. "War or no war. There's plenty for everyone, everywhere. The sun is still shining."

I may have to give up my running. "You'll probably have to put your physical strength to some better use," Herr Schmidt said. Oh, well, I suppose we are all growing up.

Sorry to be a bit gloomy, but I do look forward to this little parcel coming to me again.

Your Sabine

Renate, 1 September 1939

"This looks like it," said Christine, suddenly getting up from her seat.

The train was slowing down. Renate joined her at the window, although, there was nothing to see. It was completely dark out there. Christine opened the window. "Oooh, smell that seaside air," she cried, breathing deeply and closing her eyes.

Renate could smell something, but it wasn't the sea air as she knew it. She could smell sewage. Christine started coughing and spluttering.

"What is that smell?" she asked, waving her hand in front of her nose violently and shutting the window quickly.

"The sewage works?" said Renate, trying not to laugh.

The train let off steam and Christine jumped, then stumbled over the bags and gasmasks piled up on the floor. "Drat these ugly things," she cried. "They're even tripping me up now."

Mrs Cohen opened the door of their compartment.

"We're actually a bit early, and the families who're going to take you in won't be here yet. We'd be really grateful if some of you seniors would help with the little ones. They're very tired and they're beginning to realize that they'll be sleeping away from home for a long time. Some of them are getting a bit upset. Renate, I know you're particularly good with Daisy and Thomas Bull. They're just over there, look."

The step down from the train was quite steep, and Renate struggled to get herself, her case and gasmask down.

"That looks heavy," said Tom, as she stood beside him and dropped her case on the ground. "What have you got in it?"

"Clothes, books and some walking boots," said Renate.

Daisy began to cry. "My mummy won't be there to tuck me in tonight," she sobbed.

"No, but she'll be thinking about you," said Renate. "And I'm sure you'll be staying with a nice family with a nice mummy who will tuck you in, and if you're very good, I expect she might even tell you a story before you go to sleep."

Daisy stopped sobbing, but clung on to Renate's leg and stuck her thumb into her mouth.

"Do you think you might be staying at the same place as us?" asked Tom. There was a distinct wobble in his voice.

And I'm missing my mummy too, thought Renate. Big girl that I am. She thought it best not to mention that to Tom and Daisy.

One by one, the families started to arrive and the younger children began to disappear. The lady who came for Tom and Daisy looked cheerful and friendly. She gave them both a big hug.

"We'll soon have you two warm and tucked up in bed," she said. "And we'll get a bit of hot food into you first."

Soon there was just her, Anne and Christine left. David and Joyce had been taken to a nearby farm, and the last she had heard was David asking the farmer if he kept horses and could he help.

Even the people who were taking in the teachers had arrived.

"I'm not surprised the Johnsons are late," said the billeting officer. "They've spent most of the day helping to get the school organized."

At last, a young couple walked into the station waiting room. Mrs Johnson looked more as if she could be an older sister than a mother. She looked tired, her hair had come loose and there was a dirty smudge on her face; but she had a really friendly smile.

"You must be exhausted," she said. "I'm afraid it's going to be a bit of a squash. We only have three bedrooms, so we've put our boys into one and you three into the biggest room. I'm afraid two of you will have to sleep in a double bed and one of you will have to use the camp bed. But you are very, very welcome."

It was only a short journey to Will and Deborah Johnson's home in Will's truck.

"I'm afraid there's only soup and bread and cheese," said Mrs Johnson. "I've not had time to cook a big meal."

Renate was so tired she didn't think she'd be able to eat, but she did manage some of the soup which was quite delicious.

"You didn't tell me about the smudge on my cheek," Deborah

chided Will, as she caught sight of herself in the mirror over the fireplace.

"Well, I thought it was rather fetching, actually," said Will.

"But our guests…"

"Oh, we don't mind," said Christine. "I expect they'll rope us into doing some work tomorrow and we'll all end up getting dirty."

Renate could hardly keep her eyes open. She just wanted to sleep. She thought she would be able to sleep anywhere.

The bedroom was small, or at least looked it with the double bed and the camp bed taking up most of the space.

"I hope you'll be all right," said Mrs Johnson. She looked worried.

"Oh, we'll be fine," said Christine.

"Well, there is the walk-in cupboard where you can hang your things," said Mrs Johnson.

The three girls murmured their thanks. After Mrs Johnson had wished them good night, they started to get themselves sorted out.

"I don't mind taking the camp bed," said Renate.

"Well, we'll take it in turns, won't we?" suggested Anne.

"Course," replied Christine. "Whoever is on the camp bed has some privacy for the night, even if it's less comfortable. That seems fair to me."

It didn't take them long to get everything arranged. Anne and Renate made sure the blackout curtains were firmly in place in case one of them needed to put the light on in the middle of the night. Christine found a way of dividing the space in the cupboard into three.

"I'm so glad to be in bed," said Anne as the three of them lay there in the dark. "That train journey made me feel really tired and mucky."

"Me too. Not at all worried about sleeping in a strange bed," said Christine. "That train ride was absolutely exhausting. I don't think I ever want to go on a train again."

Renate wriggled down into the camp bed. It was a bit strange. Slim as she was, she was sure she would fall off it if she tried to turn over. Soon she heard Christine and Anne snoring gently.

Despite being tired she just couldn't drift off to sleep. It wasn't just the camp bed, though. This whole situation was so strange. She, the enemy, evacuated with the other girls and her mother still in London. The war hadn't started yet but it looked as if everybody was sure it was going to.

Sleep she did though, because the next thing she knew, she could hear seagulls screeching. They really were at the seaside. And she hadn't even fallen out of the bed.

BRIGHT NEW DAY? REALLY? OH, RENATE, WE HAVE SOME FINE TRICKS FOR YOU YET!

Renate, 3 September 1939

It felt like summer again. If she closed her eyes, Renate could imagine she was back on holiday enjoying their last day of freedom before they were back at school properly. They knew the first day would be mainly about sorting things out and getting the lovely old house where they were going to have their lessons to be more like a school but it would still be school.

"You should go for a walk along the seafront," Deborah Johnson had said that morning. "Get some fresh air. Work up an appetite. I'm going to cook you a really big lunch today."

So, here they were, walking along the promenade. The air was fresh and salty, just like it should be. The horrible smell that had greeted them two days before was gone. The seagulls were still screeching. This was so different from London.

"Let's explore the town a bit," said Anne.

They'd walked away from the sea and turned towards the town centre. There were a lot of people about for a Sunday.

"Church, I expect," said Anne. She was right. As they turned into Townsend Road, people were hurrying into the big Sacred Heart Church. Mass was due to start in five minutes.

"I suppose we ought to have gone to church," said Christine. "I guess we all need to pray a lot now."

Renate wondered whether some of her friends from her old school were going to church today and whether they would be praying as well. What exactly do you pray for in these circumstances? That you would win the war? That there wouldn't be a war? But what Herr Hitler was doing was wrong, wasn't it? So he'd got to be stopped, hadn't he?

She must have been looking very serious because Christine suddenly put her hand in front of her mouth and breathed in sharply. Then she rubbed Renate's arm. "I'm sorry," she said. "I didn't think. You wouldn't go to church at all would you?"

"I might," said Renate. Her father was Catholic after all and she was baptised a Catholic. But neither Vati nor Mutti were very religious. They were both scientists. "But no, you're right, we don't go very much."

"Well everybody's pretty worried," said Anne. "Look!"

Two elderly ladies were walking as quickly as they could into the church. Their faces were very grim.

"It's a shame to be so worried on such a glorious day," said Anne.

"Perhaps we could get a newspaper and see what's going on," said Christine. "Has anybody got any money?"

"I've probably got enough," said Anne. "I guess the station's our best bet and it's on the way back, anyway."

They turned back towards the sea front and a few moments later they were by the station.

"Oh now, will you look at that?" said Christine.

The queue at the newspaper kiosk stretched right though the ticket hall and out on to the street. They couldn't even get near enough to read the headlines.

"Maybe someone will have left one they've finished reading on a bench somewhere," said Anne.

They made their way back along the promenade. It was useless. No newspapers anywhere, nor did they even see anyone carrying one.

Suddenly some church bells started ringing. Then some more and soon a third set.

"They're finishing a bit early aren't they?" said Anne.

An awful wailing sound started up.

"What is that?" said Renate.

"Air raid warning," Christine replied. "I don't like the sound of it at all. Let's get back, quick."

Renate's legs felt like jelly. She didn't think she could move. She managed to, somehow. Soon all three of them were running into Glenmore Road. The door to the Johnsons' house was flung open.

"Oh come in girls," cried Deborah Johnson. "It's just been on the wireless. Mr Chamberlain has said so. Hitler did go into Poland. We are at war with Germany."

The wailing stopped.

"Thank goodness for that," said Mrs Johnson.

"So there's not an air raid?" said Christine, her voice hoarse and squeaky.

"No, no, of course not," said Mrs Johnson. "The war only started a few minutes ago. And it's unlikely that there would be any bombs here anyway. They would hardly have brought you to a place that was going to be dangerous, would they?"

"So why were there sirens?" asked Anne.

"Just to tell us that the war has started," said Mrs Johnson.

"They rang the church bells as well," said Renate.

"Oh, I am so sorry," said Mrs Johnson, putting her arm around Renate.

So, someone understood. She wondered what her mother thought of the church bells ringing.

TOLD YOU SO. WE'RE GOING TO GET YOU. THEY'RE GOING TO HATE YOU.

Hani, 27 September 1939

"So you'll have to go and be a soldier?" said Hani. She and Christoph were tidying up the pieces of pottery that the Special Class children had made. One or two bits needed tweaking a little to make them stand upright, but they were good on the whole.

"Well, I'd have had to do my military service about now, anyway," said Christoph. "So, I'd do my basic training and then I'd be off."

"It doesn't seem right," said Hani.

"Has to be, I guess," said Christoph.

"So, when do you think it will happen?" said Hani.

"Any day?" said Christoph. "Though, I think, actually, because some people are already trained they might delay calling me and others like me up. It will cost them to train us. The others are ready to fight."

"I suppose," said Hani. "But what would we do here without you?"

Christoph shrugged. "You'll have to find another mug, I guess. Remember, I shall be nineteen in three weeks' time."

"Wilhelm has got to start on the first of October," said Hani. "He's nineteen already."

"There you are, you see. That's war for you."

"But he hasn't done his military training yet," said Hani.

"I bet he's glad about that, then, or he'd be straight off to fight." Christoph frowned. "Not that there seems to be much going on yet. Thank goodness."

"It doesn't feel like a war at all, does it?" said Hani. She wasn't sure why she said that. She had no idea what a war was supposed to feel like.

Christoph shrugged. "Well, it's only been just under four weeks. I suppose everybody is trying to decide what they're going to do. There is something, though." He stopped working and he frowned. "My father told me. He read it in the paper the other day. All Jews living in Poland have got to move to live in a ghetto."

"What's that then? A ghetto?" asked Hani.

Christoph shrugged again. "A place where they gather them all together to live, I think. Live and let live, I suppose. I guess if you don't like Jews it means you don't have to look at them."

That really sounded bizarre.

"Do you think that will happen here?" said Hani.

"Naw!" said Christoph. "This war will all be over by Christmas. The Brits will soon show old fury-chops that he can't go round helping himself to other people's Lebensraum. I don't know what he's worried about. Look at all that open space in the Black Forest and in Bavaria. Plenty of room for everyone, I would have said."

She hoped he was right. But she was still bothered about what had happened to Frau Lehrs. Still, she couldn't help smiling at what had now become their regular name for Hitler.

"Well, that's all done," said Christoph. "We can fire them in the kiln overnight. Better start getting that lot ready to go home."

Hani suddenly sneezed. She fumbled in her pocket for her hanky. As she took it out, the beige ration card fell to the floor.

"Oh, you'd better not lose that," said Christoph, bending down to pick it up, "or you'll be deprived." He handed the card to Hani. "Just be thankful that you're still under sixteen. You get extra protein allowances."

Hani stared at the card. If this was extra, she dreaded to think what adults got. She was allowed just 62½ grams of cheese in two weeks, 125 grams of butter and three eggs. There wouldn't be any more cheesecake any time soon, then.

"Oh, don't look like that," Christoph said. "My uncle has a farm. I'll be able to smuggle in some extra supplies."

"If you're not in the army by then," said Hani.

"Even if I am, I'll ask him to look out for you," said Christoph. "Come on woman. There's work to be done."

The doorbell suddenly rang. Hani and Christoph froze. Frau Lehrs came out of the kitchen, raising her eyebrows at them. She opened the door.

"Telegram for Lehrs," they heard a young man's voice say.

Hani felt herself sigh silently with relief but then another dark thought arrived. What about if it was bad news?

Then Frau Lehrs laughed. "Oh come here, Hans," she said. "You must see this." She held the telegram out to Hani. "A Red Cross special from Renate. She is allowed just 25 words."

Hani took the telegram from Frau Lehrs.

"School now at Minehead. In nice old house. Family has twin boys. Have to help with little ones. Help on farm too. People nice. English good now. Renate."

"She's having plenty of adventures, then," said Frau Lehrs. "But I'm going to tell her not to write any more. I don't want to make it difficult for her. We'd only be worried anyway, if we didn't hear and there'd probably actually be nothing wrong. Anyway, this silly war will all be over by Christmas and that idiot man – what did you call him – old fury-chops? Maybe he will leave us alone as well." Frau Lehrs giggled.

Hani wasn't so sure though. What if Frau Lehrs and Christoph were wrong? What if it all went on for much longer? It would be horrid if she didn't know what was happening to Renate.

Someone tapped three times lightly on the door. "Ah, here we go," said Frau Lehrs. "Are you ready, Christoph?"

Christoph nodded.

Frau Lehrs opened the door. "Ah, Frau Schröder," said Frau Lehrs. "Do come in."

Hani turned to go down the stairs. She could manage Peter by herself. He was able to walk very well on his own.

Frau Schröder began to sob.

"My goodness, what is the matter Frau Schröder?" said Frau Lehrs. "Come and sit down a while." She started to steer Frau Schröder towards the lounge. "Hans, would you go and fetch Frau Schröder a glass of water. Christoph, you're on door duty."

Hani brought the glass of water to Frau Schröder.

"Thank you," she said. "I'm sorry to make such a fuss. But you know, every day when I come here I'm quite surprised to find Peter still here. One day they will come to get him. One day they will take him away. It's not just the Jews, you know. It's everybody who is defective. And my little boy's not whole."

"But he is so precious," said Frau Lehrs. "And we shall continue to look after him well. You know that, don't you?"

Frau Schröder nodded.

"We are blessed," said Frau Lehrs. "Someone, somewhere, is looking after us."

There was the sound of two sets of footsteps on the stairs coming up from the cellar.

"Where's Mutti?" Hani heard Peter say.

"You can go in the lounge," said Christoph. "Your mother's in there."

Frau Lehrs squeezed Frau Schröder's hand.

The lounge door opened and in ran Peter. "Mutti, why have you been crying?"

Frau Schröder laughed. "Because I am so happy that Frau Lehrs and Hans here have been looking after you so well. And I know they're going to carry on doing that."

I hope so, thought Hani.

"Can we go home now, Mutti?" said Peter.

Charlotte, 17 October 1939

Dear all,

I am now quite used to being an auntie. And yes, the twins do have red hair just like my own. Their little heads are now covered in sweet red curls – just like I had as a baby, Mutti says. She also says I'll have to start pinning my hair up soon. The teachers at school say the same thing. For the moment, though, I still wear my plaits. I'm not very good at getting my hair to stay up. It always comes down at school when we're doing such things as scrubbing floors. At least the plaits stay put.

Mutti says I'm going to have to think about what I want to do for my social service. I should start that in a year's time. The rest of you should be glad that you've got another year before you even need to worry about it.

I'd like to look after Ursula and the twins. She's really been unwell. She is so tired all of the time. They do that, you know, sometimes; let you look after someone in the family. I expect, though, by the time I'm ready to start she will be fully recovered. Perhaps I'll have to look after some incontinent old lady or something. I know it's necessary but, oh dear! I'm dreading it.

So, now we're at war. You'd hardly notice it, though, would you? Those of you who have brothers, will they have to go and be soldiers? I hope not.

I wonder what's happening to Renate. She's in England and we're at war with England.

I hope you're all well. I do look forward to your news.

Love to all of you,
Charlotte

Gerda, 4 December 1939

Dear all,

This war still doesn't seem real, though Thomas seems to be doing more and more training in his Hitlerjugend group. But I'm enjoying college.

I've been working hard on the farm too. With what I'm learning at college I understand much more what I'm supposed to be doing and why. Hans is quite jealous, I think. But at least he is strong and can do quite a lot of the heavy work. Father is working him hard.

"We'd better make the most of him while we can," he says. "They'll be getting him back into the army soon."

"Not if I can help it," he mumbles every time father says that.

Thomas, on the other hand, can't wait. "Do you think they'll let me do my military training early?" he keeps asking.

Honestly! You should have seen him parading around in his Hitlerjugend uniform when he first got it. Still, it keeps him out of trouble.

Vati is thinking of growing vegetables. Everyone says it's going to get difficult with food. We should be all right on the farm, I guess. Don't any of you go hungry. Do make the journey over to us and we'll feed you for sure.

Vati gets the newspaper everyday but he won't let us look at it, though he does read out odd bits and pieces. It really doesn't feel that much as if we are at war. Though I'm not sure how that is supposed to feel since it's never happened before.

Well, I'm really beginning to feel sleepy now, so I will finish.

I do look forward to getting all of your news.

Gerda

Erika, 5 February 1940

Dear all,

What a silly little thing I was about Kurt.

I was very impressed. He looked very good in his uniform. He's now in the army and I saw him the other day in that uniform – even better. But he'd got this girl hanging on his arm. Girl? Young woman, I should say. Hair pinned up, high heels, fur coat and lipstick. Do you know what? It didn't bother me one little bit. I am so over him.

That day when we went rafting he must have noticed me keep looking at him. When we stopped to dry off in the sun he put his arm round me. Then he asked me if I'd like to go for a walk with him. I was thrilled. He held my hand and we walked through the woods. Then he stopped and pushed me against a tree. My heart was beating so fast! He kissed me. But it was horrible. He was pressing really hard on to me and his mouth was slobbering over mine. He tasted of cigarettes. I pushed him away.

"Don't do that," I said.

Then he sighed. "You're a bit too young, I think," he said. "Come on, we'd better get back."

He didn't hold my hand anymore and he walked so quickly. I tripped up a couple of times but he didn't stop to help me. I've hardly spoken to him since.

But I'm over all that now. Ilse is the one who is in love. I'll let her tell you all about that herself.

Yes, the Kurt incident seems a long time ago now. But the first signs of spring are here. The sun seems stronger today and we have snowdrops in the garden.

All my love,
Erika

Ilse, 15 February 1940

Dear all,

I am in love. And I can really recommend it. It really is love, not that silly thing that Erika had with Kurt. I've heard some really nasty things about him since. But no, it's the real thing with me. And yes, it's like they say, at first at least. You can't eat, you can't sleep and you can't stop thinking about him. That stops after a bit. You just feel happy being with him.

His name is Helmut. He's good-looking as well. He has smiling blue eyes and dark brown hair. He's a bit older than us but there's no chance that he'll have to do his military service just yet.

I actually met him when I joined the choir in the next village. (Yes, I can sing now!) He has a lovely tenor singing voice and he sings many of the solo parts. I used to melt when I heard him sing. One day after choir, he asked if he could walk me home. We talked and talked and talked. We seemed to agree on everything. I felt very excited and there was a big lump in my throat, though I still managed to talk. Then after that, he walked home with me after every choir practice. One time, he held my hand. After the third time we'd walked home holding hands, he kissed me. We've kissed loads of times since and sometimes he's been very passionate. He's also told me he loves me.

It's funny at first. You wonder when he's going to call round and if he still likes you. But we're past all that now.

Erika keeps complaining I don't have any time for her now. But she doesn't mind really. I can really recommend being in love.

Ah! There goes the doorbell. That will be Helmut. Take care, and make sure you fall in love.

Ilse

Renate, 9 April 1940

"Phew!" I'm done," said Christine wiping the sweat from her face. "I really didn't imagine the countryside would be such hard work."

"This is nothing," said David. "Real farmers have to do this every day. And much more."

"Well, remind me not to be a real farmer, then," said Christine.

"I quite like it," said Anne. "It's good exercise. And it helps us to show we're as tough as the men."

"You're welcome to come and work for us any day," replied Mrs Williams. "Once this war's over."

"What war?" said David.

Renate put her fork down. Christine was right. It really was back-breaking work. It had sounded good to start with: two days off school to help to do some of the farm labouring. Many of the men had been called up and although some women were going to be arriving soon to help, they weren't here yet and they would have to be trained up anyway.

"Well, at least we can't complain about the weather," said Mr Williams. "It's exactly right for this work."

It was an incredibly mild day for April and the soil they were digging for the vegetables was just damp enough to be soft without being so wet it was heavy. Renate loved the smell of the soil. It reminded her of the countryside at home. It was all so normal. It really was hard to realise that they were at war.

The postman arrived at the farmhouse. He had quite a few letters. Renate noticed that Mrs Williams was holding her breath. She looked meaningfully at her husband.

"I'd better go and see," he whispered.

They were expecting him to get his call-up papers any day now. How would Mrs Williams manage the farm with him gone? Everyone stopped working as they watched him speak to the postman.

He waved to them and then took the envelopes inside.

"Looks as if we're okay, then," said Mrs Williams.

124

A few minutes later Mr Williams joined them. "Just business papers for the farm," he said. "We'll be all right for a while longer."

"I bet you won't get called up at all," said David. He sounded almost as if he was complaining. "I bet they'll call it all off soon. Well nothing's really happened, has it?"

"No, but..." answered Mr Williams. "I think they still believe it will, soon."

"Well, I hope we don't have to go back to smelly old London," said David. "I like it much better out here."

"A lot of the younger children are missing their parents," said Anne. "That's why so many of them have gone back to the cities. But I think their parents should be a bit tougher and make them stay. It might not be like this forever."

"Still," said Mrs Williams, "you've only got to look at Tom and Daisy. I mean, they seem fine most of the time, but Mrs Crouch says there are still tears most bed times. Tom puts on a brave face and looks very serious, but she thinks he's just holding back and Daisy, poor love, just sobs her heart out almost every night. And they've got each other. There are loads of children who are really on their own."

"Yes, it must be hard when you're so little," said Joyce. She caught Renate's eye and raised an eyebrow.

Renate felt herself blush and looked away quickly. She was suddenly very close to tears. What was happening with her father? No, it wasn't just the little ones who had it hard. Hopefully David was right. Perhaps the war would just fizzle out and that would be an end to it. It did seem ridiculous, having to take your gasmask everywhere. There were too many sensible Germans, weren't there surely? She just could not imagine Johan or Wilhelm wanting to throw poisonous gas at her and her mother.

"Hello! May I disturb you?" called a cheerful voice. "My, it's good to see all you young people working so hard. And getting a good dose of fresh air at the same time."

They turned round to see that Mrs Cohen had arrived.

"Good to see you," said Mrs Williams. "I'd better not shake hands, though." She held up her soil-covered hand.

"No, no, no need to stand on ceremony with me, my dears," said Mrs Cohen. "But I'm afraid I've got to break up your little working bee. I need a word with Renate."

Renate's heart almost flew to her throat. Had something happened to her mother? Or her father? How would they know?

"Don't look so worried my dear," said Mrs Cohen. "Yes, it's something we need to sort out, but I don't think it's anything to be scared about. Let's go over there and talk about it."

Seconds later they were sitting on the bench under the old crab-apple tree.

"I'm afraid," began Mrs Cohen, "that now that England and Germany are at war your mother has to be classed as an 'enemy alien' and you will be one too, once you're sixteen."

"Enemy alien?" whispered Renate. That sounded terrible. She wasn't anybody's enemy and she didn't feel at all like an alien.

"Silly, I know," said Mrs Cohen. "Especially when you think why you're here in the first place."

"But what does it mean, enemy alien?" asked Renate.

"Not really all that much, in your case," said Mrs Cohen. "It is mainly just a label. But it does mean that you would have to be in by ten every evening, and if you want to stay out later, you will have to get permission from the police. And you have to have permission to be near certain places – like the coast, or a munitions factory. You also have to get permission to go over ten miles from where you're staying. And you will have to report to the police station regularly."

"But we're near the coast now," remarked Renate. "The school is on the coast. Mutti won't be able to come and visit."

Mrs Cohen sighed. "Well, she will be able to come, but she'll just have to get some papers signed first."

Mutti would not like that. She wouldn't be able to go to concerts or the theatre. But then she supposed if the war did begin properly, there probably wouldn't be any concerts or shows.

"So, something you need to be careful to comply with, "said Mrs Cohen. "But nothing that should really be too difficult. Have you had any news from her?"

Renate shook her head.

"That's probably a good sign," said Mrs Cohen. "It probably means she is still busy and she is still working for the Smiths. Try not to worry. But if you are worried come and see me. Now, I'll leave you to get on with the excellent work you and your friends are doing."

Mrs Cohen waved at the others as she left.

Renate didn't move at first. She watched Mrs Cohen walk out of the gardens and then turn into the lane. She noticed for the first time that her teacher looked old. Perhaps she was finding this war – this phony war – harder than she let on. As soon as Mrs Cohen had disappeared, Renate made her way back to the kitchen garden to join the others.

"What was all that about?" demanded Christine.

Renate explained about being an 'enemy alien'.

"What a cheek!" commented Anne. "It's not as if you or your mother are going to be a spies or anything, is it?"

"I suppose they don't know that, though, do they?" replied Renate. It was very touching how her friends were always on her side. But she was, after all, German. Yes, German. Not Jewish, actually.

David suddenly stopped digging. "There's a thought," he said. "If you and your mother lived here, how could you go to the police station to ask if you can go more than ten miles away from home? The police station in Minehead is more than ten miles from the farm."

"Oh no! What a coincidence," cried Anne "Look!"

Sergeant Clarkson, the local village policeman was cycling up the lane. They watched as he propped his bike up against the fence and then walked across the yard. He nodded at them and then grinned at Renate.

"Hello, Miss Soon-to-be-Enemy Alien," he said. Then his face went very serious. "I'm afraid I've got some worrying news. Norway and Denmark have been attacked."

"What do you mean, attacked?" demanded Christine. "Bombs and things?"

Renate felt sick. Maybe it wasn't such a phony war, after all, and it was getting bigger.

ENEMY ALIEN, EH? WELL, THERE YOU HAVE IT. SEE, THE ENGLISH DON'T WANT YOU EITHER. AND WE'VE STARTED THROWING A FEW BOMBS AROUND.

Anika, 16 April 1940

Dear all,

I'm so pleased our little letter is carrying on, though I notice it is taking longer and longer to do the rounds each time. I suppose that is only to be expected. Everyone is getting so very busy. And I'm as bad – if not worse – than anyone else. Look how long I've held on to it! But let's resolve that it doesn't matter how long we take, as long as the letter gets through eventually.

So! Erika and Ilse are getting into boys. Can't say I've been very impressed by Fritz's friends. They seem just as revolting and silly as the boys who went to the other school near the WL. I will, say, though, that I'm missing them now. They used to come and play cards with me and Fritz. We even played bridge a couple of times. They're all doing their military service now. Actually, it's a bit more serious than that: they're doing their initial army training because they're going to be conscripts. Oh, Ilse, I hope Helmut won't have to do that. Let's hope this war is over soon.

So, I am bored, bored, bored. School is boring. And I'm a little bit worried. I suppose we all are a bit. That's probably why it has taken me so long to reply. I have very little to report.

I hope I'll have more exciting news next time.

Love,
Anika

Hani, 19 April 1940

"You're sure you don't want to stay on and do your Abitur?" said Frau Gödde. "You're adamant you want to leave in the summer?"

"Yes, I really am," said Hani. "I bet I wouldn't be able to finish, anyway. They'd probably bomb the school before then."

"I hope not," said Frau Gödde.

"Well, they might," said Hani. "And anyway, I want to do something practical. I want to learn to cook and look after the house." She looked up at her father.

"It wouldn't hurt," said Vati. "And you have a point. They would probably call you up to do your Reichsarbeitsdienst before you'd finished."

"Exactly!" said Hani. There was something else as well that she wasn't telling them. She hated studying. The work would be even harder for Abitur and she was finding it a struggle now. The thought of all those books and all those hours at a desk was really depressing.

"It will be difficult to come back to your studies later on," said Frau Gödde. "Even if you don't want a career, even if you get married, an education is always useful."

Didn't they get it? She wanted nothing more to do with boring old books. She wanted to do something practical. "Well, why don't I get on and do my RAD? And then I can go and get a job in the Kriegshilfsdienst? I've heard that if you go and do one of these special household management courses, you only have to do a half year of RAD. There's a school that does it in the middle of town."

"Where you're even more likely to have English bombs dropped on you," said Frau Gödde.

"You're absolutely sure about this?" said Herr Gödde.

"Yes, I am," said Hani. "What I'd really like to do is work with the Special Class all the time. But I suppose that's not an option."

Her father and mother exchanged a brief glance. Herr Gödde nodded. "Go on, tell her."

"The point is," said Frau Gödde slowly, "Doctor Kühn needs a housekeeper. If you worked for him, you would be spared both RAD and Kriegshilfsdienst."

"But what about Frau Lehrs?" she said.

"Doctor Kühn isn't allowed to employ her," said Herr Gödde. "Though I expect she would still help."

"And naturally, he also needs help with the Special Class," said Frau Gödde. "Especially now that Christoph isn't there anymore."

"This would make you working at the house all legitimate and above board," said Vati.

"But what about people like Trudi and Gisela?" said Hani.

Herr Gödde shrugged. "It shouldn't be a problem anymore. The house no longer belongs to a Jew, as far as the authorities are concerned."

Hani flinched. They still went on and on at the BDM about Jews being the enemy of the people. She just couldn't see Frau Lehrs that way.

"At least you could be Hani and you wouldn't have to be Hans anymore," said Frau Gödde, pulling the front of Hani's white shirt together. "We wouldn't be able to disguise this for much longer. When did you say the new uniforms were arriving? You're going to pop out of this shirt soon."

Hani brushed her mother's arm aside. She could be so embarrassing sometimes. She wished she wouldn't do things like that in front of Vati.

"Yes, that's great," she said. "This is really what I want to do."

"You do realise there is a risk, though, don't you?" said her father, suddenly very serious again. "Are you happy about that?"

"Yes, yes, of course," said Hani. The risk made it seem all the more important.

Frau Gödde nodded. "You will, of course, have to learn to act like a housekeeper – just in case Obersturmführer Poll or one of his colleagues decides to make another visit."

"But I can't cook!" wailed Hani.

Herr Gödde threw back his head and laughed "Well, young lady," he said, "it's high time you learnt. Even I can cook. Even Wilhelm learnt how to make an omelette before he went." His face suddenly went serious again. "I expect he knows a lot more about feeding himself now." He turned to Frau Gödde. "Do you think Rikki would give her a few lessons?"

"I'll go and ask her, shall I?" said Frau Gödde.

"You are really sure about this?" Vati asked her, after her mother had left the room.

"Yes, really," said Hani. "I'd really feel as if I was doing my bit."

"Good. Good girl," said Herr Gödde.

"Teach her to cook? Really?" Hani could hear Rikki's voice before she even got into the room. "I don't think that's right. Young Fräulein Hani working as a housekeeper."

"We all have to do our bit," said Frau Gödde.

The two women came into the lounge.

"But she's so young. She's a member of the Bund Deutscher Mädel. Lasses. Not grown up women," said Rikki.

"I really want to learn to cook, Rikki," said Hani. "Will you teach me?"

Rikki shook her head. "It doesn't seem right to me."

"Please, Rikki." Hani put her arm around the little woman and kissed her cheek.

"All right then," said Rikki. "You can start as soon as you get back from whatever you're doing with the other lasses."

She stepped back and looked at Hani. "I suppose you are growing up. Talking of which you'd better let me do something about that shirt."

Rikki bustled out of the room mumbling something about a pin.

"I guess you could start off by helping with the supper every day after school and then at the weekends you could help with the main meals. You'll soon learn," said Frau Gödde.

The doorbell rang.

"Don't you go anywhere until I've pinned that blouse for you," called Rikki.

It wasn't so bad, in the end, collecting clothes for the Winter Relief with Trudi and Gisela. They'd got quite a lot now – a wheelbarrow, a pushchair and a shopping-caddy full. They'd been given quite a bit of money, too, though whether it would go very far Hani wasn't sure.

It seemed odd, collecting for the Winter Relief barely a month after Easter, but a sudden warm spell had meant that a lot of people were throwing out some of their winter clothes.

At least the two girls were much better company than they used to be. Hani had learnt to go along with all that they said. Gisela was less bossy and Trudi didn't seem to need to make nasty remarks like she used to. Her wild hair seemed much tamer these days and stayed neatly in her two plaits. Hani thought she actually looked quite pretty now. Gisela, as usual, looked immaculate in her uniform. Hani felt quite hot and bothered, and she was sure Rikki's pin was going to give way any moment. Gisela looked as if she had only just changed into her uniform. But at least she didn't say anything about how Hani looked this time.

"I actually think that is more than enough," said Gisela. "Let's just get this back to the HJ hut and we can pack up for today."

Twenty minutes later, they were unloading what they'd collected into a cupboard.

"It's all right," said Gisela to Hani. "You can get off home. I'm going to Trudi's for tea. Her dad is coming for us in the car but he won't be here for half an hour."

Hani was only too glad to leave them. Yes, they were much better company now than they used to be but she always felt a bit as if she was in the way. She didn't know why because these days they were always quite nice to her. But it was always as if they had got some sort of secret they didn't want to tell her.

She was half way home when she sneezed. She went to get her hanky out of her pocket and found the bag of money they had been given. Oh goodness, she'd better go back and give it in. The two girls were much nicer these days, but would Gisela believe that she hadn't been intending to steal the money if she waited until the next proper meeting? Best get it back straight away.

"I'm sorry," she called as she walked into the hall.

Then she stopped dead. She couldn't quite believe what she was seeing.

Gisela and Trudi were kissing. The way boyfriends and girlfriends kissed, though she'd never even seen a boy and a girl kissing like that. Both girls' shirts were open.

Goodness, what was this?

She crept back out of the hall. What should she do? She didn't understand about the two girls. Yes, she understood about boys and girls a bit. She knew she'd had a bit of a crush on Christoph before he went away. She'd liked it when he'd put his arm round her a couple of times and she started to feel really funny, in a nice sort of way, when he was anywhere near her. Then when he'd come to see them in his uniform and he'd kissed her on the lips, she'd really have liked to kiss him for a bit longer, like Trudi and Gisela were doing right now, only she didn't think they would have been able to take their shirts off.

But two girls together?

What should she do? She shouldn't hold on to this money. She'd better let them know she was on her way back in.

"Hello," she shouted. "It's only me. I'm really sorry." She forced a giggle. "I am an idiot. I walked off with the money."

She walked slowly into the hall.

Gisela started tucking her shirt into her skirt and Trudi turned her back to her and pretended to rummage about in the clothes.

"Oh yes, thank you," said Gisela. "I should have reminded you. Just put it down on the table."

"Thank you Hani," said Trudi. As she turned to face Hani, Hani noticed that she had her shirt buttoned up wrongly. Trudi must have realised and she blushed bright red. "How did that happen?" she whispered as she tried to button up the shirt properly but in fact only made it worse.

"I'll be off, then," said Hani.

Trudi and Gisela mumbled an embarrassed "Tschüss!"

That was okay, then, thought Hani as she made her way back home. At least she hadn't got into trouble about the money. She just didn't understand about Gisela and Trudi and she didn't know who she would dare ask.

Hanna Braun, 9 May 1940

Dear all

So good to hear from you all and to read that you are keeping healthy and cheerful and quite busy. Thank you so much again for letting me contribute to your fascinating round robin letter.

I managed a day trip with my class at the end of April. We had a really interesting nature study day in the woods about an hour's bus ride from here. We did some hiking too. The countryside seems to be ignoring the fact that we are at war.

Goodness, you are all growing up.

All of you, do try to enjoy life despite everything. I'm not sure how much your parents have told you about what is going on or whether you've managed to read the papers at all. Yes there are some strange, even horrible things, happening all around us. Being at war is never pleasant, no matter how much we think it is justified. But do remember my outing with my little ones. The sun still shines and nature doesn't notice that anything has changed. And do all enjoy the things in life that are important at your age.

Get plenty of rest. Exercise well. Breathe in the fresh air. Don't starve. There are rich pickings in the countryside if you make an effort.

And I look forward to your further news.

All good wishes,
Hanna Braun

Käthe Edler, 10 May 1940

Dear Renate,

It sounds as if you are getting on well at school and you are being looked after very kindly. I am really pleased and I hope I can come and visit you soon.

Please don't worry about me, though it is all change here. I am currently alone in the flat. Mr and Mrs Smith and John have moved to Gloucester. John's school has been evacuated there and they have all decided to move to be near to him. Miriam's work is quite close so they'll be able to see more of her. Mr Smith has managed to get a transfer to a local office. There is no danger of him being called up: he is too old and anyway his work is considered important for the war effort. We are both invited to go and see them in your school holidays.

They are officially keeping me on as housekeeper but not at the house at Gloucester as that is quite small. I am to stay on in the flat and help the Hanusiaks. That doesn't take up all of my time so Mr Smith has also found me a part-time job in his London office.

I'm quite enjoying the work although it is very simple and a little tedious. It is also very aggravating to have to travel with everyone and their gas masks on the Tube. But the people are really kind and friendly. They never treat me either as if I am German or Jewish, and they do not hold back in condemning our dear Herr Hitler. (I tend to join in!) And I have been invited out several times by my work colleagues and even in a couple of cases into their homes.

Having both little jobs, and the fact that you and I are refugees and that I am a middle-aged woman have stopped me having to be interned. I'm still classed as an 'enemy alien Class B' so there is some paperwork to put in order if I am to come and see you – a little less if I meet you at your friends' farm rather than anywhere near the school. Let's hope that that can be soon.

*But I have even bigger news. A good friend of mine –
another full but non-practising Jewess – is joining me in the
flat. We shall be company for each other. The Smiths are in
entire agreement – they understand that I would feel
uncomfortable staying in their place alone.*

*I look forward to introducing you to my friend Eva. I am
sure you will like her.*

*No more news from Vati or Oma. Still, this is as we would
expect. It is really best that they don't communicate with us.
Neither should you write to any of your friends. It could make
it very difficult for them. Naturally, I am worried about your
father and your grandmother – especially your grandmother.
Goodness knows what has happened to her by now. But she
has some good friends in Stuttgart. We can only hope.*

*It doesn't feel too much as if we are at war here in
London. You can see all the signs, of course, that it is yet
expected. The newspapers make depressing reading, though.
I don't think it will be over soon. Our dear Herr Hitler is
quarrelling with so many people.*

*Take care now and carry on being good at school and for
the Johnsons. Write to me soon.*

Your loving mother,
Käthe Edler

Renate, 3 September 1940

"I shall be glad of a hot bath," said Christine.

"I bet we'll only be allowed six inches and we'll have to share the water," said Anne.

"Shouldn't whoever is going to sleep on the camp bed tonight be the one who has the water while it's hot?" suggested Renate.

"That seems fair," said Anne. "Pity we can't just have a dip in the sea."

"No thanks," said Christine. "It would be too cold and you don't know what you might find in there. Never mind that we're not allowed."

"I envy David and Joyce being picked up by Mrs Williams," said Anne. She hitched her backpack higher on to her back.

"Oh, we'll soon be there," said Renate. "Then I suppose we'll be getting ready for school tomorrow."

She'd enjoyed the camping again this year. The weather had been nice and it had been good to get away from all the talk about the war. None of the girls' parents had wanted them to go back to London for the summer. They'd spent the first couple of weeks helping on the farm and kept out of Mrs Johnson's way. Now that her husband was away, she was busier than ever with the twins. And then they'd been away at camp for four weeks.

"Yes, and we'll have to get all of our clothes washed somehow," said Christine.

It didn't take them long, though, to walk from the station to the little house in Glenmore Road.

We must be getting fitter, Renate thought.

"That's funny," said Christine as they walked up the path. "The door's not open."

Renate put her backpack down and searched for her key in the front pocket. The other two did the same.

"It's okay, I've got mine," said Anne.

She unlocked the door and the three of them made their way in.

It was unnaturally quiet. Normally you would hear the twins

playing or crying. Mrs Johnson almost always had the wireless on, and if it was a music programme she would sing along to it. There were no cooking smells either. Despite the shortages, Mrs Johnson nearly always had something bubbling on the stove or baking in the oven.

"Perhaps she forgot what time we were getting back," said Christine.

"She's probably taken the twins to her mother's," said Renate.

"Sh. Listen," said Christine. "There's somebody upstairs."

"Do you think it's a burglar?" said Anne.

"It sounds as if it's coming from Mrs Johnson's bedroom," said Renate. She put her finger to her lips and motioned to the other two that they should follow her quietly upstairs.

As they got nearer to the main bedroom at the front of the house, she was even more certain that there was someone in Mrs Johnson's bedroom. She started to open the door. Christine put her hand over hers and shook her head.

"Who's there?" called Mrs Johnson from her room.

"Thank goodness!" said Anne.

"It's only us," said Christine. "It was so quiet that we thought you'd gone out and then we heard you moving around and thought you were a burglar."

Mrs Johnson opened the door. Her hair was untidy and Renate could see that her eyes were red as if she had been crying.

"Girls! I'm so sorry about this," she said. "Didn't Mrs Williams meet you at the station?"

"We left David and Joyce waiting for her there," said Anne.

"Oh, she must have arrived too late," said Mrs Johnson. "I expect she'll come round here before she drives back to the farm." She paused to take deep breath. "You see, Will was on his way home on leave and he called to see his brother in London. He was killed in one of the air raids. They both were."

Renate felt sick.

"I'm so sorry, Mrs Johnson," said Christine, after what seemed like a very long silence.

Anne mumbled something similar.

Renate couldn't think what to say. Kind, generous Mr Johnson

139

had been killed by German bombs. The twins had lost their father and their uncle.

"I'm moving to my mother's," said Mrs Johnson. "The twins are already there. Mrs Williams has agreed to take you to the farm. I'm sure the Williams will make you very welcome and very comfortable."

The doorbell rang.

"That's probably her now," said Mrs Johnson.

The four of them made their way downstairs.

"I'm so sorry I missed you, girls," said Mrs Williams, as Deborah Johnson opened the door. "I had to wait for a herd of cows to get out of the way."

"I've told them," said Mrs Johnson.

"I'm so sorry you had to go through that," said Mrs Williams.

Mrs Johnson pursed her lips and shook her head. She looked as if she was going to cry again.

Renate looked at the floor.

"Just grab a few bits and pieces for overnight. And we can take your dirty clothes from camping back to the farm," said Mrs Williams. "I'll be doing a big wash tomorrow. Then tomorrow after school, we can come back here and get the rest of your things. Is that all right, Deborah?"

Mrs Johnson nodded. "Keep your keys until tomorrow," she said. "I'll probably be gone by the time you come round. You can leave them in the knife drawer and pull the door to behind you."

"Right, go and get your things, while I make Mrs Johnson a cup of tea."

An hour later Mrs Williams was showing the three of them their room at the farm.

"It's one of the rooms we'd got ready for the young women who were going to come and work on the farm," said Mrs Williams. "We've made it nice and warm and cosy and we should manage to accommodate all the other girls without having to put one in here. We're moving Joyce in with you so her room's empty and we can use that for the land girls."

"Now we'll be arguing about who is going to go on the top

bunks," said Christine. "I bag it's my turn – I should have been on the camp bed tonight."

"But it's a treat being on the top bunk," said Anne. "You've got nobody above you and you get a better view through the window. It was like a punishment being on the camp bed."

David and Joyce were hovering in the doorway. "Do you want to go for a walk round the farm before supper?" said David.

"Sounds great," said Anne.

"Yes, let's do it," said Christine. "Renate?"

She didn't want to go for a walk on the farm. Not now. Probably another day. She wanted to write to her mother. "No, not yet," she said, "there's something I need to do first."

"Okay," said Christine. "See you later then?"

Renate nodded.

As soon as the door had clicked to, Renate took out her notebook. She ripped two pages out. When she fetched her things tomorrow she would be able to find the envelope and a stamp. But she desperately wanted to write to Mutti. She wanted to know how she was finding living in London: watching and hearing German bombs destroying things around her and hurting people.

She started to write, but just couldn't find the words. She tore six more pages out of her notebook, wrote half a side on each and then she screwed the papers into a ball. She just couldn't get the words right.

She jumped when the door clicked open.

"There you are," said Mrs Williams. "The others are back and supper will be ready in five minutes. Oh, are you writing a letter?"

Renate sighed. "Yes. Only I can't get the words right."

Mrs Williams bent down to pick up one of the pieces of paper that had fallen on the floor. "Perhaps you'll think better tomorrow," she said. "When you've settled in properly. Now come on, don't you worry about a thing."

AYE, AYE, AYE. BUT YOU NEED TO WORRY, RENATECHEN. THIS WAR'S KILLING THE VERY PEOPLE WHO HAVE TRIED TO PROTECT YOU AND THEY'LL BLAME YOU EVENTUALLY.

Sabine, 27 October 1940

Dear all,

Goodness, how everything has changed since I last wrote.

Georg has left home now. He and his friend Thomas have been called up and they started their training at the beginning of August. We don't know where they are or when we'll see them again, but we do get the occasional postcard from Georg. It's quite upsetting. But as Fräulein Braun says, there is little point in worrying. Best to keep occupied.

And occupied I am. In September I started my new school. Not the College School like I said earlier. I managed to get a place at the Gymnasium. So, I'll be studying for my Abitur. And my main subject will be English.

"Good to know the language of the enemy," Herr Schmidt said.

Honestly, Herr Schmidt, what a strange person he is sometimes. He really enjoys his work with the Hitlerjugend. He was telling me they were doing bayonet practice the other day. Apparently, they're doing grenade throwing next week. And I thought it was supposed to be just like being in the Boy Scouts.

"I simply won't have any more time to do training with you, Sabine," he said

Well, just as well really. I have so much homework now that there wouldn't be any time anyway. But don't worry. I've not given up on the athletics altogether. The sports teacher at the Gymnasium is very pleased with me and she is looking at entering me for some inter-school competitions.

Well, I must finish now and get back down to my homework. And bliss! We have a couple of days off at the end of the month.

Your Sabine

Charlotte, 5 January 1941

Dear all,

Well yes, so much has happened. I survived the year at the Piloty School. By July, I was able to pin my hair up and make it stay. I wear it up all of the time now. I doubt you'd recognise me.

My sister Ursula is much better, more her old self. She seems to have got her old energy back. It helps that her husband, Wilhelm, is on indefinite leave at the moment. He had an accident. He fell off a motorbike and damaged his leg very badly. We're a little worried that it may have to be amputated.

And I have big news too. Ilse, I too have a boyfriend. Since September. His name is Karl, and as he works in a reserved occupation he hasn't been called up – yet. He does belong to the Heimwehr so is often on duty and has to do training. He's four years older than me. Mother and Father were a bit worried at first, but when they saw how kind he was to Oma, they were convinced. He's even had Sunday lunch with us a couple of times. I'd love you all to meet him.

And yes, of course we've kissed and cuddled and held hands. Sometimes we go for a picnic in the woods and then he lies with his head on my lap and I stroke his soft black curls until he falls asleep. I really love him!

Well, it's time for Oma's walk now. She has just woken up from her nap. So, I'll finish this now and we'll pop to the post office on our way through the village. Oma likes to chat to Frau Müller who works behind the counter there.

Looking forward to your next letters.

Your Charlotte

Erika, 10 May 1941

Dear all,

Well, I'll soon get my sister back. We go to the Schliersee for two weeks and then Helmut will start his basic training. He's recently become a Hitlerjugend leader so Ilse has had to see less of him anyway. He's been training up others. Of course, that means his army training won't take long. He'll probably be in active service very quickly.

Hopefully, Ilse's mind will soon be taken off it all. We start the Piloty School in September. I'm looking forward to it and I think Ilse is too. At least we'll feel as if we're doing something useful.

We went into Nuremberg last week. We both needed new boots. We didn't manage to get any, though. The place was so desolate. Windows boarded up. Some buildings totally crumbled. Not many people around

There were one or two shoe shops still open but they had nothing in our size. It looks as if we're going to have to get some old ones from our cousins. I hate second hand clothes – especially footwear. But we can't go on with the ones we've got. They really pinch now. Mother says she'll be glad when we stop growing.

Well, I'll stop there and hand over to Ilse.

Lots of love.
Your friend Erika

Renate, 5 July 1941

"Now then, blow out the candles and make a wish," said Mrs Williams.

"Yes, you can do it," said Christine. "Remember, the wish will only work if you blow them out all in one go."

"One, two, three," counted Anne.

"Go Renate," chanted David.

"You can do it," called Joyce.

Renate took a deep breath but she couldn't bring herself to blow straight away. What if she didn't manage to make them all go out? There were sixteen, after all, even if they didn't match. Goodness knows how Mrs Williams had managed to find them all.

"Come on then," said Christine. "Can't you think of a wish?"

Well, that wasn't the problem. Not at all. It was obvious. She wanted this war to stop. She wanted to see her father again. She wanted to live with him and Mutti like she used to. Only, she didn't want to lose all the friends she'd made here and she didn't suppose Vati would want to live in England, even after the war finished. And of course she also wanted to see Hani and her old friends in Nuremberg. It was a real dilemma.

"Come on Renate," said David. "Or we'll be late for the cinema."

She blew hard at the candles. They all went out instantly except for three that flickered and caught again before they too died.

"Hoorah!" cried Christine. "Three cheers for the birthday girl!"

Renate blushed.

"Did you remember to make your wish?" Christine whispered after they'd finished cheering.

Renate nodded.

"Eat up, folks," said David. "We need to get going in the next ten minutes."

It had got complicated. Now that she was sixteen she had become an 'enemy alien' proper. She had obtained the permission to be near the sea – with the school being so close to the beach they had to allow that. She'd also got special permission to be more than ten miles away from home when she needed to report to the police station – the nearest one was ten and a half miles from them. But she'd forgotten to ask for special permission to stay out after ten tonight. It had been too late to cycle back to the police station and Mrs Williams was out with the truck.

"It doesn't matter," David had said. "We can go to the seven o'clock showing and we'll be out by just after nine. Then as long as we pedal reasonably fast, we'll be back just before ten. And before you ask: yes, it's less than ten miles away. Nine and three quarters actually. I looked it up on the map. It's the other end of town from the police station."

So, it was going to be all right but only if they set off now.

Renate ate her slice of cake as quickly as she could. It was a bit dry but she made the effort. Mrs Williams had gone to so much trouble, and she guessed even Oma Lehrs's cakes would be a little odd if all she had to work with was carrots, powdered eggs and a tiny amount of sugar. She felt a slight pang at the thought of her grandmother and remembered the lovely baking smells that used to come from the house on Schellberg Street.

Five minutes later they were cycling towards Minehead. She had no more time to feel sorry for herself.

Renate quite enjoyed the film. They all did. It was a little bit crazy and a little bit young for them. It was about a baby elephant that had enormous ears and learnt to fly. Renate thought how much Tom and Daisy would have enjoyed it, although bigger kids could enjoy it too. It was a nice little story – lovely and colourful.

The black and white film that went with it was less interesting. Renate shuddered a little as she watched the newsreels. There wasn't any good news at all, really. But the story about the little elephant had come last and had left her feeling positive. There had been ice creams and drinks of delicious orange juice between the two films. It had felt like a real birthday treat.

It was just a few minutes after nine when they left the cinema.

Renate braced herself for a fast ride back.

"Well, even if we don't quite make it for ten o'clock," said David," I don't suppose there'll be a policeman waiting outside the farm when we get back, just to make sure you get back in time."

Now you tell me, thought Renate. For goodness sake, she'd trusted him when he'd said they'd get back all right.

Soon they were pedalling briskly towards the farm. It was harder work going back because it was uphill. It was more difficult to see, as well, because of the Blackout, though fortunately the moon was almost full and it was a clear night. Renate looked down at the ground and worked out where the others were from the way their bikes were creaking.

Even so, she did not see the big stone in the middle of the road until too late. She swerved to avoid it but the bike hit it and she and the bike fell to the ground. Her leg really hurt. She hoped she hadn't broken it.

The others stopped.

"Well, even if you haven't damaged yourself too much," said David, "your bike's going nowhere fast."

"We'll carry on up to the farm," said Christine, "and get some help. Will you stay here with her David?"

"Of course. A good idea."

Renate watched the three girls set off. So much for being home by ten.

"Can you waggle your toes?" David asked.

"I think so," said Renate. She tried it. "Yes."

"Then I don't think it's broken," said David.

Renate didn't think so either by now. It was beginning to hurt a little less but she still didn't think she could walk on it very far. "Do you think we'll get home by ten?" she said.

"I shouldn't worry about that," said David. "Even if we're back late, I doubt anyone will find out. And even if they do, it's bound to be all right in the circumstances."

Renate wasn't so sure though. The papers they'd given her said there were to be absolutely no excuses and it was up to her to allow adequate time for getting back or seek permission to be out past curfew. It looked as if she was going to foul it all up on her very first day.

But there was nothing they could do now except sit and wait.

"I don't suppose they'll be too long," said David.

Renate couldn't think what to say and so they sat in awkward silence.

After about ten minutes they heard a car engine.

"That's funny," said David. "They've brought the car. I thought they'd bring the truck."

The car came nearer and stopped.

Renate's heart sank. It was a police car. "What's the time?" she whispered.

David squinted at his watch. "Just after ten to, I think," he said.

"Hello, you two," said a familiar voice. At least it was Sergeant Clarkson. He was always so friendly. Perhaps he'd be all right about it. "What's happened here, then?"

David explained about Renate's bike. "Only she's a bit worried..."

But Sergeant Clarkson wasn't listening. He was busy examining the bike. "Oh dear, oh dear, oh dear," he said. "Bit of a mess. Tell you what; we'll just pop it behind the hedge. I'm sure it'll be safe until morning. Let's face it; nobody would want to steal it in that condition. We'll put yours underneath, David, and then anybody who sees them might think they're both wrecked. And I'll give you a lift back up to the farm."

A few moments later they were driving into the farmyard. Mr Williams was just about to climb into the truck.

"Oh, thank you Sergeant Clarkson for bringing them back safely," he said.

"My pleasure," said Sergeant Clarkson.

The front door opened. Renate could see the hall clock. It was just two minutes after ten.

"Better get in and get that door shut as soon as possible," said Sergeant Clarkson. "Blackout, you know."

"I'm sorry Sergeant Clarkson," she stammered.

"No problem," said the sergeant. "You need a bit of light to get in through your own front door."

"No, I meant about the curfew," said Renate.

"What?" said the policeman. "Oh, yes. I do believe I need to wish you many happy returns."

"I wasn't looking for birthday greetings," said Renate. "But you know, with me being an enemy alien…"

Sergeant Clarkson laughed. "That idiotic nonsense. A nice young lady like you an enemy alien. And you couldn't help riding into a big stone, what with this silly Blackout and all. No, it wouldn't have bothered me if you'd been half an hour late, even if you hadn't wrecked your bike and your leg. After all, you technically break the law every time you come and sign in."

"Oh thank you for being so understanding," said Renate, as she felt another huge stone lift from her chest. Without stopping to think, she gave the police sergeant a hug.

"Now then, don't be daft," said Sergeant Clarkson. "All my colleagues would say the same. But you'd all better get in and get that door shut before I do have to charge you with something. Good night to you all."

As they went in and Mrs Williams shut the door behind them, mumbling something about cocoa, Renate thought how nice English people were.

YES, THEY ARE NICE, AREN'T THEY, RENATE? NICER TO YOU THAN YOU DESERVE. ESPECIALLY AS THEY THINK OF YOU AS GERMAN. AND GERMAN BOMBS KILLED MR WILLIAMS AND HIS BROTHER.

AND MY, OH MY. YOU HAVE THE AUDACITY TO BREAK THE RULES OF THOSE THAT FEED YOU. TYPICAL JEW!

Ilse 10, September 1941

Dear all,

Just after Erika finished her letter, Helmut's younger brother Johan turned up to say that Helmut had been taken to hospital. He'd collapsed after doing a fifty kilometre hike. He went to bed with a fever and was so ill the next morning that his mother sent for the doctor. The doctor immediately said he had pneumonia and sent him to hospital. The doctor said that often after one of these marches he has as many as thirty boys in hospital.

I wasn't allowed to visit him for the next four days and I was too worried to write. Then, I was busy visiting him at the hospital. He was still coughing when we went on holiday.

Helmut was better when we got home from the Schliersee, but still a bit weak. They still insisted he must go away. I didn't hear from him until yesterday, and he is content and well and not yet in active service. He has almost finished his training, though. So, I'm now a little happier. I was too miserable to write before.

Even the choir has been disbanded. Too many of the young men have had to leave and we girls are getting very busy as well.

Erika didn't mention our disastrous trip with the BDM to the Starnbergersee. We had a five day camp there in July. There was a huge thunderstorm one night and our tent blew away. We got soaked.

Well, I'll finish now and get this little parcel into the post. We look forward to your further letters.

All good wishes,
Your Ilse

Anika, 15 November 1941

Dear all,

Fritz has been home on leave. He and Vati have been worrying about all the funny political things that are going on. I think Vati was pleased to see Fritz. Mutti was tut-tutting at us playing cards again and he said, "Oh leave them be, Heidi. All that counting and reckoning and second guessing is good for their Maths. That could be useful with everything that we've got coming."

Fritz has changed though. He likes to go to the inn or the café every day to read the newspaper. He won't read it at home. Partly, of course, because father won't tolerate newspapers in the house. He's started smoking as well and, especially when I get back from school, he smells of smoke. When I ask him what's happening in the news he won't tell me a thing. I do wish I knew what was happening with this war.

I don't know. I really don't. They're so full of doom and gloom, the older folk, these days. The snow will be coming soon and we'll have such glorious ice for skating on the river and snow, for snowball fights. Oh, I wish we could go skiing. They say the snow will be good this winter.

I love this time of the year. The dark mysterious nights as we get closer to Christmas. I wonder, Fräulein Braun, whether you will think this is an early Christmas present when it lands in your mail box. I'm afraid you'll have to buy a new exercise book – there won't be room to write a whole letter in the side and a half that is left.

Looking forward to all of your news.

Your friend Anika

Hanna Braun, 2 December 1941

Dear all,

How wonderful to receive your letters again. And yes, I had to buy a new exercise book. I'm sorry the paper is so poor. Our local stationer is usually excellent, so this is quite a disappointment. The effects of war, I suppose.

You all seem to be doing so well with your efforts.

It was so pleasing, to read that you are making good use of our local lakes – yes we have the Schliersee and the Starnbergersee. Don't forget, all of you, that the Innsee is also close at hand. Then there are the mountains too, quite near to us – have any of you climbed the Grossglockner or even the Kleinglockner? We are really quite fortunate having such wonderful scenery so close. We can make the most of that even in wartime – especially as it is so hard to travel.

The summer seems so long ago now, but I too had a very pleasant holiday at home. I went hiking for a week with a colleague through the Spessart. The forests are so beautiful there with their endless tracks through beech and fir plantations. We stopped each day for lunch at a simple inn and feasted on cheese, wine and bread. Definitely no sign of war, not even a stray aircraft going over.

I do wish you all success with your plans for the next year and I look forward to hearing from you again soon.

Kindest regards to you all,
Hanna Braun

Renate, 24 December 1941

"Here we are then," said Mr Smith, putting Mutti's suitcase down on the bedroom floor.

John followed him in with Renate's. The room in the little terraced house was tiny and there was just room for the two beds side by side.

"I'm sorry there's not a lot of space," said Mrs Smith. "But I think your suitcases can fit under the bed when you don't need them."

"Don't worry, Mrs Smith," said Frau Edler. "It is so kind of you to have us."

"Well, come down as soon as you're ready," said Mrs Smith. "I've made some nice soup and there are some mince pies as well."

Renate was exhausted. The train had been late leaving London and even later arriving in Gloucester. They'd had to stand most of the way. The beds looked very inviting. She was hungry though and she knew she would have to be polite. It was Christmas Eve after all. It would probably be ages before she could get to bed.

She went to the bathroom and splashed some cold water on her face.

Her mother was waiting on the landing when she came out. "We'd better get downstairs," she said.

It was cosy and warm in the small dining room at the Smiths' home. The kitchen door was open and warm air drifted in from the Aga.

The soup was delicious.

"This is lovely," said Renate.

"We grew all the vegetables ourselves," said Mrs Smith.

"You can still keep them fresh at this time of year?" said Frau Edler.

"Staggered planting's the secret," said Mr Smith. "We won't starve and we won't freeze, whatever happens. We can burn anything in that Aga."

Renate gratefully accepted a second bowl of soup.

She wasn't so sure about the mince pies, though. They were a little too sweet and a little too spicy, though if she was honest the ingredients weren't all that different from what she would have found in a Stollen – just different proportions. Mrs Smith's pastry was lovely and soft, though, and the crust seemed to just melt in her mouth. It was very filling and she began to feel very sleepy.

"You look as if you need to go to bed," said Mrs Smith.

"What about the presents?" she asked. They hadn't been able to afford much but Renate had carefully made something for everyone in the family.

"Oh, we normally open them after breakfast," said Mrs Smith. "But we might wait until after lunch tomorrow as Miriam has to work in the morning. Did you want to put them under the tree ready?"

What? No Christkind on Heiliger Abend? Well, of course she knew these days that it was the adults who put up the Christmas tree and arranged the presents underneath. But the last two Christmases she'd celebrated with Mutti, and Eva was there last year as well. They'd still put up the tree on Heiliger Abend and given each other presents after dinner.

"They do it differently in England," Mutti whispered. "They celebrate on the 25th, not the 24th."

"Yes, please," said Renate. "Can I put them under the tree? I don't want to spoil the paper while I'm rooting around in my suitcase."

"Those look very pretty," said Mrs Smith a few minutes later as Renate arranged the presents neatly under the tree.

"Thank you," said Renate. Will I ever get used to being English?

OF COURSE YOU WON'T. IT'S HARDLY SURPRISING IS IT? YOU ARE, AND ALWAYS WILL BE, JEWISH FILTH.

Renate, 25 December 1941

It was all different, English Christmas. The Smiths took them to church in the morning. Renate quite enjoyed singing the carols. They attended the family service, so the vicar made it all into a story suitable for children.

When they got back to the Smiths' house, there was a lovely smell of roast chicken coming from the kitchen.

"Miriam will be home in about an hour," said Mrs Smith. "So we'll eat at two – that leaves her a bit of time if she gets delayed."

"We'll help you with the vegetables," said Mutti.

Soon the three of them were scraping and slicing. John and Mr Smith brought in some more firewood from the store at the bottom of the garden and then arranged the Smiths' presents under the Christmas tree.

"That really is beginning to look very pretty," said Mrs Smith. "We're not going to let any old war ruin our Christmas."

Miriam arrived at just after one.

"Very good timing," said Mrs Smith. "We've finished all the vegetables now."

Miriam giggled. She was a very pretty girl, Renate thought. She'd already let her hair down and soft springy dark brown curls framed her face.

"Go on. I'm only joking," said Mrs Smith. "Go and get out of that uniform."

"Will you come and help me choose what to put on?" Miriam said to Renate.

Renate nodded her head. "Yes, I'd like that."

She followed Miriam into the small bedroom at the back of the house.

"There isn't a lot to choose from," said Miriam. "But it's still nice to get out of my work clothes." She opened her wardrobe door. "Well, what do you think?"

Renate spotted the pale blue woollen dress straight away. "That looks nice," she said.

"Yes, you might be right," said Miriam. "It's really comfortable, that one. And it's nice and warm."

A few moments later, Miriam had the dress on. She had tidied her hair and put on the slightest smear of lipstick. "Well, how do I look?"

Renate nodded. Miriam looked so pretty. "You look really nice," she said.

Miriam grinned.

Renate knew that the two of them were going to be good friends, even though Miriam must be at least six years older than her.

The lunch was delicious.

"Our good friends, the Kelletts, gave us the chicken," said Mr Smith. "It's useful these days knowing people who live on farms."

"Of course, before the war we'd have a goose or a turkey," said Mrs Smith. "But we're lucky to get the chicken. And such a tasty one at that."

Renate wasn't so sure about the Christmas pudding. It looked like the inside of the mince pies she'd had the day before. But it did look very pretty when Mr Smith poured some brandy on it and set it alight. John switched the light off so that they could see the little blue flame more easily.

She was quite surprised when she ate it. It wasn't as rich as the mince pies, and it was served with custard, which she knew and had begun to like a lot. Especially when it was made from the yellow powder instead of with fresh eggs.

"Not too bad, is it, considering?" said Mrs Smith. "I've used that packet stuff for the custard and I put a bit of grated carrot and apple in because I couldn't get much fruit."

"It's very good, my dear," said Mr Smith.

"Oh, and don't forget to watch out in case you have the sixpence in your piece," said Mrs Smith.

At that very moment Renate spotted the silver coin in her bowl.

"Lucky," whispered Miriam.

It was getting dark by the time they cleared away and started opening presents. Everyone was very pleased with what Renate had made for them.

Mrs Smith admired the embroidered needle-case; Mr Smith declared he would find the pipe-holder very useful; John was pleased about the set of bookmarks, and Mutti put on the pale blue scarf straight away.

"Now I know why you wanted me to wear this dress," said Miriam, holding up a slightly darker blue painted satin scarf. "This goes perfectly with it."

Mr and Mrs Smith had given her some new watercolour paints and a sketch pad. Mutti had given her a thick jumper.

"I hope that will keep you warm when you're by the sea," said Mutti.

Renate was sure it would.

From Miriam she had a tin of nice-smelling talcum powder and John had given her a book about wild flowers.

"I'm sorry it's not new," he said.

"It's lovely," said Renate. "It's the thought that counts anyway."

The adults had all given each other books and there were books also for John and Miriam. Renate suspected they were all from the same second-hand bookshop.

"I'm going to have to get rid of some of my old ones to make sure I have room for these on my shelf," said Miriam. "Do you like books, Renate? You could take some home with you."

Renate laughed, then groaned. "But I thought my suitcase was going to be lighter when I went home, not heavier."

The day went on as pleasantly right up until bedtime. They'd gone for a little walk after they'd opened presents. Then there'd been some games in the evening: charades, table skittles and shove ha'penny. John had played the piano and they'd all had a good sing-song. Mrs Smith seemed to keep finding more and more little snacks.

"Do you think we're becoming English?" Renate said to Mutti when they were back in their room that night.

"Maybe, a little bit," said Mutti.

"Well, I told myself I was going to like being English," said Renate, "and I do."

"That's good," said Mutti. "At least I suppose we can stop thinking of ourselves as refugees."

"Does that mean we don't need to be enemy aliens anymore?" asked Renate.

"Oh, I don't suppose they'd go that far," said Frau Edler.

BUT NATURALLY YOU ARE STILL ENEMY ALIENS. YOU ARE JEWISH. EVERYONE'S ENEMY.

Renate, 26 December 1941

"Shall we go for a long walk after breakfast?" said Miriam. "It's a glorious day. Not to be missed." She waved towards the window.

It was white outside. Six inches of snow had fallen overnight, although the sky was blue and the sun was shining. It did look inviting.

They all went in the end. Renate was glad of her new thick jumper. Although the end of her nose remained cold, her feet were lovely and warm and so were her arms. Miriam had lent her a nice fluffy hat so her head was cosy as well.

They walked up through the woods and then along the top of a hill. They had a good view of the town from there.

"It looks quite pretty in the snow," said Miriam. "I find it a bit ugly usually."

It was quite nice but now Renate was remembering the mountains in Bavaria. What was Hani doing now? What would she, Mutti and Vati be doing today if there'd been no war? And if Herr Hitler hadn't disliked the Jews so much?

"We have a lot of snow in Bavaria," said Renate.

"Yes, I'm sure you do," said Miriam. "I expect you miss your friends a lot."

"Yes, I do," said Renate. "But I've got a lot of friends here as well."

"I hope we can be friends," said Miriam, tucking her arm into Renate's.

"I'd like that," said Renate.

Mutti and Mrs Smith turned back after a while whilst Mr Smith and John strode ahead. Miriam and Renate dawdled back down the hill and into the town. Miriam kept stopping to point out landmarks to her: the hospital where she worked; where her favourite shops were, and the church hall where she and her friends met up.

"We're not religious. Not at all," said Miriam. "But they do put on some good entertainment and it is all free."

When they arrived back at the house, John was rolling an enormous snowball.

"You two took your time," he said. "Now, are you going to help me with this?"

They worked hard making the snowman. He was about six inches taller than John by the time they'd finished. Miriam found an old hat of Mr Smith's and John stole some coal and a carrot from the store cupboard to make his nose and eyes.

"What can we use for a mouth?" asked John.

"A bit of that tree?" suggested Renate, pointing to a small fir tree. "Then it will look as if he has a moustache. And not a silly one like Herr Hitler's."

"Good idea," said John.

This is fun, thought Renate, as they all admired their work. English snow is just as good as Bavarian snow – it's just different.

"English people are really nice, aren't they?" said Renate as she and her mother got ready for bed that night.

Mutti sighed. "Yes, they are. But remember a lot of German people are as well. Your father; Wilma and Johann; Herr and Frau Gödde, and Hani. And you must remember how all of your school teachers looked after you."

"My school teachers?" asked Renate.

"Oh yes," said Mutti. "They all knew you were Jewish and they didn't give you away to anyone. Nor would they let anybody do you any harm. And neither did they allow you to see some of the truly horrible things that were happening."

"My teachers knew about us being Jewish?"

"Yes, they did. And it could have made things very awkward for them. But they never complained. Not once. So you see, there are some nice German people as well. Good night, Renate."

Renate lay awake long after she heard her mother snoring gently. She could not work out what upset her most; that Mutti had

160

seemed cross or that her teachers had done so much for her and had put themselves at risk. She was only trying to do her best. She was trying to accept this new life. But it seemed she mustn't forget the old one. Oh, it was all so complicated.

GERMANS ARE ALL GOOD PEOPLE. THE PROPER ONES. NOT THE ONES YOUR MOTHER TALKED OF, WHO PROTECTED THE SCUM.

Hani, 14 January 1941

"Why do you always have to go and do cooking?" asked Peter. "And why do you always have to wear an apron like an old Hausfrau?"

"Well, you know it's because I'm Doctor Kühn's housekeeper," replied Hani.

"But you're not," complained Peter. "Frau Lehrs is."

"Frau Lehrs is getting a bit too old to work all the time," said Hani.

"No, she isn't," said Peter. "She still plays with us and she still makes us nice cake."

Hani sighed. It was true, actually. Frau Lehrs helped just as much as ever. Somehow, despite the ration cards, she still managed to make delicious cake. Her own cooking and baking was coming on but there was some way to go before she was as good as Clara Lehrs. She had to look and act the part just in case, and she did even enjoy cooking, actually. It was her turn to prepare the lunch for Frau Lehrs, Doctor Kühn and for half a dozen of the children whose parents were busy doing war work.

"I liked it better when you were Hans," said Peter. "Why can't you stay and play with us?"

Hani knew there was a pot of water about to boil waiting for her in the kitchen. She must get the Spätzle on now so that they were ready at the same time as the stew. It was always tricky getting it exactly right: cook them for too long and they would stick to the pan and if you didn't cook them long enough they were very chewy. It wasn't as easy as with the dried Italian pasta.

"I look too much like a girl these days to pretend to be Hans," said Hani. It was always difficult to decide exactly how much to tell the children. They needed to know enough to be able to act appropriately if anyone unexpected came to the house, but telling them too much might scare them and could put them and other people in danger.

"Come, on, Peter," said Frau Lehrs. "Let me read you a story until lunch is ready."

Hani made her way up to the kitchen. She'd be back down soon with the tray of meals for the children and the parents would be here soon for the others. Could she be bothered to push the big cupboard in front of the door? She ought to, she supposed. This was the only thing about working at Haus Lehrs that she hated – having to move this big cupboard backwards and forwards. But it really helped to make it look as if the basement only held the boiler room. After the last visit from the SS, Christoph, Doctor Schubert and Doctor Kühn had rearranged the garden so that you could see nothing of the extended basement from the outside of the house. It meant there was no natural light going into the classroom but it did make it safer.

It also meant that Hani was forever covered in bruises from pushing the heavy piece of furniture backwards and forwards. She decided she'd better replace the cupboard and heaved it across the doorway.

She'd been right about the water: it was just beginning to boil as she walked into the kitchen. She poured the carefully measured Spätzle into the pan. Then she had a look in the pantry. If she'd remembered rightly, there was just about enough of the apple puree left to mix with some quark and make a dessert – perhaps just for the children if there wasn't enough for the adults. She smiled at the thought of counting herself with the adults. Most of her friends in the BDM were still at school. Yes, there was enough of the apple there. Thank goodness for the apple trees in the garden and thank goodness Frau Lehrs knew how to preserve them. She took the bowl into the kitchen, found the quark and started whipping it into the apple mixture.

The water in the pan came back up to the boil and she turned the gas down.

Then the doorbell rang.

Why did people always have to turn up just before the parents were due to arrive?

She would have to go. Doctor Kühn wasn't back from the office yet and Frau Lehrs and Doctor Schubert were stuck behind the big cupboard. She wiped her hands on her apron and hurried to the door.

Hani's heart sank as she looked through the frosted glass panes in the front door. She could make out two figures, one dressed in grey and one dressed in muddy brown. She opened the door.

"Heil Hitler!" said the older of the two men.

Hani's heart skipped a beat when she saw the younger one. It was Wilhelm. He was frowning slightly and he shook his head just a tiny amount.

Hani remembered to raise her arm and reply to the officer.

"My, my, young Sturmmann Fink," said the officer, nudging him. "I think you're in with a chance there. Seems the young lady is quite taken with you. It looks as if she already has the desired Hausfrau skills. Pity she's working in a house where a Jew has lived – still lives in fact – and a pity her hair is so dark. But I expect nevertheless she's a good Aryan specimen or she wouldn't be allowed to do this job." He laughed. Then he became more serious and turned to Hani.

"Is the Jew at home?" he said. "We have some paperwork for her."

"I'm afraid she's out," stammered Hani. "She keeps out of our way most of the time."

"Well, will you give her this?" said the officer, nodding to Wilhelm.

Wilhelm took an envelope out of his small briefcase and handed it to Hani. He pursed his lips slightly and looked deeply into her eyes.

How can you do this? She knew, though, that he was only following orders.

"You won't mind, will you," said the officer, "if we take a look around? We just want to make sure that she is not hiding any of her friends here."

At that moment, Doctor Kühn arrived. "It's all right, Fräulein Gödde," he said. "I can take it from here." He turned to the two men. "I trust this won't take long," he said. "I am expecting some guests here for a working lunch. I'm sure you will excuse my housekeeper if she gets back to the kitchen."

Hani was only too glad to get back to her cooking. The Spätzle were almost done. She supposed she could drain them and leave them in the saucepan with the lid on. They would keep warm enough. She wasn't sure she'd want to eat after this, though.

She tried to keep an eye on her pots and listen to what was being said at the same time. She heard the three men go up the stairs and she could hear their muffled voices but she couldn't make out what they were saying.

By the time the Spätzle were done and she'd drained them, they were coming back down. Perhaps the lunch would not spoil after all.

Please don't let them go into the basement, she thought.

"That all seems to be fine," she heard the officer say. "May we just have a quick look at your cellar before we go?"

"Certainly," said Doctor Kühn, "though there's only a boiler room and a few jars of pickles and preserves down there."

Hani tiptoed into the hall and listened to what was going on below.

"You see," said Doctor Kühn. "The cellar only extends this far."

"Hmm," said the officer. "So what's with this cupboard? You know, people have been known to hide Jews behind cupboards. Sturmmann Fink, will you please take a look."

Hani thought she was going to faint. Any minute now that horrible SS officer was going to find out what they'd been doing and poor Wilhelm was going to be the one to drop them in it.

Three taps sounded on the front door.

Hani hurried to open it. What could she say? Out of nowhere, though, it came to her.

"Good afternoon, Herr Becker," she said. "I'm afraid the lunch will be a little delayed. We've just had some visitors." She pointed towards the cellar.

Herr Becker went white and nodded his head.

"There can't be anything behind here," she heard Wilhelm say. "It's screwed to the wall. Anyway, nobody could move that very quickly."

You think? Good for him, though. He was taking a risk but they

165

all might just get away with it. She hoped the children were keeping quiet.

"Gentlemen, can we hurry this up now," said Doctor Kühn. "I believe the first of my guests has arrived."

"Let me show you into the dining-room," Hani said to Herr Becker. "And do excuse me if I carry on setting the table while you wait."

As Hani and Herr Becker made their way into the dining room, there were another three taps on the front door. Doctor Kühn opened it himself and told a bemused Frau Schröder also to go to the dining room.

"Thank you, and good day to you," said the officer, as he and Wilhelm left. "At least you won't have to put up with the Jew for much longer. Heil Hitler!" He saluted.

Doctor Kühn shut the door without replying.

It was chaotic after that for the next hour and a half. They had to get the children who were staying fed and they had to get the ones who were going home out safely and explain to the parents who came to collect them that there had been another visit and that they'd got to take even more care in future. The children themselves, who had been really good while it was all going on, were now quite excited. Then there was the meal itself and the clearing up afterwards. Hani was surprised at how hungry she actually was now that the immediate danger had passed.

Yet still she couldn't find the right moment to give Frau Lehrs the envelope that Wilhelm had handed to her. The time did come, though, when all the children who were going home had gone, when those who were staying were safely behind the cupboard, having their nap and all the dishes waiting to be washed up were in the kitchen.

"They left you this," said Hani taking the envelope out of her apron pocket.

"Ah!" said Frau Lehrs. "I think I'll take this up to my room and read it quietly. I have a feeling it may take a little digesting."

Hani busied herself with the washing-up in the kitchen. But

even by the time she'd washed everything, stacked the dishes neatly into the rack over the drainer, scrubbed all the surfaces in the kitchen until they shone and even mopped the floor, there was still no sign of Frau Lehrs. She really wanted to know what was in the letter or at least know that it contained nothing too disturbing.

Doctor Kühn and Doctor Schubert were talking in the study. Hani knocked the door gently.

"Come in!" called Doctor Kühn. "Ha, Hani. What can we do for you?"

"I was wondering..." she said. She fiddled with her apron and looked at the floor. Perhaps she was being too nosy.

"What were you wondering, Hani?" said Doctor Schubert.

"Do you know what the letter was about for Frau Lehrs?" said Hani.

"We were just talking about that ourselves," said Doctor Kühn. He exchanged a glance with Doctor Schubert. "It could be one of a number of things."

"But don't worry," said Doctor Schubert. "We shall of course look after Frau Lehrs and make sure nothing untoward happens to her."

"Do you mind if I stay a bit longer?" said Hani. "I don't want to go home until I know."

"Well, you can help me get tomorrow's lessons ready if you like," said Doctor Schubert.

For the next hour Hani worked with Doctor Schubert on preparing some counting games for the Special Class children.

"I should get you to do this more often," said Doctor Schubert. "You're really good at it."

Hani laughed. "I would have quite liked to have been a teacher," said Hani, "if it wasn't for all the studying."

"You should be ashamed of yourself, Hani Gödde," said a voice in the doorway. "You should always follow your dream, no matter what it costs. Am I to presume you are still here because you are so nosy? You want to know what was in that letter."

"Well, it might be an idea if you told us," said Doctor Schubert, "in case it's something we can help with."

"You can't," said Frau Lehrs. "There's nothing we need worry about for a few months yet. Now, who would like some tea? And there are some vanilla biscuits I baked last night."

Helga, 18 January 1942

Dear All,

I actually got the parcel with the letters in back in December. Working with young children is not that easy, though I do like them, I really do. But it's relentless. There's always one or other of them crying and they always need help with physical things – tying their shoe laces or pulling on their boots. The mess they make sometimes when they eat! Not to speak of when we do any painting.

The little ones all have an afternoon nap. It's heaven then. And they look so angelic while they're asleep. It's so peaceful for a short while. We have a good tidy up and sit down with a cup of coffee. I felt a bit shy with the older women at first, but they're actually really friendly, even though they laughed at my idea about real clothes for the children's plays.

"There'll be a shortage of clothes soon, in any case," Frau Müller said, "if this war carries on for much longer." Oh dear, though – people are talking about the war all the time now.

I hope they'll let me continue to work with the children for my duty year. I've heard rumours that they're going to get us milking cows and digging up potatoes. Ladies, we're all changing and we'll have forgotten what we all look like anyway. So, I'm including a couple of photographs that we took in the garden. Can everyone do the same? In fact, I absolutely command it. Oh dear, hark at me. Sorry! I'm too used to having to boss the children about.

Also, I'm sending the old book on so that everyone can keep up with the letters. I guess I get to look after it when it gets back to me.

I'll finish now. I'm really tired. But I do look forward to everyone's next letter.

Best wishes,
Helga

Käthe Edler, 27 January 1942

Dear Renate,

I am writing to you with some slightly sad news. But I think you are old enough to understand this now. And before I begin, I just want to reassure you that your father loves you and I'm sure we'll all get back together as a family once this war is over.

No. I haven't heard from your father. Nor would I expect to. But I do know that at some time today he will go to Dr Burckhardt's office and he will file a petition for a divorce from me. We agreed that he would do this. You may notice that tomorrow is the three year anniversary of your leaving Nuremberg. If a wife or husband has been away from the family home for three years or more, a divorce is granted without question. I'm afraid the Nazi regime rather expects your father to apply for it. It is probably only because he is so important for the defence industry that they did not demand it even a month earlier. I expect it will be granted between March and July.

Your father wanted to leave it as long as possible, naturally, in case something came up that meant we could be together again sooner.

On the papers it will say that I left the house on the 15 November 1938 – just a few days after that horrible night when they smashed up all the Jewish shops and burnt the synagogues. Kristallnacht, I believe they call it now. That would make sense to the authorities. He will also say that he has no idea where we've been since then. You know very well that we didn't leave until 22 December and that he knew where we were, first in Stuttgart and then here in Ealing. For goodness sake, he even came to see you off at the station.

I just wanted to let you know. If something happens to me – and who knows, it's not impossible with all these air raids – the papers would come to you eventually; I just want you to understand that these lies are there to protect your father not to betray you or me.

We intend to bring the family back together again as soon as we can.

And yes, I'm afraid some of the very bombs that are coming down on London may have been designed with your father's help. Possibly that is why the Germans have not yet won the war. Your father may have been creating deliberate weaknesses.

I've written to Mrs Williams and told her to keep an eye on you.

Please be brave. You know this is for the best and it will help to protect your father.

Your loving Mutti

Hani, 11 February 1942

"Watch out! You're going to spill that," shouted Frau Gödde.

I wish she'd get out of my way, thought Hani. I wish she'd let me get on.

Hani and her mother were both working in the kitchen at Haus Lehrs. Hani was putting some water in a pan so that she could cook the turnips she had spent most of the morning chopping up. The pot was heavy as she carried it over to the stove when her mother had bumped into her, almost making her spill the lot.

Why can't she leave me alone? thought Hani. Frau Lehrs never interfered like this. Doesn't she trust me? "Will Frau Lehrs be back soon?" she said.

"It doesn't look like it," said Frau Gödde, turning her back towards Hani. "She must be enjoying her holiday."

There's something you're not telling me, thought Hani. "I don't get it," she said. "Why would somebody who is nearly seventy go on holiday for over three weeks in the winter? It's not as if she would go skiing. Not even Frau Lehrs. And she can't be visiting friends for that long, surely?"

Frau Gödde slammed down the knife she was using to cut some onions. She turned to face Hani. "All right, all right," she said. "She is visiting friends. Sort of. And I'm going to visit her on Sunday. Maybe you'd better come with me so that you can see for yourself." Frau Gödde sniffed and fumbled for her hanky. "These onions!" she said. "Next time you can cut them up."

"She's not coming back, is she?" said Hani.

"No, I'm afraid not," said Frau Gödde. "Excuse me." She picked up the scissors and rushed out of the kitchen door, making a show of cutting some sprigs from the rosemary bush.

I knew it, thought Hani as she felt the tears begin to prick at her own eyes and she took over chopping the onions.

Renate, 14 February 1942

Renate's back felt as if it had nails sticking in it. She was hot and thirsty almost all the time – except when the shivers began. And then she couldn't get enough blankets. She could just about get up to go to the toilet but her legs felt too wobbly to go any further than that.

"Shingles," Doctor Bradbury had said. "It might last just a few days or it might last quite a while. It varies from person to person. I presume you've had chicken pox?"

Renate nodded her head.

"Well. It's a sign you're growing up," said the doctor. "Children don't usually get shingles. But you're otherwise a healthy young woman. You should make a full recovery."

The recovery was a long time coming. Renate knew, though, that that was partly because it was so much easier lying here, drifting in and out of sleep, than worrying about bombs in London and bombs in Nuremberg, and whether she was English, German or Jewish and why on earth her parents had been forced – yes forced, that was the only word for it – to get divorced.

She took a sip from the glass of water on her bedside table – well, actually David's table, as poor David had to sleep on the couch in the lounge – and that was all that worried her about this. She couldn't take any more painkillers yet. She pulled the blankets round her and hoped that sleep would return so that she could escape the nails in her back for a while.

She drifted into a half sleep before voices in the hallway woke her up.

"I'm really glad you could get here," she heard Mrs Williams say. "It's been just over two weeks and there's no sign of her getting any better. She's hardly eating. The doctor is quite concerned."

"I suppose I shouldn't have sent the letter," came the reply.

Mutti? Mutti was here? Renate sat up in bed. For once, the nails didn't seem to stick in even further as they normally did with every movement.

"Oh you had to, Käthe," said another voice. "It's just a pity you couldn't have got permission to come and see her then."

Eva? Mutti and Eva were here?

"Well, shall we go and see her?" said Mrs Williams.

Renate heard them start to make their way up the stairs. Suddenly, she felt completely normal. No nails in her back, no fever or shivers and she even felt strong enough to get out of bed. Her heart was thumping.

The door opened.

"Visitors for you," said Mrs Williams cheerfully.

Mutti and Eva followed her into the room.

"Ladies, I'll leave you to it," said Mrs Williams. "I'll bring you up a cup of tea. You too, Renate?"

Renate managed to nod.

"What are we going to do with you?" said Eva.

"You've got to eat, you know," said Mutti. "You've got to get better."

"Käthe, leave the poor girl alone," said Eva. "She's been very poorly. You're supposed to be cheering her up, not making her feel worse."

"But she needs to snap out of this," said Mutti. "She must pull herself together. Huh! Shingles! When I had shingles, I still went to the opera."

"Käthe," said Eva, "going to the opera hardly requires a lot of effort. And besides, shingles affects different people differently. You ought to know that. You were studying to be a doctor."

"Not that sort of doctor," said Mutti. "To be a proper doctor. These medics just have honorary titles."

Renate was beginning to feel a bit weak again. Still, she couldn't help smiling. Her mother and Eva were so funny when they started bickering. Even so, she wished they'd stop. She wished they'd go away and leave her in peace.

"And she needs to settle down to her studies," said Mutti. "Matriculation isn't that far away."

"Käthe!" said Eva. "Let the poor girl recover from her illness before you start nagging her about schoolwork."

Renate pulled the blankets further up and closed her eyes.

The door opened again.

"Here we are ladies," said Mrs Williams. "Tea's up. And I've had a thought. I have to pop into Minehead later this afternoon. Why don't you all come with me? We can wrap Renate up warm and you can take her for a walk along the front. I would only need about half an hour and then I could come and pick you up again. You can always sit in a shelter for a while if it gets too much."

"Excellent idea," said Frau Edler. "It will certainly do her good."

I wish they wouldn't talk about me as if I wasn't here, thought Renate.

"Well, what do you think?" said Eva turning to Renate.

Mutti was glaring and frowning at her. She guessed she didn't really have a choice.

"All right then," she mumbled.

Less than an hour later, Renate was walking along the sea front, propped up on either side by Mutti and Eva. She was wrapped up in her warm jumper, thick socks, her thickest coat and two hats and a scarf. The two women were no longer speaking to each other, but neither were they asking her any questions, thank goodness.

Renate was surprised to find that she did not feel all that wobbly. It was almost as if the cold air had made her super-awake, as if it had pushed all the drowsiness away. She realised too that she had missed this salty air and the sound of the waves tumbling on to the sand. When she'd lived at the Johnsons', if the wind was in the right direction, the sound of the waves on the beach would send her to sleep. She loved living in the countryside, but school days gave her the best of both worlds; she had the countryside and the seaside on the same day. She hadn't been to school now for over two weeks, though.

There was a sudden gust of wind. A seagull circled above them, screeching. The wind seemed to wash through her, energising her and pushing away all the black thoughts that had tormented her more than the vicious spots on her back.

Stay away, she thought. Don't come back.

She took a deep breath and felt the sea air fill her. She was aware of her body getting stronger.

Eva took a deep breath too. "Hmm," she said. "It is so wonderful to breathe this fresh air. And listen." She cupped her ear. "No noisy bombs and sirens."

"Will you keep your voice down?" hissed Frau Edler. "You with your über-Yiddish accent. You'll give us away."

What on earth did Mutti mean?

"If they recognise us as being Yiddish," said Eva, "surely they'll realise that we hate Herr Hitler as much as they do."

"Not so much of the us," said Frau Edler. "I am certainly not Yiddish. I am married to a respected German Catholic, my parents were Lutheran and my mother is still Christian. The whole family has never spoken anything but Hochdeutsch."

"You're still Yiddish," said Eva. "Jüdische Deutsche. Yiddish."

"You don't really care what people think do you?" asked Renate.

"Of course not," said Frau Edler. "But you see… we never got permission to be so near to the sea. There wasn't time to get the extra paperwork done. So I think we should be a bit careful."

"So, why didn't you say when Mrs Williams suggested coming here?" asked Renate.

"Your mother could see you really needed some fresh air," said Eva. "And with the two of us to prop you up… Mrs Williams wouldn't have had time to do that."

Renate suddenly remembered that she had meant to like being English. If she didn't they'd won, Herr Hitler and his lot. But could liking being English include breaking the rules sometimes? She remembered how Sergeant Clarkson had said that these particular rules were a bit daft. That was a good enough reason to like being English, wasn't it?

There were Mutti and Eva as well, being naughty, going to the seaside when they shouldn't.

Resolution number two, thought Renate. Do not obey rules blindly.

Well, well, well. Dear Mutti. She normally did everything according to the rules and here she was, being defiant. She liked it. But there was just one thing she needed to check first.

"Mutti, are you sure you and Vati didn't really want to divorce?" she said.

"Of course not," said Mutti. "And naturally, we both love you."

That was all right then.

"There's Mrs Williams," said Eva.

They made their way back to the car. Renate knew she would be better soon and she knew she would work very hard for her matriculation exams.

SO YOU'RE FEELING BETTER, HUH? PITY. YOU DON'T DESERVE IT. YOU BROKE THE RULES. YOU CAN'T GO ROUND BREAKING RULES. YOU WILL BE PUNISHED FOR IT.

Hani, 15 February 1942

It had taken them longer than it should have to get to the station. The train out of Stuttgart had been incredibly slow because of the weather. At least now it wasn't snowing any more but it looked as if it might start again any minute. It was only just after eleven and it was as gloomy as if it were four o'clock. The wind was pinching at Hani's nose and making it feel as if it was going to fall off. But apart from her face, she was really warm. Her thick coat, lined boots and woollen scarf and hat were keeping the cold out very effectively.

Besides, the basket and bag she was carrying were really heavy. Both she and her mother were sliding all over the place with every step they took. It was difficult to make much progress.

"What time do you think we'll get there?" asked Hani. "How much further is it?"

"We're about half way," said Frau Gödde. "It would normally only take about half an hour to walk from the station. But we can stay overnight if we have to. You won't mind sleeping on Frau Lehrs' floor, will you?"

"No, of course not," replied Hani. "But what about the school?"

"They'll have to manage without us for once," said Frau Gödde.

It wasn't that simple, though. Couldn't she see that? Hani was supposed to be Doctor Kühn's housekeeper. Wouldn't it be funny if she wasn't there? Look well if they had another visit from the SS.

"Shall we rest for a few minutes?" asked Frau Gödde.

Hani nodded. Then she almost regretted agreeing. Straight away her feet began to ache with the cold.

"Hello there," called a voice suddenly.

Hani and her mother turned to see a boy sitting on a horse-drawn sled. The sled looked as if it would fall part any minute. It was piled quite high with logs. You could see the horse's ribs. Hani thought the boy could do with a good meal as well. And he must be so cold. He had no gloves on and wore a thin coat. Under his hood Hani could see a black skull cap. She guessed he was a little older than her.

"Are you folks going into Rexingen?" the boy asked.

"We are indeed," said Frau Gödde. "We are going to see Clara Lehrs."

"Frau Lehrs," said the boy. "She is living in the house next to ours. An amazing lady. Come on, get on, if you can perch on top of the logs. My name is Shmuel, by the way."

It was good to be able to put the heavy bags down, but the sled was a little cramped and the undernourished horse could not quite go in a straight line. The sled creaked in a threatening way.

"Maybe I should walk," Hani suggested.

"No, no," said Shmuel. "Adiv is strong really. He will be offended if you get out and walk."

The road levelled out after a while and the sled started going much more smoothly and less noisily.

"It is good of you to come and see Frau Lehrs," said Shmuel. "I have lived here all of my life. When I was little, all of my cousins and aunts and uncles used to come from all over Germany. No one comes any more. We hear nothing from them. A lot of the others who used to live here have gone away."

Just a few minutes later, the sled stopped.

"This is Frau Lehrs' house," said Shmuel. "She lives on the second floor, the third room on the right. Just go straight on up. And knock on our door when you want to go back to the station. Adiv and I will take you back."

Shmuel watched as Hani and Frau Gödde unloaded the bags and the basket from the sled. "You have brought many presents for Frau Lehrs," said Shmuel. His deep brown eyes grew round.

"Here," said Frau Gödde, reaching into the basket and pulling out a wholemeal loaf. "For you and your family."

"Thank you, thank you," said Shmuel hugging the loaf as if it were a new puppy.

Two men wearing wide-brimmed hats were standing in the doorway of Shmuel's house.

179

"They are waiting for the logs so that they can get them ready for the fire this evening. My father and my uncle," said Shmuel. He waved to them. "Go on in. I'm sure Frau Lehrs will be glad to see you."

The two men waved to Hani and her mother then turned to help Shmuel unload the sled.

The door to the house was already partly open. Hani pushed it further and it scraped on the floor. There was snow inside the hall. It was very gloomy. Hani put the basket down and slid her arm up the wall, trying to find a light switch. Her hand touched it. She flicked the switch but nothing happened.

"The bulb must be gone," said Frau Gödde. "Let's wait a bit until our eyes get used to the dark."

Sure enough, a few seconds later, Hani could see how threadbare the carpet was and where the stairs were. The floor was free of dust and there were no dirty marks on the walls, but the paint was flaking off in places. It felt and smelt cold and damp.

Hani and her mother made their way up the two flights of stairs and started along the corridor.

"This must be it," said Hani, counting the doors. She knocked the door.

"Come in," called a familiar voice.

Hani pushed open the door. There was a strong smell of paraffin in the room and a little warmth coming from a small stove. And there was Frau Lehrs, dressed in very dark clothes and wrapped in two shawls. Hani could swear she looked thinner, paler and older than normal.

The room only had a few bits of furniture but Frau Lehrs had arranged them very neatly. A pretty cloth covered a little table and on it were a few photos Hani recognised and a book Frau Lehrs had been reading. One of the photos, Hani realised, was of her and Renate.

Frau Lehrs got up out of her seat. "Frau Gödde! Hani!" she cried. "How nice to see you. Come in. So kind of you to come and see me."

"We've brought you a few things," said Frau Gödde.

"Oh, that is so generous of you," said Frau Lehrs. "I'm afraid I have nothing to offer you. But come and get warm."

The fumes from the stove were quite strong and Frau Lehrs must have been able to tell that Hani was trying not to breathe them in.

"I'm sorry about the smell," she said. "You do get used to it after a while. They won't let us buy any fuel for the central heating. But there was a good supply of paraffin on one of the farms. And then every evening we gather in the big living room of the house next door and sit round a log fire."

"That's what Shmuel had been collecting the logs for," said Hani.

"Yes, he's a good boy," said Frau Lehrs. "He and his brother. Now let me see what you've brought me. I'll have to give some to the family next door."

"But we brought it all for you," said Frau Gödde. "We've already given him a loaf of bread."

"Oh, but the young people need the extra food more than I do," said Frau Lehrs.

"How are you, really?" said Frau Gödde, helping Frau Lehrs to unpack the bags and the basket. There was more bread, some apples, some large overstuffed Maultaschen, Spätzle, two cabbages, some sugar, a dark Pumpernickel loaf and some peppermint tea.

"Oh, I'll do," said Frau Lehrs. "We have just about enough. They're letting us keep everything from the farms at the moment, though soon there won't be any eggs. We're having to kill off the chickens one by one."

"How are you getting on with everybody?" asked Frau Gödde. "Is it strange for you, being with so many practising Jews?"

"Everybody is really kind," said Frau Lehrs. "They don't mind at all that I've become a Christian. And I do go to the synagogue with them on a Saturday now. It's the same God, after all. But you know, everybody here is a bit afraid, despite their faith. Now, can I make you a cup of tea? I've only peppermint tea, I'm afraid."

"No, no, Frau Lehrs," said Frau Gödde. "I've told you, these supplies are for you."

"Very well," said Frau Lehrs. "Let's sit down and make ourselves cosy. And you can tell me all about what's been happening with the Special Class. No more unexpected visits, I hope. I guess it's easier now that I'm out of the way."

Hani was about to start telling Frau Lehrs about the latest developments at the school, when the door suddenly burst open and a little girl with dark curls and deep brown eyes ran into the room. Hani guessed she was about three or four. She was well dressed for the cold, but her jumper and leggings had great big holes in them. Her nose was running.

"'Rau Lehs, 'rau Lehs, tell me a story," said the little girl.

"But where is Mutti, Kyla?" asked Frau Lehrs.

A young woman came running into the room. Her clothes were worn as well. She looked tired. Her dark hair was plaited and wound into coils over her ears, but many strands were escaping, including some that were getting in her eyes. "I am so sorry, Frau Lehrs," said the young woman.

"It's all right, Selda," she said. "You can leave her with us. You should go and get some rest. But let me just introduce you to my good friends, Frau Gödde, and her daughter, Hani. They have been so helpful to me."

"Any friend of Frau Lehrs is a friend of mine," said Selda. She shivered and swayed a little.

"Go and lie down," Frau Lehrs commanded. "We'll amuse Kyla."

"Thank you, Frau Lehrs. You are so kind."

"And remember," said Frau Lehrs. "It will get better. You're almost through the worst stage. And the spring is on its way."

Selda nodded and smiled.

"The poor girl," said Frau Lehrs, after Selda had left the room. "She is in the first stage of a new pregnancy. Her husband died just a month ago. Influenza and malnutrition, we think. And this child has so much energy. The poor woman is exhausted. I shall have to see what I can give her from what you have brought."

"But it's for you!" protested Frau Gödde.

"She needs it more than I do," said Frau Lehrs. "Now come on.

Let's see if we can sing some songs and tell some stories with this young lady." She looked over the child's head. "Don't say anything about the Special Class in front of any of the people here," she mouthed. "What they don't know can't hurt them."

Hani actually enjoyed playing with the little girl. She had a very sweet singing voice and knew most of the songs that Hani herself had sung as a child. There were a few more as well in Yiddish that Frau Lehrs half knew.

"A long time since I've sung any of those," she said.

Kyla gobbled up the stories too. Little Red Riding Hood, Sleeping Beauty and Cinderella. Then Noah and his Ark, Moses in the Bulrushes, and Abraham and Isaac.

"Tell me the one about the tower falling down," said the little girl.

"Oh, that's not such a nice one," said Frau Lehrs.

Suddenly the room lit up with a pink glow.

"Will you look at that?" said Frau Lehrs, picking up the little girl and holding her up to the window.

The grey clouds had rolled away now and there were just a few white ones against a pale blue sky. It faded to pink where the sun hung low. The snow-covered hills, no longer hidden by the mist, now reflected the setting sun.

"See," said Frau Lehrs. "The greyness always goes eventually."

The door opened gently. It was Selda.

"They'll be getting the fire ready in the big room next door," she said. "Are you going to come along, Frau Lehrs?"

"Well, you look better my dear," said Frau Lehrs. "You know it is fine for you to leave this little one with me any time you like. She is such a good girl."

"Will you come with us?" said Selda to Hani and her mother.

"We ought to get back now, really," said Frau Gödde. "We'll come again in two weeks' time. Is there anything particular you'd like us to bring you?"

"You might look out some clothing for this poor young woman and her child, if you have the chance," said Frau Lehrs.

Selda blushed and looked at the floor.

Hani thought immediately of the Winter Relief collection. Could she find something there? Dare she look? Perhaps she could go out and pretend she was collecting again? Or maybe some of the parents of the children in the Special Class could help? Did she herself have anything she could spare? She would try to think of something.

"I think we could walk back to the station," said Frau Gödde once they were outside. "It's a shame to disturb Shmuel and make that poor horse work again. It'll be easier now that the bags are empty."

But Shmuel spotted them leaving.

"Come on," he said. "Adiv and I will be proud to take friends of Frau Lehrs back to the station."

It was actually easier going back, as the sled was carrying just three people and not the heavy logs and bags as well.

Water was dripping from the trees.

"The spring is coming," said Shmuel. "Adiv will soon be able to eat the fresh grass again."

They arrived at the station twenty minutes before their train was due.

"Will you come again to visit Frau Lehrs?" asked Shmuel.

"Yes, in two weeks' time," said Frau Gödde.

"On the same train as today?"

Frau Gödde nodded.

"Then we shall meet you," said Shmuel. "And I hope it will be with the cart, not the sled."

Hani watched him and Adiv make their way back along the road to the village. She hoped he, Frau Lehrs and Shmuel were right about the spring coming soon.

Sabine, 23 March 1942

Dear all,

Life goes on as usual at school. The exams are fast approaching.

Father says I must work hard at my sport, but that also I should remember the duties of a young woman. He tells me how proud he is of my mother – always working hard for the family, making lots of lovely food and doing her duty by going to church. That would drive me mad I think. I'm so glad they don't want me to do all of that sort of thing just yet.

I've been working part-time at the telephone exchange. I'll go full time there once I've finished the exams. I think it counts as essential war work. We handle 6000 daily call sheets! I wonder whether I've handled any calls from you. People say they can recognise my voice. My call sign is U3. Look out for that on your call sheets. They really work us hard but it's good when you get your pay and can go and buy yourself something nice.

I've been doing some work for my grandparents. They've suggested I could do my duty year helping them, but the telephone exchange is also calling. I did some work in the garden while I was there. I loved getting my fingers in the soil. It made me feel strong. The photograph I've included is of me working in their lovely garden.

I'll just leave you with this quote from Goethe:

"We humans often complain that of good days there are few and of the bad ones so many, and – as it seems to me – often unjustly. If our hearts were always open to enjoy the good things, which God has prepared every day for us, then we would also have the strength to endure the evil."

Well, I'll finish now. I look forward to hearing from you all.

Your Sabine

Charlotte, 27 March 1942

Dear all,

So nice to get your letter and of course, to see the photos. I'm including one of me and Karl. Yes, he is still my boyfriend and he is still doing war work here at home. So far, there seems no chance of him being called up.

Oma became so frail that she had to go into an old people's home. So, I'm now working at the rectory. Our deacon had been called up and they were short-handed. I started off doing just half days. They sent me to do a typing course so that I can write all the letters professionally. I've also had to have organ lessons – it's more different from playing the piano than you would imagine. The organist was called up too! I was very nervous the first time I played but I'm getting used to it now. We're very busy at the church – Easter is coming and there are also lots of confirmations.

In my 'spare time' (Ha! Is there such a thing these days?) I've taken a course in dress-making. I've managed to make myself one or two dresses and several for the twins. Not from new material, though. Mutti and I have been recycling dresses we'd grown tired of.

Hopefully, the work at the rectory will count as my duty work and then in 1944 I can breathe a sigh of relief and start to live my own life again. Mind you, I quite enjoy the work, but I expect once the war is over, all the men will return and there'll be no need for me to work there any longer. I wonder when that will be.

All my very best to each one of you,
Your Charlotte

Gerda, 3 April 1942

Dear All,

I'm helping mother in the dairy quite a lot now, as well, and I think I'm looking forward one day to being a farmer's wife and helping a handsome young husband run his own farm. I like helping with the animals as well.

Our crops are doing well, especially the potatoes. The farm next to us is for sale – quite cheaply too. The family who own it are Jewish and have to go away. Such a pity we can't buy it now for Hans to run when he gets back. Then we could have one big family farm. A pity girls can't become farmers in their own right. I might even start a political movement – the Association of Women Farmers – now how does that sound?

Well, I'm getting muscles in my arms. Do you know how heavy a milk churn is? Or a cheese that needs turning or a full pail of milk?

But I wonder how you get to marry a farmer if you don't go to agricultural college? My mother was lucky. My grandfather was a farmer and my father was apprenticed to his farm. My father won't take an apprentice, and even if he did, it wouldn't be a nice-looking young man, of that I'm sure. The college was my only chance and there just wasn't anybody there.

Thomas is settling down a little, thank goodness. He even said the other day that he was getting tired of all the marching and would rather stay at home and work on the farm. I'm glad he's stopped being so fanatical about it all. I suppose he will be called up as well soon.

In response to the 'call from above' I've included a photo of me and Mutti outside the dairy. Don't we look like a pair of good, honest, hard-working German women?

Looking forward to the next round of letters.

Your Gerda

Renate, 18 June 1942

Renate woke up in the unfamiliar bed. Where was she? And what was that noise? It was that wailing noise again. Like they'd heard on the day war broke out and like she'd heard several times since, when she'd been here with Mutti and Eva. It was screaming at her urgently now. She had to get out.

Where were Mutti and Eva?

Already down in the shelter?

There wasn't time.

She would have to shelter under the table.

They were really close.

They're dropping the bombs now, she thought.

Nothing for several seconds. Then the loudest bang she had even heard. Then another and another. The smell of smoke. It was getting hotter there. Was the house on fire? Or the one next door?

The noise stopped.

Now the other siren. The All-Clear.

Then she was outside. Lots of women in long white overalls and tin hats. Some men were carrying people – or were they bodies – out of what was left of the houses nearby.

She didn't recognise the street at all.

It occurred to her suddenly that she didn't know whether she was in London or Nuremberg.

She woke with a start.

"Come on girls," called Mrs Williams, peering round their bedroom door. "You'll be late for school if you don't get up now."

"Have there been any more bombings?" asked Renate.

"No more on London," said Mrs Williams. "And no more on Exeter or Bath either. Don't worry, much as we love Minehead, they don't think it is an important tourist resort."

Renate shuddered as she remembered the sound of the aircraft bringing the bombs.

SEE, TOLD YOU WE'D GET YOU. AND WE'LL GET YOU AGAIN AND AGAIN AND AGAIN. YOU CAN RUN BUT YOU CAN'T HIDE. WE'RE GOING TO GET YOU.

Renate, 20 August 1942

"Renate, thank you for coming in today. Please take a seat," said Miss Faversham.

Renate sat on her hands. She had to do that to stop them shaking. Why had Miss Faversham sent for her? Still in the holidays? It seemed to her that the end of the summer always brought bad news – the war started right at the beginning of September and Mr Johnson had been killed in London in the summer. What now?

"Oh, don't look so scared," said Miss Faversham. "I have some good news, actually."

Good news? That happened sometimes?

"Really?" said Renate.

"Yes," said Miss Faversham. "Your matriculation results. They are absolutely fantastic. You have passed every single subject. That can't have been easy. So I wanted to tell you personally."

"Goodness!" said Renate.

Miss Faversham laughed. "Is that all you can say?"

"I'm surprised, that's all," said Renate.

"Well, you shouldn't be," said Miss Faversham. "You deserve it. You've worked very hard."

"I tried my best," said Renate.

"And it paid off," said Miss Faversham. "And I hope you're going to stay on and do the Higher School Certificate? I assume you are as you're still living here?"

"Yes, I am," said Renate. "But that was because I thought I'd have to repeat the year. Yes. I would like to start my Higher Certificate."

"Good," said Miss Faversham. "And I expect you're most interested in the sciences – Biology, Chemistry and Physics?"

"Yes," said Renate. Of course she was. Especially Biology. She was so interested in what made living things 'living'.

"Good," said Miss Faversham. "So, I look forward to greeting you back into the sixth form at the beginning of the new school year."

Renate couldn't quite believe what she had just heard. She had passed every single subject in the matriculation exams. Even English.

"Good news, eh?" said a familiar voice as Renate made her way out of Miss Faversham's office.

"I'll only be about ten minutes with Miss Faversham" said Mrs Cohen. "I'll treat you to an ice-cream if you can hang on. As a celebration. For how well you've done in your exams and for how English you've become."

Renate felt warm inside as she watched her favourite teacher go into the Headteacher's office. She was going to be a proper English sixth-former in September.

DO YOU DESERVE THIS? DO YOU REALLY? YOU LUCKY, LUCKY UNTERMENSCH.

Hani, 22 August 1942

"Please don't say anything to anyone," Gisela pleaded.

"You know we could get into a lot of trouble for this," said Trudi.

I don't care, thought Hani. I'm not going to tell anybody. She didn't understand it. She had a vague feeling it wasn't quite right. But it didn't bother her personally. She'd caught Gisela and Trudi kissing passionately again. In fact, it had been clear when she woke up that they'd actually shared a sleeping bag. But that was their business and it didn't actually bother her. It made her feel a little sick actually, if she stopped to think about it for too long. But she wasn't going to think about it for very long. She had plans of her own.

"Take as much as you like from the Winter Relief stock for your friends," said Gisela. "We won't tell either." Gisela was pale and Trudi was looking at her with tears in her eyes.

"It's all right," said Hani. "I won't tell anyone anything."

Was that why they'd been so helpful in finding some clothes for her friends? Had they realised she had seen them the first time?

None of that mattered. Even if they hadn't been helping her she wouldn't tell anyone. Everyone had their secrets didn't they? Now, it was important to get packed up as quickly as possible. Peter would be waiting for her. Her tummy fluttered at the thought. She mustn't keep him waiting. She really mustn't. He would have to go without her if she wasn't ready in time.

"Come on," she said. "Let's get this tent packed up."

In fact, she needn't have worried. By the time she'd put her camping equipment onto the truck that was taking the girls' things back and then found Peter, he was still busy loading their truck.

"Hey, here she is," he said. "The woman of my dreams." He pulled her to him and kissed her lightly on the cheek. "I did dream about you last night," he said.

She wished he'd kiss her like he had last night. Oh yes, she could understand kissing now and what it felt like. Being near him was even more exciting that it had been being near Christoph.

"Won't be long," he said. "Then when we've dropped these clowns and all their stuff off, we've got plenty of time to get to Stuttgart. I've managed to put together a little picnic. I know where we can stop off on the way back."

Ten minutes later, the truck was all packed up.

"You lot in the back, and you right next to me in the front," he said, taking Hani's hand and helping her up into the cab.

Hani felt like a queen, sitting next to Peter. He was so good-looking and his uniform suited him. She did catch one or two girls staring at her as they drove past. She wondered if they were jealous. Every so often, where the road was nice and straight, he would squeeze her hand, or rub the top of her leg. He even leant over a couple of times and kissed her. "Won't be long," he said. "We'll soon get rid of this lot."

Half an hour after they had set off, they stopped in a little village and the younger boys unloaded their tents and bags, then packed all the camping equipment away.

"Ten more minutes," said Peter, as the boys waved them off. "And then we have about an hour to eat and do whatever else you like before we need to drive on to Stuttgart."

They stopped right at the bottom of a hill. Peter led her down to a place next to the river. There was a lovely view of a waterfall. The picnic didn't take long to eat as it was just a couple of bread rolls with some cheese and apples.

"Pity we haven't got out swimming things with us," said Hani. "It would be nice to swim."

"Who needs bathing costumes?" said Peter. "Nobody would see us here."

"We can't do that," said Hani blushing.

"No, we probably shouldn't," said Peter. "Besides, I'd really rather actually do this." He leant over and kissed her.

She didn't want him to stop. They kissed and kissed and kissed, only pausing occasionally to breathe. Peter pushed his hand up under her shirt. She liked the feel of his fingers on her skin. She did the same to him.

"Hmm," he mumbled. "That feels good. Oh, that feels so good."

He pulled away from her suddenly. "Let's go for a walk," he said. "This is getting dangerous." His voice was quite hoarse.

They walked along the river for a while. They held hands and occasionally Peter pulled her to him and kissed her again. But he got quieter and quieter and then suddenly sighed.

"What's the matter?" asked Hani.

"I'm just thinking about what I've got to do when I get to Stuttgart," he said.

"What have you got to do exactly?" asked Hani.

"It's not nice," he said. "But don't bother your pretty little head about that."

Then it was time to go.

"Write your address down for me," said Peter, just after they'd got back into the truck. He handed her his notebook and a pencil. "I'd like to see you again."

Hani felt a little tingle of excitement inside. She wrote down where she lived.

Peter didn't say much on the rest of the journey, but Hani was quite happy just to look at him from time to time and remember all the kisses and how affectionate he'd been.

Too soon, they arrived just outside the Killesberg Park.

"I'll leave you here," said Peter. "You don't want to see what's going on in there. You'll be able to get a tram home all right?"

Hani nodded. She had just about the right money left in her purse.

She waved to Peter. He gave a quick little wave and a grin. Then his face went serious again. He looked so worried. She supposed she'd better go and get the tram. If she hurried, she would get back about the same time as if she'd gone back with the girls and there would be no questions. She guessed she could rely on Gisela and Trudi to keep quiet.

Then she realised that she was still holding Peter's notebook.

No, she thought. I'll never see him again.

The truck was disappearing into the park. She started to run after it.

More and more trucks were arriving. There were lots of soldiers around and some more Hitlerjugend leaders like Peter. Suitcases were being loaded on to some of the trucks, and there were lots of old people. They were all wearing labels with numbers on them.

She couldn't see Peter.

What was going on here? What were all these old people doing here? Why were they wearing labels? Why the trucks?

"You look lost, my dear," said an old gentleman.

"I'm looking for my boyfriend," she said.

"Oh, I hope you find him soon," he said. "It's good to stay together. We've been together for over fifty years." He squeezed his wife's hand. "And now we're going to a nice old people's home in the east."

That didn't sound so bad. Why had Peter said he wasn't looking forward to doing this job?

Then she saw him.

"Excuse me," she called. "Peter." She started to run towards the truck.

"Hani!" called a voice suddenly. "I'm so glad I've seen you."

Hani recognised Frau Lehrs' voice but couldn't see her. She looked round frantically for her. But when she saw her she gasped. She hardly recognised her. She was so much thinner than the last time she'd seen her, even though that was only three weeks ago. Her back was very bent.

"Frau Lehrs!" said Hani. "What's happening?"

"They're taking us away to an old people's home in the east," she said. "I've had to give them the last of my money. But there will be plenty of food, and fuel for heating, and even entertainment. They have some splendid concerts, apparently. They have promised to look after us well. The worst is over now." She gave one of her usual cheerful smiles but Hani thought there was a dullness in her eyes.

A soldier started moving the group.

"Oh, here we go," said Frau Lehrs. "We're off to get the train from the Nordbahnhof. Give my love to your mother."

"Yes," murmured Hani. She stared at the label pinned to Frau Lehrs' coat. 811. There was something else playing at the edge of her mind. The Nordbahnhof. She'd seen the big trains there last month. Long trains, with lots and lots of trucks. The sort of trucks that you moved animals in. And that face looking out of the window at the top of the carriage.

You didn't put labels on people and transport them in cattle trucks if you were taking them to a nice cosy old people's home. Peter had said he had something not too pleasant to do.

She watched Frau Lehrs and the others. They each had just one very small suitcase. This wasn't right. This wasn't right at all.

She started to run. She didn't bother with the tram. She needed to keep moving. Besides, she'd left her purse in Peter's truck. She ran and ran and ran. She ran the three kilometres home hardly pausing for breath.

She realised she had also dropped Peter's notebook. That didn't seem to matter anymore. And her key was in her purse. She had to ring the doorbell. Rikki opened it. She burst into tears and Rikki hugged her.

Mutti came into the hallway. "What on earth's the matter?" she asked.

Her father came out of his study.

"There was this boy, Peter," said Hani between sobs.

"What?" said her father. "Has he hurt you?"

Hani shook her head. "He was helping to get them to the trains," she said. "They're going to the east in cattle trucks. It's not right. It's not right."

Her parents didn't say anything. Rikki carried on holding her.

"I'm so sorry you had to see that," said Herr Gödde at last. His voice wobbled. "I'd hoped the rumours weren't true."

"Mutti," said Hani. "Frau Lehrs was there. She said something about concerts, but Peter said he had something nasty to do."

"Dear God," said Frau Gödde, taking Hani into her arms. "She was wrong about the spring coming then. Dear God, how will it all end?"

Ilse, 4 September 1942

Dear all,

Just as I was about to start writing, I received a message from home that our father was extremely ill. I had to return every weekend to see him. He died just two weeks ago. The doctor says his heart was very weak. I think it was broken. He hated the fact that we are at war.

Erika and I are going to run the family business together. We have managed to obtain an exemption from the duty year. Father's business is considered essential for the war effort. The factory makes spectacle frames. Both Erika and I have to do some training so that we understand the business better. Most of the men have now been called up, but Frau Griebel, father's personal secretary, has been such a great help. She has been with the firm since before Vati took it over from Opa. She understands absolutely everything.

One comfort is that I have heard from Helmut. He has been sent to France. He is well and not engaged in any active fighting. He can't say much in his letters, though, about what it's really like because they are censored. But he does think he might get some leave over Christmas. That will be marvellous. The pastor at our church has asked if he will sing a solo if he can get to the Christmas Eve service. I do so hope he will.

Mother is struggling a little. She is so young to be a widow – just 45. Father was 48.

The responsibility weighs heavily on us. I think our days of playing tricks on people are over. We dress differently all the time now, so that everyone knows which sister they're talking to. Mother doesn't seem to mind that at all these days.

We hope you are all well, and that we will have more cheerful news next time round. We certainly look forward to your news.

Your Ilse

Anika, 17 September 1942

Dear all,

I am no longer living at home, and mother brought the letter over to me when she came to visit at the weekend. I am doing my placement with a well-known family in Ludwigshöhe. I'm not allowed to tell you who they are. I've been here since June.

They do have a maid, but there are four children and I also have to look after the garden, which was in a terrible state when I arrived. Plus the mistress of the house was away for July and August so I had to run the household. I've learnt so much. Thank goodness I went to the Piloty School. It really prepared me well for that.

Well, the half year is nearly over now. Only having to do a half year is another advantage of having been to the Piloty School. When I get my life back I'm intending to go to drama school. I have decided I want to become an actor and play tragic, dramatic roles. I've already started back at dance school – there happens to be one not far from here, so what with the work in the garden and the dancing my muscles ache so much every night. But it will be worth it, I expect.

I'll have to take some tests next spring to see if they will allow me to enter the school. Please keep your fingers crossed for me.

Erika and Ilse, I was so sorry to hear about your father. Please give my regards to your mother. Yet I'm also quite excited for you – getting to run the family business. My, my, we women are coming up in the world.

Well, I must finish now. Tomorrow brings another whole round of hard work. Looking forward to the next round of news, as ever.

Your Anika

Helga, 10 November 1942

Dear All,

Would you believe it? I've had chicken pox! I caught it of course from one of my little charges. I woke up feeling really groggy. I took some aspirin and felt more or less all right for most of the day. I went to bed early. Well, I woke up still feeling bad, but you know, sometimes by the time you've actually got out of bed, it's better. The spots went septic and I was delirious all of the time. They sent me off to my aunt's to convalesce and I had a lovely time, eventually, enjoying the Bodensee. I was glad to get home though, and actually glad to get back to helping at the nursery. And of course, I was glad to find the circular letter waiting for me.

Today has been hard. The first day back at the nursery. There was a lot to do. Not to worry though. They are so sweet, these little kids.

Before the chicken pox episode, I was on a pharmaceutical course. I had to learn about all sorts of medicines. I was sent on a residential course in Würzburg. It was a bit like our old holiday home in Mostviel but a little more elegant and a little more comfortable. We were not woken with a whistle every day but by the radio. And instead of our beloved peppermint tea in the evenings we had a glass of wine. The course lasted eight days. I also learnt first aid. I will have to renew my knowledge about the drugs and about first aid every six months and take a short test. If I fail the test, I have to, at my own expense, go on a longer course. One half day a week I work at the local chemist to help to keep my knowledge up to date. I am now the medical expert of the nursery.

Well, I'll stop writing now so that I can let the not-so-little parcel get on its way.

Love to you all,
Your Helga

Käthe Edler, 9 November 1942

Dear Renate,

At last I have a reply from Butlers. It wasn't their fault they didn't reply. Their offices and warehouse were set on fire by an incendiary bomb. They've only just started operating again. They have a real mess to clear up.

That means, of course, that those few bits and pieces that we managed to bring with us from Germany are now gone; except for a little table linen and a few items of cutlery that I took out of storage to use in the flat.

So, it seems that Herr Hitler won in the end. If he couldn't take away our most precious belongings, he wasn't going to let us have them either.

Never mind though. You are doing well with your studies. That is the main thing.

I've had an idea. As you're all coming to London for Christmas, why not invite some of your English friends for a German Heiliger Abend on the 24th?

Ah, we could use the white tablecloths!

Mutti

Sabine, 16 November 1942

Dear all,

The postman arrived just under a week ago and said, "I have got something very special for you today." It was of course the class letter! What a joy!

So, my time at the Gymnasium is well and truly over. I did rather well in my Abitur and I hope you won't think I'm being too big-headed in telling you about it. It was a good time and I made some nice friends. But it wasn't the same as our dear old Wilhelm Löhe school.

I did have to do a half year duty in the end. I was sent to a family where I had to do a lot of cooking and looking after children. The cooking was fine, the children weren't. Helga, I do admire your patience. It's made me think really quite hard about whether I do after all want to become a teacher. And of course, this was all in North Germany. They are so different from us Bavarians! I can tell you, I am glad to be home.

They are quite happy that I do the second half of my duty year at the telephone exchange. Then May next year, I should get my life back and can start planning a proper career. So, ideas, please, what can one do with a good Abitur majoring in English? Apart from getting a degree and becoming a teacher. I would like to study further, of that I am certain.

Oh, it is so good to be back in Bavaria. The Isar valley, the Allgäu, the Salzburg Alps and the Zugspitze. Listen to me, I'm getting sentimental.

So I'll finish now and send the parcel on its way.

Hoping to hear from you all again soon.

Your Sabine

P.S. Erika and Ilse – so sorry to hear about your father. My thoughts are with you.

Charlotte, 8 December 1942

Dear All,

It is good to hear from old friends. I have made lots of new friends, as well, including, of course, dear Karl, who, I'm very happy to say, is still here and has not yet been called up. We are hoping because he has a very important job overseeing the delivery of medical supplies he won't be, in fact.

I'm still working at the rectory. I quite enjoy the work, but I'm still sure that once this war is over, the men will return and I'll no longer have a job. I think I might then like to train as a primary school teacher.

The church very kindly sent me on a course for Sunday School teachers. I thoroughly enjoyed it! Even the 'teaching practice', when I had to take a Sunday School lesson at the local church. The class was mainly BDM girls. The superintendent on the course said I did well. I was so proud.

I realise how lucky I am. I met a girl on my course whose family is all split up. Her mother is at home in Rimmelsberg. Her father is in South Africa, has been for two years, where he is interned. At least they can communicate with him but letters take three to six months to get there. One brother has served on the Russian front and is now in officer-training school in Pomerania. Another brother was killed in action during the battle of Stalingrad.

The course lasted a week and we had two afternoons free. We made the most of our beautiful surroundings and went for a couple of longish hikes.

Well, I'll finish now and send the letter further on its rounds.

Your Charlotte

Renate, 20 December 1942

Renate closed the lid of her suitcase. She'd got very good at packing. Just some clean underwear, a spare blouse and skirt, an extra jumper, her best dress and one or two books. She hadn't done anything about presents yet, though. She would have a few days in London to do that. The girls and David were sorted out anyway with the cinema tickets.

Then as soon as Christmas was over, she would have to hit the books again. This Higher Certificate was really hard. Perhaps Mutti could give her some help.

They were getting the train first thing tomorrow. It was supposed to take four hours.

That's if there are no bombings on the line, thought Renate. She had read in the paper about somebody being held up on a train for six hours the other day because somewhere further up had been bombed. What would London be like? They'd been saying that we were getting on top of things. Perhaps old Hitler would leave them alone a bit.

We? Where did that come from? Was she beginning to think of herself as English?

"Are you still fiddling about, Renate?" said Anne who had just appeared in the doorway. "Come on! The Williams are dying to get started on their mini-Christmas."

"I'm coming," said Renate.

Goodness, English Christmas today, then a German one on the 24th and then another English one with the Jenkins on the 25th. Her stomach churned at the thought of her mother's little soiree. They should sing German Christmas carols for their guests, Mutti had said. She had forgotten a lot of the words, though, and of course, her singing wasn't all that good. Even more worrying, she was beginning to forget her German. How could that happen?

"I'm dreaming of a white Christmas," came Bing Crosby's voice out of the gramophone in the lounge.

Mr and Mrs Williams were already sitting there. Mrs Williams had on her best velvet red dress and Mr Williams had put on a shirt and tie. The table was covered with plates full of sandwiches, mince pies, fruit and nuts.

"And did I hear that you lucky girls were going to go and see *Holiday Inn*?" said Mrs Williams. "That will be a nice Christmas treat."

"And me!" said David.

"I didn't think it was the sort of thing a chap would want to see," said Mr Williams.

David blushed.

"Get away with you," said Mrs Williams. "It would do you good to see it. Come on, now everyone. Get stuck in. And Merry Christmas to you all. Let's hope this war is over soon!"

Yes, that of course and she hoped they would all enjoy the cinema visit. It would cost Mutti quite a lot of money. It was to be the present from Eva as well. But Mutti was still insisting on the German Christmas evening.

Oh, she hoped it would be all right.

"Come on Renate," said David. "Stop daydreaming. It's Christmas."

SEE, YOU CAN'T QUITE STOP BEING GERMAN, CAN YOU? AND YOU'RE NOT EVEN THAT, REALLY, ARE YOU? NOR JEWISH. MISCHLING SCUM!

Gerda, 26 December 1942

Dear All,

We have acquired the farm next door! The government gave my father a very attractive loan and it was going at such a reasonable price that we could hardly refuse. It's an investment for Hans. So, you can imagine, we are busy, busy, busy.

We expect Thomas to be called up any day now. I don't know how we would manage without him. Some of the local Hitlerjugend boys help at crucial times, such as harvest, and we always have at least two girls doing their duty year here, but the work always takes longer when you have to explain to someone what you want them to do. We really need extra help from people who know what to do.

Hans has been injured, so spent a short time in hospital and was then allowed a few days' leave before he returned to light duties. His injury is keeping him away from active service for a while still. I'm pleased to say that he and Thomas really get along quite well now.

In September I was exhausted. One day, I just could not get out of bed. One of the duty year girls had to help Thomas with the milking. "See, we can manage without you, sis," said Thomas.

The doctor said I must have some rest. So, a friend of mother's took me to the mountains. For the first two days I did little but snooze in the garden but then we did some walks. Despite the rationing we managed to eat well. I returned a week later fully restored. Isn't the time passing so quickly? I'll send on the letter now and I'll look forward to the next instalment.

All good wishes,
Your Gerda

Erika, 14 January 1943

Dear all,

Thank you all for your kind wishes about father.

Ilse and I are getting on with learning all about the business now. Mother is now having more good days than bad ones, so most days Ilse and I trundle off to the office, briefcases in hands. We did ask my uncle if he or his boys wanted to join the firm, but he was adamant that he had no interest at all in business. So, yes, we are very modern women. Of course we have to wear smart clothes. You have to feel sorry for us.

We're currently on a big run of frames for the troops. That is our war effort.

After Easter next year, I am going to Munich to take a general business course. I'll have to leave everything to Ilse, but I'm sure she'll manage. Then, the next year it will be my turn to look after the shop while she does the same course.

Just before Christmas, one of the girls from the Piloty School who lives in a really big house in the middle of Nuremberg invited us all. It was a really lovely evening. I realise now that we did make some good friends there. I have this feeling that you never lose friends, even if you fail to keep in touch. You just accumulate more and more friends as you go through life. That has got to be good, hasn't it?

You know what? Our handwriting is changing! Is that because we are becoming more mature? Isn't that strange?

Now, I'll pass over to Ilse, who has some VERY BIG news that will delight you all!

Best wishes,
Your Erika

Ilse, 16 January 1943

Dear all,

Yes, I have the most spectacular news. Helmut and I are engaged to be married. When he came home on leave six months ago, he asked me to marry him.

"Will you marry me when it's all over?" he said one evening as we walked home from church.

I really blushed then but I don't think he noticed. My ears were thundering with the blood rushing into them. But I did manage to say, "Of course I will."

He put his hand in his pocket and pulled out a little box. "This was my grandmother's," he said. "Maybe we could get it altered if it doesn't fit."

It was a perfect fit. I've worn it every day since. Erika and Mother are delighted.

I wouldn't be happy about giving up my work completely. I'm really enjoying running the business with Erika. All of the women in the office and in the factory are hard-working and cooperative and not at all phased by having two girls younger than themselves in charge. It's quite exciting to think that the army chose us to supply most of the spectacle frames for the men.

Handling big sums of money and such big orders is a bit daunting. We don't pay ourselves a huge wage, but there is enough to support both of us and mother. It's difficult looking smart and business-like all the time. I wish we could just wear suits like the men, just ringing the changes with different ties and shirts.

Well, I'll stop now and get this letter on its way.

All my love,
Ilse

Renate, 1 February 1943

The queue in the post office went out of the building, round the corner and half way down the next street. She'd already been waiting twenty minutes and was just at the corner now.

It's a good job I came on my bike, thought Renate. I'd have missed the bus.

It was tempting to give up and come back tomorrow, but she needed those stamps. Mutti would get worried if she didn't get her letter and they often got held up anyway.

She could see what the problem was once she was in the doorway. It was only Mr Higgins senior serving and he did get mixed up with his change sometimes.

The queue moved eventually and at last she was served. She took the stamps and watched patiently as Mr Higgins counted out her change with his shaky hands. As she was about to leave, young Mrs Higgins appeared from the back room.

"Isn't Angela here today?" asked Renate.

"Oh, you haven't heard?" said Mrs Higgins. "She didn't tell you?"

"Tell me what?" said Renate. She hoped Angela wasn't ill.

"She's been called up," said Mrs Higgins. "She's had to go. You know they're calling up all young women aged nineteen now, don't you?"

Nineteen! She had read about that. But Angela was only just nineteen and they'd only brought the rule in a couple of weeks ago. Goodness! She'd be eighteen herself soon. They wouldn't call her up, would they? She'd heard that some German Jews had joined a special part of the British Army.

"Anyway, I'd best get on and give Arthur a hand," said Mrs Higgins. "But I just had to do some stocktaking today. You don't know of a young girl who would like to train up as a Post Office clerk, do you?"

"I'll try and think of someone," said Renate. She thought she would quite like to do that herself, but it seemed important to stick to her studies.

"So we've been giving Berlin a battering," she heard one of the men say as she made her way out of the door.

She wanted to stop and ask if they'd heard anything about Nuremberg but she didn't dare – not because she was shy or bothered about her English anymore but because she was afraid of what they might tell her.

And then she had the peculiar and slightly frightening thought that Angela might soon be organising bombs to be dropped on her father.

TUT, TUT, TUT. WHICH SIDE ARE YOU ON, ACTUALLY, RENATE? YOU JUST CAN'T MAKE YOUR MIND UP, CAN YOU? ABOUT TIME YOU DID.

Anika, 1 February 1943

Dear all,

Your photos are all intriguing. I think we should try to include one every time we send a letter.

Well, I got into the drama school in Munich. It was very nerve-racking. I had act from a script I'd not seen before with a professional actor. They allowed me just ten minutes to read it through. Then two of the teachers from the school, all cold and business-like, asked me about whether I was up to the strenuous exercises every day, what was my favourite piece of literature and had I been to the theatre often. I think my voice went a little squeaky. I was more nervous in the interview than I had been in the auditions. They accepted me, though, and I am now well into my course.

I stay with my aunt there during the week and come back home here at the weekends. Occasionally they want us to go and see some play or opera or other. At least I get free tickets for me and my aunt, which she very much appreciates. I come home every evening absolutely exhausted and at the weekend I mainly sleep.

My singing voice has improved. My body is becoming so much more subtle with all the dancing. And I am certainly learning all about straight acting. That, of course, is where my real passion lies. I long to take the female lead in a truly tragic play.

We hear from Fritz very occasionally. He tells us a nothing about his war effort. We don't actually know exactly where he is.

Well, I must go now. I have to learn a whole part by next week for a play we're rehearsing.

My love to you all.
Anika

Hanna Braun, 14 February 1943

Dear all,

You may have heard, perhaps, that my dear mother died just six weeks ago. She was 92 and not particularly ill. As I said last time, though, she was getting increasingly frail. She died very peacefully in her sleep. She went to bed early on the Tuesday evening and when I went to wake her on Wednesday morning she had already died. There was a faint trace of a smile on her lips.

My goodness girls – aren't you growing up? Such interesting lives you're all leading.

My work carries on as usual at the little school. Some students grow up and leave but there is a steady stream of new ones coming to the door. There is a lot of work, but not nearly as much, I don't think, as what my friends from college who teach in state high schools have. They are exhausted. There is actually a shortage of teachers, with virtually all the men away.

The weather is very spring-like at the moment. The sun is quite strong today. The days are getting longer. Isn't it fantastic how nature carries on as if nothing has happened? It seems not to know there is a war on!

Do take a few moments, however, to think of those who are less fortunate than ourselves. Some of your school friends are losing brothers, fiancés and fathers in this war.

Girls take care, and continue to send me your news.

All good wishes,
Hanna Braun

Hani, 9 March 1943

"Well, Fräulein Gödde," said Doctor Schubert, "I suppose we'd better let you go and start getting the lunch ready. It's a pity as we're all having so much fun."

"Oh. Can't she stay a bit longer?" said Peter.

"I like Hani's games," said Liesel.

"Why does she have to go?" said Dieter.

Always asking why, thought Hani.

"Because she has to, or we'll all starve," said Doctor Schubert.

Hani sighed. "Yes, I suppose I should go and make a start," she said. She really liked cooking now. It was just that she liked working with the children even more. Perhaps she ought to have trained to be a teacher. Maybe those hours with the books would have been worth it.

"Let's do the counting game just once more," she heard Doctor Schubert say as she pushed the cupboard back in front of the door and started to make her way up the stairs.

She was halfway up when the sirens began.

She hated that sound. It seemed to tell you to rush but she couldn't move now. They'd had raids before but never when the children had been in school. They'd either been in the evenings when they were at home with their parents, overnight or early in the morning before they'd arrived.

They had a drill. They'd practised it. She knew what to do. It was just that her feet seemed to be stuck to the floor. She gripped the handrail. The wail from the sirens seemed to get louder and even more piercing.

Frau Gödde appeared out of the kitchen and Doctor Kühn came out of his study. "Come on ladies," he said. "Into the cellar room and I'll put the cupboard in front of the door."

"Is that really necessary?" said Frau Gödde. "In an air raid? Wouldn't you be safer in the classroom with us?"

Doctor Kühn shook his head. "We can't be too careful," he said. "I'll be perfectly safe in the boiler room and at least I'll be able to eat a few pickles if I get hungry."

Hani managed to turn and she and her mother made their way into the classroom. The sirens were still screeching as Doctor Kühn slid the cupboard across the door. Several of the children had their hands over their ears and some of them were rocking backwards and forwards.

It was quite cramped in the classroom with the two extra adults in there. Today of all days every single student had turned up.

The sirens stopped.

"I expect they'll be here any minute," whispered Frau Gödde.

"Let's sing a few songs," said Doctor Schubert.

"I want my lunch," said Peter. "I'm hungry."

"Well, let's just hope the British airmen are hungry too," said Doctor Schubert. "And that they go home and have their lunch soon."

Before too long the children were singing quite cheerfully. Normally they had to keep as quiet as possible. But today their noise helped to drown out the sound of the aircraft overhead and the bombs dropping. Hani hoped, though, that from the outside the bombers were drowning out the sound of the children singing.

The ground shuddered as a rather large bomb exploded. Some dust fell from the ceiling.

"Gosh, that was near," said Frau Gödde.

"The house won't fall down on us, will it?" said Liesel.

"No, I don't think so," said Hani. "Frau Lehrs and her son made it really strong." She knew she mustn't let the children know how scared she was. Somehow, having to help them made her feel braver.

"And this is a very fine cellar," said Doctor Schubert.

There were several more explosions, also quite near, though not as loud as that one. The house shuddered each time.

Hani could smell smoke.

At last, though, the engines of the aircraft became quieter. The explosions became less frequent and sounded further away. Then, all the noise stopped.

"We'd still better wait for the all-clear," said Doctor Schubert.

"And you'd all better keep quiet now."

Most of the children put their fingers on their lips. One or two of them giggled.

A few moments later, the steady note of the siren announced the all-clear and it was precisely at that moment that Hani's legs began to shake.

"Are you all right?" asked Doctor Schubert as she almost fell over whilst trying to stand up.

"I think so," said Hani. "I've been sitting funny."

Then she heard the sound of the big cupboard being moved. The classroom door opened.

"Ladies, I think the allied forces are allowing us to have our lunch now," said Doctor Kühn.

"Well, that's everybody," said Frau Gödde as she closed the door behind the last of the children to be collected.

Every single parent had been late arriving. Some streets had been blocked so they'd had to find another way to Haus Lehrs. They had also stayed a while to tell them about the damage they'd seen.

"It seems that it wasn't too bad, then," said Doctor Kühn. "Not too many reports of injuries or deaths."

"What about that really big explosion we heard?" asked Hani.

"Yes, I think that was rather close," said Doctor Kühn. "But I'd imagine it hit one of the fields at the back. Not the woods, thank goodness, or they'd have probably caught fire. So, although it scared us, they would have been disappointed."

"I wonder whether we got any of the planes down," said Doctor Schubert.

"I hope not," said Frau Gödde. "Those pilots and crews are people just like us."

"Well, maybe they'll leave us in peace for a while now," said Doctor Kühn. "And maybe we can enjoy our day off tomorrow. You do think I was right, don't you? Closing the school for the day?"

"Yes, of course," said Doctor Schubert. "The children were exhausted."

"Good," said Doctor Kühn with a sigh. "And let's be thankful it was a largely unsuccessful raid."

An unsuccessful raid? thought Hani. Let's hope they don't have a successful one sometime soon. It had most certainly been frightening enough.

Renate, 15 March 1943

"Oh what can I do for you?" said Renate.

The little black and white kitten seemed to be following her.

"Shouldn't you still be with your mummy?"

The kitten mewed and rubbed her face against Renate's leg. "You're very cute," she said. "But I don't have anything for you."

"Oh, it's that one again. She doesn't seem to know which one is her mother and, to be honest, I can't say I'm all that sure either." Mrs Williams pointed to the two nursing cats that were nested cosily inside the barn.

The big tortoiseshell had given birth to five kittens the day after the little black one had had her four babies. The kittens didn't seem to mind which mother they fed from and the two mothers seemed equally content to offer their milk to any kitten that came calling. Except this little black and white one who never seemed sure where she should go.

Mrs Williams bent down to tickle the kitten but the little animal ran towards Renate.

"She seems to like you," said Mrs Williams.

"You're sure it's a she?" said Renate. "How do you know?"

"I'm just guessing," said Mrs Williams. "But I'm fairly certain. I've seen so many kittens. I'm sure she's a girl."

The little cat was now standing behind Renate.

Mrs Williams shook her head. "She won't survive unless she feeds," she said. "She's too young to be weaned. Neither of the two cats seem to want to tolerate her."

"Can't we give her a bottle?" said Renate.

"We could," said Mrs Williams. "But there's no guarantee... I wouldn't want you to get too attached to her."

"I'd like to try," said Renate.

Mrs Williams sighed. "All right," she said. "I'll go and make up a bottle. I'll warm the milk and dilute it a bit. See if she'll let you pick her up." She made her way out of the barn and back to the farm house.

"Come on, you," said Renate, slowly bending down.

The kitten rubbed her head against Renate's hand. She didn't struggle at all as Renate picked her up and carried her outside. She sat on the bench under the crab apple tree.

"We'll have to give you a name, won't we?" said Renate, whispering into the kitten's fur. "Little miss doesn't-know-where she belongs."

You're just like me, she thought.

The cat started purring. She was such a pretty little thing, Renate thought. She was mainly black with just a few white patches – on her face, her chest and her two front paws.

Mrs Williams reappeared from the kitchen.

"You two look cosy," she said, handing Renate the bottle. "Have you thought of a name for her?"

"I'm going to call her Molly," said Renate. "Molly Mittens."

"Suits her," said Mrs Williams. She rubbed Renate's shoulder. "This might work, but it might not."

Renate nodded. She offered Molly the teat of the bottle. It was a little big for her tiny mouth – one they usually used for the lambs whose mothers had rejected them. Even so, within seconds little Molly was sucking heartily and the bottle was emptying rapidly.

"I'll leave you to it," said Mrs Williams. She patted Renate on the shoulder again. "It'll be hard work but she looks like a fighter."

I'm not going to let anything nasty happen to you, Miss Molly Mittens, thought Renate.

Molly stopped sucking for a moment but kept the teat in her mouth. She blinked up at Renate, then closed her eyes again and carried on sucking.

No, you belong now, thought Renate. You belong to me. I'm your mummy now.

SEE WHAT A MESS YOU ARE? EVEN A KITTEN CAN FIND OUT WHERE IT BELONGS. BUT YOU CAN'T. THAT'S BECAUSE YOU DON'T BELONG ANYWHERE. YOU'RE A NOTHING.

Helga, 26 March 1943

Dear all,

I've been too ill to write. I had an obstinate 'flu that would not go away. Then I was just beginning to get better and we had those two terrible attacks last week. Have you seen the state of the city?

The doctor says I need to go away for a rest cure. Fat chance!

I'm continuing to work with children – I've actually been helping recently with some of the Kinderlandvershickung programmes. Just with the children who are sent for the holidays. We try to give them as much fun as we can. They do get terribly homesick. I don't think the people who send them – including their own parents – realise this, though. I'm really glad we don't have to work with the children who are permanently away from home. I don't think they should be away from their families for such a long time.

I do think it is good for young children to be with others of their own age and to learn a bit. But they definitely need also to spend time with their parents and brothers and sisters. Home is important!

Oh, it reminds me a bit of Mostviel sometimes! The singing, the story-telling and the fun in the dormitories – I'm not quite sure you knew about those pillow-fights and midnight feasts, Fräulein Braun.

And yet it's different with these children. There are certain things we have to make sure they learn before they go home, so there's quite a bit of pressure to get things done. Greetings to all of you and especially to Fräulein Braun.

Your Helga

Sabine, 2 June 1943

Dear all,

It is now just over six months since I last saw the Rundbrief and so much seems to have happened to all of you in that time.

I am no longer working at the post office telephone exchange. I was able to use my languages a little and I felt as if I was really doing something for the war effort. But the authorities didn't think so!

They sent me on the other half of my RAD course – last winter. Our barrack was at the top of a hill, in the Rhine valley. It was so cold that the bedclothes were completely stiff in the mornings. And we couldn't get out through the doors as the snow was piled so high. We had to go out through the windows!

My father has been posted to France, so mother is glad that I am now back in Nuremberg. The post isn't all that good. Sometimes a letter will take two months to arrive – other times though it's just a matter of days. They don't always arrive in the right order.

I am actually working in a chemistry laboratory. I have to test various materials and see that they are strong enough to be used for our war effort. Several times I've dropped some acid or other chemical on my stockings and caused a great hole to appear.

My biggest news is that I am now engaged – I have been for four months actually. His name is Walter. He was on leave from the Russian front. But we had a few days together and hopefully he will get some more leave soon. He's back at the front now. Naturally, this is more worrying than my father in France. Let's hope this war will end soon.

Lots of love to all of you, especially to you, dear Fräulein Braun.

Sabine

Renate, 15 June 1943

"What's the matter, Christopher?" said Renate. "You look really fed up. It can't be that bad, surely?"

"I think I messed up my English exam," said Christopher.

"How?" asked Renate.

"I was so angry about that wretched book they made us study that I didn't answer the questions on it very well," said Christopher.

"Which book?" asked Renate.

"Siegfried Sassoon's 'Memoirs of a Fox-hunting Man'," said Christopher.

"Never heard of it," said Renate. She'd had to do Dickens and Shakespeare and some poetry for her English matriculation exam. Those had been reasonably straightforward, though the language in Shakespeare had been a bit confusing. Then again, she expected her old classmates from the Wilhelm Löhe School were complaining just as much about Goethe and Schiller.

"So what's wrong with the book, then?" said Renate.

"Well for a start, it's about fox-hunting," said Christopher. "I think it's cruel. And not only is the guy obsessed about it – spends all of his time and money on it – but he complains all the time because he is only allowed £450 of his £600 a year allowance. His solicitor holds back £150 for savings. He never has to work for a living. We'll all have to work and I bet we won't see that much money in three, four or five years."

"What are you on about, Christopher?" said Christine who had just walked into the dining hall. "Why are you on your soap-box?"

"Because of Siegfried Sassoon and his fox-hunting," said Christopher.

Renate had thought she'd heard right the first time. Siegfried. A good old German name. She shuddered inside though. Siegfried was a hero in an opera by Wagner and Herr Hitler loved Wagner. So why were English schoolboys being asked to read books about something they'd never be able to do and written by somebody who sounded as if they'd stepped out of a German opera?

"There's nothing wrong with fox-hunting," said Christine. "They have to be kept down or they attack the farmer's livestock. We should know. We live on a farm."

"We have hunting in Germany, too," said Renate. "Wild boar, deer, foxes, pigeons, ducks and other things, I think."

"Yes, but fox-hunting here isn't about finding food," said Christopher.

"Well neither is it in Germany," said Renate. "It's about a sport. The hunters don't usually eat what they've caught."

"Yes, but it's stupid here," said Christopher. "It's all about silly ceremonies, expensive clothing and blood-thirsty hounds."

"Oh come on," said Christine. "It's just English tradition. We're full of tradition."

"And silly outfits," said Christopher.

Renate remembered pictures she had seen of English fox hunts. Yes, the clothes did look a little impractical and slightly old-fashioned. But were German hunting clothes any better? She couldn't actually remember. She supposed that was partly because she wasn't the slightest bit interested in hunting. She never even thought about it before, really. Perhaps Christopher was right: it was a bit cruel.

However, as Christine said, England was all about traditions and actually that was part of what she liked about it.

"Anyway, if any more of those flying bombs come across," said Christopher, "maybe they'll get me and it won't matter how badly I've done in the matric."

"Flying bombs?" said Renate.

"Keep up girl. Yes, that's what you're sending to us now," said Christopher. "Remote control bombs, sort of. When the engine stops, you worry: that's when the bomb is falling."

That was terrible. Could that be something her father had worked on?

"Christopher Rowland, apologise to Renate at once," said Christine. "It's not her fault at all."

"Sorry," said Christopher. "I didn't mean anything by it. I was just so fed up about the exam."

Renate shook her head and waved him away. That was so scary. He was right to be annoyed.

"I think you'd better leave now, Christopher," said Christine.

Christopher went bright red and mumbled something that sounded a bit like another apology as he left the hall.

"Are you all right?" said Christine. "You've gone really pale."

STILL DON'T FIT IN, DO YOU? NO MATTER HOW HARD YOU TRY. DO YOU LIKE OUR NEW TRICK THEN? CLEVER, AREN'T WE? BOMBS THAT DON'T NEED PILOTS. WE'LL GET YOU. WE'LL GET YOU YET.

Renate, 16 August 1943

"When did you say you start?" said Christine. "You're going to look very smart, that's for sure. But I'm not sure about the colour. Can't tell whether it's brown or dirty mustard."

David was showing off his new Home Guard uniform. It did rather suit him, Renate thought.

"First of September," said David.

"But what about school?" said Renate.

"I'll have to fit school and studying round Home Guard duties and working here," said David.

"Speaking of which, we'd better get back to it," said Anne.

They'd all stayed behind at the farm to help with the harvest this year and to give some of the land girls a bit of a break. Renate was pleased. It had meant she could stay with Molly. Although Mr Williams had not been called up, he had to take on more Home Guard duties as more of the young men went off to the army. He would be training David himself.

Most of the harvest work was done now and Mr Williams had asked them to help him clear a ditch after they'd had a break. It was a lovely sunny day but it had rained heavily after a storm the other day and now the water was spilling over the top instead of running away because the ditch was clogged with debris.

Mr Williams was waiting by the ditch when they got back there. He had a selection of spades, forks and rakes with him.

"Doesn't David look smart in his uniform?" said Christine to Mr Williams.

"He probably does," said Mr Williams. "Though it certainly won't stay smart for very long. They're not really very well made. They're getting flimsier and flimsier all the time."

"Do you think we'll see much live action?" asked David.

Mr Williams laughed. "In Minehead?" he said. "No, I don't suppose there'll be a lot but there will be all of the drills and the training. You can get pretty mucky just doing that."

"So you don't think they'd try and invade through this coast?" said Joyce.

"No. It's too far west," said Mr Williams. "Besides, we're giving them a bit of a thumping around Cologne and Dortmund. And in the industrial areas. Plus they're having trouble with the Russians."

Renate's mouth went dry. She tried to swallow but couldn't.

Mr Williams handed out the spades.

"Come on then folks. Let's get to it." He tapped Renate on the shoulder. "Don't worry too much," he said. "There's not so much happening in the south. And you know what we say: no news is good news."

She hoped he was right.

"Anyway," said Mr Williams. "There's not a lot you can do about it from here. But you can do something about this ditch."

Yes, I jolly well can, thought Renate. She started digging. Each forkful was heavy. Lifting it made her back ache, and the muck kept slipping back into the hole. But at least the gunge was soft even if it was heavy. I'll get this ditch clear if it kills me, she thought. Nobody talked much as they worked. There wasn't enough energy left.

Gradually a mound of twigs, leaves and some nasty looking mud piled up at the side of the ditch. Suddenly there was a loud gurgling sound and the water started flowing freely.

"Hoorah!" cried Anne.

"Job done!" said Christine.

"What about this then?" said David.

He was holding the fattest worm Renate had ever seen.

"I'm coming to get you!" shouted David.

"Get away from me with that thing," cried Joyce.

"I'm a lovely wiggly worm," said David, running after Joyce shaking the animal at her.

Christine picked up a clump of mud-covered leaves and threw them at David.

"Oi!" shouted David, picking up another clump of leaves and threatening to throw them at Christine.

"Come on," said Anne, nudging Renate and picking up a handful of wet grass.

Renate did the same and soon all four girls were chasing David up the path.

"Good job you haven't got that uniform on now!" cried Christine.

"Get off you mad women," cried David. "You're ganging up on me."

Suddenly he fell, face down on the mud. His grey shirt now became black, as did his trousers and his face.

The four girls stopped dead still. Then Christine began to giggle. Then Anne, and finally Renate and Joyce.

"Oh, you can't go into the house like that," said Joyce.

Renate suddenly had a bright idea. "We'll have to put the hose on him in the farm yard," she said.

"Great idea," said Christine. "Come on!"

"I'm not a bloomin' fire," said David.

Seconds later the water was streaming over him and he was alternately screeching and laughing. Renate didn't think she had ever laughed so much at anything.

The back door suddenly opened and Mrs Williams came out, followed by Molly who immediately began running round, trying to join in the fun.

"What the...?" Mrs Williams' eyebrows were raised and her mouth was wide open. Then she started laughing as well. "Well, I guess it will save me having to wash them," she said. "But I think you should come in now and get those wet things off. We don't want you catching cold."

I think I like being English, thought Renate. They know how to have fun.

Molly wandered over and rubbed her head against Renate's legs.

YOUR FRIENDS ARE HAVING FUN AND YOUR LITTLE CAT LOVES YOU. DO YOU DESERVE IT, THOUGH RENATE, DO YOU? AFTER ALL YOU ARE NOTHING BUT SCUM.

Charlotte, 18 August 1943

Dear all,

So lovely to get the class letter again and to hear of all your news.

It did manage to find its way to me in my hostel (I have started my teacher training course – two of the men returned from active service so I lost my little job at the rectory) but I had to leave suddenly as I was called home because my mother died. With all the fuss I forgot to pack it, and so it stayed there, safe in my locker, until I went back seven weeks after the funeral.

Karl is still very much part of my life and he has been great at this sad time. I am so glad that he didn't have to go and fight because he is doing war work here at home.

Despite all the sadness, it was really good to read of all your news. So many of us are finding our careers and even if we're not yet doing exactly the work we want to do, most of us seem to have a quite clear idea of what we are planning for the future.

Sabine, many congratulations on your engagement. What cheerful news to read!

Eventually, though, I had to give up my teacher training course because of my mother's death. I now work at home as a housekeeper for my father and I also help him in the office. I am learning a lot but also feel that I've grown up very quickly.

I'll stop there for now. I wish all of you, especially you, Fräulein Braun, all the best. And so I send the letter further on its journey.

All my love,
Your Charlotte

Erika, 18 September 1943

Dear all,

"Yesterday and the day before yesterday I did my duty, but what is duty without the presence of love?" (Goethe)

How lucky we all are in our work. It seems to me that we all love what we're doing, so none of it seems just like duty.

We have learnt so much in a short space of time. We have a routine which is very enjoyable, but we are also always looking at ways of actually bringing in more money – without cheating everybody and, in fact, always offering a good service. Naturally, the war creates plenty of work but finding people to do it is a little difficult. As is getting people to pay for it!

My latest enterprise is learning to drive. That is a challenge. Of course, it's not easy to get petrol but it will be so useful to be able to drive out to see important clients.

Did you hear that the RAF knocked out another weather station near here the other day? That's bad for the farmers and for our own Luftwaffe, I guess, not being able to predict the weather. I wish it would all end soon.

Ilse and I had to go into Nuremberg last week. What a dreadful sight! Rubble everywhere and many buildings not recognisable. It's so depressing. Still, I guess some of the English towns look as bad. It all seems a bit senseless, really.

Anyway, I'll finish now and pass the book on to Ilse.

I look forward to more of your news.

All my best wishes,
Your Erika

Ilse, 15 October 1943

Dear all,

I was actually just sitting down to start writing this letter when we received a telegram to say that Helmut had been injured. He had hurt his leg and his arm quite badly. He was transferred to a hospital quite near here and so I was able to visit him most days. And thank goodness, they managed to save the leg.

He is making a good recovery and will be back at work soon. They're keeping him on office duties in Munich for the next six months, which is a bit of a relief, actually.

We did some work for a local farmer and he gave us half of his potato crop. The only problem was that we had to help him with the harvest. Well, I did; Erika was too busy learning to drive. To be quite honest, I actually enjoyed getting out into the fresh air and getting my hands dirty. My back was sore for days afterwards, however. Never mind, we have enough potatoes to last us to the end of the war, I should think.

I do hope it will end soon. I would love to go out and buy myself some new clothes, but it seems pretty impossible. Mind you, I have learnt to sew and I managed to make a really good dress from quite a complicated pattern. It isn't easy, though, getting the material.

When the war ends, when the war ends, though...

Let's hope the peace comes soon.

I'll leave you all now and let the class letter get on its way. I look forward to more news from you all.

All my best greetings to all of you, and especially to Fräulein Braun.

Your friend Ilse

Renate, 22 October 1943

Renate was getting good at this now. She'd found a way of getting the peel off in just four cuts of the knife and of getting the core out easily.

"Like this," she said, showing Christine. "You just cut it into four and scoop the core out of each quarter. Then slice it through."

"There's enough for another pan load, now, I think," said Christine.

Renate smiled to herself. Christine was useless at peeling, coring and slicing the fruit. Much better that she got on with the cooking.

The scent of apple was stronger than Renate had ever known it before. It was on her hands – in her hair probably too – and was filling the whole kitchen. It wasn't an unpleasant smell, but she didn't think she'd want to eat another apple for a while. Even Molly had had enough of it and had left the kitchen in a bit of a sulk.

"There must be getting on for about fifty pounds here," said Mrs Williams. "That will be more than enough apple puree for us for a few months. The rest can go to market – and you can take some to school for the other families."

"So we can stop after this load?" said Christine.

"I think so," said Mrs Williams.

At that moment, the kitchen door opened and David walked in.

"Ooh! Apples," said David.

"I guess we're not going to starve," said Christine, "even if they ration more things."

"There are some advantages of living on a farm," said Mrs Williams. "Though the hard work isn't one of them."

"I'd like to be a farmer," said David.

"I'm sure you'd be a fine one," said Mrs Williams, "but I'd get out of that uniform if I were you."

It seemed Mr Williams was right about the uniform. It was wearing out already, yet he's hardly had it two months.

"Yes, but may I have an apple first?" he asked.

"Go on then," said Mrs Williams. "You probably deserve it."

Renate suddenly remembered her grandmother's house. Oma used to puree the apples from the two big trees at the back. Plus there were the black cherries and the plums. They didn't have plums quite like those in England.

She wondered whether all the gardens had rows of vegetables in them like the English gardens all seemed to have. Would her grandmother's garden look like that now? And what about the garden in Nuremberg?

Joyce and Anne arrived in the kitchen.

"That's it then," said Anne. "All the potatoes and onions stowed away and ready to go to market."

"But there'll be plenty for us," said Mrs Williams.

"Do you think they'll have rationing in Germany?" Renate said.

"I guess so," said Mrs Williams. "But a lot of what they need doesn't have to come across the sea like it does for us. They can get most things from other places on the continent. And let's face it, they're occupying quite a lot of those other countries now."

Renate tried to imagine what was going on back in Germany, but she couldn't remember what her friends looked like. She couldn't remember what Oma looked like. She couldn't even remember Vati's face. But she could see the garden on Schellberg Street very clearly. The lawn had gone from the back and the roses from the front. They'd been replaced with rows and rows of vegetables.

YES, WELL, I EXPECT THEY'VE FORGOTTEN ALL ABOUT YOU TOO. WHY WOULD THEY WANT TO REMEMBER YOU? A NOBODY LIKE YOU?

Anika, 22 October 1943

Dear all,

My, aren't we all busy, with RAD and war work. The skills we've picked up between us. Have you all seen the state of the town centre? I find it quite shocking. Yes, I suppose it's true, the Luftwaffe has done as much damage to English towns. But those lovely old buildings almost completely destroyed. And people's homes. Where have they all gone to live, I wonder?

Some of them are still in hospital. We were ordered to go to the hospital and sing to some of the patients who had been there for quite a long time. We were warned that we were to put on a brave face and look beyond the injuries.

"You'd better not faint or vomit," said the doctor.

I don't think she really liked the idea of us being there.

I think it did the patients good. They seemed to enjoy listening to us. I find singing also cheers me up. Do you and Helmut find that, Ilse?

My brother Fritz is still away on active duty. We haven't heard from him for ages and we're hoping no news is good news. He is at the eastern front, so it is quite a worry. I do hope this dreadful war ends soon.

I'll end now and send the class letter on its way. I look forward to hearing from you all again soon.

All my love,
Anika

Hanna Braun, 7 November 1943

Dear all,

As usual I was delighted to read your news. You are all so busy and active it makes me tired just reading about it.

You may have noticed I am still living in the old family house. It proved impossible to sell – maybe we will try again after the war is over. My two brothers are happy for me to housekeep for them. So, there is very little possibility of me being a teacher again – unless the war ends and we do manage to sell the house. It is quite a big house to look after.

My war work consists partly in providing accommodation for people who have to work away from home. Some come for a few days, others for a few weeks. They're mainly young women about the same age as all of you. I don't envy them at all, not having their own space to live in but I try to make them as comfortable as possible. And I do enjoy their company.

As I would yours. Yes, it would be lovely to meet you all again, face to face. It probably won't be possible until the war is over. Shall we make that a plan, though? You would all be very welcome here as soon we can meet easily again.

Do continue to send me your news, and do go into the details of what happens in your daily lives. That is all so interesting

Yours,
Hanna Braun

Helga, 19 November 1943

Dear all,

The class letter again to be whizzing around at the moment. Is this a sign that we are getting into some sort of routine? Are we getting used to being at war?

At this time of year there are fewer children coming to the camp. I have to spend quite a lot of time in the office and I sometimes think they are inventing work for us. Lists, lists and more lists. They love their lists. And we have to make tons of notes on every child that we come into contact with. They're even now asking us to measure their noses and look at the shape of their ears. Ridiculous! Goodness, I hope I'm the right shape. Isn't one of the points about life that we're all different?

Even with all of these lists they couldn't find enough for us to do and we've been doing some work on a local farm. Of course this time of year there is less light, so we have to go home by four o'clock. So my days are quite short and not as physically demanding as being with young children all day and looking after them in the evening as well.

One advantage of going to the farm has been getting a supply of eggs. Baking is such fun at this time of the year. It will soon be Advent. One of my favourite times. Even this silly old war cannot spoil that.

Well, I'll finish there, wish you all a wonderful Advent time and get this letter on its way,

All my very best wishes to all of you and I especially wish you a very happy birthday in the next few weeks, Fräulein Braun.

Yours,
Helga

Renate, 20 November 1943

She was running through the streets. She couldn't find her way to the shelter. Wasn't it round the next corner? The sirens were wailing. They always seemed to say, "Go! Your life is at risk." They made her feel sick.

She knew she had to run, but she didn't know where to. She didn't even know where she was. Was this London or Nuremberg? Or even Berlin? She'd been to Berlin once before but it hadn't looked like this. This could be any war city; there were ruined buildings and fires everywhere.

The sky lit up. She could see the bombs falling from the aircraft. Where were they going to fall?

There was a loud bang just beside her. She screamed.

"Renate, wake up," said Joyce. "You've been having nightmares."

"Were you dreaming about an air raid again?" asked Christine. "It seems so odd because you've never actually been in one."

"Unless you count the false alarm when we were at the cinema last Christmas," said Anne.

"Yes, it was such rotten luck," said Joyce. "It had just got to the good bit."

It had been Berlin, Renate decided. If it had been London she would have been with Mutti or Eva, or one of her friends' families and they would know where the shelter was. Vati would have known about the ones in Nuremberg. And if she'd been in Stuttgart, Oma would have known the way. Stuttgart? She'd not thought of Stuttgart before. Would there be bombs in Stuttgart too?

OH, RENATE, RENATE. WHO ARE YOU? WHO DO YOU FEAR THE MOST?

I'm German.

NO, YOU'RE NOT. IF YOU WERE, YOU WOULD BE HAPPY ABOUT THE GERMAN BOMBS FALLING ON LONDON.

I'm Jewish.

NO, YOU'RE NOT. DO YOU GO TO THE SYNAGOGUE ON SATURDAY?

Am I Yiddish?

NO, YOU SPEAK HOCHDEUTSCH.

So, I'm English.

YOU DON'T SPEAK ENGLISH PROPERLY. AND WHY ARE THE ENGLISH THROWING BOMBS AT YOU IN BERLIN? NO, YOU ARE NOTHING. YOU ARE A DIRTY MISCHLING. A DISGRACE.

"Renate, are you talking to yourself?" said Christine.

"Am I?" said Renate.

"You seemed to be mumbling something," said Christine. She laughed and sat on Renate's bed, putting an arm around Renate's shoulders. "You looked really funny."

"I was probably still half asleep," said Renate.

"No problem," said Christine. "We'll just have to wake you up properly. Going out and collecting some logs in this cold weather should do the trick. The alarm's going to go off any minute now, anyway."

The door opened and a small black and white head pushed through. Molly jumped on to Renate's bed, but when she reached out to stroke the now quite big cat, Molly turned her back towards her. She was right, of course. Renate wished now she hadn't looked at Mr Williams' paper the other day. He'd left it on the dining table and she couldn't resist, especially as it said something about Berlin on the front page. The city had been heavily bombed. The Germans were also losing against the Russians. That might mean the brothers, fathers and cousins of some of her old friends were being injured or killed. She couldn't be on any side in this war. Did that mean she belonged nowhere?

Sabine, 24 November 1943

Dear All,

I really enjoyed reading all of your news – the good and the less so good. Helga is right. Advent is a very special time and some of my best memories of our little school are from this time of year. All those cards and gifts we made for our families. And then at home on Sundays, lighting the candles on the Adventskranz. Next Sunday we shall light the first one.

My work has changed a little again since I last wrote. I am still working at Siemens, but now work in the pharmacy two days a week. I run a surgery for foreign workers and often have to use my French or English. Not of course, that we have any French or English people working for us, but often those are the only languages we share. It feels good, actually, getting to use my languages.

I've included a photo of myself and Walter (my fiancé). Do carry on putting photos in every time you send the class letter on.

Walter is now away in the east, which I find slightly worrying. We hear very little from him and have no idea when he'll be home again.

Please God, let this war finish soon.

I do hope you are all really keeping well and cheerful and not just putting on a brave front in the letters. My Oma always used to say, "Smile, even if you don't feel like it and then you will feel like it." I think she's right, actually. It does work.

So, that's what I'm doing right now as I end this letter and get it into the post.

All my best wishes,
Your Sabine

Renate, 18 December 1943

The thread on the sewing machine snagged again and broke. This machine just wasn't working properly. Maybe the needle was too fine for the thread. It had seemed such a good idea at first, making a pretty nightie out of warm material for Daisy for Christmas. The pattern had been cheap with a coupon out of the newspaper, and she'd found some pretty red and yellow material in the remnant box outside the big shop in town. It had gone quite smoothly at first. But now the last little bit was taking forever because of the wretched machine.

Molly wasn't helping either. She was giving Renate a look that suggested only sarcasm. "What? You can't even sew a simple child's nightie?"

"It's all right for you," mumbled Renate. "You have your clothes with you all the time. It's cold for us in the winter."

The door opened and Renate felt herself go bright red. Mrs Williams had caught her talking to the cat yet again.

"Playing up, is it?" said Mrs Williams as she put the bucket of coal down on the hearth. "You might have the tension wrong. I'd have a look for you, but my hands are filthy."

"It's been fine up until the last ten minutes," said Renate. "I'm tempted to do the last bit by hand."

"Well you could," said Mrs Williams. "Sorry I can't be much help. I don't have a lot of time for sewing." She put the bucket down near the fire place. She walked over to the table where Renate was working. "I won't touch it," she said. "But it does look pretty. Why don't you finish it by hand? And are you going to put some of your lovely embroidery on it?"

"I suppose I could," said Renate.

Except she quite liked the sound of the sewing machine. It drowned out the thoughts that were going round and round in her head.

THEY'RE GANGING UP ON YOU NOW. CHURCHILL, ROOSEVELT, STALIN. ALL YOUR FRIENDS WILL BE GONE. AND IT WILL PARTLY BE YOUR

FAULT BECAUSE YOU'VE BECOME ENGLISH. YOU'RE NOT A VERY GOOD GERMAN HAUSFRAU, ARE YOU? CAN'T EVEN SEW A CHILD'S NIGHTIE. YOU'RE NOTHING. YOU'RE A DISGRACE.

"The others will be back soon," said Mrs Williams. "I'll go and put the kettle on. You look as if you could do with a nice cup of tea. And they'll want to warm up."

That sounded good. She must be becoming English. She looked forward to the strong English tea with milk in it.

YES, THEY'RE GANGING UP ON YOU. YOU'RE A DISGRACE. YOU'RE NEITHER ONE THING NOR ANOTHER.

I really must stop reading the newspaper and listening to the wireless, she thought. It's best to just get on with ordinary things. The trouble with that was, though, if she hadn't looked at the newspaper she would never have found the coupon for the pattern.

She took her sewing out of the machine and threaded a needle with red cotton.

She heard the back door open and then the voices of the others.

"Go and tell Renate the tea's ready in the kitchen," she heard Mrs Williams say.

Thank goodness they were back. The chatter would drown out those silly thoughts.

Charlotte, 27 December 1943

Dear all,

It has been quite a grim time, hasn't it, with all the attacks and the bombing raids. Some of the aircraft seemed to come right over our house recently. It was very frightening. No matter how often it happens, you don't quite get used to it do you?

Christmas was strange for us this year. It was the first one without Mother. We spent Heiliger Abend with Karl's family and they are going to come to us for Sylvester. We shall see the New Year in together. However, there is still a big gaping hole. It's odd to think that we are so afraid of losing out fathers, brothers and fiancés (though I'm lucky to have Karl at home) in the war effort and my mother dies of an illness that could strike you at any time. Or maybe it was the worry of being at war that made her ill? Who knows?

I tend to spend the mornings cooking, cleaning and doing other housework, then in the afternoons I type letters, answer the phone and do the bookkeeping for Vati. This is all good practice for later – I shall be doing the same for Karl. I expect Vati will have to hire a housekeeper and a secretary then.

Karl still has to take some exams so that he can get promotion before he will be able to afford to take on a home of his own. It's hard to do that during war time. So in the meantime, I can carry on improving my housekeeping and secretarial skills.

It's all so uncertain, isn't it?

I can only now wish you all the very best for the New Year and hope that we can all enjoy the peace soon.

All my best wishes,
Charlotte

Hani, 4 February 1944

"All you have to do is walk forward and hold the flute up to your lips," said Hani. "You don't have to play it. The people watching will hear the music in their heads."

"Why?" said Dieter.

Why what? wondered Hani. Why had he only got to walk forward, or why had he only got to pretend to play the flute or why would the people watching only hear the music in their heads?

The end of term play was going to be performed in mime. Hani had her own question too. How were they going to fit everybody in to the cellar room? It was crowded enough with just the class in, let alone their parents as well.

"Clara Lehrs would have insisted," Doctor Shubert said. "It's really important to make school as normal as possible for them."

Yet they'd not done it before. They'd been too shocked for the first few weeks after Frau Lehrs' deportation to think of anything. Hani had first thought of this and Doctor Schubert had eventually agreed with her.

"Why?" said Dieter again impatiently?

And another question she couldn't answer was why Dieter always asked why. Then again, why shouldn't he? She often wanted to ask why about a few things herself.

"Look, this way," said Hani. She pulled Dieter on to his feet. "Like this."

Dieter shuffled forward.

"That's it. And now put your flute up to your lips but don't blow. Pretend to be playing it," said Hani. She waited for the inevitable "Why?" but oddly it didn't come for once.

Dieter frowned.

"Come on young man," said Doctor Shubert. "You know you're going to look really very handsome in the red tunic and the golden crown that that Frau Gödde has made for you."

"Why?" said Dieter.

Doctor Schubert rolled his eyes at Hani. "Keep up the good

work," he whispered. "We'll get there eventually."

Even though Dieter was difficult, Hani was enjoying this. Would it be too late for her to train as a teacher when the war ended? She'd even be willing to put up with all of the studying now. She would like to work with special children like Dieter, Peter and Liesel.

"Come on Dieter," she said, pushing the little boy gently forward. "Like this."

"Why?" said Dieter.

"Because it's fun," said Hani, "and you will be good at it. Not like the silly way I'd do it." She pulled a funny face.

Dieter giggled. "It's fun," he said. "Hani's a silly."

He took the three steps forward and held up the flute to his lips. He fluttered his fingers up and down on the holes and cocked his head slightly to one side. He really looked the part.

"Bravo," said Doctor Schubert, clapping. "Well done," he said, patting Hani on the shoulder. "You are an absolute natural. You must consider taking this up properly."

Hani felt her cheeks burning. She felt too embarrassed to look directly at Doctor Schubert. She stared at the floor.

The doorbell rang.

Now Hani looked up at Doctor Schubert.

He nodded his head briefly. He turned to the children and immediately put his fingers to his lips. They all stopped what they were doing and sat as still as statues.

Her mother was already outside the room when Hani got through the door. Together the two women pushed the heavy cupboard in place in front of the door.

"You go and open the door," whispered Frau Gödde. "Put your apron on first. And if they come in and find me cooking in the kitchen you can say I'm the hired help."

They moved upstairs as quickly and as quietly as they could. Hani quickly grabbed her apron from the kitchen and tied it on. Then she hurried to the door. Through the glass panel she could make out a man standing in the porch. He didn't seem to be wearing any sort of uniform.

Hani took a deep breath and opened the door.

She recognised the man straight away. He was one of the neighbours. He was quite elderly. He'd never been particularly friendly. He'd never complained about anything either. They just didn't know whether they could trust him or not.

"I'm sorry to have kept you waiting," said Hani. "We've been having trouble with the hot water. I was down in the cellar trying to get the boiler working again." Her heart was thumping. She had no idea whether he was a friend or an enemy.

"Arthur Ehrlichmann," said the man, extending his hand towards Hani. "I have been Frau Lehrs' neighbour since they built the house," he said.

"I'm Hani Gödde, Doctor Kühn's housekeeper," said Hani, shaking his hand.

"Ah, so Frau Lehrs no longer owns the house," said Herr Ehrlichmann. "She hasn't..."

"She's had to go and live in an old people's home," said Hani.

"Ah, I see," said Herr Ehrlichmann. "I thought I hadn't seen her for some time. Is she well?"

"I really don't know," said Hani. "I work for Doctor Kühn. He owns the house now."

"Good, good," said Herr Ehrlichmann. "I just wondered about Frau Lehrs. A good Christian woman."

"I've heard that too," said Hani.

"Well thank you," said Herr Ehrlichmann. "I'm sorry to have kept you from your work." He turned to go and then he hesitated. "Just one thing, though. Did I see Doctor Schubert here the other day?"

"I don't recall the name," said Hani, "though sometimes Doctor Kühn lets his visitors in himself if I'm busy in the kitchen."

Herr Ehrlichmann shrugged. "I may have been mistaken," he said. "But I know he used to do a lot of good work at the Waldorf School before it was closed. Frau Lehrs used to tell me all about it. And Doctor Kühn. That name is familiar too. Did he not also work for the Waldorf School?"

"I'm afraid I don't know anything about Doctor Kühn's work," said Hani.

"Very good. Very good," said Herr Ehrlichmann. "I am sorry to disturb you. But will you tell Doctor Kühn that I called and that if I can help him in any way, he should just call on me?"

"I'll do that," said Hani. "Thank you. Good day to you."

"Good day to you too, Fräulein Gödde," said Herr Ehrlichmann, raising his hat.

Hani shut the door behind him and watched through the glass door as he made his way slowly down the path, turning once to look back at the house.

"What did he want?" said Frau Gödde, making Hani jump.

"I don't know," said Hani. "I really don't know."

The plates were still on the table two hours after they had finished their lunch. They had gone over and over the conversation Hani had had with Herr Ehrlichmann. Was he just being concerned, or was he actually trying to find out more? Hani really couldn't make it out.

"You don't think he's trying to get at me, do you?" asked Doctor Schubert. "Technically you could argue I am half Jewish."

Doctor Kühn waved his hand dismissively. "If they'd have wanted you they would have taken you by now," he said.

"Do you think Herr Ehrlichmann might have an idea about the Special Class?" asked Frau Gödde.

"He seemed to think it was a good idea," said Hani. The elderly man had seemed very nice, actually, but she'd been constantly taught to be careful about whom she trusted and she knew she shouldn't trust anybody she didn't know enough about.

"I think it's probably best to assume there is a problem," said Doctor Kühn. "I think we should plan to take more care."

"Do we need a way the children can escape from the cellar room?" said Doctor Schubert.

"We ought to make one, but I don't know how we can," said Doctor Kühn.

"A false wall at the back – another cupboard in front of the door and a staircase that leads into a shed," suggested Doctor Shubert.

Doctor Kühn sighed. "Yes, I suppose we must do that," he said.

"It will be a lot of work, though and who can we get to help?"

"My husband will help," said Frau Gödde. "And he can find some other people who will be willing to work with us."

How can he? thought Hani. How does he know all these people he can trust?

Gerda, 1 March 1944

Dear all,

The class letter went to the old address and now I am back on the family farm. It took them a mere six weeks to send it on!

The work is almost identical at home. Milking, harvesting, repairing fences, baking, mending, pickling, cooking, cleaning – and looking after children.

A family now lives in the other farmhouse rent-free and the mother works on the farm. Her husband is away at war, naturally. She has five teenage boys, all staunch and loyal Hitlerjugend members. They're a bit too 'Hitler' and not quite 'youth' enough for my liking – they take themselves rather seriously and never seem to have any fun. They are really helpful on the farms, though, and of course their training has made them very fit and able. I do hope the war will end before they are called up. The oldest is 17. Then 16, 15 and twins aged 14.

Hans is at home with us now. He has now been invalided out of the SA. He is at home convalescing. He can't walk yet but the doctor said he will walk again – even if it is with a limp. Someone told me that if he marries and has children, they will not have to do military service as their father had made sacrifices for his country. It would be nice if it were true.

Never mind, I'll remember what Sabine's Oma said about smiling and try to do that. Being busy helps anyway.

Maybe this photo of me in my work overalls will make you all smile a little. My love to you all and do all try to stay cheerful.

Your friend,
Gerda

Erika, 2 April 1944

Dear all,

It has been a difficult time recently. We have had the saddest news from our aunt, our father's sister. Both of our cousins have been killed in action. And then, on top of that, my aunt and uncle lost their home in the recent raids. This makes the war seem very real somehow.

I have to say, though, that our work keeps us busy and occupies our minds so that we don't have to dwell on it all too much. We both enjoy the work so much. We're now looking for new ideas and taking the firm forward. But it would be even better if the war would finish – as long as we don't get a string of men coming back looking for work and trying to take over.

I'm now getting used to driving the car. It certainly makes getting into town a lot quicker. Of course, we have to be careful about not using up too much petrol. You should see the look on the faces of some of the business men we go to visit. Eyebrows are raised, I can tell you.

Some people near here are saying that we're actually losing the war now. What do you think? What will it be like if we lose? How will they treat us, the British, the Americans and the Russians? Does that mean my cousins will have died for nothing?

Sorry to sound so gloomy. But I am actually very worried.

Never mind, though. This letter will always cheer me up. So I'll pass it on to Ilse quickly and hopefully she will get it on its way again soon. And be warned – Ilse has the most amazing news for you!

Greetings to you all, especially Fräulein Braun.

Stay safe,
Your Erika

Renate, 24 April 1944

"Is it like this because it's Good Saturday?" said Renate.

"Nothing very good about it if you ask me," said Eva. "Now Karsamstag that would be a thing."

Renate couldn't remember what "kar" meant – except that Karfreitag was the Friday before Easter and Karsamstag was the Saturday before Easter and everybody was always a bit sombre and serious on those days.

"Well, there's not a lot to see here," said Frau Edler.

Most of the shelves in the Food Hall in the basement of the big department store were empty. There was a long queue for fish, though.

"Scallops," said Eva. "They're queuing like that just for scallops."

"I don't think we need to have fish two days running, do you?" said Mutti.

Suddenly, Renate noticed a group of women watching a demonstration. "You don't think they might be doing something with chocolate do you?" she said.

"I doubt it," said Mutti. "But let's have a look."

It was just a talk about how to make things from dried eggs.

"Come on, we'd better go and get that pot before they're all sold out," said Mutti.

They walked up the stairs. Not all of the lifts were working. "Leave them for the old and infirm," said Eva.

Half of the floor of the ironmongery department was closed off.

"Here they are," said Mutti. She picked up the ugly pan.

It looked to Renate just like an overgrown saucepan. The enamel was a sickly beige colour. "So what's it for?" asked Renate.

"For boiling that chicken we've managed to get," said Mutti. "There's no way we can fry or roast it."

"This is an extremely popular line," said the woman who served them. "They really can help your food go a long way and be really tasty."

It's a saucepan, thought Renate.

"Well, we've got your pan, now, Mrs Practical," said Eva. "So let's go and have a look at the fashions."

"We haven't got any money or clothing coupons to waste," said Frau Edler.

"Oh no, Mrs Practical, of course not," said Eva. "But we can look can't we?"

The clothes department was nearly as empty as the Food Hall had been. There were plenty of stockings, though, and a long queue of ladies waiting to buy them. Unsurprisingly, there were no silk ones, Renate noticed – just lisle – and no fully-fashioned ones either. She would need some more stockings soon. She could get away with long socks for school and slacks for on the farm but for Sunday best and going out she needed something a bit more grown up, especially when she was in London.

The make-up counter was almost empty, too. There were just a few pots of face-powder set out with big spaces between them. There seemed to be only one make.

The lady in the hat department looked fed up.

"What, no customers?" said Mutti.

"Well, you can see why," said the lady, pointing to a few rather ugly hats on her counter.

"Yes, I see what you mean," said Mutti, trying on a pink felt hat. She pulled a face when she looked at herself in the mirror.

"Can't get the material to make anything decent," said the young woman.

Renate closed her eyes. She imagined what this shop would be like normally. The Food Hall would be full of delicious sights and smells and there would be no queues. The make-up area would be bubbling with different colours and perfumes. There would be more than two types of stocking, two weights and three colours. There would be dozens of different choices and there would be silk ones and fully-fashioned ones. Mutti and Eva would be able to spend hours trying on hats. And nobody would be buying sickly-coloured poultry-boilers. They would be looking forward to a roast chicken dinner. It would be lively and colourful here. There would be music, and lots of people rushing about, excited about their shopping. Yes, this English department store was lovely. She had been right. She would like being English. Especially if this war ended, so she and Mutti and Eva and Molly could all live together. Perhaps Vati as well.

IT'S NOT FOR YOU THOUGH. YOU DON'T DESERVE IT.

"Goodness, Renate, what are you doing?" said Mutti. "Are you going to sleep standing on your feet? Come on, let's get home and get this fowl cooked."

Renate, 6 June 1944

Renate looked at the big clock at the front of the hall. Good, she still had thirty-five minutes to go. There was time for the last question and to read everything through. Why was it always so hot when the exams were on? Guaranteed, as soon as they were over, it would start raining. In fact, it had been pretty disappointing on the days in between the exams. Just every day that she had one... Well, it was warm and stuffy today. She didn't mind though. In an odd sort of way, because she was slightly uncomfortable, she worked even better.

A breeze wafted in through the open window, almost blowing her question paper off the table. She just managed to catch it in time. The cool air gave her another surge of energy.

Thirty minutes to go.

Her friends thought she was mad. She enjoyed exams. She got excited about them. This one – the first part of her Biology – seemed quite easy. The main problem was trying to write down everything that she knew. She'd worked hard. She'd really enjoyed studying all the sciences but Biology was her favourite.

Normally, by this stage of an exam, she had settled right down. But there was something about today. Something really special. The fluttery feeling in her stomach was still there. It wasn't nerves. It was the excitement of knowing that she was about to show off all that she knew. The feeling usually went after about ten minutes. But it had lasted until now and was showing no signs of going away soon. Perhaps it was just because she was so keen about Biology. She always found it exciting. Yes, it was probably that – partly. She knew, though, something else really important was happening today. How did she know that? Was it something somebody had told her about but she'd forgotten?

Twenty-five minutes to go. She was halfway through the last question. In five to ten minutes she would finish and then just have enough time to read through all her answers.

Miss Faversham came into the hall and said something to Miss

Samson. Both women looked her way. Miss Samson nodded and Miss Faversham smiled at her.

She finished her last question and read through all her answers. Everything seemed to be in order.

"Pens down," said Miss Samson. "Renate, leave your papers on your desk. Take your personal belongings and go and see Miss Faversham."

The fluttering in Renate's stomach got worse as she made her way along the corridor across the big hallway and up the stairs to Miss Faversham's office. She was nervous now, but she was still excited as well. What was going on?

"So how was the exam?" asked Miss Faversham after Renate had sat down in the seat opposite the head.

"Fine, I think," said Renate. She was being modest. It had been easy.

"Good," said Miss Faversham. "We're expecting you to do well. A girl with the talent you have should be going to university, but…" She looked down and then out of the window. She took a deep breath and turned back towards Renate. "They wouldn't admit you to a British university at the moment. You are still an enemy alien. And even if you weren't because you are not English you would not be able to get a grant."

Ah, that again.

"Still," continued Miss Faversham, "it looks as if the war might be over soon. Especially with today's news."

Today's news? What had happened today?

"Listen, I have a proposal for you," said Miss Faversham. "How would you like to stay on at the school another year? You can help out with the younger children and that will get you out of other war work and you might be able to study for one of the new A-levels. That would make it even easier to get into university once the war is over. I think the new Education Act will come out in your favour – once we've overcome the enemy alien problem. Staying on a year will buy you some time and you can keep up with your studies. What do you think?"

"Yes, I think I'd like that," said Renate. Had she picked up some clues that this was going to happen? Is that what all the excitement was about? Maybe. But it did still feel as if she was waiting for something else.

"Just one more thing before you go," said Miss Faversham. "Have you – and indeed your mother as well – considered becoming British? That would certainly ease getting a place in higher education, though again I doubt anything can be done before the war ends. Or I suppose you might want to go back to Germany? Anyway, after today's news, you might be able to make some decisions sooner rather than later."

Renate wished she knew what the news was but she would feel silly asking.

The bike ride home seemed to take longer than ever, yet when she turned into the farmyard, she couldn't quite remember how she had got there. She'd had a lot on her mind. Staying on an extra year at school sounded excellent. Going to university would be great – if she could get over the usual old problem. And what about becoming English? What an idea! Surely Mutti would want to go back to Germany when it was all over? But the idea of her staying here and becoming properly English? And what was the news that Miss Faversham had mentioned?

David and Mr Williams were in the yard mending a fence.

"What's been happening today?" called Renate "What's the big news?"

"You've not heard?" asked Mr Williams.

Renate shrugged and shook her head.

"I suppose you wouldn't have," said Mr Williams. "Most of the British and the American armies are invading France. Thousands crossing from just along the coast from here. They've dropped paratroopers into Holland. It should all be over quickly now."

"Yeah, we'll soon zap him!" said David.

There was an awkward silence. David's face went bright red and he looked down at the ground. Renate felt her own cheeks burn, and she too looked away.

Mr Williams put down his tools, walked over to Renate and put an arm around her shoulders. "We're all hoping, praying and keeping our fingers crossed that all your relations and friends will be safe," he said.

"It's all right, Mr Williams," said Renate, looking straight into his eyes. "I think I'm going to be a real English girl soon. And you can zap Herr Hitler as much as you like. Be my guest."

She bent down to tickle Molly who was rubbing her head against her legs and purring.

BUT YOU CAN'T BE ENGLISH, CAN YOU? AND DON'T THINK A FEW SOLDIERS CROSSING THE WATER WORRY US. NOT AS MUCH AS HOW UN-ENGLISH YOU ARE WORRIES YOU. THEY'VE GOT SOME SENSE, ANYWAY, THE BRITISH. SEE, YOU'RE NOT GOOD ENOUGH FOR THEIR UNIVERSITIES.

Hani, 8 June 1944

Hani looked at her clock. It was only five in the morning, but already she could hear voices coming from her father's study. He'd had breakfast meetings before but this was ridiculously early. Still, she may as well get up now. She probably wouldn't be able to get back to sleep. Besides, if she went downstairs, she might be able to find out what was going on.

A few minutes later she found Rikki in the hallway carrying a tray laden with coffee cups, a pot of hot steaming coffee and a bread basket piled high with Bretzel.

"Is that real coffee?" asked Hani. It certainly smelt like it.

"Oh yes," said Rikki. "They got me in early and decided to serve some of the good stuff. On account of the news."

"The news?" asked Hani.

"Oh yes," said Rikki. "Two bits. The English and the Americans are over here now. Took everybody by surprise and came over where the Channel's wider. And young Wilhelm is being sent home. He's lost his leg." Rikki's lower lip quivered and her eyes filled with tears.

"Wilhelm's been hurt?" said Hani. "That badly?" She suddenly felt sick.

"Well, Herr Gödde said straight away that he would find him a job in his office once he's well enough to work," said Rikki. "Now, if you'll excuse me, I'd better get in there before this lot gets cold."

"But who are all those people?" said Hani.

"Well, I don't rightly know," said Rikki. "And it's not my place to ask. But I do know this. They're good people. Just like your mother and father. And I also know they're waiting for their breakfast."

She bustled into the study.

Hani waited for a while in the hallway. She tried to listen to the conversation in her father's study, but they were all speaking very quietly and her father had probably pulled the curtain across the inside of the door.

Frau Gödde appeared in the hall.

"What's going on, Mutti?" asked Hani.

"I wish I could tell you," said Frau Gödde. "But it's still better if you don't know." She sighed. "It might soon be over. We might be about to lose the war. There will be a lot to be sorted out then. Whatever happens remember this: your father is a very good man. And so are all of those people in there with him. But there are some people around who are not so good, and when they know we're losing they may get even nastier."

"Are they all people who work with father?" asked Hani.

"Most of them," said Frau Gödde. "And because they've been involved with war work it might be harder for them once it's over."

The door to the study opened.

"Let's hope so," she heard her father say. "But there is, of course, some way to go."

"Come on," said Frau Gödde. "Let's go and get breakfast."

Hani and her mother decided to walk to Haus Lehrs. Frau Gödde's bike had a puncture. Hani knew how to repair them now but it was such a bad one it would have taken them too long. They didn't say much as they walked. Hani found it difficult to work out whether her mother was glad because the war was almost over or worried about what might happen to her father before the end or what the Americans might do to him afterwards.

It was a mild day and the sun was just beginning to come out. The pavements were wet because there'd been a thunderstorm during the night. It now promised to be a pleasant and not too hot day.

"It's such a pity they can't play outside," said Frau Gödde. "But maybe they'll be able to in a few weeks' time." She sighed. "Though we'll have to be even more careful until then."

Hani was about to ask her mother how long she thought it would be until the end of the war, but a woman was walking towards them on the same side of the street. She knew not to talk about the Special Class in public.

"Grüß Gott," said the woman.

Hani was so surprised that there had been no "Heil Hitler!" that she almost forgot to reply.

"Grüß Gott," replied Frau Gödde, nudging Hani.

She just about managed to mumble a reply.

Then they turned the corner into Schellberg Street and Hani's heart missed a beat. There was a young man standing on the front doorstep. He was dressed in a familiar brown uniform. Hani was sure it was Peter. He stood as tall and straight. He had the same short brown hair. How had he managed to find out where she worked?

"Let's go round the back," said Frau Gödde. "Then you can get into your work clothes and open the door to him and act as if you didn't know he was there."

Hani's heart continued to thud. She felt really sick again. Her hands were shaking so much she could hardly tie her apron or open the door. She managed though she didn't know how.

It wasn't Peter. It was just someone who looked like him. She would have to get rid of him as quickly as possible. The children would be arriving any minute.

"Can I help you?" she asked, ignoring his salute.

"We're trying to find out what happened to the Special Class that used to go to the Waldorf School," said the young man. "I wondered if I could talk to Doctor Kühn."

"He's not in at the moment," said Hani. "Can I tell him you called?"

"Yes, please do," said the young man. "My name is Werner Kaufmann. When would be a good time to call?"

Hani saw Dieter and his mother arrive at the front gate. Frau Leman stopped suddenly and waved to Hani that she would go round the back.

"Well," said Werner Kaufman. "When would be a good time?" He turned to look at where she was staring. Fortunately Frau Leman and Dieter had already disappeared along the side path.

Werner Kaufman sighed. "I hope you're not trying to hide anything from me," he said.

When would be a good time? After all the children had gone home, surely?

"About half past three?" she said.

"Very well," said Werner. He bent his head towards her. "Listen," he said. "We've heard a rumour that some of the defective children have been coming here. They've ordered us to set fire to the place if we find any evidence. None of us actually want to do that. Please, if you're doing something you shouldn't, you'll have to stop it or at least be really careful. Tell Doctor Kühn I called. Heil Hitler!" He saluted, clicked his heels and set off down the garden path.

Hani shut the door and leant against the wall. She was finding it hard to breathe. How had they found out about the Special Class? Could it have been Gisela and Trudi? Herr Ehrlichmann? One of the other BDM girls? Surely not one of the parents, though maybe one of the ones whose child had become too old for the class?

She took a deep breath and went to find the others.

"He called them defective children," she said. She couldn't get that phrase out of her head. It was like with Peter all over again. Peter had seemed nice but he'd helped to transport the old people to the east, whatever that meant. Werner had seemed nice and it was good of him to warn them but he thought of the children in the Special Class as defective.

Doctor Shubert sighed. "That's how he's been taught to think," he said. "You mustn't blame him."

Frau Gödde was not saying much. She looked a little pale.

"I'm afraid I think it is going to get worse," said Doctor Kühn, "before it starts to get better. They'll be using every old man, young man, woman and child to be doing their dirty work soon. They're getting desperate. I doubt they'll win, and I'm sure they know that, but they've got to put on a good show."

Frau Gödde cleared her throat and hurried out of Doctor Kühn's study.

"I think we'd better have an evacuation drill," said Doctor Kühn.

It all went quite smoothly in the end. The children stowed everything away neatly into the box under the floorboards. Those who could walk filed through the door and up the stairs quietly. Hani and Doctor Schubert were able to use the special hoist they'd made to get the others up to ground level. Doctor Kühn put the cupboard in place in front of the secret door and then the other cupboard in front of the door to the cellar room. The children quickly made their way into the shed. It had all taken less than three minutes.

Doctor Kühn came into the shed from the garden.

"That was very good," he said. "I think we'd better practise that at least twice a week. Now, just as quietly as you came up, back down to the classroom."

Twelve pairs of eyes looked from her to Doctor Kühn.

"It's important," Hani whispered.

Dieter went to open his mouth, but then turned and started to lead the way back down the stairs.

Doctor Kühn opened the door of the shed. Hani caught a glimpse of a face at an upstairs window. Herr Ehrlichmann. Had it been him then? Could he see what was going on now?

"Come on then, quickly," said Hani, as the last two children made their way to the staircase. They just had to get this right.

Ilse, 27 June 1944

Dear all,

So good to hear from you and read all of your news. I really admire my sister for not spilling the beans about my big news.

Helmut and I are married. We decided we could wait no longer. Now I am expecting a baby – due in November. I was terribly sick for the first three months and very tired but now I seem to have some energy back though I am beginning to expand and it's more difficult moving around. Poor Erika has to do a lot of the work on her own though she never complains. She says, though, that I am the brains in the firm. I have to admit I do seem to be full of bright ideas now that I can think again. Is it being pregnant that makes that happen?

Well, I really thought this horrid war would end when the Brits and the Americans invaded France. But now we've invented this flying bomb. It's quite nasty by the sounds of it. An unpiloted plane dropping a bomb anywhere. Just think what it would be like if you heard one of those up above. At least with a pilot in a plane might consider avoiding ordinary people.

Are some of the Hitlerjugend boys getting more aggressive? Thank goodness I'm not a boy and in fact thank goodness we no longer have to be members of the BDM.

Still, it's a beautiful day today and if all of the plants are still growing life must be fine, mustn't it? You've got to live in hope, haven't you? I actually feel quite optimistic that the war will end soon. Let's hope so.

So now I'll send this letter on its way and look forward to your further news.

My love to all of you,
Your Ilse

Anika, 17 September 1944

Dear all,

I had been having quite an exciting time of it until that Herr Goebbels closed all the theatres. I'm very pleased to say that we have been a little subversive. Nothing too political, though between you and me we have one actor who does amazingly funny impersonations of Herr Hitler. Yes, I'm afraid we've been making people laugh and wearing frothy costumes and generally being a little bit frivolous. My goodness don't people need that in these dark days? We've had to be a bit careful – the Nazis don't like this sort of showy theatre. But we got away with it.

Now, though, I expect I'll have to do something sensible like work in a munitions factory or help with the post. Still, from what you all tell me, that sort of work isn't all that dull. I expect I'll get used to it.

Yes, haven't you all been busy! And Ilse about to become a mother. That is truly remarkable.

Yes, Ilse and Erika, I think you are right about the Hitlerjugend boys. Some of the girls are marching around like soldiers, too. Is it my imagination or is it getting a bit chaotic? People seem to be rushing all over the place but nobody seems to know where they are going. Never mind. Let's make this letter a point of stability in our lives. Let every girl pass it on as quickly as she can and fill it with interesting news.

I'll do my duty right now and send it off straightaway.

Greetings to you all,
Your Anika

Hanna Braun, 27 September 1944

Dear all,

So good to get your news again. Two of you engaged and one married and about to become a mother. My goodness! And the first time I met you, you all had plaits and knee socks.

As for me, well in the mornings, I am my own maid-of-all-work. Keeping the big house warm and clean and cooking for all the guests is quite a chore.

In the afternoons, I work as a clerk for the local hospital. I order medical supplies. Often they send the wrong item. It's not my fault but matron is a dragon – yes that old cliché, but it's true – and I have to endure her wrath several times a week.

How glad I am then to get home to my girls even though it means cooking a huge evening meal for them. We've all got to know each other really well. It feels like a big family.

At the weekends, I'm often visited by my sisters-in-law – the men are away fighting. It's good having the children around again and it reminds me of why I liked being a teacher. Girls, this war cannot last too much longer. I think the next months will be hard, though. Still, I can't imagine that the invaders would be too cruel. Yes, Anika, you are right that it is chaotic now and I think it will get worse. Maybe that is what it needs to do in order to become better.

So, our little book is getting full. When it gets back to the last but one girl to have written in it, she can keep it – or perhaps even burn it.

Herewith my own photo: sitting outside under the cherry tree in the summer. Who would have thought there was a war on?

Take care all of you, and carry on sending the interesting details about your daily lives.

Your Hanna Braun

Helga, 7 November 1944

Dear all,

Look what I found in the paper the other day:

"2 November 1944. Born to Helmut and Ilse Lehman, a son, Rainer Harald, 2.40 a.m. 3.7 kilos. Mother and son well. Congratulations from Erika and Leopold Naumann."

So, Ilse is now a mummy. What a thought!

Did any of you read or hear Herr Himmler's speech yesterday? We must murder any of the enemy we find in our town and we're even to murder anyone we see or hear being disloyal to Germany. I personally don't think I could murder anyone, though I'd certainly hit out hard enough at anyone who tried to harm any of the children I have to look after. Not enough to kill them, though. Herr Himmler is a frightening man – even more frightening than Herr Hitler, I think. They say he will take over if anything happens to Herr Hitler.

I'm still working with my groups of children and as usual, it's my job to look after the youngest. Even they are becoming more aggressive. I do wonder whether they understand all these slogans they chant. They're very intolerant of weaker children. I'm not sure that's right. Some people are naturally physically weaker than others. And now we have to also award each of them points for how 'Aryun' they are. Ridiculous! We even had one child join us whose mother was not married. He had the most beautiful blond hair and big staring blue eyes. His mother seemed to be very proud of the fact that she had done her bit for the Reich. But what will it be like for that poor little boy without a daddy?

Yes, let's make this letter the one stable thing in this confusing time.

Lots of love to all of you,
Your Helga

Renate, 15 November 1944

"The wretched thing won't stay closed," said Christine. "Whatever you do, there will be a gap and light will show. Why's it suddenly doing this? It's been fine up until now."

"Oh, you're only fiddling with that so that you can get out of all of this mending and altering," said Anne. "I don't think the Blackout police are exactly going to come looking up here are they?"

"Give me that black sweater and a couple of safety pins," said Christine.

Joyce handed them to her.

"There," said Christine after she'd pinned the sweater across the gap. "Freddy's old pullover has come in useful after all."

Why did they still have to do this? It had looked as if the war was going to end very quickly back in June. Now it was still dragging on. "He's an obstinate old bugger," she said.

"Renate! I'm surprised at you," said Joyce. "You can't use words like that."

Even Molly had jumped off Renate's lap as if she didn't approve of her mistress' language.

"Why not?" said Renate. "It means dredger in German and that's what he is – the dredgers."

"Who? Freddy?" said Anne. "Anyway you're getting dredger and dregs mixed up."

"No, Adolf Hitler, of course," said Renate. "Anyway, he thought he was the dredger – getting rid of all the dregs but he's actually the dregs himself."

"Gosh, Renate, you're clever," said Anne. "I couldn't have said all of that in French."

"Yes, but you're not living in France," said Renate. "Anyway I've forgotten most of my German. Except Bugger. Well actually, it's really Bagger."

"I thought he was supposed to be dead?" said Christine. "That's the gossip."

"I won't believe it until somebody says it's true," said Renate.

Anne laughed. "Do you realise what you've just said?" she said.

"I don't care," said Renate. "It's a pest. Another winter of not being able to see in the dark. Not enough clothes for the children. Or we wouldn't be doing this. And he's still throwing things at us. He's a bugger. He's the dregs."

"Hey, Renate," said Anne. "It's not like you to be so stroppy. What's up?"

She took a deep breath. "You know those new rockets? The ones you can't hear? That have done so much damage on this coast?"

The three other girls were staring at her now.

"Go on," said Christine.

"Well, I think my father might have helped to design them," said Renate. How had she dared to say that? But it had been bothering her all day. She had to tell somebody. And these three were her best friends.

The others carried on staring.

Renate's mouth was dry. Had she spoiled everything?

Christine shrugged. "It's war," she said. "It can't be helped."

Anne picked up a pink cardigan that had two huge holes at the elbows. "I don't think we can repair this," she said, "but we could unravel the wool and somebody could knit it into something else."

Renate shivered.

"Shall we put some more coal on?" said Anne.

"Better not," said Christine. "Mrs Williams said we should only use one bucketful. There's a shortage."

"Perhaps we can look for logs again at the weekend," said Joyce.

YOU SEE? ROCKS AND HARD PLACES. WE'RE NOT GIVING UP. NOT YET.

Hani, 19 November 1944

"I'm afraid they fetched him last night," said Doctor Kühn. "They said he has to go to a work camp."

"But I thought he only had two great-grandparents who were Jewish?" said Frau Gödde. "Surely according to the Blutschutzgesetz that's not enough?"

"They're using the slightest excuse, now," said Doctor Kühn. "And I think it might be since their suspicions about our little school started. We're doing everything we can to get him back."

"My husband might be able to help," said Frau Gödde. "I could go to his office and speak to him."

"That would be splendid," said Doctor Kühn. "And I must go and see one of my contacts too." He turned towards Hani. "Which rather means you'll be in charge of everything today. I promise you I'll be as quick as I can. Will you be all right with that?"

Hani nodded.

"You'll need to be brave," said Doctor Kühn. "Now that he's turned the whole population into soldiers everybody who does anything remotely like the right thing is in danger. But goodness knows what the Americans will make of it all once they arrive."

Hani swallowed. She nodded again.

"Good girl," said Doctor Kühn. "I know you can do it."

Half an hour later, all the children had arrived and were more or less settled in the cellar room.

"Where's Doctor Schubert?" asked Liesel.

"He's had to go to a business meeting," said Hani.

"And where's Frau Gödde?" asked Peter.

"She's had to go to another meeting," said Hani.

"Good," said Dieter. "That means we've got you all to ourselves."

That was something, she supposed. At least they seemed to be glad to have her as the teacher for today.

She started them on some number work. They seemed to settle well.

All of a sudden, though, she heard a movement upstairs. She put her fingers on her lips. The children copied her and sat very still.

"Hani, where are you?" called a voice.

Gisela? What was she doing here?

"Look we know what's going on. We want to help you. This is really important," said another voice.

Trudi? Oh, God, what did they want? Hani nodded to the children and put her fingers on her lips again.

She went through the door but before she could pull the big cupboard across Gisela had appeared on the stairs. "Don't worry," she said. "We know all about it and we're not going to give you away."

"Nor do we want to hurt the children," said Trudi. "But you've got to get them out. In ten minutes the other girls will be here and we're to set the house on fire. We'll try and keep it to the cellar. They asked the boys to do it but they refused and now they're in a lot of trouble. We'll be in even more trouble if we don't do it."

"We're not going to hurt people just because they're a bit different," said Gisela. She exchanged a meaningful look with Trudi. "We're here to help you. But we've got to get them out quickly."

Hani tried to swallow what felt like a tennis ball in her throat. It wouldn't go away. Somehow, though, she managed to explain about moving the cupboards.

Seconds later she was organising the children to escape.

"We've got to hide everything in the cellar," she said. "And get up into the shed. You remember what to do. Just like we've practised."

In very little time they were on the staircase. Fortunately today there was only one child there who needed to use the hoist. Anneliese was small and light and it only took Hani a few seconds to get her up the stairs. She heard Gisela pull the cupboard across the doorway and then the second one into place. Then, she and the children made their way into the shed.

"Lie down as quietly as you can," she said. "Make yourselves as small as little sleeping hedgehogs." She covered them with the tarpaulins that Doctor Kühn had put in there just two days ago. That was such a good idea. No one would be able to see them and it might also protect them from the worst of the smoke.

It seemed to take hours before the BDM girls arrived but soon after she heard a few voices there were black clouds billowing from the cellar and the choking smell of smoke. Some of it was coming under the door of the shed.

"That should get the vermin out," she heard one girl say.

"Well, we'd better hope there are some vermin in here," she heard Gisela reply. "Just get on with it and hope that we're not ruining Doctor Kühn's house for nothing."

The smoke was beginning to make one or two of the children cough. There was not much she could do about that. She could go outside and look. In fact it might be that they were beginning to look for her. But she daren't leave the children on their own.

There was suddenly a scraping noise from the side of the shed. Hani held her breath. Then a panel came away.

"Come on," said a voice. "They can hide in my cellar. They'll be away from the smoke then."

Herr Ehrlichmann!

"Don't look so afraid," he said. "I thought something like this might happen. I took the liberty of loosening a panel in my fence and in your shed the other day. If they're quiet, nobody will know. The steps into my cellar are just the other side of the fence and nobody will see them with all of this smoke."

The children didn't speak or make any fuss as they made their way into Herr Ehrlichmann's cellar.

It was bigger but emptier than the one in Haus Lehrs and there were no windows at all. The children had to sit on the bare floor, but they didn't seem to mind.

"They'll be all right with me," said Herr Ehrlichmann once the children were settled. "You'd better go and see what is going on or they'll wonder where you are."

Hani made her way to the street in front of Haus Lehrs. A fire truck was there and Doctor Kühn was now talking to one of the fire officers.

"Ah, Hani," he said. "Thank goodness you are all right. We were getting concerned."

"I was helping Herr Ehrlichmann with his delivery," said Hani. "Everything is stacked away neatly in his cellar. What's happening here?"

"The good girls of the BDM decided it would be helpful to set my cellar on fire," said Herr Kühn. "They think we're keeping defective human beings down there." He turned back to the fire officer. "You don't seem to be attempting to put the fire out," he said.

"That is correct, sir," said the fire officer. "We've been ordered not to spare the lives of the defects."

"Have you actually bothered to check that there is anyone down there?" said Doctor Kühn going red. "And that if there is, that they are indeed defective, whatever that might mean? You are allowing my property to be badly damaged and you are possibly failing to save human life. My housekeeper could have been down there. Thank goodness she was at the neighbour's house."

The fire officer frowned.

"Well, man, what do you intend to do?" said Doctor Kühn.

"All right," replied the fire officer. He turned to his men. "Put the fire in the cellar out."

Twenty minutes later, the flames had gone and the cellar was steaming gently.

"Now, if you would be so kind as to go and see if you have killed any defective or undefective human life, or even a grey-coated rat, I would be very grateful," said Doctor Kühn.

Two of the fire officers went down into the cellar.

Hani dug her nails into her palms while they waited. Ten minutes later the men came back up.

"Nothing down there," said one of them. "Just a few pickles and preserves, an old boiler and a cupboard full of linen. There doesn't seem to be any structural damage."

Hani's hands relaxed.

Gisela stepped forward. "We're so sorry Doctor Kühn," she said. "We'll help you to clear up the cellar."

"Thank you, my dear," said Doctor Kühn. "That is really kind of you. Don't apologise. I know you were only acting on orders."

By seven o'clock that evening, most of the dirt from the smoke had been scrubbed away. The BDM girls, apart from Gisela and Trudi had gone home. They were now in the cellar room with Doctor Kühn and Hani.

"Here goes," said Doctor Kühn.

Hani held her breath.

Doctor Kühn lifted up the loose floorboard and took out the box of the children's work and books. He opened the lid. The contents of the box seemed to be undamaged. "Perfect," he said.

Hani breathed again.

"Fantastic!" cried Gisela, hugging first Hani and then Trudi. "You'll be able to carry on with the school."

"Well, the walls could do with a lick of paint first," said Doctor Kühn. He grinned at Hani. "And I'm afraid you'll have to carry on being the teacher until we get Doctor Schubert back."

The front door opened.

What now? thought Hani. She heard footsteps on the stairs. She exchanged a glance with Doctor Kühn. He looked as worried as she felt.

The door to the cellar room opened. It was Doctor Schubert.

"They let me go," he said. "It seems we have some good friends."

He collapsed and Doctor Kühn caught him.

Renate, 23 January 1945

The pictures in the newspaper seemed to come to life. She could see the tanks making their way along the streets that she knew. Were they flattening things down in front of them? She couldn't quite see. Then there were the soldiers, marching, marching. American soldiers. British soldiers. Russian soldiers, and the Germans waiting for them. Young boys and girls, younger than her. Waiting. Waiting to use their training as nastily as they could. The paper said they would do that because they knew they would be in trouble. So best to try and kill the soldiers or be killed. These would be the younger brothers and sisters of her friends. And the old men? Would they be as old as Oma?

She saw her Oma's house on Schellberg Street. It hadn't been bombed. Would the soldiers come and take her Oma away?

But the children on the street in front of the house looked hungry. The food shortages were worse there, they said. Perhaps it was better if you lived in the countryside though, like it was better here on the farm.

She looked at the picture of the French women who had been let out of the prison. That was a nicer picture. The women, full of joy. Life beginning again.

NOT FOR YOU THOUGH, RENATE. YOU DON'T DESERVE THAT. WHAT ARE YOU ANYWAY? YOU CAN'T BE ENGLISH. YOUR FATHER MAKES BOMBS THAT DON'T SAY THEY'RE COMING AND THEY'RE THROWN AT THE ENGLISH. YOU CAN'T BE GERMAN. THEY THREW YOU OUT. YOU'RE NOT EVEN A JEW. YOU NEVER GO TO THE SYNAGOGUE AND THEY LET A GENTILE CHRISTIAN PRIEST BRING YOU INTO THAT FAITH. YOU'RE A DIRTY LITTLE MISCHLING. A DISGRACE.

HOW DO YOU LIKE ENGLAND NOW THEN?

IT'S NO GOOD, ALL THIS WORK. IT WON'T CHANGE ANYTHING. YOU'VE GOT TO STOP EVENTUALLY. THEN YOU'LL JUST HAVE TO FACE IT. YOU DON'T FIT IN. WORKING HARD DOESN'T MAKE YOU GOOD. THAT WAS A MYTH. ARBEIT MACHT NICHT FREI! WORK DOES NOT FREE YOU.

SWANNING AROUND, PLAYING SCHOOLGIRLS WHILE YOUR MOTHER LIVES IN FEAR FOR HER LIFE AND WHILE YOUR FATHER WORKS HARD TO

DESIGN THE RIGHT WEAPONS TO MAKE THE WAR END QUICKLY.

YOU DIRTY LITTLE MISCHLING. DIRTY LITTLE MISCHLING. YOU DISGUST ME.

Molly jumped up on to Renate's lap but Renate pushed her away. It wasn't that simple. Molly always found everything too easy.

"Come on Renate, we're going to be late," Christine called from the back door. "You haven't even got your coat on yet."

Renate went to stand up. She couldn't move. She went to say something but the words stuck in her throat.

"Renate," she heard Christine call. "Come on."

She heard Christine's footsteps cross the kitchen. She had black blobs in front of her eyes now.

"What on earth's the matter?" she heard Christine say. "Renate are you all right?"

Renate felt herself whirling through a dark space. Christine, the farmhouse kitchen and the newspapers were gone.

The children must get some food. It was up to her to bring it to them. Surely there would be apples on the trees in her grandmother's garden? Wouldn't that help? Or perhaps she could take some of the potatoes and onions they'd put in the cellar?

She must look for Mutti and Eva. Were they under that rubble? Was that the all-clear sounding? Could she go now? Would somebody come and get her out of here? Please?

She had to finish that essay, and she needed to get into the laboratory to finish the experiment.

HA! NO CHANCE OF UNIVERSITY YET. THE WAR IS STILL GOING ON. NO UNIVERSITY PLACES FOR MISCHLINGS.

SEE, WE DON'T WANT YOU. THEY DON'T WANT YOU EITHER.

It sounded like the SS man from the train.

She heard a cat meow. There was something important about the cat but she couldn't remember what.

There weren't enough logs. Why weren't there enough logs? Had something happened to David?

What? There were bombs in Nuremberg? Was Vati's house all

right? No, it wasn't Vati's house. It was the Family Edler's house.

Heil Edler.

No, there are no bombs. Sleep. Warm. Sleep.

The blackness came.

Renate didn't know where she was when she woke up. Sunlight was streaming in through a thin yellow curtain. She was aware of a soft bed. She could hear voices. Then she realised that there were other people in the room.

"Oh, you're quite young really," said a voice. "You looked really old when you came in. You've been asleep a long time. I expect you needed it."

Renate sat up. The voice, she discovered, came from a middle-aged woman in the bed opposite. She looked around the room. There were seven other beds and all their occupants were staring at her. She pulled the covers up under her chin.

"Oh good, Miss Edler, you're awake at last," said a pretty, young nurse. "I'll get Doctor Murphy."

"How long have I been asleep?" asked Renate.

"Well, they brought you in Tuesday morning," said the lady who had spoken to her earlier, "and it's Thursday lunchtime now."

Sabine, 27 January 1945

Dear all,

Two days after the book arrived Walter actually came home on leave, completely unannounced. He looked terrible. I could see that he was terrified to go back. That in turn left me totally depressed and I got through Christmas and the New Year like a clockwork doll.

The raid on 2 January shook me. Of course Walter and the other men have a duty to stop this sort of thing happening. Have you seen what they've done to our beautiful old town? I hate seeing the walls and the castle damaged like that, not to mention our churches. The British men who flew those planes across were putting their lives at risk and perhaps also have wives, girlfriends and fiancés waiting at home for them.

Are you all as afraid as I am? I want the war to end but probably, now I'm thinking, that means we'll lose and what will that mean? What will they do with us? Is it all right in this class letter to talk about our fears? Do we have to pretend to be jolly all the time?

I am constantly hungry. They say that's how sharks feel. Well, I'm glad I'm not a shark. This time of year is particularly bad because there's not much even to forage in the countryside. Sometimes grateful patients give me a loaf of bread or a few apples or potatoes. We had a good supply of potatoes in our cellar, but some of them were frozen and then when they thawed they were quite rotten. We ate them anyway. They were awful.

I'm sorry to be so gloomy. I'll end this now and get the letters back on their way. Maybe by the time it gets back to me – if it makes another round – things will be better.

Do take care all of you.

All my very best wishes,
Your Sabine

Renate, 1 February 1945

"There, you can look now," said Christine. "Open your eyes."

Renate took her hands away from her face and looked in the mirror. Was that really her, that young woman looking out? Putting her hair up had made her look older but she'd looked so German with her plaits coiled round her ears.

"You do like it, don't you?" said Agnes, the hairdresser who had come to the hospital that evening.

"It looks really lovely," said Joyce. "Don't you think so, Renate?"

"Will you cut mine like that?" said Anne.

"Yes, of course," said Agnes. "But maybe you'd better come to the salon." She looked down at the hair all over the bathroom floor.

"Oh, don't worry about that," said Christine. "We'll soon clear it all up."

Renate still couldn't believe what she was looking at.

"You're really lucky that you have such a nice natural wave," said Agnes as she looked at Renate through the mirror. "It will be easy to keep it like that. You'll just need to set it each time you wash it."

"You're not saying much, Renate," said Christine. "Don't you like it?"

"Of course I do," said Renate. "It's lovely."

"It makes you look really pretty," said Anne.

"Well, I'm glad you're pleased," said Agnes.

A nurse popped her head round the bathroom door. "Goodness," she said, looking first at the floor and then at Renate. "Girls, you need to finish up now. And tidy up this mess. Renate needs to get some rest."

"Oh, we'll do this very quickly," said Christine. "Do you have a dustpan and brush?"

"Follow me," said the nurse. She hesitated in the doorway and turned back to Renate. "It makes you look so English. It really suits you."

Renate looked back at her reflection. She did look English didn't she?

She waited for the voice to start arguing with her but it didn't come.

"Still admiring yourself?" said Christine when she came back. "Come on girls," she said, handing the dustpan to Anne and the brush to Joyce. "Let's get this cleared up before matron has fifty fits."

"Thank you for thinking of this," said Renate.

Her friends were great. And nobody was arguing.

Renate, 5 February 1945

"No, you are not going mad, Renate," said Doctor Murphy. "Those weren't really voices in your head. It was just your own mind, trying to sort things out."

"But it sounded so nasty," said Renate. "Like, I think, the SS man who came on to the train."

"You've probably been reading too many newspapers, watching too many newsreels or listening to the wireless too much," said Doctor Murphy. "Everybody has been getting a bit hysterical recently. It's not just you, you know. Besides you were physically exhausted. Why had you been pushing yourself so much?"

"I just wanted to shut out the voices," said Renate. "I didn't want to think any more. And I wanted to be good."

"And do you still hear the voices?" said Doctor Murphy.

"No," said Renate.

"And do you feel fine physically?" said Doctor Murphy.

"Yes," said Renate. She did, in fact. Giving in to the tiredness had actually been good. She'd forgotten what it felt like to have enough sleep.

"Then I'm going to prescribe for you plenty of fresh air, plenty of fun with your friends, not too much study and plenty of sleep. Can you stick to that?"

"Yes, I think so," said Renate.

"Then I am going to let you go home. No more tablets. But I want you to spend a little more time with me first."

"Oh?" said Renate.

"What did you think of when I said home?" asked the doctor.

"Well, the farmhouse and Mr and Mrs Williams and all my friends who live there. And my cat, Molly."

"Good, good," said Doctor Murphy. "I'm glad you said that and I'm glad you used the word 'friends'. You have some very good ones there. Look at all the flowers they brought you, and the fruit and even chocolate and sweets. Despite the rationing. Look how often they came to see you, too. Never mind the new haircut. You are very well regarded, Renate Edler. And you have a cat. Tell me about your cat."

"Her name's Molly," said Renate. "Molly Mittens, because of her two white front paws. Her mother rejected her and I fed her with a bottle when she was a baby."

"She must give you a lot of pleasure," said Doctor Murphy.

"She does," said Renate. "And I'm really looking forward to seeing her again."

"I'm sure she'll be pleased to see you, too," said Doctor Murphy. "And it's good to care for another living creature. It makes us more human, somehow."

Renate felt herself blush. "I suppose I should be more grateful," she said.

"No, no, no, don't do that," roared Doctor Murphy. "You must have some respect for yourself. You are Renate Edler. A smart young woman who has a lot of very English ways, who speaks English very well now, without any trace of a German accent, and we forgive her the odd little mistake now and then because they are usually absolutely charming. She still has a few German ways, but these are very good and nothing at all to do with some of the silly things that have been happening recently. And she probably has a few cultural ways from a very old religion that she should be happy to be connected with. You see, it is good to have a mixed background. It makes you special. And everybody is special anyway, as an individual, because everybody is unique. Do you get my meaning?"

"I think so," said Renate.

"Then you may go," said Doctor Murphy, "and you may go home tomorrow."

Renate felt lighter as she left Doctor Murphy's room. So, it was all right, was it, being a Mischling? And suddenly she couldn't wait to see Molly – her own little Mischling.

Renate, 3 March 1945

"It was supposed to be a surprise," said Christine. "David wasn't supposed to bring you back yet."

"It was raining," said David. "We were getting soaked."

"Well, couldn't you have taken her somewhere else?" asked Christine.

David shrugged. "Sorry. I couldn't think. Anyway, I thought you'd be finished by now."

"Oh, well now you're here you can blow up some more balloons," said Christine.

"Why are there so many balloons?" said Renate. There looked as if there were hundreds of them. Blue ones, yellow ones and red ones.

"Practically the whole school is coming," said Christine. "And the whole village."

"The whole school and the whole village?" said Renate.

"Yes, to your party," said Christine. "And you'd better put Molly somewhere safe or she'll get trampled, there'll be so many people here."

"My party?" said Renate. She pushed her face into Molly's fur so they couldn't see how red she'd gone. The cat started purring. "You'd want to come to a party wouldn't you, Molly?"

"Yes, your 'welcome home, we're glad you're better and we really love you, Renate's party," said Christine. "Everybody is bringing a plate of food to share."

"And I am making a huge cake," said Mrs Williams who had just walked in with Anne. They were carrying armfuls of crepe paper streamers. "Now why don't you girls go and make yourselves beautiful. I've already sent Joyce up. David and I can finish off here."

They were putting on a party for her. That was amazing. She suddenly felt very warm inside.

Molly licked her nose.

Charlotte, 4 April 1945

Dear all,

I am glad to read that you are all safe, reasonably well and that nobody is giving up. You Fräulein Braun are so busy and really doing exactly the same sort of things that we are all doing. I am determined despite everything to do all I can to make life nice for me and everybody I know.

Yes, some horrible things are happening. What about that nasty raid we had two weeks ago? More damage to our lovely old city!

Yet there was Easter. The spring is here. It always fills you with hope, doesn't it, because of all the new life that comes then? Nature doesn't give up even when humans are behaving disgustingly. Our vegetable plot is putting up shoots, so soon there'll be some good fresh food.

I am now quite a good cook and housekeeper. I can turn out a healthy meal even with the poor supplies we have. Vati is a little more cheerful these days. He is quite resigned that in probably less than two years, I shall be married to Karl and he will have to find himself a house-keeper and a secretary.

Both of my men are at home. I feel sorry for those of you whose fathers, brothers and fiancés are away, fighting for our country. When there is an air raid and I know that Karl or father are in town I am. It's nothing having your men away at the front and not having any idea what is happening to them, though.

Do, all of you, keep safe and well and also cheerful if possible.

Your friend,
Charlotte

Renate, 12 April 1945

"And you're feeling quite fit and well and really recovered now?" asked Miss Faversham.

"Yes, I really am," said Renate. She did feel very different. She looked straight into the eyes of her Headteacher. She sat up straight. She no longer stared at the floor or her hands. Her English was all right, she knew, and she had stopped worrying about making mistakes.

"Good, good," said Miss Faversham. "I am so pleased to hear it. But I'm afraid this war is still not over though I imagine it will only be a matter of a few weeks."

"I hope so," said Renate. She thought fleetingly about her friends and relations in Germany. She still hoped they were all right, although there was nothing she could do about it now.

"Only worry about what you can change and accept that you cannot change everything," Doctor Murphy had said. "And even when you recognise what you can change, don't actually worry about it, just get on with whatever needs to be done."

Once the war was over, she would contact everybody again. That would be a little scary, but for the moment, all she could concentrate on was making sure she was well and was doing the best she could in these last three months at school.

"I'm afraid it is still not possible for you to get into an English university," said Miss Faversham. "Even if the war finishes tomorrow, it will take several months if not years to get everything back to normal."

"It's what I expected," said Renate. She knew it wasn't her fault. Nor was it anybody else's – well, except maybe that nasty Herr Hitler and his friends'.

"I do have a suggestion, though," said Miss Faversham. "A good friend of mine is taking on some new laboratory assistants in a biology research organisation in London. I've recommended you and he's agreed to interview you, if you're interested."

"That sounds really good," said Renate. "And of course, I'll be able to live with my mother and her friend Eva."

"Good," said Miss Faversham. "Here are the details." She handed Renate a piece of paper. "It will be interesting work and will keep you in touch with your subject. If you do well, they may even agree to pay for you to study."

"Thank you," said Renate. "I'll miss the school, though." She folded up the piece of paper and slipped it carefully into her pocket.

"You'll be welcome to visit any time," said Miss Faversham. "I expect we'll all be returning to London soon as well. Come and see us when we get back."

Renate, 4 May 1945

"So they offered you the job straight away?" said Mrs Cohen, taking a sip of her lemonade. "That is good news. What was the interview like?"

"They were really friendly," said Renate.

"Good," said Mrs Cohen. "And did they tell you all of the duties you'll have to perform?"

"I'll have to help set up the experiments, help read the results, use the microscopes, feed the animals and wear a white coat," said Renate.

"My goodness, you will be busy," said Mrs Cohen.

The waitress arrived at the table, carrying two huge plates of food. Renate had not seen so many vegetables on a plate for a long time, nor had she seen such a large piece of steak – ever.

"Gosh!" said Mrs Cohen. "It looks as if rationing doesn't apply here."

"That's our aim," said the waitress. "We want to make people forget about the war. Mind you, it looks as if it will be over any minute now."

Renate's heart skipped a beat. Soon she would be able to find out about her father, her grandmother and her friends.

"This looks like hard work as well," said Mrs Cohen, after the waitress had left them. "Come on then, eat up. You'll need to keep your strength up for that new job."

The small orchestra in the corner was playing something loud and startling, so they couldn't talk for a few minutes. Renate concentrated on her food. The steak was delicious, if a little chewy. The mashed potato was beautifully creamy – she could swear it had real butter in it. The vegetables were just right – soft enough to eat easily yet not so overcooked that they'd lost their flavour. She made a mental note to come here again – maybe after she'd had her first pay packet. Perhaps she could treat Mutti and Eva. And wouldn't it be grand if Vati could come over to London once everything was settled?

"I'm done," said Mrs Cohen, half an hour later. "They really overdo it here." Her plate was still a third full.

At least Renate didn't feel so bad now about leaving a couple of mouthfuls of potato and a few vegetables. She'd managed all of her meat.

"So, when will you start?" asked Mrs Cohen.

"As soon as school finishes," said Renate. "Twenty-third of July."

"No summer holiday then?" said Mrs Cohen. "Won't you miss the seaside? And the countryside?"

"A little," said Renate. She looked around the restaurant. This was a really exciting place. The young waitresses in their black and white uniforms bringing their plates of steaming food, the hum of people chatting, the sound of cutlery and in the background the coffee machine whooshing and swishing. Not to mention the orchestra. It was all so energetic and busy. When she looked through the window she could see traffic and pedestrians making their way purposefully along the Tottenham Court Road.

"Everybody seems very cheerful," she said.

"Well, I think that young lady was right," said Mrs Cohen. "It's really only a matter of days now."

A good-looking young man sat down at the next table to theirs. He smiled and waved to Renate.

"Yes, I think I'll be happy being a city girl for a while," said Renate. She remembered being in Selfridges with her mother and Eva when they bought the poultry boiler. She wondered how long it would be before the shop was full and busy like she'd imagined it. "An English city girl."

"I'm glad to hear it," said Mrs Cohen.

Renate, 8 May 1945

"Three o'clock today?" said Christine. "It's definitely all over by then?"

"That's right," said Mrs Williams. "The peace begins at three o'clock this afternoon."

"It's a pity we've got to go to school," said Christine. "They ought to let us off to celebrate."

"They might let us out early," said Anne.

"I expect the little ones will be excited," said Renate. Secretly she was relieved to be going to school. If the war was ending today, life was going to change again – hopefully mainly for the better, but there were so many questions.

Would her mother want to go back to Germany?

Did she? What about her new job?

What about Molly?

What was it going to be like seeing her father, her grandmother and her friends again?

At least at school she would be so busy she wouldn't have time to think.

"Well, we've had an idea," said Mrs Williams. "We thought we could have a barn dance. If you ask all the people at school and we'll send one of the girls round the village. We'll ask everybody to bring food like they did for Renate's party. And we'll donate a couple of barrels of cider. There are plenty of people who can play for us and at least a couple of folk who know how to call out the steps."

"Could I borrow the truck today?" said David. "Only if I take everybody to school and bring them back, we'll be home sooner."

"I don't see why not," said Mrs Williams. "We won't need it today. We'll be too busy getting the barn ready. And yes, it will be a good job if you come home early. You can all help us finish it off."

She turned to Renate. "This should complete your experience of England nicely," she said. "You can only be truly English when you know how to do some English barn dances."

Renate found herself grinning. It sounded like fun.

Hani, 10 May 1945

It felt more like a party than a school day. The parents hadn't just dropped the children off and gone home; they'd stayed to chat. Frau Gödde was busy making cups of coffee – still the ersatz sort, of course; it was going to take a few weeks or even months – maybe years – before everything got back to normal. Nobody seemed to mind that, though.

"School will take place upstairs in the lounge today," Doctor Kühn had said. "There will be no hiding in cellars behind cupboards any more. And they shall go outside into the fresh air for their break."

"Do they really need a break?" asked Hani. School hadn't exactly started yet and half the morning had already gone.

"Oh, with this many people here, nobody will be able to concentrate," said Doctor Kühn. "They're all here, aren't they, today?"

"Yes, and a few others," replied Hani nodding towards Günter, a young man old enough to be called up for the army if he hadn't been disabled.

"And we've had more people asking if their children could join the school," said Doctor Kühn.

"I like it when there are so many people here," said Hani.

One or two of the students had stopped coming to the school after the fire. The cellar room had never been quite the same again. It still smelt of smoke. And it had somehow seemed even gloomier down there.

Hani had carried on helping Doctor Schubert. Since he'd been arrested he seemed to lack his normal energy and some days was too tired to teach at all. If she was honest, she had been was glad that there were often no more than six students there. She was getting better and better at teaching but she did not have the training or experience that Doctor Schubert had.

"Let's hope Doctor Schubert comes back soon with some good news," said Doctor Kühn. He had gone to talk to the Americans who had taken her father away. Doctor Kühn took her arm. "I'm sure he'll put in a good word for your father."

"We'll just have to keep busy," Frau Gödde had said. "I'm sure they'll be fair."

Hani could tell her mother she was just putting on a brave face. There were dark circles round her eyes and she'd heard her moving around in the night. She wasn't sleeping very well at all.

Yet Hani couldn't help catching the jolly mood that everyone seemed to be in. They were certainly busy today.

Gradually, though, the parents drifted away. She managed to get the twelve members of the class into the lounge. She just about had them settled when the door opened. Doctor Kühn came in accompanied by a small girl.

"This is Gerda," he said. "I told her parents she could start today. Children, I'm sure you'll all make her very welcome."

Thanks, thought Hani.

"Okay, Gerda," she said. "Come and sit next to me."

The little girl sat down on the floor and promptly stuck her thumb in her mouth.

It was hard to get the children to concentrate. Some of them looked uncomfortable sitting on Frau Lehrs' lovely furniture.

"Please stop that," said Hani as one of the boys fiddled with the fringe on one of the upholstered chairs.

The children were all squashed two or three to a chair anyway and were constantly accidentally sticking their elbows into each other.

If this is going to become the permanent school room, we're going to have to change the furniture, thought Hani. But what would happen to Frau Lehrs' beautiful things?

Eventually the children settled a little and something that seemed a bit like a lesson began to take place.

Then there was another interruption. There was a tap on the door but before Hani could answer, in walked Doctor Kühn, Doctor Shubert, her father and the American officer who had called at her home a week earlier.

Hani gasped. Then she got out of her chair and rushed up to her father and hugged him.

"Vati, are you all right?" she asked.

"I'm fine," he said, returning the hug but then pushing her away gently. "It looks as if you all are too," he added looking round at the children

He looked well, too, she thought. The Americans hadn't treated him too badly.

But where were her manners? She turned and shook hands with Doctor Schubert. "I'm so glad to see you," she said. "We're a full house today." He still looked thin but at least he was smiling today.

"Good morning, Fräulein Gödde," said the American officer. "So, I hear you've become a teacher."

An American who speaks German? thought Hani. That's unusual isn't it? Well, he did have a bit of a funny accent but he seemed to understand what people were saying.

"This is the class I told you about," said Doctor Schubert.

"My wife has worked here for several years and my daughter for a little less time," said Herr Gödde. "As I said, we helped to get several children out of the country including our daughter's best friend. And my wife and daughter used to visit Clara Lehrs when she lived in the ghetto in Rexingen. This house used to belong to Frau Lehrs."

Vati had helped Renate to get to England? That she had not known.

The American officer nodded.

Herr Gödde frowned. "Though they don't normally have their lessons in the lounge," he said.

"Can you show me the cellar room where they usually learn?" asked the officer.

"Of course; follow me," said Herr Gödde. He left the room with the American and Doctor Kühn.

Doctor Shubert stayed behind.

He would, thought Hani.

"Don't mind me," said Doctor Schubert. "Just carry on as if I wasn't here."

Hani took a deep breath and continued telling the children the story of the hare and the tortoise.

"I thought we should have a little celebration," said Doctor Kühn. He was opening a bottle of red wine. "Not least of all about the fact that shortly I shall be able to use the cellar for its true purpose and store all my wine down there."

They were sitting in the dining room. Doctor Kühn had insisted that they should dine in style today. The American Officer had been perfectly happy about the way they had looked after the Special Class and even praised them. He'd appreciated that everyone had had to be very careful.

There had already been some discussion about how the Special Class might carry on and how they might set about finding Frau Lehrs and bringing her home.

"There is, of course, some way to go," said Doctor Kühn, as he poured the wine. "It will be quite a long time before we can get good supplies of food and fuel. We have lost the war and that will always be a little uncomfortable." His face suddenly became very serious. "There were some things very wrong about this war and what it was hiding. And we have to face that."

He finished pouring the wine. "But everybody around this table has something to celebrate today." He looked directly at Hani. "Especially the youngest person sitting here." He exchanged a glance with Frau and Herr Gödde who both nodded.

"I have arranged with the Waldorf Schools Association to award a stipendium to Fräulein Johanna Gödde, to study to become a teacher of children with special educational needs. They have waived the requirement for her to obtain any more qualifications. She has more than proved herself with her work here. Her parents have kindly agreed to cover her living costs. She will start her studies in September."

Hani felt herself blush.

"So, ladies and gents, will you please raise your glasses to Fräulein Hani Gödde?" said Doctor Kühn.

Gerda, 8 June 1945

Dear all,

Exactly one month now since the war ended. It has been good to be without the air raids.

Thomas is in a military hospital close by and is expected to make a full recovery. He is blind at the moment. He should get most of his sight back and with some good nutrition, he will soon be on his feet again. Hans is now fully recovered and able to help on the farms.

Where will Thomas get his good nutrition from? We have to supply the American troops. They often come up to the house to take a bath, using up all our hot water. Not many of them speak any German. I find their accent so difficult to understand if they speak English. They're really quite fair, though, about the provisions they take from us and they do leave enough for the family and for the Müllers next door.

One of them brought some chocolate and a pair of the new nylon stockings for me the other day. He's a very sweet boy, but I don't like him in that way at all.

The Müller boys are really scared of the American soldiers. I've heard about young boys trying to fight professional soldiers and getting killed or badly injured in the attempt. But it's clear they are not quite sure how to behave around the Americans. Frau Müller hasn't yet heard from her husband and she is a bit tense. Father has said she can stay on.

It's going to be messy for a while yet, I suppose. But at least there are no more bombs and no more people getting killed. And the sun is shining today.

Do let's keep in touch and let's not allow the chaos to stop our dear class letter carrying on its rounds.

My love to all of you,
Your Gerda

Renate, 1 August 1945

Renate's back ached. She'd been pretty well on her feet all day, except for the last hour when she'd been bent over a microscope. The stool had been too high so her back had cricked. Now her feet were aching again as she trudged up the long road from the station.

She hoped there would be enough hot water for a bath before supper, she thought. It was nice that she, Eva and her mother were now renting a flat. They had spent so much time living in other people's homes. It was good to have a place of their own.

At last, the house was in sight. She found some new energy as she made her way up the path, through the front door and up the stairs to the first floor flat.

"I'm back," she called from the hallway.

Molly trotted out of the kitchen, rubbed her face against Renate's legs and started purring.

Her mother came out of the lounge. She held a letter. Her lips were pursed in a straight line and she was frowning slightly. "I think you should read this before you do anything else," she said.

So much for the hot bath, then, thought Renate.

"I'm quite certain I know what it is," said her mother. "I have had a similar letter. It is as I expected, and frankly, I'm quite relieved. But I think you should go to your room and read it on your own."

Renate recognised her father's handwriting on the letter. She trembled as she carried it upstairs, followed by Molly. She sat on her bed and just about managed to hold her hands steady long enough to open the envelope. Molly hopped on to the windowsill and stared out of the window whilst Renate read the letter.

Nuremberg, 15 July 1945
My dearest Renate,
What a joy to receive your letter. It arrived on your birthday, even though you posted it almost two months before. I am so pleased that you and your mother are alive

and well. I mean that most sincerely. And to think that you are now twenty! No longer my little girl but a grown up woman. How are you enjoying your job? I hope you do manage to get to university eventually.

It is six and a half years now since your mother and I put you on the train for England. What an anxious time that was for me. Especially when I read in the papers about the attacks on London, where I was sure your mother was still living. I hoped that whichever school you went to had had the sense to move somewhere safer and I was very glad to read in your letter that that was the case.

Your mother seems to have explained about the divorce very well. You must understand that at the time I filed those papers I still did love your mother and hoped that you both would be able to return one day and that we might all live together again as a family. I had no choice about the divorce. If I hadn't filled in the papers I would have been put in prison.

You know also that I was involved in war work even before you left Germany so there was no way that I could leave with you or your mother. If I'd tried to, it may have meant the two of you would have not been able to get away. Neither could I refuse to work on the very weapons that were causing havoc in England. I did go a little more slowly sometimes... I hope I didn't prolong the agony.

I have spent these years not knowing whether you were both still alive and being very sad that I did not know how you were growing up.

Your mother has also written. She says that you are very settled in England and that she herself also feels more English than German now and not a bit Jewish! Not that there would be anything wrong with the latter. Not at all. We kept from you that you were Jewish because of the terrible things that were happening at the time. But I knew very well that your mother's parents were Jewish and it did not bother me personally one little bit. Anyway, your mother tells me the

English have been very good to you. She will leave the final decision to you – whether you stay in England or come back here to Germany.

Your mother and I have been apart a long time and we are officially divorced. Yes, I'm afraid the old Nazi divorce does still count as real. It might be very difficult to get used to each other again. I personally think it might be better for you and your mother to take on English nationality. But that doesn't mean that I won't support you both still. And of course, we shall all remain the best of friends.

The most difficult piece of news to tell is that I have married again. I'm afraid I fell in love. The war was difficult and Ingeborg was so kind to me. I was actually completely convinced that both you and your mother had died. That seems unforgivable now. But Ingeborg helped me through the darkest times. I hope you can forgive me and I hope that you will meet her one day soon and that you will like her. She deserves to be liked.

Hopefully, they will lift the travel bans soon. You are then, of course, most heartily invited to Germany and I would also like to visit you in your new home in England.

Do keep on writing.

Your loving father,
Hans Edler

Renate put the letter down on the bed and hugged her shoulders. Thank goodness her father was alive and well. It sounded as if he didn't want them to go back, or at least wasn't expecting them to. She couldn't believe how relieved she felt. She didn't have to go running back to Nuremberg and try to be a daughter to her father again. And it sounded even as if Mutti didn't want that either.

Molly jumped off the windowsill on to the bed and started purring loudly at Renate. Renate stroked her gently.

If she was honest with herself, she really wanted to stay here.

This was her home now.

Goodness, what would her father make of this higgledy-piggledy flat here in West Hampstead? It was big enough and comfortable enough but needed a bit of care and attention. The garden was so shabby. It was nothing compared with the lovely one in Nuremberg. Or the one at Oma's house in Stuttgart. But at least Molly loved it.

He hadn't said anything about Oma. Perhaps he'd not been able to find out anything yet.

But he was alive and well! And he'd remarried. What did Mutti make of that? Renate couldn't believe how little it bothered her. In fact, she was rather glad that Vati wasn't lonely. But Mutti?

There was a little tap at the door.

"Yes," said Renate, not really surprised at how hoarse her voice sounded.

Eva popped her head around the door. "I've run you a bath," she said. "You looked as if you needed it."

"Thank you," said Renate, still hoarse.

Eva came right into the room then. "So," she said, "you are well and truly a young English lady now."

"Is Mutti all right?" said Renate.

"She is fine," said Eva,

"Good," said Renate. "Yes, England really is my home now."

"I am so pleased," said Eva. "I like England too. Now, go and have your bath before the water gets cold."

Molly meowed as if agreeing.

Erika, 10 August 1945

Dear all,

I'm not sure which was the more chaotic time – the end of the war or the beginning of the peace.

Ilse will certainly not have time to write now. I'm running the business almost single-handed. And of course, I'm enjoying being an aunty.

Yes, Rainer Harald was born on 2 November 1944 at half past two in the morning. He was supposed to be born in the maternity home near you, Fräulein Braun, but he decided to come into the world very quickly and was actually delivered by a local midwife. He is adorable and is now crawling all over the place. Ilse was very tired at first, getting up two or three times in the night to feed him, but now he goes to bed at seven in the evening and sleeps through until six in the morning at least.

Ilse and Helmut are going to move to their own home shortly. Helmut is going to come and work in our family business, though, so I shall still have some contact.

Surely life will get back to normal eventually? I'm really looking forward to when I can go into town and buy myself a whole new outfit, have my hair done and get some new make-up.

Then there are the real ambitions. Above all, that there should never be another war like this one.

What about the rest of you? Will you write down your ambitions in the next round of letters?

Your friend Erika

Hanna Braun, 22 August 1946

The day seemed to be dragging. She had managed to obtain the cream, the vanilla, the sugar and the nuts and had baked a huge Bienenstich and she'd also managed to buy enough quark to make a quite large Käsekuchen. She had put the prettiest tablecloth she could find on the outside table. She'd rolled down the canopy so that the terrace was shaded. The weather forecast had promised warm sunshine all afternoon. It would be so pleasant sitting outside – even if what she was about to tell them was quite serious. She worried whether this was really right – sitting outside as if it was a normal Kaffeeklatsch when she knew she had got to give them a bit more of the truth about the times they had just been through.

She went back into the kitchen. Was everything ready for the coffee and the tea? She really had no idea which they were going to prefer. The last time she had seen them they had been young teenagers who were only allowed peppermint tea. Now they were all grown-up young women – in fact, two of them were housewives, and one of them was even a mother. Two of them were running their own business.

At least she had managed to get some real coffee beans – and not too stale at that. She had ground up plenty. If there was any left over, maybe one of the girls might like to take it home. She took the lid off the tin and closed her eyes so that she could enjoy the smell even more. Yes, it smelt beautifully fresh.

She took a deep breath to steady her nerves. They had been so careful with the Rundbrief. They had never written anything too controversial, but had any one of them been able to read between the lines successfully? Had none of them ever asked why she had stopped teaching or had they not asked because they actually knew and understood these things?

She would really have to make sure they knew about Sister Kuna, and about Father Maxfeld. About Renate and why she had to go to England. Thank goodness England had been kind to Renate! Yes, it was time now for the truth.

She heard a car stop outside. Oh! She seemed to have some other visitors. Could she put them off? She really wanted to have the girls to herself. She made her way round to the front of the house. Three pretty, young women were getting out of a car. Each of them wore a full-skirted flower-patterned cotton dress, white gloves and a smart little hat. Two of them looked like identical twins though their dresses were a different colour.

They were identical twins! Of course, Erika and Ilse. And the other young lady? Maybe Helga? What had she been expecting? Little girls with pigtails and knee-socks? That was silly.

The young women were chattering excitedly.

Helga suddenly noticed her standing there. "Fräulein Braun!" she called.

One of the twins – maybe Erika? – locked the car and all three young women made their way over to her. My, oh my!

"Come through girls," said Hanna. "I thought we'd sit in the garden. It's so nice today."

"You mean to say you don't have any American soldiers living here and you don't have to ask permission to use your own garden?" asked Helga.

"No, I've been fortunate," said Hanna. "They allowed me to keep the place to myself. I suppose because I often offer accommodation to migrant workers. I was full at the time they came in."

"I wish we'd done that, don't you, Ilse?" said the twin who must be Erika.

Ilse is wearing the yellow frock, thought Hanna. Erika is in blue. I'll have to try to remember that.

"Definitely," said Ilse. "Gosh! Do you remember Captain Thomas and those horrible cigarettes he used to smoke?"

"Yes," said Erika. "I could never understand what he was saying. He always had chewing-gum in his mouth."

"We also had a young American officer billeted with us," said Helga. "He was rather nice, actually. He was really missing his wife and daughters, though. I think he was glad to go home."

"And they've all gone now," said Ilse.

"There's still a lot to be done," said Helga. "Have you seen the centre of town? It's a real mess!"

"It's gradually getting sorted, though," said Erika. "And at least now we can put our Sunday best frocks on and come out to tea. Mind you, I'll be glad when we can buy some new things."

"Is everybody coming, Fräulein Braun?" said Helga.

"Yes, everybody who contributed to the Rundbrief," said Hanna. "Apart from Renate, of course." She thought fleetingly of the other girl they would never ever see again. Should she tell them about Elfriede as well? This was going to be difficult. The mood seemed too buoyant. Had organising a Kaffee und Kuchen afternoon been such a good idea? Yet they still deserved to celebrate the fact that they'd made it through the dark times, didn't they?

She heard another car stop.

When she arrived at the front of the house four more young ladies in colourful cotton dresses were getting out of a taxi. She could just make out which were Sabine, Anika, Charlotte and Gerda.

"Let me pay," she heard Anika say, "as it's my fault for wearing such high heels. I'll pay on the way back as well."

"Fräulein Braun!" cried Gerda, running over to her.

Gerda was probably the only one who could run – the other three were all wearing high heels, though Anika's were certainly the highest. It was obvious why they had needed a taxi up from the station. Despite her flat shoes, even Gerda looked very grown-up in her bright red dress that was held in fashionably at the waist by a wide white belt.

Grown-up indeed, thought Hanna.

"Come round to the garden, girls – or should I say, ladies," Hanna said. "The others are already there."

There were squeals of recognition followed by hugs and kisses and laughter as the seven girls were all together for the first time in over seven years.

Hanna busied herself in the kitchen making the coffee for the girls and a lemon tea for herself. She was glad they had come through pretty much all in one piece. It was good to smell coffee brewing again in her kitchen. This was the first time since the war began that she had made proper bean coffee. She liked the smell of the real thing even if she didn't drink it. The old ersatz coffee had smelt of nothing in particular. The liquid bottled coffee the Americans had supplied had smelt more like vegetable stock and even the soldiers themselves had often pulled faces at it.

This seemed more like normal German life.

As she waited for the coffee to be ready, she could hear snatches of conversation from outside.

"It's a lovely photo, actually. I wonder if there'll be some more nice young men available soon."

"So, what's it like, being a mother? Are you still enjoying it?"

"Gosh, can you remember how rough the sheets were? The first three nights I came out in a rash. Then I got used to it."

"Where did you get stockings in such a nice shade?"

"Which stockings? This is actually cold tea. Anyway, how can you bear to wear stockings and a corset this weather?"

No, the mood was definitely too light. Maybe she should leave it for another time to tell them about Sister Kuna, about Father Maxfeld and about Elfriede Kaiser. She probably didn't want to discuss either why exactly she had stopped teaching.

The coffee was beginning to bubble.

She placed the Käsekuchen and the Bienenstich on the tray with the plates and forks and carried it out into the garden.

"Here we are ladies," she said. "Helga, could you start serving everybody while I go and rescue the coffee?"

"My goodness, Fräulein Braun," said Sabine. "You have been busy."

"Bienenstich and Käsekuchen!" said Helga. "So long since I've had that. This is so generous of you, Fräulein Braun."

Anika, Hanna noticed, was looking at her thoughtfully. She seemed the quietest of the girls at the moment. Odd, thought Hanna. Anika was a very glamorous young woman and normally talked exactly as you would expect of a sophisticated actress. She'd always had a strong personality, but today she was curiously quiet.

Hanna felt a little bit uncomfortable as the young woman stared at her.

"So which will you have, Anika?" Helga said to Anika.

Anika ignored her. "Fräulein Braun," she said suddenly, her deep brown eyes staring straight into Hanna's. "Why exactly did you stop being a teacher? You were so good at it. We all used to enjoy your lessons so much."

The others murmured agreement and suddenly there were seven pairs of eyes staring at her.

Hanna took a deep breath. "I'll just go and get the coffee," she said. "Then I'll tell you."

Her heart was pounding as she went into the kitchen. Today was going to be more than just Kaffeeklatsch after all.

Anika, 25 August 1947

"Come on Anika, for goodness' sake, you're just not concentrating," said Berndt. "We open in ten days and we've not got this scene right yet."

"I know. I'm sorry," said Anika. "I've just got something on my mind."

"Let's take a break, then," said Berndt. "Maybe you'll get into it after a coffee?"

"Was that a hint?" said Anika.

Berndt shrugged. "If you like," he said. "You must admit, that coffee you've got is a bit special. It'll be even more special if it wakes you up enough to get this scene worked out."

"Okay," said Anika.

While she busied herself in the kitchen, she tried to imagine what it was going to be like in four days' time when they all met up again. They all knew so much more than they did a year ago when they'd had the Kaffeetisch at Fräulein Braun's house. And there would be an extra guest there this time: Renate. What could they say to her? She was sure everyone would feel awkward. Yet her letter had been friendly enough.

She slipped it out of her pocket again and reread the last part.

...So now you have all my news. I hope that makes up for almost ten years of not contributing to the class letter. I have to come to Nuremberg to meet up with my father again and get to know his new wife. It would be lovely to meet all of you or at least some of you again. I would like to know what the war was like for you. Do you think it would be possible to arrange something? I'm writing to you, Anika, as you were the next one on the list for the class letter...

Would what she had arranged be all right? They were all going to have coffee and cakes at the little patisserie opposite where the school used to be. Was that the right thing to do? Should they have met in one of their homes? Or was it better like that, on neutral ground?

All the girls except Ilse had replied to her invitation. They'd all thought it was a good idea. Even Ilse. Erika had replied on her behalf and said she would be along.

Anika could think of hardly anything else. What would it be like? She wasn't exactly looking forward to it and every time she thought about it her stomach flipped over.

"I suppose you're still worrying about that meeting," said Berndt, as she walked into the lounge with the coffee on a tray.

She nodded.

"Well stop worrying," said Berndt. "Everybody agrees with what you've done. It might be a bit awkward but you'll all only be together for a couple of hours. And it's the right thing to do, isn't it?"

"Do you think we should apologise to her?" said Anika.

"Wait and see if it seems the right thing on the day," said Berndt. "I don't suppose she's coming to tell you off. She's going to be in Nuremberg. Why shouldn't she want to see her old friends?"

"I guess you're right," said Anika.

"Come on then, let's drink this wonderful coffee and get on with that scene," said Berndt. He kissed the top of her head. "And stop worrying so much."

"I'll try," she said. She took a sip of her coffee. "Oh gosh. It's so good isn't it? I'd forgotten how wonderful real coffee could be."

"It's not quite as wonderful as the sight I have in front of me," said Berndt, raising his eyebrows and half smiling.

Anika felt her cheeks burning. "That really doesn't help," she said. "You are such a distraction, Berndt Maier!" She picked up a cushion and threw it at him.

Berndt chuckled as he ducked out of the way, almost spilling his coffee.

The doorbell rang.

"My goodness, it is getting exciting round here," said Berndt.

"Parcel for you," said the postman as Anika opened the door.

"Thank you," she said taking the packet from the postman. The weight of it felt familiar and she recognised the handwriting on the back. Surely it was Ilse's?

"Lucky you, getting a parcel," said the postman.

"Yes, indeed," said Anika. "Very lucky." She closed the door and stood staring at the parcel.

"Aren't you going to open it?" said Berndt, who had now appeared in the hallway.

"Yes, of course," said Anika. "But I know exactly what it is. Come on, let's go and sit down and I'll show you."

"Wow!" said Bernd an hour later after they'd read all the way through the volume of letters. Some of the girls' writing had been a bit hard to read and they'd spent some time looking at the photos. All of them had left their pictures in the book.

"We didn't have a clue, did we?" said Anika.

"Nobody did," said Berndt, kissing the top of her head again. "Well, at least not many people did."

"I wonder why she's sent it now, though," said Anika. "And she still hasn't actually said she'll come to the gathering."

Berndt started rummaging in the paper that Anika had dropped on the floor. "Look, there is something here," he said. He handed her a piece of notepaper. "What does it say?"

"Dear Anika," she read.

"I'm sorry it's taken me so long to reply to your lovely invitation. Rainer Harald continues to take up a lot of my time. Of course, I'll be delighted to attend the Kaffeetisch. I'd like to apologise to you and the others also for hanging on to the class letter for so long. Poor Rainer Harald. He gets the blame for everything. But believe me, being a wife, business woman and mother is very time-consuming.

"I haven't bothered adding another letter because we did all meet up last year and we're soon going to meet again. But I had this idea. Why don't we give Renate the books? That would give her a really good idea of what happened after the school closed and during the war years. Maybe you could even take them to her father's house so she has a chance to read them before she meets us? Anyway, I'll trust you to make the right decision and I'm sure everyone else will agree.

"I'm so looking forward to meeting up again. And it will be especially nice having Renate along as well. All best wishes, Your Ilse."

"That sounds like a really good idea," said Berndt.

"It does, doesn't it?" said Anika. It was as if a great stone was being lifted off her chest. "Now do you think you might be able to concentrate?" asked Berndt.

"I think I just might be able to," said Anika.

"Good," said Berndt. "But I insist on giving you one more distraction first. To test out this theory, you understand." He pulled her to him and kissed her long and hard on the lips. "Now miss," he said as he came up for air. "Let's nail down this part once and for all. With passion, please."

Hani, 26 August 1947

Something felt very familiar about this. And yet it was different. Almost nine years ago she had been getting the garage room ready for her and Renate to sleep in. Well, Rikki had been getting it ready and she was just helping in a bossy sort of way. Today she was getting the guest bedroom ready for her friend and Rikki was helping her just a little bit. Her former nanny was frail now. The war had taken it out of her, especially when Wilhelm came home minus a leg. The Göddes had kept her on of course, although it was more them looking after her these days. Still, she tried her best.

"Well, I'm glad that you're being a bit more sensible this time," said Rikki, as she plumped up one of the pillows. "I'm sure Renate will be pleased that she won't be expected to sleep outside in the garage room." The old lady swayed a little on her feet and then had another coughing fit.

"Sit down, Rikki, and take it easy!" said Hani as she pulled the cover on to the feather bed.

"Oh, I'm no good to anybody," said Rikki, wiping her mouth.

"You are," said Hani. "You can help me decide which flowers to put in here and which towels."

"The towels with the yellow edge, of course," said Rikki, in what Hani called her bossy voice, "and yellow roses to match. They're best this time of year."

So not all that much has changed.

"I'll leave you to it then," said Rikki. "You seem to have everything under control." She pulled herself out of the chair and hobbled out of the room.

Hani was quite glad to be left alone as she busied herself with getting the towels and the roses ready. She could relish the excitement of looking forward to seeing her best friend again. They'd exchanged a few letters and it seemed as if their friendship had taken up where it had left off. Almost. They'd both avoided talking about Frau Lehrs.

I just hope there'll be no 'chicken pox', this time, she thought.

There probably wouldn't. All sorts of other things could go wrong though, she knew. The transport systems were still not working all that well. Only people on important business were allowed to travel. Renate had got special permission because she was coming to a science conference in Stuttgart. Please let her get here all right, she thought.

She knew Renate's letter off by heart. Especially the last paragraph:

And will you come to Nuremberg with me after the conference? I'll need you with me to give me some courage. I'm a little apprehensive about meeting Vati again and about meeting his new wife. And please come with me to the meeting with the girls. They might feel a bit awkward. If they can see I'm easily friends with another German girl they might relax a bit. Of course, while I'm in Stuttgart we'll have to look up some of the places we always went to.

Not once had she mentioned her grandmother.

Hani flopped down on to the chair where Rikki had been a few moments ago. The excitement she'd felt earlier was replaced with a slight dread.

There was a light tap at the door.

"May I come in?" called Frau Gödde.

"Of course," said Hani.

"My goodness, this looks pretty," said Frau Gödde. "She'll feel very welcome." She sighed. "Though I'll have to apologise as well. Making her room pretty isn't really enough on its own."

"You'll embarrass her," said Hani.

"Maybe," said Frau Gödde. "But we've got to talk about it at some point."

"I guess," said Hani. "But how?"

"I don't know," said Frau Gödde. She stroked Hani's hair. "I really don't. But I suppose we'll just have to find a way. I'm sure we'll think of something once she's here."

Hani pursed her lips and nodded her head.

"I think I'll go for a walk," she said.

"Good idea," said Frau Gödde.

Hani couldn't help it. She had set off for the woods and had tried to tire herself walking through there. But she just had to come back via Schellberg Street. An hour after she'd left the house she found herself standing in front of Haus Lehrs. Yes, it was still called Haus Lehrs as if it was hoping Clara Lehrs would just walk through its doors again any minute now.

There was no sign of life at all. She'd heard that the Waldorf School was now open again and she presumed the Special Class was there. Anyway it was the school holidays. Doctor Kühn was away a lot too, travelling up and down the country, helping to re-establish all the schools. He'd even come to her college a couple of times to deliver a lecture.

Still, the garden had been well looked after, she noticed. The grass had been cut, the roses pruned and there were no weeds anywhere in the flower beds. There were still a few vegetables growing but now there were more flowers again. Frau Lehrs would like that.

She rang the doorbell but there was no answer. The step had been cleaned, that was obvious, and the glass in the door sparkled.

Then she heard footsteps coming up the path from the back garden.

"Fräulein Gödde," said a familiar voice. "How very nice to see you. I won't shake hands – I'm covered in dirt. And how good that you've come at precisely this minute. I was about to have a break and make some tea. Will you join me?"

"Herr Ehrlichmann," stammered Hani. "What are you doing?" The old man was wearing dirty overalls and he was holding a garden fork in his soil-covered hands.

"I'm looking after the garden for Doctor Kühn and Frau Lehrs," said Herr Ehrlichmann.

"But surely…" Hani started and then stopped herself.

"There's not enough work for a younger man," said Herr Ehrlichmann, "and besides, I enjoy pottering around in the garden

– and doing a bit of housekeeping. But come and have some tea and tell me all about what you've been doing."

"So that's the big dilemma," said Hani, as she toyed with the cheesecake on her plate. "I don't know how much she understands about what's been going on here. On top of her having such a difficult time about whether she was German, English or Jewish. Now that she has got that all sorted out I don't want to present her with some other problems."

"Ah yes, Renate," said Herr Ehrlichmann. "I remember when she came here when she was just a toddler. Running all over the lawn. I met her father too, a couple of times. A nice chap. Don't be too hard on him. He just got caught up with everything. And when there was no news—"

"But what can I tell her if she asks to come here?" said Hani.

"Just bring her," said Herr Ehrlichmann. "We'll show her where you held the school. And your mother can tell her how kind her grandmother was to the other people in the ghetto."

"Yes, I suppose that would be a good idea," said Hani.

"And of course, no news is good news, as it was in her case," said Herr Ehrlichmann. He frowned slightly. "It will be easier for her to get news, being a relation," he said. "And the news might be bad. But you know what?"

"What?" said Hani.

"You can't do a lot more now," said Herr Ehrlichmann. "Except be her friend. And you know what else Clara Lehrs would say?"

Hani shook her head and blinked back the tears that she felt forming.

"She would say, 'You may as well have another piece of this excellent cheesecake,'" said Herr Ehrlichmann, grinning. "Now, I'm afraid I cannot bake like Frau Lehrs can, but the good news is that this came from that lovely cake shop, the one opposite the synagogue that was all but destroyed in November 1938. Some of the family survived and they are back in business. You see, there is good news sometimes. So, eat up!"

Hani laughed. It was going to be all right. Renate was still her best friend – even though she was English now. This wouldn't be easy but it would be all right in the end.

Renate, 27 August 1947

Renate was beginning to feel nervous. The journey so far had not been too bad. Yes, she'd felt queasy on the ferry but the Channel had been much calmer than when she had gone in the other direction almost nine years ago. And she hadn't actually been sick this time. She was travelling in daylight, though that was a little depressing, actually; everywhere there were still signs of the war – abandoned farms, empty buildings and boarded up windows. Now they were getting very near the German border and she was feeling very nervous.

Another young woman in her compartment was standing up at the window. She had been asleep all the way from Hook of Holland but had woken up as the train started to slow down. "I can see Germany," she said excitedly. Renate's stomach flipped. She thought she was going to be sick now.

Keep calm. Take a deep breath, she told herself.

The train stopped. She heard the door to their carriage open and shut. Then there was the sound of polished boots walking along the corridor.

Surely they hadn't still got the SS here. Were they still going to be nasty just because they were in uniform?

The ticket collector who'd called by earlier, a serious-looking passport control man and a customs officer came into their compartment.

"Just these two young ladies, here," said the ticket collector.

"Right ladies," said the passport control man, "may I please see your passports?"

At least he's being polite, thought Renate. "Here's mine," she said, handing her brand new British passport to the official. She saw the eyes of the other girl in the compartment go round.

"Oh, you're English," said the official. "But you speak very good German."

"I used to be German," said Renate, rather regretting how cold she'd managed to make her voice sound.

"Ah, I see," said the official, looking away from her. "And can you tell me why you're travelling to Stuttgart?"

"For the Science and Industry Conference," said Renate.

The other English girl held out her passport for the official to examine.

"He wants to know why you're coming to Germany," Renate explained.

"I'm going to a science conference in Stuttgart," said the other girl.

"Really?" said Renate. Well, at least there would be one familiar face when she got there.

"We won't keep you much longer, ladies," said the customs officer. "Can you just show me what you have in your suitcases?"

"Just spare underwear, the normal toiletries, night things and conference papers," said Renate as she and the other girl opened their cases to show that they had shopped at more or less the same shops and also had the same paperwork.

"Ah, I see," joked the customs officer. "Twins!"

The other two men laughed.

"Thank you ladies," said the customs officer.

"Have a good journey," said the passport official.

A few moments later the train started moving again.

"Good that we're going to the same conference," said the other young woman.

Her name was Edith and she could actually speak German quite well. It was just that she was more used to reading and discussing scientific articles than speaking to customs officers. Renate was actually glad of the company. It stopped her feeling too nervous about going back.

"You speak really good English, though," said Edith.

"Well, I've lived in England almost nine years," said Renate. "And I was rather thrown in at the deep end. In fact, I have to concentrate to get my German right now."

"It must have been really funny, though, having to leave like that," said Edith. "Really scary."

Had it been scary? Well, the SS guard coming on the train had been scary. But the rest of the time it had just felt like a dream or even a nightmare. She had been sure she would wake up at any moment. "People have been very good to me in England," she said.

Not everybody had been as lucky as her though, she knew. At least both her parents were alive and well and the families she'd lived with had treated her kindly. She'd made a lot of new friends.

"I expect it will be hard to find out about your grandmother," said Edith.

Renate sighed. "Yes, it will be hard," she said. "And I'm actually expecting the worst. But the very worst of all is that I don't know how to talk to my German friends about it. They might think I'm accusing them of something."

"Gosh," said Edith. "And I'm nervous just about the conference. I'm sure you'll find the right things to say, though."

"I'm so glad about the conference," said Renate. "I wouldn't have been able to come otherwise."

She remembered the reaction of her mother's new friends when she'd announced she was going to be allowed to travel to Germany.

"Can you find out anything about my brother?"

"Will you look into what happened to my niece and nephews?"

"Can you find out if my aunt is still alive?"

She had taken a few notes, though she doubted she'd have enough time to even find out about her own grandmother.

The train pulled into Stuttgart station. Renate's stomach started churning again.

"This is it," said Edith as the two of them took their cases off the luggage rack. "Good luck with everything. See you tomorrow!"

Edith scuttled off in search of a taxi, leaving Renate standing on the platform waiting for the steam to clear. Her heart was thumping and her mouth was dry. Would she even recognise Hani? Would Hani recognise her?

There was suddenly a powerful smell of Bratwurst and mustard. It seemed such a familiar station smell. She hadn't realised how much she'd missed the firm meat-packed German sausages. English ones just didn't taste of anything much. More memories flooded in – not of the time when she left but of a time much earlier than when she'd been a very little girl and before there were swastikas everywhere. She closed her eyes and remembered other German food – Apfelstrudel, her grandmother's Käsekuchen, and the Zwiebelkuchen, soft and sweet with cooked onions, that they loved to eat in the autumn. She hadn't realised she was that hungry, but she could eat all those right now.

She opened her eyes again. The steam had almost gone. There were no swastikas. No black or grey uniforms and certainly no one wearing the six-pointed star that showed they were Jewish. Just normal people walking along knowing where they were going and what they were doing.

There was a young woman about her own age standing on the platform. She was wearing a pretty navy blue dress, a button-hole of white flowers and a thin white beret. She was quite slim but there was a familiar roundness about her face. Could it be?

"Renate?" said the young woman.

"Hani?" replied Renate.

The last of the steam cleared. Of course it was Hani. Unmistakeably.

Seconds later Renate was having the breath squeezed out of her as her friend gave her the biggest hug ever.

"Are you hungry?" said Hani, when she at last let her go. "Only the patisserie near the synagogue has opened again. They came back and they do the most amazing cheesecake. Even better than before. Almost as good as your grandmother's. I thought we could pop in there before we go back home."

So, not all that much had changed, even if Hani was a bit slimmer now.

"I'm really hungry," said Renate. "That sounds like a lovely plan."

Hani frowned slightly. "Actually there's a lot I want to tell you about your grandmother," she said. "Things I didn't really want to put in a letter."

It was that simple in the end.

Renate suddenly thought of her grandmother's home. Now she

wanted more than anything else to see the house again. "Before we go for cake can we go to Schellberg Street?"

Hani nodded. "That's probably a very good idea. Let's take a taxi."

As they walked to the taxi rank Renate took a deep breath. There were still some things she had to do before it could all be all right.

Fact and Fiction in *The House on Schellberg Street*

Much of what is told in this story actually happened. Some more of it probably did. Some parts are complete guesswork but they do offer a plausible explanation for some things that really did happen.

Fact

20 Schellberg Street / Haus Lehrs

This house does exist. It has a Stolperstein laid in front of it. Stolpersteine commemorate victims of the Holocaust.

Not only was Clara Lehrs a victim of the Holocaust but she can also be described as a resister. When the Waldorf School was closed in 1938 she allowed her home to be used to house the 'Hilfsklasse' that had operated at the school. Before that, anyway, the house, which she built with her son, Ernst Lehrs, had been used for Waldorf School boarders.

No one is quite sure how but the 'Hilfsklasse' did survive the Holocaust and managed to carry on almost uninterrupted throughout and after World War II.

Käthe Edler and Adolf Hitler

It is true that Käthe Edler was once shown into an anteroom next door to one where Adolf Hitler had a meeting. It is also true that she had a small gun in her bag. It never occurred to her to shoot him.

Renate's story

Renate came to England on the 28 January 1938. We are now fairly certain that this was with the Kindertransport. Various pieces of information we have from Renate herself and from Käthe Edler now point to this, though her son, Martin James, thought that some sort of private arrangement had been made. She really was born in a thunderstorm and christened 'Klara Renate' instead of 'Renata Clara'.

Dates, weather and war news

All of this has been thoroughly researched.

Fiction

The German girls' letters

A group of German girls did write a class 'Rundbrief' ('round robin' or class letter) and did include their class teacher Hanna Braun. They were the girls from the Wilhelm Löhe School, class Vb. The letters filled three volumes in exercise books and started when the girls left the school when it stopped being a church school and was taken over by the state – with all that that meant.

I have had access to the second volume of letters – as far as we know to date, the only one remaining. Much of what they contain is only of interest to the girls who wrote and read them, though they give us several clues about what life was like for young German girls of that era. So, my version of the letters is completely fictional.

The essence of what is in the real letters does, however, influence the text in the novel. Even the style of the letters is imitated.

Hani's Story

Hani and her parents are completely made up, as are all the characters with whom she interacts, except Clara Lehrs, Karl Schubert and Emil Kühn. These three characters are also fictionalised.

Does the version of this story in *The House on Schellberg Street* offer an explanation of how it might have been possible for the 'Hilfsklasse' to survive and carry on after the end of World War II?

Renate's story

The other schoolchildren, the children she meets on the Kindertransport, the teachers at the school, and the families she stayed with, are all made up.

You can read more about fact and fiction in *The House on Schellberg Street* on the web site:
http://www.thehouseonschellbergstreet.com

Glossary

Abitur
This is roughly the same as our A-Levels. It is still used in Germany today and is the qualification you need for getting into university.

Adventskranz
This is a Christmas wreath that sits on a table. At coffee and cake time, between four and five in the afternoon, in Advent, the candles are lit.

Apfelkuchen
Apple cake

Apfelstrudel
Apple pastry – lots of apple and a very thin pastry. The pastry should be so thin that you can read a newspaper through it.

Arbeit macht nicht frei
Over the entrances to the concentration camps was the motto 'Arbeit macht frei' – work liberates you.

BDM
Bund Deutscher Mädel. This was the main youth movement for girls aged 14-18 and it was compulsory. They wore a very smart uniform. They did many of the same activities as the *Hitlerjugend* and similar to our own Guide Association. There was also some Nazi indoctrination involved.

Bienenstich
Literally 'bee-sting'. A sweetened pastry, covered in nuts, and filled with vanilla cream.

Blutschutsgesetz
This was one of the race laws passed in Nuremberg in 1935. It was made in order to keep the German race pure. It forbade marriage between Jews and Germans. It also defined being Jewish as having three or more Jewish grandparents. If you had two German

grandparents, as was the case for Renate, you were *Mischling*. Mischlings were also not allowed to marry Germans.

Christkind
Literally 'Christ child'. He delivers the Christmas presents on Christmas Eve.

Ersatz
This was a substitute for coffee that was made of ground hazelnuts. The word literally means 'substitute'.

Fasching
The time before Lent begins. From the Thursday before Ash Wednesday until the Tuesday, everyone enjoys themselves.

Führer
Literally 'leader'. This was Hitler's nickname.

Gymnasium
Roughly equivalent to our grammar school, though a higher percentage of the German population attend. In Renate's day there was a type of middle school system: students left basic education at 14, either leaving school completely or going on to a grammar school or a vocational school.

Heiliger Abend
Christmas Eve. In Germany, presents are exchanged on this evening. For younger children, the parents decorate the tree behind closed doors and ring a little bell when it is done. The children enter the room and find the presents stacked up under the tree. The Christkind, the Christ child, has brought the presents.

Heimwehr
This was the equivalent of our Home Guard. Younger and older men, and those who were unfit for normal military duty, or involved in other essential war work, used to fit Heimwehr duties around their main job. There was some training.

Hitlerjugend
This was the main youth movement for boys aged 14-18. They did many activities the same as the Scouts. There was also some Nazi

indoctrination involved; a training ground for the *SA* and the *SS*.

Jungmädel
This is the organisation for girls aged 10-13.

Kaffeeklatsch
This is the slightly mocking name for a group of people, usually mainly female, who meet to gossip over coffee.

Kaffeetisch
Another word for *Kaffee und Kuchen*, though possibly with more of a sense of occasion.

Kaffee und Kuchen
A German afternoon ritual, involving coffee and cake, a little like our afternoon tea.

Käsekuchen
This is a cheesecake made with *Quark*.

Kindertransport
10,000 Jewish children were evacuated by train from mainland Europe and brought to Britain. Many of the children never saw their parents again. We decided only to help children, as allowing whole families to immigrate may have taken jobs from British families and sparked anti-Semitism here. Families had to find £50.00 sponsorship. This would be £3,000 today. The Quakers helped with this initiative a lot. Many of them accompanied the children on the journey. If any one of them did not return to the mainland the Germans would have stopped the Kindertransport.

Kinderlandvershcickung
Literally 'sending of children to the countryside'. Children in some of the big heavily bombed cities were evacuated. However, they were only rarely billeted to individual families as British children were. Most of the time they went to camps especially designed for them.

Kriegshilfsdienst
This followed the *Reichsarbeitsdienst, (RAD)* and was training for war work. This included sorting the post for the troops, air traffic

control, work in munitions factories, working on farms – a little like our land girls – and looking after children on the *Kinderlandvershcickung.*

Kristallnacht
This took place during the night 9-10 November 1938. Kristallnacht is sometimes translated into English as 'The Night of the Broken Glass'. Shops and businesses belonging to Jews were ransacked by SA and SS personal and civilians. One international reaction to the Kristallnacht was the setting up of the Kindertransport.

Landschulheim
A type of hostel in the countryside or by the sea where school groups can spend some time.

Lebensraum
Literally, 'Living Room'. Hitler wanted more space for Germans. He'd worked out that Germany was overcrowded.

Maultaschen
Literally 'mouth pockets'. Big squares of pasta stuffed with a meat mixture. There are several different recipes; popular in south Germany.

Mischling
A Mischling is a person who has two Jewish grandparents. They are too Jewish to be considered German but not Jewish enough to be considered Jewish. This was determined by the *Blutschutzsgesetz* that was established in Nuremberg in 1935, leaving many people, including Renate, without a clear identity.

Mutti
Mum, mummy.

Obersturmführer
This rank, in both the *SA* and the *SS* is the equivalent of first lieutenant.

Oma
Grandmother, granny, nana.

Pumpernickel
The ultimate in black bread. It is made from coarsely ground rye.

Quark
Curd cheese. You can get this in England now sometimes. In the 1940s it was unheard of. It makes much better cheese cake than ordinary cream cheese.

RAD
Reichsarbeitsdienst. Literally the 'Reich's Work Service'. Young women had to work for one year for the *Reichsarbeitsdeinst.* They were then taught a variety of skills including household management and childcare. They would then go on to their *Kriegshilfsdienst.*

Reichbürgergesetz
This defined who was and who was not a German citizen. Jews and some other groups of people could not be German citizens. They were subjects – and this included being subject to the laws of the country. Certain privileges only open to German citizens were denied them.

Rundbrief
Literally the 'round letter'. The round robin letter the girls sent to each other. They sometimes call it the class letter.

Spätzle
Long, flat, egg-rich pasta, a little like flattened spaghetti. They are very popular in south-west Germany, near Stuttgart.

Stollen
A yeast-based cake, a little like a fruit loaf. It contains dried fruit and often has marzipan in the middle. It is eaten at Christmas.

Sturmmann
Literally 'storm trooper'. The lowest rank in the army, equivalent to our private.

Sylvester
New Year's Eve. Saint Sylvester has his saint's day on 31 December.

Tschüss
'Bye'.

Vati
Dad, daddy.

Zwiebelkuchen
A type of onion quiche, usually eaten in the autumn.

Coming soon

Quotes

It captures time and place so well and also, takes no sides, makes no judgements but shows what happened to these families, no matter which side of the channel. We see that people are people, children are children and how in the darkest of times there is always light.
Debz Hobbs-Wyatt, author of *While No One was Watching* and free-lance editor.

This intriguing book is based on a true story. It makes innovative use of the 'perpetrator' voice and will interest young and adult readers alike.
Antony Rowland Professor of Modern and Contemporary Poetry, Manchester Metropolitan University.

Having spent many years researching this area for my own novel… I was really struck and impressed by the historical accuracy…I had to keep reminding myself it was fiction, as I could easily have believed it to be original material from the period.
Anne Booth, author of *Girl with a White Dog.*

From reviews on Amazon

Highly recommended to adults and young adults alike.

This is a great cross-over book with an appeal to teenagers and adults alike.

Like many good stories, it's a mixture of real-life and imagination, and it rings true.

In an added twist, the personification of the Third Reich has a voice in this book, and makes its own unpleasant but effective contributions to the story.

This was a fascinating and thought-provoking read.

Renate's story and transformation into a young English woman comes across as realistic.